Delidolu

Joan Kim Erkan

Joan Kim Erkan was born in Wales an educated in London at the Central School of Speech and Drama. She has spent most of her life in Turkey with her husband, Aydın Osman Erkan and two daughters.

At the author's request proceeds from this book will be given to OMM (Odunpazarı Modern Museum), Eskişehir.

LADY WHO

1476/1 Sok. No:10/51 Alsancak-Konak/İZMİR

WRITER: Joan Kim Erkan
COPYREADER: Ayşegül Utku Günaydın
PROOFREADER: Armağan Tuna
COVER DESIGN: Emine Tusavul
GRAPHIC DESIGN: Aynur Sarıbüyük

PRINT: Ertem Basım Yayın Dağıtım San. Tic. Ltd. Şti.
Başkent Organize San. Bölgesi 22 Cad. No:6 Malıköy, Temelli, Ankara
Tel: 0 312 284 18 14

First Edition: September 2021 (2000 copies)

ISBN: 978-625-7314-50-3
Publishing House Certification No: 45041
Printing House Certification No: 48083

delidolu.com.tr

LADY WHO

Memories of a not so ordinary life in Turkey

Delidolu

Contents

To my family
Erol and Rana, Ceylan, Alican and Chantal, İdil,
Emrecan and Selina, Erol Emil and Oskar Ali

Many people in Britain use endearing nick-names left over from their childhood and the title of this book is a pun on my nick-name which is Kim and was fine until I came to Turkey. But in Turkish, Kim means 'Who' which is rather unfortunate and is met first with a look of surprise, a pause and then a smile or hoots of laughter. Conversation goes something like this:

'Merhaba, senin ismin ne?' (What is your name?) - Benim ismim, Kim (My name is who), 'Ne?' (What) - 'Kim' (Who) and on it goes but it broke the ice, I made friends and no-one ever forgets my name.

Preface

This book is about my life and the people I met in Turkey in six decades as a *yabancı gelin*, 'a foreign bride'. It has been a time of immense change. Within a few decades, from its agricultural roots with a largely rural population, Turkey has burst onto the global stage as a secular democratic country and consequential regional power in the Middle East. It has been a rocky ride kept in motion, not by governments or ideologies, but by the fortitude, resilience and tenacity of the Turkish people, whose hard work, earthy good humour, and strong sense of community have overcome geopolitical challenges facing a country located at the crossroads of Europe and Asia.

Not in our wildest dreams could we have imagined that during our life-time, Istanbul would become a megacity and change beyond recognition – one census estimated a population growth of nearly 450% between 1960 and 2000. In 1959, when I arrived, the population of Istanbul was 1.2 million. Unprecedented urbanisation resulted in massive physical changes as the influx of migrants from Anatolia was accommodated. We watched as familiar places – part of the identity and childhood of the citizens of Istanbul – vanished into rubble. People mumbled and grumbled 'everything's changing'. Parks became shopping malls, and that relaxing Sunday family drive along the shore of the Bosphorus to Belgrade Forest became a traffic nightmare. Glorious, wild beaches on the south coast disappeared and entrances to antique sites newly discovered by visitors were bombarded with tourist shops and cafes.

Memories of things we hold dear or wish to let go change according to our circumstances. But the overall memory-picture that I and the citizens hold of Istanbul from those years never changed. This is not mere nostalgia, for they were years beset with difficulties. Each decade presented different obstacles to be overcome: shortages, street fighting and military coups or, after a decade of prosperity, a decade of economic disaster. Nor was it all the fault of the wrecking ball and dust of construction work as the city became a mega-city.

It went deeper. What concerns many people is that amongst the rubble of familiar childhood places they are at risk of losing their true identity as a compassionate, caring community and their culture and traditions as a secular country.

Listening to these 'everything has changed' moans, I realised they were connected with the threads from my life's tapestry in Turkey. This is what has inspired me to write a book, so that my grandchildren might know the Turkey that welcomed me as a foreigner all those years ago. I was destined to meet many extraordinary people in my life and this book is about some of those who have enriched my journey as a *yabancı gelin.*

My own Welsh childhood was spent listening to my elders, especially my father and his brother Uncle William, who related stories of the Second World War, of brave young cousins who fought and died, of local eccentrics and the best choral singers, all told with quick wit and a touch of sarcasm. You can imagine my delight to discover everyone but *everyone* in Turkey has a story to tell. It is the best of these stories that I recall here.

I refer to some men as *Bey* which means sir, and some women as *Hanım* which means lady. These are titles used out of respect for their position or age. It was how I was introduced to them and have addressed them, so.

All historical and political opinions are mine and mine alone.

I appreciate that I have lived a charmed life in a fascinating country, one that is frequently misunderstood by those who have not been fortunate enough to acquire a taste for *Turkish Delight.*

I am deeply grateful to everyone who generously gave their time and shared their stories with me. Thanks to Rosa Vane who edited the first draft, to novelist, teacher, Roger Norman for his guidance, help and encouragement during our discussions about Turkey and the book in Eskişehir, John Scott, editor of *Cornucopia* for his advice and valuable suggestions throughout. I have benefitted in countless ways from the help of journalist, author and translator, Zeynep Avcı and graphic designer and friend, Emine Tusavul who has guided me through to the final process. Thanks to Nihat Odabaşı for his beautiful photographs. Very special thanks to Erol and Rana Tabanca for their constant, patient interest and enthusiasm, without which this book would never have been finished.

From London to Istanbul

'The journey of a thousand miles begins with one step'.
Lao Tzu

It was St. Valentine's Day, 14th February 1959.

'Someone's knocking,' my husband, Nil murmured sleepily. It was the steward.

'Good morning,' the steward said, his smile cheering a dawn wake-up call. 'Too early for breakfast, so I'll prepare a tray for you on deck.'

Istanbul approached from the sea is said to be one of the most beautiful sights in the world and I had no intention of missing a chance to see it at its best.

Ignoring Nil's grumbles, I made my way to the upper deck. The ship's gentle roll rocked its sleeping passengers as a golden dawn rose over the vastness of the sea. Cold and crisp, sea and sky merged into harmonious shades of blue. Wrapped up in a thick blanket, I nestled into a deckchair to savour the final stage of our journey. Migrating birds head for Turkey on their flight to warmer lands and, at the age of 22, I was about to follow them.

As Nil, wrapped up in a blanket, threw himself into a nearby deckchair, a waiter arrived with a tray of freshly baked bread, white cheese, olives, tomatoes and steaming tea.

I had met Nil Arbel, my husband, a tall, fair, good-looking Turkish student at the School of Aeronautical Engineering in Chelsea, when I was studying at the Central School of Speech and Drama based at the Albert Hall in London. I lived in Onslow Gardens with other music and drama students as well as Myshka Kuleshka, a Polish relative of the landlord who was a little older and enjoyed mothering us. Nil lived at Joe's house in Cranley Gardens, the next street, with other Turkish and Greek students. There was a large Polish war-veteran community in South Kensington, the members of which had escaped to Britain during the Second World War to set up the Polish Free Army. Myshka invited us to a party hosted by our landlord, veteran freedom fighter Mr. Zavidski and Joe, Nil's landlord.

Nil was European, worldly-wise, well-travelled and full of surprises. He went out of his way to charm me. If I mentioned a play, exhibition or event, tickets would appear. He played the piano at parties, frequented the best restaurants, and spoke Swedish, Turkish and French at the embassy functions to which he invited me. Nil was not shy to express his feelings and I was more than flattered.

In the common-room of the Central School, I rubbed shoulders with future greats of the British stage: Judy Dench, Vanessa Redgrave, Mary Ure, Jeremy Kemp and Philip Bond. Kenneth Tynan and Peter Hall judged our end of term performances, John Gielgud and Laurence Olivier came on visits to Miss. Thurborn, the autocratic school principal.

At Uncle William's house in Wales, I had met Richard Burton with his Welsh actress wife Sybil. When he learned I was in my first year at Central School, he was kind enough to send two tickets for *Macbeth* at the Old Vic Theatre with an invitation backstage after the performance. I met him again a year or so later, this time with Elizabeth Taylor a few weeks after they had completed Cleopatra, the magnificent film that fired their stormy love affair. Hiding from the press – since both were married at the time – they escaped to Cwmavon in Wales, the village where both Richard and I had been born. While there, they visited his family and his old friend, my uncle. Invited to lunch, my cousin and I scrambled through my aunt's wardrobe for something glamorous to wear. Thank heavens we found only scarves to throw over our shoulders because Elizabeth Taylor turned up simply attired in a black cashmere jumper and pleated skirt. She was very beautiful with fine, transparent skin, dark red lips and magnificent deep, velvet eyes that followed Richard's every move. Petite, with a tiny waist, her natural friendliness put us at ease as she spoke of the tedious hours spent on Cleopatra's make-up and enthused at what a wonderful experience it had been playing opposite a magnificent actor such as Richard Burton. 'He taught me so much,' sighed the highest paid Hollywood actress of the day. With a twinkle in her eye, she repeated the rude Welsh words Richard asked her to pronounce to amuse his men friends. For a stage-struck drama student, it was a magical afternoon. I remember telling my cousin, 'I want to fall in love like Elizabeth Taylor.'

Theatres at that time played to packed houses, and writers and directors dared to create controversial plays. Even so many theatres were closing due to a lack of government support. The director George Devine, a larger-than-life character, poured his energy into everyone's favourite playhouse, the Royal Court at Sloane Square.

The Central School was invited to the final dress rehearsal of Arthur Miller's *A View from the Bridge* before its premiere. Waiting to take our seats we stood in the small, packed bar, where John Osborne, Peter Cook, Laurence Olivier and Joan Plowright often wandered in for a drink. As the lights dimmed, Marilyn Monroe, in a figure-hugging black suit, her silver-blonde hair shining like a halo, wiggled down the aisle followed by her husband Arthur Miller. After the play, he rose to answer questions but all eyes were on his wife and with a wry smile he invited her to the stage to say a few words. She was lovely, natural and funny.

In the late 1950's, the first great age of TV and the odd noisy glamour of Pop Art, London was swinging to the sound of rock and roll starring Bill Hayley, Fats Domino and Elvis Presley, the King. Dressed-to-shock hippies roamed along Kings Road where Italian coffee bars were the place to be seen, and out of work actors waited on tables or modelled in fashionable boutiques. Iconic designers began changing the shape of the female body with precision cutting and sharp, clean designs. Andre Cortèges, Pierre Cardin, Yves Saint Laurent, Pucci's divine Mondrian designs and Mary Quant's white mid-calf-length boots filled the shop windows. It was the right time and place to be a drama student. Even if such a fast Bohemian lifestyle was out of our reach, just being there was excitement enough.

Somewhere along the way I fell in love and decided to marry Nil Arbel. It was much against my parents' wishes, and the mother of one of my friends took me aside to tell me that I was making a terrible mistake. Still there came a moment when I found myself at a church near the Albert Hall, inquiring whether it was possible to be married there. The young priest suggested that he came for coffee that evening to discuss it with both of us. When he arrived, we chatted about his hitch-hiking days in Greece and Turkey before he had decided to take up the priesthood.

Then, in more solemn tones, he explained it was not possible for us to marry in a church because Nil was a Moslem. I was very disappointed and Nil sensed it. 'If a church wedding will make you happy, then we'll have a church wedding,' he said. 'I will convert. I never had any religious instruction anyway.' The priest's eyes lit up at the thought of a convert, which irritated me. 'Of course, I am upset at marrying without my parents' blessing and without a church ceremony,' I told Nil. 'Even so I can't let you change your religion for my sake because I will never change mine for you.'

It was Nil's loving support that overcame all my doubts and brought me to the Chelsea Register Office on March 14th 1958. As we waited in the lounge, an official ushered me into his room where he stood in front of me peering at my face. 'It is my duty to inform you that Moslem men are allowed four wives,' he declared. 'Did you know that? I suggest you think very carefully, young lady, before marrying. It's not too late to change your mind.'

At that moment I would have married Nil Arbel simply to spite the world. In a quiet, controlled voice (when angered I become quiet), I told him to check his facts about marriage laws in different countries before voicing ignorant opinions. In 1928, I informed him, marriage laws in Turkey had been reformed according to Swiss law.

Without a word, the official opened the door. I would have marched straight out of that registry office had Nil not stopped me. Thank heavens the registrar was all smiles and wished us well. After lunch at the Savoy Hotel with Myshka, Petros, Nil's

Greek friend, Mr. and Mrs. Zavidski and Joe and his wife, we drove to Bath for a honeymoon weekend before returning to London and our studies.

Three months later my mother telephoned to invite us to stay for a weekend. My parents were tense and overly polite – so unlike my father – while Nil, desperate to make a good impression, tried too hard to please (in all the wrong ways) but the ice was broken and I was happy with the thought that I was free to visit home or telephone my parents whenever I wanted.

In those days of innocence, it wasn't unusual for a waiter in a Kings Road restaurant to bring a card from a theatrical agent or photographer at the corner table requesting permission to take a photo. Even then we all knew the perils of the casting couch and I felt that I didn't have that core of inner steel, dedication and confidence demanded of an actress. When Patricia, an acquaintance who owned a modelling agency off Bond Street, asked me if she could take some photographs, I agreed. Much to my surprise a week or so later she sent me on my first assignment, an outdoor shoot on Hampstead Heath. It was a miserable cold grey day, but the photographer, knowing it was my first job, was kind and funny and helped me to smile. A few days later the same photographer asked me to model for a TV advertisement for a fashionable shirt company. I was the background figure hanging onto the arm of an incredibly handsome man. Later, another call came. This time the incredibly handsome man hung onto *my* arm as I smiled at the camera wearing an exquisitely cut shirt for women. 'Cool,' I thought and spent all my earnings buying that very shirt, which I wore forever. So began a not too serious career as a model.

Nil and I had rented a flat in Onslow Gardens. Friends dropped in to cook, study or just chat. I was getting regular work, which pleased the agency and, as I was earning my own keep for the first time, pleased me too. I went to Wales as often as possible to appease my guilty conscience and see my parents. Life was hectic but fun. Then Nil received a letter from his father saying that it was time for him to return to Turkey to prepare for his compulsory military service.

We spent Christmas with my parents, I hate goodbyes. My mother smiled through her tears as she made me promise to 'write and telephone every Sunday'. I had telephoned my parents on Sunday mornings ever since I had left home. My father was tight-lipped, disapproval written all over his face. He held me close. 'Remember I am just a telephone call away,' he said. 'Take care.'

Turkish customs forbade the entry into the country of all sorts of things at that time, but Nil was returning indefinitely and was allowed to take all his personal and household goods. He was inundated with telegrams and telephone calls from people in Turkey asking for medicines, cosmetics, electrical items, underwear and anything cashmere. 'Buy everything you need now because there is nothing you will want to buy there,' he kept warning me.

I was busy packing family photographs, prints, books and silly trinkets I thought I couldn't live without and didn't heed his words. I lived to regret it.

We spent the New Year with Nil's uncle, Ambassador Selahattin Arbel, and his wife, at the Turkish residence in The Hague in the Netherlands, an utterly charming, tall, narrow building on a quiet tree-lined canal. We had stayed there twice before, once to attend the opening of the World Fair in Belgium, and another time for a never-to-be-forgotten week.

On that occasion, while his wife was in Istanbul visiting their daughter, Selahattin Bey had moved to a suite at the Steigenberger Kurhaus Hotel, a palatial hotel on the promenade at Scheveningen, from where he kept an eagle eye on the restoration works in progress at the Residence. We arrived at the hotel during the afternoon to be informed that the ambassador had been called away, but that we were to be in the dining room at 7.30 p.m. sharp and he would join us later.

The stately ballroom sparkled with a thousand stars as we were led to a table in the centre of an already crowded room. My eyes widened and jaw dropped as I realized that the sparkles were not from stars on the ceiling, but from the emeralds, diamonds, dazzling pearls, earrings and brooches, medals and ribbons adorning ladies in sumptuous evening gowns and gentlemen in immaculate evening dress. And there was I in a Harrods full skirted dress with a tight bodice and narrow straps, sans jewellery. Totally out of place. As if that wasn't enough, I was hungry not having eaten since breakfast. When a chef set up a Guerdon to slow-cook a steak flambé, the odour of the steak simmering in wine, cream and herbs was torture. I munched on the bread rolls glaring at Nil, who was deep in conversation with a bejewelled lady and her handsome grey-haired husband at the next table.

Selahattin Bey appeared in time for dessert, pausing at each table to say a few words until he reached us. 'Thank you, my dears,' he purred, just like a Cheshire cat. 'You saved the day. This gathering is one of the most important dates on our diplomatic calendar. As one of the organizers, it would have been a scandal had my table been unoccupied.' He beamed with pleasure. 'I do hope you are enjoying yourselves.'

'I wish you had warned me,' I mumbled petulantly. 'I would have brought something more appropriate to wear.'

He laughed. 'Look around you, child. Youth is beauty and beauty, youth.' Then, in his sanguine manner added, 'Youth cannot be bought, so stop fretting. My guests are charmed by my young relatives. Nil will provide the jewels you need when the time comes, never fear'.

That evening from the balcony of the hotel we watched the most magnificent fireworks display I have ever seen in my life.

When we visited Selahattin Bey and his wife on our way to Istanbul, Safiye, their daughter was there. She had come to give birth in Holland. Voluptuous yet ethereal, her long black dishevelled hair framed a lovely oval face. She constantly argued with her father, adored her mother, and pined for her husband who was due to arrive nearer the birth. Every morning, wrapped up against the bitterly cold winds, we walked along the promenade and lunched at a small Vietnamese restaurant on the waterfront. Safiye hugged me when we were about to leave. 'You'll love Istanbul. When I come, I'll introduce you to my friends' she promised. Safiye and I became friends, but a few years later, still very young, she died giving birth to a third child in Istanbul.

We drove to Paris to spend five wonderful days at a small hotel in Saint-Germain that Nil knew from his student days. It was snowing and Paris was magical in its white cloak. We walked along the Seine, spent a day at the Louvre, and dined at the Trocadero, but it was the evening watching my first cancan revue at the Moulin Rouge – a theatre filled with history – that I remember most vividly.

In the mornings I would dip flaky *croissant au beurre* into a bowl of steaming black coffee, copying my favourite actress, Jeanne Moreau. The croissant was too buttery and the coffee too bitter and I longed for tea and toast.

Edouard Mesley, Nil's friend from London, arrived to take us to his family home outside Paris. His parents lived in a rambling, old French farmhouse with a mill and stream flowing through the land. Two frisky dogs greeted us at the door. The sun sparkled on the snow as we walked across the fields, and the nights were full of stars. Madame Mesley spent her days in the large kitchen amongst shining pots and pans, jars of homemade jams and pickles, casks of wine, and dishes of butter and cream. She entertained neighbours, read newspapers and cooked up mouth-watering meals without ever leaving the kitchen. In the evening we would gather around the large table in the dining room for a Madame Mesley feast: pâté, steaming rabbit casserole, tender duck with wild mushrooms and pork or boar washed down with gallon-size bottles of tart wine. Edouard's father was a typical French countryman; solid-looking, reserved and serious. He would appear at lunch and dinner time to pour the wine before sitting down, whereupon he would complain about the weather, the government, expenses, and Edouard. Nevertheless, with typical Gallic charm, he never once left the table without complementing his wife on her cooking.

The Mesleys owned a modern poultry farm for intensive indoor broilers. Thousands upon thousands of poor chickens were kept in enormous, immaculately clean box-like structures equipped with a complicated mechanical system to control heating, lighting and feeding. We were never served chicken.

One afternoon, against his father's advice, Edouard insisted we drive to Paris for dinner in his father's new 1959 Peugeot car, even though the weather forecast warned of an impending storm. On the outskirts of Paris, the blizzard made visibility minimal and Edouard decided to turn back. The car hit an icy patch, skidded out of control, and somersaulted into a ditch. I remember being dragged out of the car and then Edouard and Nil carrying Valerie, Edouard's girlfriend, to the roadside. Not long later an ambulance arrived. I must have fainted, for I woke in a crowded hospital ward with a splitting headache. After causing a fuss in school French, I found Nil in a private room conversing with a pretty French nurse.

Except for a few bruises and scratches, Nil, Edouard and I escaped unscathed, but poor Valerie broke her hip and to our horror the car was beyond repair. Fury and high blood pressure made Monsieur Mesley's cheeks even ruddier as he brushed away our apologies with a shrug, but later on his scathing outbursts to his son behind closed doors in the library echoed through the farmhouse. Madame Mesley's cooking tasted bland without its generous pinch of love.

To escape the atmosphere in the house, every morning I walked the dogs across snow-covered fields. The air was invigorating and I shook heavily laden branches of snow over the leaping dogs. I went to a smoke-filled café to warm my hands on a bowl of steaming soup, smiling hello to staring locals.

Nil and I realized that our presence was not helping the situation, so we decided to leave early. We begged Edouard to join us for a few days but he refused, and we bade an apologetic goodbye to our hosts who were, I am sure, delighted to see the back of us.

Sheer panic kept my hand clutched on the lock of the door as Nil drove down the breathtakingly panoramic but precipitous road from Cannes to the Riviera. Nil, a gambler at heart, headed straight for the casino. I was wearing trousers and was therefore refused entrance to the Royal Casino in Monte Carlo. Delighted to escape a boring evening, I walked around the town then sat in a café, nursing a glass of wine and watching the tanned winter yachting crowd.

With all our cash in the hands of the croupier, we drove on to a hotel in Naples, pre-booked (thank heavens) by Selahattin Bey. Nil went off to the shipping office and returned with tickets for the Ankara, a cruise ship owned by the Turkish Maritime Line, and enough Italian liras to tide us over for the three days we had in Naples before boarding. I looked forward to the voyage; it would give me time to gather my thoughts before meeting my Turkish in-laws and whatever lay in store for me in Istanbul.

At sea, we read books and walked the deck before dinner at the Captain's table. Other guests included a friendly Turkish couple and their recently qualified doctor son, two Turkish ladies who kept us amused with stories of their adventures, and a handsome naval officer, who spoke English with an Oxford accent. One of the ladies, wife of an industrialist, asked if I would take a fur through the customs for her because it was forbidden to bring furs into the country.

That first glimpse of Constantinople, former capital of the Byzantine and Ottoman Empire, was unforgettable. In the misty morning distance, its celebrated skyline formed a unique pattern of towers, domes and slender minarets belonging to famous churches, mosque and palaces, arsenals of faith, conflict, intrigue and war. Who can tell what went on behind those walls? It was breathtakingly beautiful. As the ship sailed on, the buildings appeared to change shape while remaining as solid as if they had been there forever, witnessing the passing of centuries.

The ship moved into the port of Istanbul escorted by a flotilla of fishing boats, tugboats, paddle-boats, and ferry-boats. Sirens blared, bells rang, and seagulls swooped, circled and cried. Boatmen secured thick twines of ropes to huge iron rings. Porters, young and old, ran barefoot up the gangway into the bowels of the ship to reappear carrying bags, suitcases, bundles of all sizes and shapes on their backs, shouting, 'Make way, make way', as they scurried down the gangway to throw their load on a luggage cart, then scramble back for a repeat performance.

The large hall of the *Yolcu Salonu*, 'the waiting room', echoed with people shouting and waving their arms. Luggage was shuttled to and fro while police and officials blew repeated blasts on their whistles. Nil pointed out his parents standing on a balcony above the maddening crowd. Ambassador Bedii Arbel, tall and upright in a long black coat and crowned with a shock of white hair, waved his hat. His wife, Afife Hanım, was wrapped in fur, her face hidden under a wide brimmed hat. Next to her was Nil's aunt, Professor Fazila Giz, who had stayed with us in London a few times while attending university seminars. Slim and of average height, she seemed taller in her well-cut, classical black suit which set off her slender figure to perfection. Her dark hair, knotted at the nape of her neck, framed a long, sensitive face with brown expressive eyes, often wreathed in smoke from her strong Turkish cigarettes.

We navigated our way past porters and passengers down the gangway. Police blew whistles to control the noisy crowd milling around the custom buildings. Nil told me to wait in a corner of the customs-house. The noise was deafening, the crowd extraordinary. I spotted the car containing my precious belongings swinging in the air at the end of a steel cable as though about to crash onto the pier. I tugged an officer's arm, pointing anxiously to the vehicle. 'That's my car!' 'Good, very good,' he smiled, walking off. As soon as the luggage was checked, our dinner companion appeared to collect the fur. She presented me with a box of Turkish delight and handing me her card insisted I keep in touch before disappearing into the crowd.

In possession of our car once more, Nil drove to the entrance of the customs-house, hand on the horn. Here we were met by his parents and his aunt. Under her hat, Mrs. Arbel had porcelain-white skin, piercing blue eyes and red lips. 'Welcome to Istanbul, my dear,' she said, squeezing my hand. 'Welcome, welcome, my dear,' echoed my father in law. 'It's too noisy here. Let's be off.'

With my face pressed to the window of the car, I caught my first glimpse of Istanbul, a city with a population of less than a million and a half, a city of mosques and churches that divided Europe from Asia and was to become my home.

Meeting My In-Laws

The Arbels lived in Şişli in a residential cul-de-sac overlooking wide open spaces. Two sentinel cypress trees guarded the entrance of the building. 'I had this apartment built and the trees planted,' said Afife Arbel over her shoulder as she ushered me up the steps.

A large hall opened onto a series of rooms: sitting rooms, dining room, Bedii Bey's study, and bedrooms. The kitchen was the domain of Anna, a dour Russian with a partiality for Turkish vodka.

'Make yourself comfortable, my dear,' Afife Hanım pointed to a table laid for tea with a fine china tea set and small cakes on a silver platter. 'We drink more tea than you English. The first thing you will be offered here will be a glass of tea or Turkish coffee which you always accept. It's rude to refuse.'

Bedii Bey and Afife Hanım were a handsome couple. Bedii Bey had a long scholarly face topped by a thatch of white hair. He was aloof by nature, Nil had told me he tested the patience of his staff with occasional outbursts, irritating obstinacy, and a preference to write poetry or paint rather than attend to the mundane tasks of diplomacy. Afife Hanım had a beautiful heart-shaped face, startling blue eyes and blonde hair, loosely caught up in a bun. She was known for her intelligence and sharp wit and for her heated responses (in five languages) when angered. Neither she nor her husband suffered fools gladly.

My parents-in-law spoke French to each other, Russian to Anna, French or Turkish (depending on the subject) to Nil, and Greek to Maria, a lovely Greek lady who had been with them since she was 15 years old and was now part of the family, coming twice a week. Her daughter and son-in-law looked after the Arbel's summer house in Büyükada. English was spoken at the table for my benefit.

The large high-ceilinged rooms were furnished with heavily carved English and French antiques and a magnificent Chinese rosewood trunk. The floors were covered with Persian carpets. Paintings by Bedii Bey, and their famous artist friends from their days in Paris – İbrahim Çallı, Namık İsmail and Bedri Rahmi Eyüboğlu – lined the walls from ceiling to floor. Two massive antique Chinese vases dominated the entrance to the dining room, where a mahogany table, dark leather armchairs and dresser left little space to move. The dresser was filled with silver cutlery, delicate Lemoyne tea sets, elegant gold-rimmed embossed dinner sets and beautiful hand-painted Meissen and Sevres plates – all remnants of Afife Hanım's impressive collections and treasures from grander days. The only form of heating in the apartment was a large ornate porcelain stove in the sitting room. The doors of rooms were kept open to let the heat fill the whole apartment and Bedii Bey kept himself warm with a cape-like Scottish blanket over his shoulders.

When you live in Turkey as a foreigner, you are a yabancı. When you marry a citizen of that country, you are forever known as a yabancı gelin – a foreign bride. I was fortunate to have married into a modern and educated family of scholars, doctors, intellectuals, academics and diplomats who spoke English and French, thereby removing any immediate necessity for me to learn Turkish. Loyal to the legacy of Atatürk and proud to be Turkish, I was warmly welcomed.

Tradition and hospitality are the cornerstones of Turkish culture. Since their nomadic days on the steppes, travellers are considered *Tanrı misafiri*, 'guests from God', welcome to share table and shelter. For centuries, friend and foe, merchant and soldier, diplomat, teacher and preacher, poet and painter, attracted by the Ottoman Empire's turbulent history, wealth and power, were drawn like bees to a honey-pot and enjoyed Turkish hospitality. Many who came stayed on.

The Ottoman Empire was more tolerant to religious minorities than were Christian countries. Greeks, Anatolian Orthodox Christians, descendants of Byzantium and Rome (known as Rum in Turkish), Bulgarians, Armenians and Kurds were all considered subjects. Jews expelled from Spain were offered asylum in the 16th century and when the Caucasian War ended in 1864, more than a million and a half Circassians escaped Russian persecution by sailing across the Black Sea, offered sanctuary by Ottoman Sultan Abdulaziz, son of the all-powerful Circassian, Valide Sultan. And so it came to pass that, within Istanbul's walls, ethnic minorities lived in particular neighbourhoods, working side-by-side with the Moslem majority. Proud of their ancestors, these groups all delighted in sharing family stories. (There was a sort of familiarity in their social attitude that was refreshing.)

The Arbels were no exception. Bedii Bey's parents were Circassian exiles who had settled in Izmir and sent their three sons to be educated at the French Lycée in Istanbul as boarders. Muvahhit, the eldest, joined a band of young liberal-minded actors called Sanatçılar (artists) while his younger brothers, Bedii and Selahattin entered the Foreign Service. Actor-playwriter Muvahhit cut a dashing figure on stage and had a reputation as a lady's man. Seeing him on stage in İstanbul, a young girl fell madly in love with him. Bedia Şekip, a student at the French Dame de Sion, was so besotted by Muvahhit that she sat in the front row at every performance until she caught his eye. After a short courtship, despite strong opposition from her conservative parents, they married in 1921. Muvahhit became her devoted husband and mentor. She became one of the finest actresses of the Republic of Turkey and one of the two first Muslim actresses in Turkish cinema. On 31st July 1923 they had the honour of performing in front of Mustafa Kemal Pasha at the Palas Cinema in Izmir.

When her husband was diagnosed with TB, Bedia moved her small son, Sina and ill husband to Büyükada, the largest of nine islands in the Sea of Marmara archipelago, where she had spent a happy childhood. She was convinced that the sweet-smelling pine forests, soft sea wind and quiet, calm island life would restore her husband's health. Sina remembers these as the happiest days of his childhood, running wild in the forest and swimming in the sea while his mother nursed, read to and fed his father until his death in 1927.

I was thrilled when Sina invited us to dinner to meet his mother, then in her 80's. Bedia Muvahhit was elegant in a simple black dress with a large diamond pin, her short, dark hair framed the still handsome face and lively eyes that had captivated audiences in the theatre and cinema for more than seventy years, as one of Turkey's leading state artists. Still involved in the theatre world and friend of the famous, she had many amusing stories to tell, recalling her husband as 'my mentor and my love'. His last words to her were to make her promise to continue her dedication to the theatre world he loved so much. 'He died with a smile on his beautiful face and I kept my promise,' she told me with pride.

She spoke of the euphoria of those pioneering days as a young actress in the newly formed Republic. At that time, it was considered improper for Turkish women to act in the theatre. Female parts were mostly played by Armenians, Greeks, Russians or young boys. Dedicated to the spirit of Atatürk, intellectuals such as Muhsin Ertuğrul, Adnan and Halide Edib Adıvar, Cahide Sonku, Vasfi Rıza Zobu and Dacat Güler were the pioneers of culture, art and freedom of speech, working tirelessly to modernize the Turkish theatre and establish a film industry. (The list of theatre figures is too long).

Muvahhit's brother's, Selahattin and Bedii, became respectively Ambassador to Pakistan and Consul General in Marseille, at a time when Turkish diplomats were closely involved in the dramatic events of the Second World War.

In 1933, Atatürk had offered sanctuary in Turkey to German professors of Jewish origin under threat from Nazi persecution for their left-wing ideas. As a token of gratitude, these professors taught at universities and were instrumental in introducing major reforms within the educational system.

During the Second World War, the Turkish government, led by İsmet İnönü, issued a decree extending transit visas to all Jews who had obtained visas from other countries. In addition, as one of a few neutral countries in Europe, Turkey maintained diplomatic representation with Germany and German-occupied countries to ensure that Turkish Jews would not be subjected to the same racial laws applied to French Jews. In 1995, for the first time, in a paper on the historical data of the role of Turkish Diplomats between 1940-1944 it was revealed that saving Turkish Jews in France were actions taken by men of conscience, members of the Turkish diplomatic corps who risked their careers and often acted on their own against their government and that of the U.S and the U.K.

Led by Ambassador Behiç Erkin, Turkish Ambassador to Paris and later Vichy, diplomats, Bedii Bey, Necdet Kent, Namık Kemal Yolga, and Mehmet Fuat Carim and others used their political clout to intervene by providing false papers and certificates of Turkish citizenship to those finding themselves at the centre of the tragic events unfolding in Europe. Turkey was in the unenviable position of attempting to maintain neutrality while in dire fear of being invaded by Germany and after great pressure from Germany Ambassador Behiç Erkin was recalled to Ankara and in thus doing so the rate at which Jews were repatriated to Turkey was greatly diminished. Bedii Bey was rightly proud and humbled of the part he had played.

Afife Hanım played her part and did her best in protecting Jews from the Nazi persecution. Nil recalled how they were sitting in the Paris Embassy garden one day when a Jewish woman with a child appeared, clinging to the gates and begging to be allowed in. His mother ran to open the gate to see two German officers approaching. Pulling the terrified woman and child inside, Afife Hanım locked the gate. 'My maid,' she announced haughtily, in impeccable German.

One afternoon as we sat in his library going through albums of photographs, newspaper cuttings and letters, yellowing with age, he began, 'The Turkish Foreign Service played an honourable role in saving thousands of lives and I am proud to have been a part of it.'

On his desk next to a silver framed photograph of Atatürk was a silver-framed autographed photo of King Gustaf Adolf VI of Norway. During his tenure as Ambassador to Norway, Bedii Bey had befriended King Gustaf Adolf VI. The two men had much in common – French literature, art, chess – and were often seen deep in conversation strolling in the palace grounds or sitting in a corner, painting or playing chess. Fearlessly independent and outspoken, Bedii Bey was overheard by an underling at the embassy criticizing Turkish Prime Minister, İsmet İnönü. The underling squealed to the ministry in Ankara and Bedii Bey was instantly recalled.

Displeased, King Gustaf wrote a personal letter to İnönü expressing his concern and displeasure that a representative of the Turkish Republic, an ambassador of such standing and a valued friend, had been recalled on unsubstantiated rumours. In the most gracious terms, he indicated his sincere desire that Ambassador Bedii Arbel return to his post. Bedii Bey was summoned to Ankara where İsmet İnönü spoke of his displeasure at such indiscretions from a senior ambassador. He warned him to be more discreet in future and ordered his return to Norway within ten days. Bedii Bey thanked the prime minister, shook his hand and walked out of his office. On his way out of the ministry, he penned a letter of resignation.

Amongst the photographs Afife Hanım showed me, there was one I especially remember, it was a faded picture of a child with a rather petulant expression on her pretty face and long blond ringlets sitting on a carpet playing with a chest of gold coins. As though speaking to herself, Afife Hanım murmured 'Those coins were to finance that little girl's dream to become a doctor'. It was a photograph of herself. She had changed those gold coins into German Marks when she went to study medicine in Germany. In her third year the mark devalued and she was forced to return to Istanbul. Soon after she met and married her husband and together, they embarked on a diplomatic career. But the desire to become a doctor remained.

Afife Hanım was the youngest of four siblings born into a wealthy landowning family in Bosnia. After the sudden death of their father, Süleyman Kaptanoğlu, his wife, Fatma Hanım and her children, Gülsüm, Cemal, Tahsin and Afife moved to Istanbul where her three sisters resided.

Gülsüm, the eldest sibling, was soon married to Mehmet Şevket Pasha, former Governor of Baghdad and Commander of Edirne, and Fatma Hanım joined her daughter and son-in-law in a charming wooden villa in Arnavutköy, a village on the European shore of the Bosphorus. Şevket Pasha was a handsome, larger-than-life Circassian known affectionately in military circles as deli (mad) or mağrur (proud) Şevket. He frequently and loudly voiced his disapproval of pashas, including his wife's relatives, who spent more time at the Sublime Porte seeking favours from the Sultan than with their troops in the field. There is a story that he sold the family gold to provide shoes for his men when funds from the Sublime Porte failed to arrive. A law unto himself, Mehmet Şevket Pasha was an accomplished rider who rode a fine white stallion named Ferhan and under his tutelage, his regiment became a crack cavalry force in the Ottoman Army. I heard two stories concerning this beloved horse. One is that the horse died the same day as his master. The other was that, on hearing the Pasha was unwell, the Sultan sent an envoy to inquire if there was anything he needed. The only request that came back was for Ferhan to be kept at the royal stables at Yıldız Palace. This magnificent white stallion became the Sultan's favourite horse to ride to Friday prayers at Yıldız Mosque and the stables were renamed Istabl-ı Amire-i Ferhan.

Şevket Pasha's wife, Gülsüm was pregnant with her fifth child when her husband suddenly died of a heart attack in 1916.

As was the custom in those days Gülsüm remarried but sadly after three years or so she too died and her five children were left orphans.

It was these five orphans, Fazila, Mehmet, Mahmut, Faize and Mehmet Şevket, (called Ahmet) who, years later, became my adopted Turkish family. I enjoyed an intimate relationship with each member of the Giz family and never felt the emotional scars of a traumatic childhood or problematic upbringing. Their parents were loving memories in the past. Their concern had always been to address the actual circumstances they found themselves in at any given time. They rallied without self-pity or regret. Their attitude was pragmatic, coloured with a tongue-in-cheek humour of childish squabbles and embarrassing pranks played on each other which underlined a loving bond. The stories were of their lives, the drama of growing up in a new republic, of their student days in America and Europe. They were never judgmental, welcoming cousins whenever they visited with genuine warmth. Books and articles testify to the academic excellence of the extraordinary Giz family. Their children and grandchildren, husbands and wives are as much part of my life today as their parents were when I first arrived in Turkey.

The Magic of an Imperial City

My mother-in-law, Afife Hanım insisted on taking me on my first outing to what she called the Grand Rue de Pera, İstiklal Caddesi in Beyoğlu. As we walked down what was and is the main shopping centre in Istanbul, she kept up a running commentary on the splendour of the late 19th century art nouveau buildings, once home to embassies.

Beyoğlu was cosmopolitan. People considered themselves citizens of the world and dressed up. Women wore furs and hats and men looking smart in long overcoats and flat caps strolled along to meet friends in fashionable cafes. The most colourful shop windows were confectioners, jewellers, shiny with gold rings and bracelets and the *bol kepçe* restaurants. *Bol kepçe* means a 'full ladle' of freshly cooked food in large trays displayed in the window, so a customer can point to the dish of their choice.

Afife Hanım marched into Tanca, the famous shoemakers, to inquire if her shoes were ready and on the spur of the moment instructed him to make a pair for me. My first bespoke pair of shoes were so comfortable and special that I became a regular customer. We popped into the cinema (at that time there were half a dozen cinemas in Beyoğlu) to see what was playing. Films were our one common interest. She was fond of American films and knew the names of most actors. Bedii Bey and I had art in common: he spoke, I listened.

Our next port of call was the bank. As Afife Hanım entered, the bank manager jumped from his chair to button his jacket. Refusing his offer of tea, we went downstairs to the vault where he opened drawer after drawer of magnificent silverware the Arbels had used in former days.

In front of Galatasaray Lycée, established in 1481 – making it the oldest high school in the world with instruction given in French – Afife Hanım reeled off the names of famous graduates and friends. We walked through Balık Pazarı, a colourful fish and flower market with restaurants favoured by socialist writers and artists pass Pera House, once the British Embassy and now the British Consulate, hidden behind a high wall at the corner of a seedy street lined with small hotels, restaurants and souvenir shops. We stopped at Marquis Cafe for afternoon tea. The scene was quintessentially 1950's. My mother-in-law, having made her entrance, began, as whimsical and charming as she was eccentric, to chat in French to friends wearing a variety of hats, plum-coloured lipstick and red nail vanish, while I devoured tiny cakes and a welcome pot of freshly brewed tea.

Off again, we stopped at Narmanlı Han, a charming *han*, 'Caravanserai' to leave a note for Aliye Berger-Bronai, artist, socialite and friend of the Arbels, who was the youngest of six siblings born into the prominent Shakir family of Istanbul and held court in her artistic salon in Beyoğlu, before arriving at the oldest and shortest underground funicular railway in Europe, built in 1875. This carried us down the hill to Karaköy, where Afife Hanım hailed a taxi to take us home.

I gazed across the Golden Horn at the magnificent buildings of the old city and at boats of all sizes criss-crossing the Bosphorus to villages on the Asian shore. The city which in the 16th century Petrus Gyllius wrote, 'It seems to me that while other cities are mortal, this one will endure as long as there are men on earth'. It reminded me of the setting for an opera. People in strange costumes jostled, shouting their wares; flower-sellers hunched on stools smoking, their billowing trousers as colourful as their flowers; horse driven carts galloped by; buses spouted black smoke; large American cars serving as taxis honked; sea-gulls following fishing boats and, above all this noise there was the faint cry of the *müezzin*, carried by the wind, calling the faithful to prayer. The buildings had a benign, neglected look, whereas the streets were a mayhem of noise, smells and people. I loved it, I found the energy of the streets completely unique.

Afife Hanım's conversation sparkled with anecdotes featuring artists and celebrities, and grand receptions. She told me the story of a ball they attended at which the British Ambassador's wife had flirted outrageously with Bedii Bey. An infuriated Afife Hanım, obviously jealous, complained in her five languages to a friend in the powder room when an attendant flew in demanding she lower her voice.

Turks are cat lovers and cats are considered sacred. Istanbul's streets are full of them. The story goes that the Prophet Mohammed found a cat sleeping on his robe and, rather than disturb it, he ordered the robe cut. Most homes care for one or more overfed cats. These felines greet you at the door, preen on cushions, and watch the world go by from windowsills. Old ladies carry brown paper bags with scraps to feed street cats, calling them by name. I often bought liver from a shop in Beşiktaş for Nil's aunt Fazila's three cats who lived in the garden. Dogs, for their part, had to be protected from the authorities who considered them dirty. This attitude has thankfully changed and today cats and dogs are loved and cared for alike.

I finally persuaded Nil to hand over the car keys. The first time I drove alone in Istanbul was the most terrifying experience of my life. I drove along Cumhuriyet Road, the main boulevard past the Hilton Hotel to Taksim Square, and down the hill to where the road divides – right to Galata Bridge and the old city and left along the Bosphorus shore road as far as Rumelikavağı, a tiny fishing village of nets, boats, trawlers and fish restaurants.

I drove at a snail's pace – not so much to avoid the few cars and *dolmuş* 'shared taxi' on the road, but due to a train of camels, horse-driven carts and *hamal* 'porters' bent double under heavy loads, balancing the weight with rope pulleys, shouting, *'Yol verin, yol verin!'* (Let me pass!) Then there were the pedestrians who would casually look in the opposite direction at the approach of a car! My destination was the old city. I crossed Haliç Bridge, which rides on broad pontoons and opens for an hour at dawn to allow boats to leave and enter.

Haliç, the Golden Horn, wasn't golden at all. It was a dirty, scary area of crumbling buildings and evil-smelling rundown buildings. I sat in the car as pleased as punch at having driven to the old city. When I had safely parked and locked the car on the corner of a narrow street of wooden houses, I began my wandering adventure around alleys and side streets to The Grand Bazaar. It was fascinating, I felt the physical intensity and earthy vibrant energy in the people and streets rather than anything eastern or exotic, although there were some strange costumes. Streets seemed not merely a means of getting from A to B but more like stage settings for a Turkish film with their clamour and noise and galloping horses.

Groups of moustached thick-set men in patched trousers stand at street corners or drink tea in local cafes playing dominoes, *tavla* 'backgammon' and card games. Turks are expressive, each word punctuated by gestures. Men greet each other with a kiss on both cheeks, walk arm in arm, shrug their shoulders, raise their eyebrows and nod instead of speaking. Outside the post offices and government buildings, retired bureaucrats in dark suits, shiny from wear, sit on stools in front of portable typewriters typing documents for a small fee for those who can't read or write. Shopkeepers sit on stools in front of the door waiting for a *simit* 'a delicious, fresh bagel-like ring of bread covered with sesame seeds cooked in wood-ovens'. *'Taze simit, taze simit'.* He is followed by young boys swinging brass trays of freshly brewed tea in tulip glasses. It's breakfast time in the bazaar.

School children in black uniforms with crisp, white collars and large white bows in their hair wave good-bye to their mothers, who leaned out of cushioned window-sills to lower a basket attached to a rope. *'Bakkal! Bakkal!'* (Grocer, Grocer), they shouted until the man in question pokes his head out to put the usual morning order into their baskets: a loaf of bread, white cheese, cigarettes and newspaper. As they pull up the basket, they continue chatting to neighbours waiting their turn. The grocer records this transaction in a big black book in the hope that one day he'll be paid, and I am sure he was. Lunchtime is heralded by men pushing covered barrows of rice, beans, *köfte* 'meatballs', followed by a barrow of sweet deserts such as *baklava.* This was street food at its best, long before it became popular in the west.

Most weekends found me in Sultanahmet with Nil or a friend. Crowded, noisy, disorderly, dirty and smelly – it was the Istanbul that I had expected. I loved the energy, humour and good nature of the people on the streets. My favourite places were Kariye Camii (former Church of St. Saviour in Chora), and Süleymaniye Camii. The latter is a city within a city, a magnificent mosque complex built by the great Ottoman architect Sinan, and a worthy monument to Suleiman the Magnificent. We would stand in silent awe under the cavernous dome, before moving on to Haghia Sophia, or wandering in the dark, musty claustrophobic harem quarters at Topkapı Palace (glad not to have been an odalisque at court), or strolling down narrow streets, wondering who lived in those dilapidated but delightful wooden houses with bay windows and lines of washing in Fener and Balat. Giggling children ran behind the car shouting. 'Look, a woman driving,' they hooted. But when I spoke to them, they scattered.

We bought simit or fresh warm bread from flour-covered men wearing striped pinafores and no shirt while pounding dough for *francala,* a soft centred white loaf with a golden crispy crust. It was the tastiest bread I have ever eaten. Hawkers selling combs, comics, books, lighters, fuel and razor blades on street corners shouted obviously rude remarks to amuse their companions. Cheeky waiters blocked our path. 'Very good food. You German?' Why did everyone have to be German? Back then, you saw few unescorted foreigners – other than hippies on their way to a pudding shop, which, we were told, purveyed other substances besides puddings. Young men would stare, but never threaten. On the contrary, people went out of their way to be helpful. The city soon lost its strangeness and many further secrets remained for me to discover.

The Tourism Office's advertisement for Istanbul in the sixties and early seventies ran as follows: 'Sights and sounds and smells of Istanbul, a city which straddles two continents, Asia and Europe.' Sights and sounds were obvious – but it was the smells that excited the memory and remain. You were sprayed with lemon or rose cologne when visiting a friend or leaving a restaurant. The cologne mixed with the pungent smells of fried fish sandwiches cooked under Galata Bridge, mussels and lobsters sold along the shores of the Bosphorus which in turn combined with the gypsy's fresh flowers. Restaurants smelt of good food, aniseed, and cigarette smoke, while bakeries gave forth their wonderful whiffs of hot fresh bread.

Each street and every corner hummed with the magic that was Istanbul. The city never slept. As the sun set, night-revellers took to the streets: young men wandered arm-in-arm with nowhere to go; well-dressed theatre-goers enjoyed a rakı and *meze,* 'hot and cold starters' before a show; artists, newspaper reporters, and blue-collar workers met friends in Beyoğlu's Greek meyhanes, tavernas, Armenian and Russian restaurants, or The Çiçek Pazarı's fish restaurants. Ladies of the night – young or old, skinny or plump – sat smoking on the doorsteps of derelict houses in the back streets of Beyoğlu and Karaköy waiting for clients. Small restaurants stayed open till dawn serving tripe soup to revive those who had over-indulged.

With each decade that passes Beyoğlu reinvents itself – its shops, restaurants and music – according to the mood, politics and people that walk its streets.

On my way home from my expeditions, I'd stop at the Greek delicatessen at the corner of Güzelbahçe Sokak to buy 'meze' for my father-in-law. The owner Aleko, fat and friendly, would welcome me with paper thin slithers of ham served on the blade of a long flat knife, or a chunk of cheese with brown bread and a green olive for me to try as I chose from an array of *dolma* 'rice stuffed vine-leaves', cheese or meat *börek* 'filled dough' and trays of sweet deserts. I always bought too much.

Transport around town was by tram, bus and shared taxi, the *dolmuş*. This was an ideal form of transport, quick, inexpensive and practical. It even dropped you off in front of your door. The dolmuş was a big, comfortable petrol guzzling, shiny American car of the 40's or 50's – Oldsmobile, Cadillac, Packard, Chrysler, Plymouth or Buicks, with room for two passengers in front and three in the back travelling along a fixed route. I used to pay for two tickets in the front, to enjoy the ride. These cars inspired an interest in old cars and many Turkish men began to collect them. The Rahmi Koç Museum has a stunning collection.

Being a creature of habit myself, I was delighted to learn that, on these early excursions, if you visit a place a few times you become, *bizden* 'one of us', a familiar face welcomed and looked after. It's such a simple human interaction, one that takes away the strangeness and the differences and makes you feel safe and has worked so well for me over the years.

The Many Delights of Turkish Cuisine

A love for good food and the delights of dining was an important part of life, socially and at home. There was no opportunity for me to cook at the Arbels. Twice a week Afife Hanım and Anna would huddle around the breakfast table discussing menus before Anna went to market. She would return in the late afternoon dazed and smelling of alcohol. No-one was welcome to mess about in her kitchen, I believe Afife Hanım tolerated her in order to practice her Russian. Besides, most days Nil and I were invited out to lunch or dinner – often together with my parents-in-law – to welcome back Nil after a five-year absence and out of curiosity to see the *yabancı gelin.*

I discovered pretty soon that when you marry a Turk you marry his family and I, despite the ups and downs, have been incredibly fortunate. I squealed with delight when I first tasted leeks simmered with carrots and rice in olive oil, after a childhood of boiled leeks or leek soup. This became 'Kim's favourite' and appeared on most family tables. The leek, with the daffodil, is the Welsh national emblem and we wore them on our lapels to school on St. David Day, March 1st, my birthday. Legend has it that the leek was once worn on the caps of Welsh soldiers to distinguish them from the enemy.

As we frequented the same restaurants, everyone knew everyone in those days. A family Sunday lunch included a leisurely drive along the Bosphorus to Abdullah Restaurant at Emirgan, a large wooden house set in a garden of fruit trees and vegetables that stretched to the shore of the Bosphorus. Children played hide and seek amongst the trees while their parents enjoyed a hearty lunch. Except for Sunday, every morning at 7 a.m. sharp, top-hatted and perfectly attired, Abdullah Bey would stand at the gate waiting for his car to take him to market.

Süreyya's in Bebek was a popular lunchtime venue for businessmen and in the evening a place to socialize with friends over dinner. Süreyya was a large imposing

Russian who waited and bowed his head in welcome before leading regular customers to their favourite table. He carried a small silver fork in his top pocket which he would take out to check on a dish that displeased him. If it was not up to par, a Molotov cocktail exploded in the kitchen. After his death, the restaurant was taken over by a young lady specializing in *nouvelle cuisine.* The few times we went there after it had changed hands, two old waiters who were delighted to serve familiar faces monopolised our evening. They hovered over our table, complaining: 'It's not the same as in the old days. People are big spenders but they don't know how to order or how to behave.'

But it was the Park Hotel that held its place as everyone's favourite. My in-laws never refused an invitation to the Park Hotel. Built next to the German Consulate on grounds belonging to the late Ottoman Grand Vizier, Ahmed Tevfik Pasha, it had a breath-taking view of the Bosphorus and Old City and a popular patisserie. During the Second World War it was one of two noteworthy venues catering to a horde of diplomats, officers and foreign spies in Istanbul which, as in Egypt, was a centre for political intrigue. The other was the Pera Palas near the British and American Consulates. The Park Hotel's spacious dining-room, with its pristine white linen and embossed silver cutlery, served famous guests such as Mustafa Kemal Atatürk, writer Yahya Kemal and Prime Minister Adnan Menderes.

The Hilton was the meeting place for the young crowd. A number of international films were set in Istanbul and all one had to do to see Hollywood stars was to take afternoon tea in the lobby, dine and dance at the rooftop restaurant, gamble in the Casino or become a member at the best tennis club in town.

Moda, on the Marmara Sea shore, was another marvellous place for lunch. Many of our friends lived there and we must have spent hours sitting in the car waiting to cross the Bosphorus by car-ferry. Moda has in parts retained its delightful Victorian Englishness and narrow cobbled streets when it was home to British, Levantine and Greek traders and businessmen in the 19th century and when Moda Yacht Club was established. The Greek Orthodox and Anglican churches are still active here. One of Moda's leading families was headed by James Whittall who set up J.W.Whittall & Co in 1873. My friend, Feyhan Sporel's mother was a Whittall with wonderful stories of her youth in Moda told over lunch elegantly served by a butler. Feyhan still resides in the same apartment overlooking the sea but longs for the old days and ways.

No matter where you go in Turkey, or what time of day it is, you will be offered a glass of tea or diminutive cup of Turkish coffee. Turkish hospitality is generous and instinctive and can at times be overwhelming. Every self-respecting Turk, male or female, is interested in food. Ingredients are fresh and cooking for a family dinner is given the same attention to detail as for a dinner party.

Food is indeed a passion. Turkish cuisine is a combination of tastes and recipes from the Aegean, the Mediterranean, Asia, the Balkans, the Caucasus, Middle East and Greece. As Musa Dağdeviren, a famous Kadiköy chef, has written: 'Food has no ethnicity, only geography'. Inherited from the Ottoman kitchen, classical Turkish cuisine is fine and delicate in taste, time consuming to prepare and a dying art. No two people ever cook a recipe the same way. The plus side of this is that it lends itself to contemporary fusion foods which are so popular these days. Added to this is a diversity of tastes because of different ingredients grown in a country extending from the warm sunny south to the vast plains of Anatolia, from the wet Black Sea coast to arid lands of the Arabic world. The Aegean and Mediterranean produce herbs and sweet-tasting olive oil to add to its abundance of fish and fresh vegetables while Central Anatolia and the South-East are famed for stronger flavours – spicy meat dishes and rich sweet desserts, baklava, *künefe* and *kadayıf* 'shredded wheat in syrup'. As well as being a vegetarian paradise, this culinary diversity serves to make travelling around the country a gourmet's delight.

We often arranged to have Sunday breakfast/brunch in a restaurant on the Bosphorus or at Polenezköy, the old Polish settlement of farmers beyond the Beykoz Forest. An array of cheeses, soft white, or strong yellow, green and black olives, large ripe tomatoes and cucumbers, butter, home-made jams, honey, fruit, eggs cooked with tomato and peppers and mopped up with fresh *francala* bread or *simit,* all washed down with umpteen glasses of tea.

Rakı, the national drink, is an aniseed-flavoured liquor, rather like Arabian arak and Greek ouzo, sometimes called 'lion's milk' because it turns white when water is added. It is sipped slowly between mouthfuls of 'meze' and puffs. It is an acquired taste, one I never acquired. I would drink beer or a glass of whisky on the rocks until such time as Turkish entrepreneurs started producing their own excellent Turkish wines.

Dark, sweet and strong, Turkish coffee should froth just as it is lifted from the heat. It is served *şekerli, orta* or *sade* 'very sweet, a little sweet, or bitter'. There is a Turkish saying: 'My desire is not for the coffee or the coffee house but for the talk that goes with it.'

Drinking a cup of Turkish coffee after dinner is not only good for the digestion but comes with a tradition of reading the coffee cup or fortune-telling, *fal.* After enjoying the coffee, place the saucer over the cup, turn the cup and saucer three times in the air, make a wish and set the cup and saucer upside down on the table. The sediment of the coffee grounds forms patterns on the sides of the cup and in the centre of the saucer, which a professional fortune teller or intuitive friend can interpret. I am not a coffee drinker but am a staunch believer in coffee cup readings. You would be amazed at how many times my *fal* has been true.

There is never any lack of conversation at a Turkish gathering. People are there to enjoy themselves so it's usually lively and good spirited, except perhaps when it comes to football teams or politics, when the discussion may become heated. Patriotic and military-minded, men revel in telling stories about their time in the military service. The country is known as a male dominated, patriarchal society, but I found that women played a very significant role in the tight-knit communities of a traditionalist society. There is a strong sense of family custom in which after the head of the family, the elder brother is called *abi,* and the elder sister, *abla* (never by their first name) are respected. The Turkish men I met treat women well, with respect and an old-fashioned protectiveness. They pay the bill and insist on seeing you home safely. Prone to superstition, they have a surprising tendency to self-criticism: *bizden adam olmaz* 'we will never be men' was a phrase I often heard. They criticize themselves, their countrymen, and of course the government, but woe and behold a foreigner who dares do so! When things go wrong, there is always someone else to blame. In politics, this often translates as some kind of foreign intervention.

Many households, large and small, have some domestic help, often a live-in retainer who is treated as part of the family and remains with the family until they retire. Women are proud hosts and housewives, always hospitable and capable, they openly express concerns of their social status, inequality in the work-place and education for their children. Feminism maybe discreet, subtle but I soon realized, in their own quiet way, they know how to get what they want.

Generally, Turkish men appreciate and expect good food because their mothers and wives are good cooks. Whole reputations are dependent on one special dish with a single secret ingredient. Recipes are passed down from one generation to another, but for eager foreign learners, it's frustrating. A recipe comes without measurements – all you will be told is: 'a pinch of this, a tablespoon of that, a water glass of oil and the rest according to your eye!'. Did you know that there are more than forty ways of cooking a 'börek' or an aubergine and there is a dessert made from *hamsi* 'anchovies'? The quality of olive oil is a matter for serious discussion.

Turkey was one of the last paradises for smokers. Everyone puffed away happily on Turkish or American cigarettes without any thought for the consequences. Doctors generally held a more permissive view of health which included a nightly glass of rakı, a cigarette, and a sensible diet of olive oil, seasonal vegetables, fruit, fish and meat. Fast-food didn't exist until McDonald's arrived in Taksim Square. However, a ban on smoking and the opening of fitness centres has aroused a growing awareness in health-care. Today many healthy Turks, young and old, come rain or shine, walk or run along the shores of the Bosphorus.

Mustafa Kemal Atatürk and Other Notables

When I arrived on the 36th Anniversary of the Republic, the country was emphatically Atatürk's Turkey. There were photographs of Kemal Atatürk in every home, shop, restaurant and office, and statues in every square and his name dominated political conversations. Everyone had an Atatürk story.

Those who survived the War of Independence described how a straggling army with little military power gathered behind a man who ordered them 'not to fight, but to die' for their country. He was a man of such charisma and passion that he became the voice of the nation, leading them to freedom, victory and the founding of the Republic of Turkey. His strength came from ordinary men and women in towns and villages who did their bit against the powerful Allied Forces.

An old lady recalled her experience when just four or five years old she lived in a large house in Alsancak, Izmir. One day her father swept her up in his arms and carried her to the attic in the house and laying her on a bed promised an ice-lolly if she could keep her eyes closed until he told her to open them. A few moments later foreign soldiers with guns entered to search the attic and seeing a child asleep, left quietly. Her face broke into smiles as she went on, 'I became very good at closing my eyes for those ice-lolles and was delighted to learn that the bumpy mattress hid a stock of guns'.

In a delightful little book called *A Taste of Old Istanbul*, Jak Deleon recalls a lesson in hospitality by Atatürk at Pera Palace Hotel:

> *'After the First World War, Istanbul is under the occupation of the allied forces, their Commander General Harrington is dining at the Pera Palace Hotel with his aide-de-camp. A man with a pensive and determined look on his face is sitting at another table. General Harrington signals for the headwaiter to ask, 'Who is that person?'*

The waiter's answer is clear: 'The hero of the Battle of the Dardanelles, Mustafa Kemal.' Harrington is taken aback. 'The legendary Mustafa Kemal? Please ask him to honour our table and have coffee with us.'

The waiter conveys the message to Mustafa Kemal, to which he replies, 'According to Turkish tradition, it is the host who invites. Despite the fact that they are commanders of the occupation forces, they are nevertheless our guests. They will have to leave one day. If they wish to have coffee with me, they should come to my table.' General Harrington and his aide were delighted to join Atatürk at his table.

Another coffee story that I like is that when a guest noticed that a waiter was not writing down orders for coffee at Atatürk's table, he asked the waiter, 'How will you remember who wants which coffee?'

The waiter replied, 'I know how the Pasha likes his coffee. No-one is likely to complain at his table.'

And there was a conversation I had with the intelligent daughter of a cousin which I have never forgotten. It was the beginning of 2000 when I asked her and her boyfriend, both university students, what they thought of the social changes which were taking place in the country. Her answer was quick and precise 'Our democracy is young and as a nation we are spoiled. We didn't fight for democracy or for our rights as you did in Britain. We fought to rid the country of Allied troops, the occupation forces, the British, French, Italian and Greek not for civil rights.' Her friend piped up, 'Atatürk was a reformer and an educator who wanted to give people a knowledge of facts through education, science and technology. He gave us the Latin alphabet, freedom of speech, he gave Turkish women the right of education and the vote before women in many European countries aquired theirs. Because we didn't have to fight for these rights, instead of nurturing them, we take democracy for granted.'

I was fortunate to meet quite a few extraordinary personalities. These include Ambassador Muharrem Nuri Birgi, a colleague and friend of Bedii Bey. My parents-in-law invited Nil and I to the Park Hotel to celebrate my birthday when in walked Nuri Bey. Afife Hanım purred, 'Nuri you must join us for dinner. It's Kim's birthday.'

'Happy birthday, darling. I'd be delighted to join your little party,' he replied cupping my hands with a kiss. Turning to my mother-in-law, 'Afife, darling, age has not changed you,' stroking her mink wrap, 'or dimmed that wicked twinkle in your eye.' They spent the whole evening gossiping and giggling in French. The next day Nuri Bey sent me a huge bunch of flowers with a well-thumbed Turkish/English dictionary.

I had already met Nuri Birgi when he was Turkish Ambassador to London. The former head of the Turkish Diplomatic Service, he was a dapper, brilliantly intelligent bachelor with an impeccable command of French and English. Soon after Nil and I married, he invited us to the Turkish residence in Grosvenor Square for lunch. His mother, a formidable Greek lady, presided over the table which included Turkish guests and the most obnoxious red-nosed Englishman I have ever met – obnoxious not only for his large intake of alcohol but for the disparaging remarks he made against the British. Conversation around the table was in Turkish so I sat there quietly admiring the fine blue and white Chinese porcelain collection on the dining-room wall when my host leaned towards me, 'Did you understand what my mother said to your husband?' he asked.

'No, I don't speak Turkish,' I replied.

'Well,' chuckled Nuri Bey, 'she asked Nil why he married a *gavur* – a rude word for a non-believer – when he should have married a nice Turkish girl from a good family like himself. And now I wish to put a question to you: What made you, a pretty young, seemingly intelligent English girl foolish enough to marry this spoilt Turk?'

I fell in love with Nuri Bey then and there and we kept in touch. He would introduce me as 'My dear, sweet friend, who insists on marrying Turks', but he did approve of my second husband and often invited us to lunch.

Though Nuri Birgi, ambassador extraordinaire, charmed his guests with his rather wicked wit and sense of humour, he wasn't always kind when it came to my mother-in-law. 'Afife', he warned me, 'can be quite impossible at times. She makes a habit of arriving late, wearing the most outrageous hats and furs. You will have your hands full with her, my dear'.

In 1968, Nuri Bey purchased Çürüksulu Mehmet Pasha Yalısı, an 18th century *yalı* 'waterside residence' in dire need of repair set in a garden overlooking Leandros (Maidens') Tower in the Sea of Marmara from his friend, Belkıs (Çürüksulu) Râtib. After selling the last of her jewels for the upkeep of her home, she was forced to sell the yalı and who better to care for it than her friend, Nuri Birgi who sold all three of his properties to purchase the property. With the help of his architect friend, Turgut Cansever, he restored the residence to his taste with the blue and white china collection dominating the dining room just as it had in the Turkish Residence in London, Nuri Bey set about landscaping and planting a rose garden.

I was often called upon to fill the chair of a guest at a lunch party who'd had to cancel at the last minute. The evening before or on the morning of the party, an exasperated voice would be on the telephone to me begging me to come and of course if I could, I went. No one ever refused Nuri Bey.

On one occasion, Belkis Kemali Söylemezoğlu, known as Benli Belkıs, as much for her beauty as for her marriages, walked into Nuri Bey's drawing room with the aura of a Fifties Hollywood star, blond hair, red lips and cigarette holder elegant and confident. Over lunch, which included Doctor Jenni and Emil Franco she was charming, funny and captivated us with stories of her Georgian family and life. I often exchanged greetings with her when I passed through the Hilton lobby where she, as elegant as ever, was taking tea with some high ranking military American guest.

Nuri Bey took a schoolboy's delight in shocking friends with impish, often unkind remarks.

One evening, during the interval of an Aphrodisias fund-raising event at Atatürk Cultural Centre, I saw Nuri Bey leaning against an empty bar looking rather frail. I walked over and was about to speak when, raising his hand, he said, 'Don't say I look well. I'm not. Don't ask if I am enjoying the concert. I'm not. I want to sit down. I'm thirsty and I want to go home.' I found a chair behind the bar and went off to get him a drink. On my return he was surrounded by friends. I gave him the drink he grimaced, blowing a kiss. That was the last time I saw him. Ambassador Extraordinaire Nuri Birgi was honoured with a state funeral.

He was cared for by a devoted German house-keeper. Not a wealthy man, in his last years, his needs were met by a close family friend, Selahattin Beyazıt. On his death he bequeathed the yalı to Selahattin Bey who has maintained it in pristine condition. Even though the present owners, one of Istanbul's most loved and socially active couples, Selahattin Bey and his wife, Ayşe Hanım open the doors of the residence to entertain guests for many charity evenings, the house seems frozen in time, soulless without its former owner's wit and presence.

A visit to Halide Edib Adıvar – novelist, professor, and companion – in-arms to Atatürk during the War of Independence was not only a pleasure, but a privilege. Before her retirement, Halide Hanım chaired the English Language and Literature at Istanbul University. Although she was quite bit older than Fazila, both were graduates from the American College for Girls and as colleagues at the university, a friendship had blossomed. Fazila often visited her and this time she had kindly included me in an invitation to tea.

A housekeeper opened the door of her modest house opposite Istanbul University and led us into a room lined with books where Halide Hanım sat at a table laid for tea. Smiling behind large round glasses, her skin was as white as her hair pulled back in a bun. She quizzed Fazila on the university, 'Oh dear, oh dear,' before going into a tirade, lighting a cigarette and lapsing into English. As her housekeeper poured tea, she explained how one day, during one of the many crises at the Royal court where her father served as private secretary to Sultan Abdülhamid, he had come home carrying a frightened, little black orphan in his arms from the harem at Yıldız Palace.

Since that day they had been inseparable.

Born into an elite, wealthy family, Halide Hanım was educated at home. She began writing articles on the social and political dilemma of the country and its fight for independence. A pragmatic reformer she became known as a 'firebrand' (as well as other, less polite names). She married Dr. Adıvar and together they fought side-by-side, she, first as a corporal then a sergeant with Atatürk in the War of Liberation. A difference of opinion between the more conservative members of the progressive Republican Party and their leader caused a few, including Halide Hanım and her husband, to leave, (some say flee) the country. They first went to France then England before settling in America. They returned to Turkey after the death of Atatürk in 1939.

A prolific novelist, socialist, feminist and academician she published twenty titles and was, at the time I met her, in the process of finishing a manuscript. The main theme of her novels was women's rights and their low social and political status in Turkish society, her main characters were strong women who devoted their lives fighting for the cause. Age had not diminished Halide Hanım's passionate fighting spirit for justice and woman's rights, nor softened her critical attitude to the government in power, she was always out-spoken and independent. Nearing 80 when I met her, in the nicest way she questioned me on the reasons why I had married a Turk then turning to Fazila began, in flattering terms to compare me with a mutual foreign friend they both knew. Halide Hanım died in 1964, by then one of the few survivors of the Turkish War of Independence.

Another of Fazila's colleagues was writer, translator and teacher, Prof. Dr. Mina Urgan. Mina would arrive at Fazila's apartment, dominate the conversation, fill the room with smoke for an hour or so, then march off.

She would greet me with a quote from Shakespeare, T. S. Eliot or Oscar Wilde and had collaborated with Scottish writer historian, Lord Kinross on his book, 'Atatürk, The Rebirth of a Nation'. Mina presented me with the book one Christmas saying of Atatürk's reforms, the shape of social life changed, women were no longer kept at home, they could go out with boys, have fun together, eat and drink together. Mina instilled a love for English literature in her students. White haired, short, rather plump, a cigarette never out of her hand, she translated many masterpieces, including works of Shakespeare, from English to Turkish. On her retirement, she wrote a book entitled *Bir Dinozorun Anıları* (A Dinosaur's Memoirs) published in 1998, which became a bestseller and has been reprinted over 70 times. This was followed by *Bir Dinozorun Gezileri* (A Dinosaur's Travels) another bestseller. Her success amazed and rather troubled her and her reaction, 'How come?' was typical.

The only person who could persuade Fazila Giz to do anything against her will was her younger sister, now Mrs. Faize Bekata. It was to placate her, Fazila finally agreed to move into the garden flat in Ayaspaşa the Bekatas had recently acquired. For months she stepped over crates of books to get into bed, though that didn't bother her as much as it did me. Her concern was the garden, 'I shouldn't have moved,' she moaned, 'I don't have time to tend to the garden'.

I had the key to her flat and from experience had learned the best way to handle Fazila was to do what was needed without her knowledge, then suffer the consequences. My second husband, Aydın Erkan knew all there was to know about soil and plants. He organized gardeners and lorries of earth to come to Ayaspaşa one Friday morning after Fazila had left for the university. By the time she returned home that evening, four men had, more or less, levelled six trucks of earth. Fazila was delighted. The next day she and Aydın drove to Belgrade Forest to buy trees, shrubs and plants, and together, they spent a glorious Sunday planting, while I unpacked crates of books. Tired but content Fazila was delighted with her garden and comfortable bedroom with her library in place and I was left to care for an exhausted husband, complaining of backache.

Across the road from Fazila's flat was a large wooden *konak* in a garden, home to Latife Hanım, ex-wife of Atatürk. In her book *Madam Atatürk*, İpek Çalışlar writes:

> *'Her family purchased a four-storey wooden mansion overlooking the Bosphorus in Ayaspaşa, this was one of the finest houses in Istanbul right in the heart of the city… Latife lived on the top floor… with a close circle of family and friends and her memories. She spent many hours in her room and took long walks in the garden over-looking the Bosphorus shaded by magnolia trees. From the window she could see Mustafa Kemal's comings and goings from Dolmabahçe Palace and rumours abound that the state kept a close eye on his ex-wife when she stood looking out of the window.'*

One afternoon, Fazila announced we were invited to tea. As we crossed the road, she repeatedly warned me not to mention Atatürk or ask questions. Latife Hanım had dark hair, a round face, wary brown eyes and a narrow mouth. She greeted us in a pleasant but rather dark room, as the shutters were half closed and introduced her guests, a tall slim aesthetic-looking man, a cousin, who was delighted to see Fazila and a lady friend. She was not beautiful nor did she ooze charm but was cultured and self-contained. She spoke of a visit to London adding, with the glimmer of a wistful smile, Paris was her first love. I recalled what Lord Kinross had written in his book, 'of his feminist reforms the personal symbol had been Latife…intelligent though she was, she lacked the gift of handling human beings'.

Over tea, conversation, partly in Turkish and partly in English centred around health, gardening, and old friends. It was pleasant and unremarkable. I sat there wondered how she had survived such a public break-up of her marriage, the emotional pain and public humiliation? One moment, First Lady of the Republic married to a man who was a legend in his life time, her every move and gesture photographed, imitated, newsworthy and the next moment removed from the world around her. Within two years and a few months it was over – her position, love, marriage, expectations, life – and she was forced into seclusion, never to be mentioned in public. Her demeanour, conversation and body language gave no hint of her past, she was no aging celebrity. The gravity and seriousness of her manner had moulded and aged her expression. As we walked back to her flat with a smile of approval, Fazila said, 'she might invite you again'.

Latife Hanım moved to an apartment in Harbiye where on 12th July 1975, she died. She deserves recognition and respect for the discretion and dignity she showed in the latter part of her life. On March 17th 1976, a year after her death, her family entrusted her personal possessions and papers to Professor Enver Ziya Karal, then president of the Turkish History Society. When and if they are ever disclosed, will they reveal unknown facts concerning the Republic? Or her traumatic marriage? Or just the bittersweet story of a woman spurned in love?

Finally, I turn to Çelik Gülersoy, for as a friend of his wrote, 'no book on Istanbul would be complete without mentioning certain people whose influence vision and effort has left a strong imprint on the city.'

Çelik Gülersoy's name is synonymous with the first wave of the preservation and restoration of Ottoman buildings. Tall, impressive, with charming, old-fashioned manners, his father had died when he was five years old and he devoted his life to caring for his mother. He was director of the Turkish Touring & Automobile Association, founded in 1923, and affiliated to various international tourist and automobile organizations that issued licences to every vehicle entering or leaving the country. This steady cash flow financed Çelik Bey's vision to convert Ottoman buildings into touristic venues-hotels, restaurants, parks and hunting lodges. In 1984, his pioneer project was the restoration of a 19th century mansion, Yeşil Ev in Sultanahmet into a boutique hotel with twenty-nine rooms, a hamam and delightful conservatory dining room in the garden. It became the in-place to stay, even though some critics ranked it, kitsch. In 1986, the walls of Topkapı Palace in Soğukçeşme Sokağı became the backdrop for a street of elegant Ottoman hotel rooms. In one of these buildings he created a library and underground restaurant, Sarnıç. Çelik Bey's golden years stretched from 1977-1990, during which he developed hotels, köşks, pavilions, hunting lodges and mansions in royal gardens.

I would book visiting guests into Yeşil Ev or Soğukçeşme Sokak. This way they would avoid traffic, and see the beauty of mosques in the morning mist, or lit up at night from their bedroom window. Çelik Bey was an enormous help, and a fount of knowledge. He opened many doors for me, normally closed to the public, so my guests could research archives. He enjoyed the company of like-minded people insisting he host breakfast concerts of classic Turkish music in the library. However, this used to cause problems because of tight schedules and limited time: although guests appreciated the concert and delicious breakfast it took up a whole morning, and I began to receive 'not on the programme' complaints. Not wanting to disappoint my friend, I found a way around the problem by changing the itinerary slightly to include a choice between a free morning shopping or concert breakfast. I also included a Happy Hour with Çelik Gülersoy as our guest before dinner at the Yeşil Ev on the last evening. It worked. Believe it or not, most people chose breakfast and thoroughly enjoyed Happy Hour with Çelik Bey.

During the Istanbul Music Festival, if Çelik Bey was in his office I would join him for a glass of wine before a concert. A pioneer in his field, he was generously awarded for his work by Turkish, Italian and French governments. It included a 'first' from Europe Nostra as the only person to be presented with two awards for his work on historic preservation. Çelik Gülersoy died in 2001 and is buried at Demirciköy.

Büyükada

Breakfast at my parent's house in Wales had been quiet, with a quick peck on the cheek before I left for school. In fact, one of my father's rules was no bad news before breakfast or a meal (a comfort at exam result time). At the Arbel's home in Şişli, breakfast began with a morning argument between mother and son. Obsessed as she was by Nil, Afife Hanım didn't seem happy at his return. I began to wonder if I was the problem. Perhaps she didn't want to share her son? Having been so beautiful in her youth, she might resent a younger woman being around as some do as they grow older. I realized Nil and his parent were able to argue then walk away as though they hadn't crossed words. I wasn't able to do that, and, being pregnant, my over-active hormones didn't help. Afife Hanım's mood swings made my days uncertain. One moment she was kindness itself, the next manipulative and uncharitable – not to me, but to those around her. I realized this must have been the way they had communicated since Nil was a child, it was a part of their complex mother-son relationship. I just happened to be there.

She could be so tricky. Whenever we were invited out together just before we left, she would drape one of her fur stoles over my shoulders. On our return, I placed the fur carefully on a chair in our bedroom to find in the morning it had disappeared when I asked Anna if she'd taken it, she snarled, 'Only Madam is allowed to touch her furs, they are locked in a cupboard.' When I asked Afife Hanım over breakfast about it, 'Yes dear, I put it in the cupboard.' This weird fur, fox, or mink scenario continued until the weather warmed, whereupon I never saw the furs again.

As part of their social life, ladies held weekly afternoon tea or bridge parties. Afife Hanım never did. She rarely entertained and when she did it was on a grand scale, amusing her guests with endless stories and playfully flirting with their husbands. She kept in touch with her nieces and nephews especially when Faiza, her favourite niece, came to stay with her sister, Fazila, and the family gathered together. Once a month she and Bedii Bey lunched with a lovely Swedish lady and her diplomat Turkish husband at the Park Hotel.

Bedii Bey had many friends who would drop by in the evening for a glass of rakı, a chat, or game of chess before dinner. Afife Hanım either adored or ignored them. There was Nubar, a portly Armenian who lived in Büyükada but spent winter weekends in town. Afife Hanım did not approve of Nubar because he would arrive with a bottle of rakı to add interest to their game of chess. Not good for Bedii's health, she complained loud enough for him to hear. She saw to it that Bedii Bey had just one glass of rakı diluted with water.

In mid-May, the Arbels moved to Büyükada – *Prinkipo*, as Afife Hanım called it – in the Marmara archipelago also known as Princes Island because it was where troublesome Byzantine and Ottoman princes, as well as a few foreign dissidents, were exiled. One of them was Leon Trotsky who after his flight from Russia completed his autobiography and the History of the Russian Revolution during his exile on the island from 1929 to 1933. Motor transport is forbidden, instead tasselled horse-drawn carriages, phaetons, with their drivers hunched in overcoats, line the square near the pier waiting to take passengers to their front door from the ferry. The housekeeper, Hatice's husband, Hasan was the proud owner of a horse and carriage. In the mornings he brought newspapers, milk and groceries and would ring his bell whenever he passed. If he was free, he would drive us around the island. Horse's hooves set the pace of life for the residents living in those turn-of-the-century white villas, with gardens amassed with bougainvillea, wisteria, oleanders and roses. The local permanent residents added to the colour and charm of the island, Turkish fishermen and Greek taverna owners lived side by side with a sprinkling of Armenians and handful of Jews. In spring, konak shutters were thrown open, lawns manicured and garden debris raked in preparation for the arrival of their owners for the summer season.

The Arbel konak, its paint flaking off under overgrown wisteria, was a stone's throw from Luna Park at Maden Square, end of the Grand Tour. An uphill walk took one to a popular spot - the highest peak of the island where Greek monks from the Aya Yorgi Monastery produced home-made wine to sell to those who climbed the hill to watch the sunrise and sunset.

Nil and I joined Bedii Bey and Afife Hanım at weekends. They appeared happier and more active on the island. Hasan took me on a tour and I fell in love with Büyükada. Bedii Bey set up his easel on a balcony while Afife Hanım would work in the garden. Everyone knew each other on the island, most evenings neighbours, Turkish, Greek, Armenian, retired diplomat friends, dropped by for drinks hosted by Bedii Bey in white flannels and shirt, and Afife Hanım in a colourful summery kaftan. On Saturday evenings we dined at the Anadolu Club.

My pregnancy passed quite easily with the help of Dr. Spock, the pregnant woman's bible at the time. I asked Afife Hanım what arrangements I should make and spent the afternoon listening to her own difficult birth with Nil, the possible complications her doctor had spoken of and how she had silenced him with an instruction to save the child at all costs. She had been in her mid-forties at the time, living in Germany, I was horrified I might have to make such a choice. Finally, she telephoned her nephew, Dr. Mehmet Giz instructing him to make the arrangements, he was delighted and immediately got down to work. His choice of gynaecologist was Dr. Kazım Arısan from the Güzelbahçe Clinic, he insisted that he and Şevket Bey whenever possible accompany me on my monthly visits – for reasons which soon became obvious. They were classmates at medical school and looked forward to a monthly chat. For my first visit I prepared a list of questions. It was after all my first birth and in a foreign country. Dr. Kazım answered one or two questions politely before he said, 'Look here, young lady, you are not the first, nor will you be the last, woman to give birth in Turkey. I am a good doctor and that is why you are here. The hospital is the best in Istanbul. Our women give birth in fields. You are young and healthy. I assure you that the care you receive here will be far better than you would receive in England. No more questions, now, be a good girl. Follow the nurse into the other room, she knows what to do while my friends and I catch up with our news.' Every appointment was the same.

On 26th July, 1959, Fazila, Nil and I drove to Faiza's summerhouse at Dragos to spend the day. It was hot. I floated in the cool turquoise Marmara Sea in a frilly skirted bathing costume, while her young children, Nur and Fatoş tried to immerse then splash my baby bump sticking out of the water. Nur remembers her great aunt, Afife Hanım as 'the most magical story teller'. After lunch we picked cherries from a tree in the garden and hung the biggest, darkest, shiniest ones as earings from our ears, then licked the sweet juice from our fingers. The children climbed up to the highest branches to pick the sweetest fruit. Tired but happy we drove home in the late evening. After a quick shower, I fell asleep to wake in the early hours of the morning with labour pains.

Dr. Kazım Arısan and his team attended the birth of a beautiful girl born on 27th July 1959. Mehmet held my hand throughout and I remember others coming in and out of the room, smoking and talking. Baby names had been a hot subject of conversation. Bedii Bey had suggested St. Cyr, a French writer he admired. I was sure it was the name of the French Military Academy. Afife Hanım wanted her brother's name, then mother's name, then her own. One day I came home from the market. 'I heard a lovely word, a name for a girl,' I said. '*Lahana*. Pretty isn't it.' 'Yes, dear,' sighed my mother-in-law in utter disgust. 'I hope you didn't buy one and won't name your daughter, *lahana* because it means cabbage.'

I chose Ceylan which means gazelle from a book. Nil, as usual, made no comment. A day after the birth, Nil handed me the baby's birth certificate: *Ceylan St. Cyr Afife Arbel.* To keep the peace, Nil had pleased everyone.

Ceylan's cot was in the far corner of an empty nursery and, though it was summer, she was brought to me wrapped under a blanket. One nurse used to hiss and spit around her, muttering '*tu tu çok çirkin, çok çirkin*' ('very ugly, very ugly') under her breath whenever she was around the baby. I complained to my doctor. He laughed, explaining that it was part of a ritual to ward off the evil eye and spirits because she was so beautiful. The *nazar boncuğu,* a blue stone with an eye in the centre, is a motif, talisman, to keep evil at bay and ward off negative thoughts and actions. Since then the *nazar boncuğu,* in all forms, can be found in every room of the house. We are great believers in *nazar boncuğu.*

I received a tearful letter from my friend Myshka in London, saying her three years engagement to a medical student had ended. I suggested a change of air was just what she needed, and invited her to help me with the baby, I offered to buy the ticket and pay a small pocket money salary. She accepted. I was delighted, Myshka was a friend, who loved children and at the same time would be a companion for me. Her mother had died when she was young and her father, an ex-officer in the Polish Free Army had remarried an Irish lady who gave birth to 5 children and Myshka had been roped in to help.

Ceylan, Nil, Myshka and I moved to Büyükada and my parents-in-law moved back to the city. Ceylan spent her first months following the sun around on balconies in a cot, shaded by fragrant pines and oleanders. Friends arrived by boat from Istanbul for the day, Jane White, a fellow student from Central School flew in from Cyprus and Nil's Greek friend, Petros fell in love with the island and stayed on and on. We swam, walked in the forest, shopped once a week, and lunched on fish at tavernas on the jetty. Occasionally friends of Nil's parents invited us to the Anadolu Club. A surprise telephone from a school friend, Catherine Fitzmaurice, added an unforgettable weekend to this near-idyllic life. Catherine's sister was PA to an eminent surgeon at St. Thomas' Hospital. He had been invited as guest speaker to an international medical conference in Istanbul. However, this rather eccentric gentleman would only accept invitations to places he had contacts. I was the only person they knew in Turkey, so had to help out. I agreed to invite them to the island for a weekend if Catherine promised to visit. A few weeks later Nil went to the Hilton Hotel to meet our guests. Delighted with the cool ferryboat and horse carriage ride after the heat of a city, they stepped off the phaeton screeching, 'This is heaven. It's Heaven! Thank you so much for inviting us,' thus setting the tone for the weekend.

The fiftyish surgeon (who will remain anonymous) was portly, bald with an interesting face, curious piercing eyes and an energetic air. His wife had shoulder-length blond hair and a ready smile. I showed them to their room. By the time dinner was served they had already explored the house, admired Bedii Bey's paintings, and climbed down the steps with Petros to the rocky cove we shared with our neighbour, an ex-president of parliament.

The next morning, while Myshka and I prepared lunch and Nil shopped, Petros took the guests for a morning swim. With Ceylan in my arms I climbed down the steps to join them as a shout came up, 'Come in Kim! Strip off! It's wonderful.'

There, on a rock jutting out of the sea, was the eminent surgeon, his wife, and Petros, standing, waving and shouting – quite naked. When Petros saw me, he threw himself into the water to swim ashore, sheepishly wrapping a towel around himself. I whispered at him, 'Petros, are you mad! The neighbours can come down any moment, and we'll land in jail for indecent behaviour. Quickly get them into the water.'

Waving I shouted, 'Lunch ready soon. I'll dip Ceylan in that little pool before I put her to sleep.' and made a quick get-away to warn Nil, who rushed off to see if our neighbours were in residence. He was relieved when the housekeeper reported they were not expected until the following week.

The eminent surgeon and his wife kept us in hysterics with tales of nudist camps. During the day they swam with Petros while we made feeble excuses. On the evening of the Gala Dinner at Dolmabahçe Palace, they appeared downstairs, elegant in evening attire – but he was wearing one black sock and one brown sock. 'My dear wife brought one of each,' he laughed, as they climbed into a friend's motorboat to be taken to Dolmabahçe pier. The dinner was a huge success and his speech received a standing ovation.

On their last evening, Bedii Bey arranged that the President of the Anadolu Club and a few friends invite us to the Club for dinner. Over plates of 'meze', fresh fish and rakı, our guests listened enthralled to stories of the island's famous exiles and its part at the end of the Second World War. We kept in touch. They lived in a heavenly house in Regent's Park and at one of their soirees, I danced in their small but absolutely charming ballroom. We discussed plans for another visit, but it never came about. Three or four years later, however, a rather bedraggled exhausted young man did knock on our door in Istanbul. He turned out to be their son returning from months travelling through Iran and eastern Turkey. I threw him in the bath from where he reappeared handsome, and quite as charming and talkative as his delightful parents.

Summer days gave way to autumn. Trees turned reddish gold. The evenings grew cool. It was time to return to Istanbul, but I insisted on staying. Myshka and I took it in turns to shop and care for Ceylan who intoxicated with fresh sea and Pine tree air was no trouble at all. She slept and slept again. We lit fires in the sitting room and stoves in the kitchen. We collected wood and twigs so that we could roasted chestnuts. Shops and restaurants pulled down their shutters and friends left. That winter it snowed in Büyükada. It was so quiet, the clip-clop of hooves muted by the snow, the air was invigorating, snow-brushed trees surrounded a grey-blue sea. We left the island in late November.

The Coup

Until the end of the Second World War, Turkey was ruled as a one-party state with a population that was 90% Muslim and a Greek, Jewish and Christian minority. In January 1946, Celal Bayar, Adnan Menderes and two others formed the Democratic Party. Its landslide victory over CHP and public support in 1950 marked the beginning of multi-party politics in Turkey. The transition has proven a rocky road with a great deal of opposition.

Prime Minister Adnan Menderes formed a new government with Celal Bayar as President. To conciliate the party's religious, conservative followers in 1950, the government passed laws which still have negative reverberations today. The most controversial dealt with religion: the *ezan* 'call to prayer from the minaret of mosques' was changed back to Arabic from Turkish, and permission was granted to open *İmam Hatip* religious schools to train Imams and priests. In addition, the popular educational *Köy Enstitüleri,* 'village institutes', set-up throughout the country by Atatürk were closed. At the height of the cold war between Russia and the west, American President Truman wrote to President Ismet Inönü complaining that the Village Institutes resembled the Soviet System but the ınstitutes did not closed until 1954 under the Democratic Party. Never the less blame fell on Menderes and the Democrat Party.

On 17th February 1959, I was horrified to see blood flowing in street gutters outside the apartment. It was the blood of animals, slaughtered as a sacrificial act of gratitude for the Prime Minister, who had escaped unhurt from a plane crash. Adnan Menderes was flying to London to sign the London Agreement on Cyprus with British Prime Minister, Harold Macmillan, and Greek Prime Minister, Constantine Karamanlis, when the flight was diverted to Gatwick Airport due to poor visibility. It crashed and caught fire in Jordon's Wood, Surrey, during its approach. Five members of the crew and nine passengers died. The Prime Minister walked off the plane unscathed, to a hero's welcome at home and the slaughter of all those poor animals.

Adnan Menderes was born into a land-owning family in the province of Aydın. He grew up amongst farmers and villagers and from a young age felt empathy for those working on the land. One of his election campaign promises was to modernize agriculture and the lot of the farming communities. True to his word, his first task as Prime Minister was to set up an agriculture credit system providing farmers with credit to buy modern agricultural machinery and import cotton seeds from America. Wasteland was distributed and roads built, unpaved perhaps, but nevertheless lifelines connecting villages to towns. Between 1950 and 1960, agricultural output doubled and the national product increased fourfold. Agriculture flourished, and so did life in villages as stone houses with running water and electricity replaced mud-brick huts. High on the agenda was a network of roads connecting villages to towns throughout Anatolia and plans to build a bridge across the Bosphorus were on the drawing board. But at the same time public debt tripled.

Adnan Menderes underestimated the opposition and the importance that the middle class, academics, socialists and city dwellers gave to political expression and freedom of speech. When the government refused to increase military expenditure, the army entered the political arena and the Prime Minister did not respond wisely to the rumblings by disgruntled officers in military halls. From the very beginning Menderes's relationship with the opposition party was uneasy, the CHP was a well-established experienced party while the Democratic party was young and unexperienced. Menderes did not trust the close affiliation between İsmet İnönü and the army.

With inflation rampant and the economic situation worsening, the general sense of discontent further increased following the constraining laws against the press and political activities imposed by the government. Tension gathered momentum as young army officers sided with workers and students took to the streets. The city was rife with rumours of a military coup. Factories were closed, classes cancelled, workers marched and students demonstrated in the streets demanding the resignation of the Prime Minister and government. Riots and clashes between police and students turned nasty. The government's muzzling of the opposition and media added fire to the flames. On 27th May 1960, as Adnan Menderes and his entourage were driving from Eskişehir to Ankara, the Democrat Government was overthrown in a bloodless military coup.

Nil had left to perform his six months military service as English teacher/translator to officers in Amasya. Myshka, Ceylan and I had moved into an apartment behind Şişli Mosque, overlooking the green playing fields of a school. Afife Hanım rang the bell every other day to check on her granddaughter. Early in the morning of the day of the coup, a banging on the door woke me. It was Yusuf, the doorman. He rushed past me into the sitting room and turned on the radio, gesturing me to sit. It was a declaration by Colonel Alpaslan Türkeş, former President of the Nationalist Movement Party. At 3 a.m. that morning, Turkish armed forces had taken over the country. There was a curfew. Yusuf warned us not to leave the apartment, he would buy what we needed. With each hour I grew more agitated. I had no idea what was happening and didn't even have a telephone to call someone. By the afternoon, ignoring Myshka's pleas, I decided to go to my parents-in-law's apartment, which was nearby.

The usually busy street was deserted, curtains drawn, shops shuttered and locked. Silence prevailed except for distant rumblings. I turned the corner into the main Şişli Mosque Square and froze. On both sides of the boulevard, soldiers, rifles in hand, stood in-line as tanks rolled past. It was like a scene from a Second World War film. No one noticed me in the shadow of the doorway. I don't know how long I stood there, watching, undecided whether to return home or try to pass those soldiers. I had to cross that road to reach the Arbel apartment and I did so want to speak to Bedii Bey. Taking a deep breath, I walked towards the line. Guns crashed in front of me blocking my path. A soldier shouted and an officer ran towards me, screaming in Turkish, 'Stop, stop! Where the hell do you think are you going?'

'I am going to my parent-in-law's house at Güzelbahçe Sokak, across the street,' I said in Turkish, then in English. 'I am British.' 'British or not, it makes no difference, don't you know there is a curfew?' he barked back in English. 'And it is forbidden to leave the house'.

'My husband is in the army and I have a baby at home and don't know what is going on.' I could hear my voice rising in panic which made him angrier.

Cursing, swearing, he swept the guns aside with his hand, shouting at a soldier to come over. 'This soldier will take you to the house and bring you back. Be quick,' he said ordering us to return to the same spot.

The soldier pulled me across the road before a tank rolled past. We ran down a side street to Güzelbahçe Sokak. Anna opened the door. Shocked to see me she smothered me in wet Russian kisses shouting for Afife Hanım. Afife Hanım pulled me into the sitting room, telling Anna to feed the soldier. Bedii Bey, with his usual calm, assured me that there was nothing to fear, that the coup was not unexpected. 'We must be patient and wait. In the meantime, obey orders until the curfew is lifted. I suggest that you, Myshka and the baby come here.' I agreed.

Thanking the soldier, Bedii Bey urged him to see I reached home safely. Afife Hanım hugged me, Anna handed me a bag of food, and we headed back to the same spot where the officer had entrusted me to the soldier. He was there, walking up and down. He crossed the road, lowered the guns and rushed us across the road. 'Never do that again. This isn't England,' he said, and, relieved to see the last of me, raced off before I could thank him. The soldier and I hurried through the deserted streets back to the apartment where Myshka, with Ceylan in her arms, watched anxiously from the window.

The coup, bloodless and swift, the work of a group of junior rank officers, was applauded by socialists, academics and workers in large towns especially Istanbul and Ankara. In most rural areas, especially the Aegean, citizens were subdued. Following a long and drawn out trial at a military compound on Yassıada, the last island of Marmara archipelago, 123 members of the party were acquitted, 31 sentenced to life-imprisonment and 418 sentenced to lesser prison terms. Fifteen received death sentences, which were later revoked. The government was imprisoned. Prime Minister Adnan Menderes, Foreign Minister Fatin Rüştü Zorlu and Minister of Finance Hasan Polatkan were hung. This remains a black spot in the political history of Turkey.

Sir Bernard Burrows, British Ambassador to Turkey between 1958-1962, writes in his book *Diplomat in a Changing World* that Menderes had been reckless both in dealing with the opposition and in embarking on a massively under-financed development programme. But, he adds, 'this should not obscure his basic commitment to the good of Turkey as he saw it, which was a more powerful motive than any idea of personal aggrandisement.' A Turcophile and unflappable diplomat with many friends in Ankara, Burrows continues, 'My wife had cakes baked at the Embassy kitchen and we sent them, by devious means, to our friends who were in prison to supplement their regulation diet. This must have been well known to the Turkish authorities, but they never raised any objection'.

The new constitution, drawn up by the National Unity Committee is the most liberal constitution ever to be drawn up in Turkey. It was a reaction against political abuse and anti-democratic policies and set out to stabilize public order, prevent terrorism and abuse of power against the media and universities, and to stimulate economic and social reform. It included a remarkable tolerance for political activities. Citizens and students were given civil rights, freedom of speech and expression, the right to belong to associations, to set up societies and institutes, and publish books. The result was a surge of energy in production, construction and manufacturing in the private sector. Factories produced black and white televisions with three channels, electric equipment, refrigerators, washing-up machines for the home, and the semblance of a telephone system. Until then the radio was the main source of news and entertainment.

Much of the social life for expatriates and foreigners living and working in Istanbul during this time took place either at the British Consulate social club or the magnificent grounds and wooded hills of Robert College, which in 1974 became Bosphorus University, and Rumeli Hisarı where academics and writers lived and were as famed as much for their partying, some of which I joined, as for their literary output. This community centered around a charismatic American/ Irish, teacher and writer, John Freely and his wife, Gillian, Toots to friends. Everyone seemed to have strolled somewhere around Istanbul with John as part of the brilliant book he and Hilary Sumner-Boyd wrote, '*Strolling Through Istanbul*'. One evening I found myself sitting next to James Baldwin, champion of U.S civil rights at dinner, I was surprised that he seemed so consumed in his own world rather than the goings-on in Turkey. It was here I met Ann Bruno, an American journalist, a large, impressive lady who knew everyone and was invited to every party, be it Turkish or foreign. I remember discussing politics with her at the Daily News office in Babıali.

Another member of this happy community I came to know well was Godfrey Goodwin, professor of art history at Robert College who wrote '*The History of Ottoman Architecture*' and his wife, Dolores. At 80 years old Godfrey still taught summer courses and took tours to Edirne. One evening at dinner at the home of Mary Berkmen, he related a story, I have no idea if it's true, but it was a great tale.

Waiting at a bus station at the end of a hitch-hiking tour in Greece when he was a student, Godfrey saw a road sign to Istanbul and on the spur of the moment jumped on the bus. Walking down the gangway he was rudely pushed from behind twice, the last time into the back seat of the bus only to see a bedraggled bear and his owner plonk themselves next to him. The bear keeper shared his meal, bread, cheese, olives and nuts with the bear and Godfrey and when they arrived at the bus station outside the city, he insisted on taking Godfrey to a safe boarding house to spend the night. 'That is when I decided, sometime in the future, I would come to teach in Istanbul'.

The late Norman Stone academic, historian and author, told me he decided to settle in Turkey on his first visit when he saw two policemen smoking under a non-smoking sign 'my sort of country' he thought and was quite satisfied to follow any medical advice given by his smoker doctor friends. Norman was great company, he was good-hearted, intellectual and a constant source of humour. A member of the Crimean Church community in Istanbul, he inspired countless students and did much to promote Turkey in his books and articles.

Unfortunately, when I moved to Aydın I lost touch with many in this vibrant group from Robert College who wrote and taught and did so much to preserve the cultural wealth of Turkey. I personally have never considered myself an ex-patriate or ex anything. As long as I am allowed to be myself, I fit in.

The new freedoms and technology allowed people to become active in social movements. Experimental theatre groups put down roots, and actors including Yıldız and Müşfik Kenter and Haldun Dormen, and musicians such as Hikmet Şimşek, Timur Selçuk and Zülfü Livaneli came to the fore. Youth festivals took place, and Yapı Kredi Bank instructed Ruhi Su to organise the first music folklore archive. Books by Yaşar Kemal that were previously outlawed were published and translated. In addition, feminism boomed: women made their voices heard, led by Şirin Tekeli and Duygu Asena.

The strange phenomenon about the sixties and seventies was even though they were decades of dire shortages, the cold war, the Kremlin glowering over Turkey's shoulder and the arrival of American troops, teachers and a fair amount of spies to preserve an international balance and thriving P.X black market those years are remembered with nostalgia as the Golden Era of friendship, culture, theatre and art and agriculture!

In 15th September 1984, General Turgut Sunalp stood up in Parliament and made an extraordinary apology for the 1961 hanging of Adnan Menderes, Fatin Rüştü Zorlu and Hasan Polatkan, adding that the executions were events 'that could no longer be forced into the acceptance of the public conscience' and 'had always been productive of unease and disturbance'.

Amasya

My first journey outside Istanbul, in the later months of 1960, was to Ankara, capital of Turkey and Amasya – to keep up the moral of a disgruntled husband in the military service. I flew to Ankara to stay with Faize and Hıfzı Bekata, newly appointed Minister for Foreign Affairs in the Republican People's Party (CHP), for a weekend before taking a train to Amasya.

At the airport the taxi driver beamed when I gave him the address. 'Ah, Hıfzı Bekata *Beyefendi* (sir). Good man, one of us.' He then proceeded to relate how he and his sons had demonstrated against the former government. He refused to accept my fare, carried my luggage to the door, and with a broad smile said, 'You are our guest. Give Hıfzı Bey my greetings.'

It was a large, comfortable house set in a shady garden. Later it became the Tunisian Embassy. Faize and Hıfzı's daughters, Nur and Fatoş, took me to my room and sat on the bed plying me with questions. Faize's brother Ahmet and his wife Zeliha Giz joined us for dinner adding their voices to the heated debate of whether it was safe for me to travel alone in Anatolia. Hıfzı and Ahmet blamed Nil: 'he's doing his military service like everyone else, there's no need for you to go. Stay here.' Faize and Zeliha agreed. But having come this, far I was as eager to see Amasya as I was to see Nil.

The next morning Faize took me on a walking tour around the town that Atatürk had chosen as the capital of the Turkish Republic. We climbed the hill to the Byzantine fortress, old castle and city to see the panoramic view of modern Ankara, met Faize's colleagues at the university and called on Ambassador and Mrs. Burrows for tea at the British Embassy. That evening we dined at the Gar Gazinosu.

Ankara, with a population of one and less than a half million, was more orderly than Istanbul. Except for the old quarters round the citadel, it was well-planned, green and clean, peopled with diplomats, bureaucrats and an army of office workers who kept the wheels of the ministries, banks and offices turning. People flocked to listen to classical music at concert halls, watch plays and ballet performances at the Ankara State Conservatory. Many restaurants had live music with dancing and a show. The quality of life and cultural activities in some respects in Ankara was far superior to those in Istanbul.

At the station the following day, Faize implored the guard to keep a watchful eye on me. Opening a carriage-door he helped me in. Then, with a grand gesture, locked the door, holding the key high so Faize might see, calling out 'Don't worry, she will be perfectly safe. I'll open the door at Amasya.' There were no corridors joining compartments. Faize grinned smugly at my expression of horror.

The train chugged across the flat arid Anatolian plains until it reached Amasya where the guard, full of smiles, unlocked the door and delivered me like a parcel to my waiting husband. Amasya was a surprise. A pleasant surprise. It was extremely cold as we hurried along the bank of the Yeşil Irmak River, past a row of quaint but dilapidated timber-framed Ottoman houses with large bay windows to the Belediye Gazino Oteli, the only hotel in town. There were few people on the street, but I noticed that every time a woman in a long black garb passed, she'd tilt an umbrella ever so slightly so as to hide her face. Amasya was a conservative, traditional town.

We were shown into a large and bare but clean room. Nil's face lit up as Marlboro cigarettes, Nescafe, chocolates and six cans of beer toppled out of my suitcase. In the empty hotel restaurant, we were given a table in a corner reserved for families near a big black stove. It was hot and smoky but the food was delicious – mounds of warm flat bread, thick, hot soup, and rice with meat sweetened with apples. Next morning Cihat, a Caucasian officer friend of Nil, joined us for breakfast. Handsome in his uniform, he was eager to show me the town before taking us by local train to visit relatives in a nearby Caucasian village.

Cihat explained Amasya's fascinating geography to us. The town was built on both sides of the Yeşil Irmak River and was well protected, shadowed by craggy mountains and forests. Historically known as the city of kings, young Ottoman princes were sent to Amasya as governors, a sort of royal apprenticeship, before being thrown to wolves and intrigues at the Sublime Porte in Istanbul. Amasya is picture perfect, a symphony of natural beauty, architecture, rock sculpture, classical ruins and derelict buildings. The mountains cast a shadow over the winding river and Ottoman mansions on its banks. As though that was not enough, Amasya grows the smallest, sweetest, crispiest red apples in the world.

We climbed ancient stone steps passing mosques and ruins hidden by shrubs and trees, and crossed a bridge to the opposite side of the gorge to see five arched royal tombs of Pontic Kings carved into the rocks. We then went on to the military barracks, once an Ottoman palace, where Nil and Cihat spent their days. Amasya,

Cihat told us with pride was the place where four friends, Mustafa Kemal, Ali Fuad, Rauf Orbay and Refet Bele met to sign the draft of the Declaration of Independence and the start of the resistance movement. 'The independence of the country was in danger. The capital was under Allied occupation and the Government, subject to foreign control, hence incapable of governing'.

The local train blasting black smoke chuffed its way inland to a tiny station, where a man with a wooden cart and horse waved us to climb aboard before trotting us off to the village. It was a Circassian village. Young girls, their long hair free or loosely covered with fine white muslin, waved from windows of *kerpiç* 'mudbrick houses'. Children skipped around the cart when we stopped outside a two-storied wooden house, home to the *muhtar* 'village headman', who greeted us on a wooden balcony over-looking an apple orchard. His two daughters kissed my hand and his wife smiled a greeting as she served glasses of tea. After a while we were taken to stables where four handsome horses stood ready to ride. Our guide Hasan, the muhtar's seventeen years-old son, led us past sweet-smelling apple orchards and fields to open pastures, familiar to the horses, who set off at a wild gallop.

We stopped at Borabay, a crater lake famed for trout fishing, to picnic on pasties covered with poppy seeds and delicious yoghurt drink, and to listen to Hasan's family stories. Circassians don't inter-marry, but most of the villagers were somehow related and owned orchards. Hasan was proud of his cousins living in Amasya and Istanbul, four professional soldiers, two doctors and teachers. We returned along the river route, so beautifully fragile it seemed surreal, but after hours in the saddle, I was relieved to see the village.

Removing our muddy boots, we sat on a divan, a long, hard settee built round the room. Trays of steaming lamb cooked with apples, rice, yoghurt, beans, towers of warm, fresh bread, olives and cheese, cold olive oil leeks and fried aubergine were set before us on low round tables by the muhtar's wife, a smiling motherly woman who, with her daughters, sat near the door ready to serve. The muhtar held forth on politics, football, and the apple market while male relatives sat smoking and flicking worry beads. No sooner was one plate finished then another appeared with yet another glass of tea. Full to bursting, I whispered to Cihat, 'please tell them I can't eat or drink another drop'.

'Leave food on your plate and tea in your glass or put a spoon on top of the glass, then they'll know you don't want more,' he replied. And I had been brought up to finish everything on my plate, thought I!

It was time to leave. The muhtar handed us two baskets of small rosy apples. 'Next time you must stay. I do not insist today because my brother died yesterday and I do not want to burden you with our loss,' he said looking grave. Humbled by their quiet dignity, overwhelmed by their generous hospitality and good manners we thanked them and offered our condolences. The village women were friendlier than those in town, waving goodbye as we climbed into the cart.

The hotel lobby was filled with army officers. Three obviously highly ranking officers blocked the stairs. When they saw me, they stepped aside so we might pass. I smiled and bade them good night in Turkish, and they returned with a salute and a nod. Nil, head lowered rushed past me upstairs into the room. 'Why the hurry', I inquired.

'Didn't you see who they were? One general and two majors stood aside for me, a private to pass. Thank heavens I was in civilian clothes and they were too busy ogling you to notice me, otherwise I would spend the rest of my life in a military jail,' he replied.

The next day we drove to Samsun, then an uninteresting port town on the Black Sea. Someone mentioned Bafra leaf tobacco was grown in Samsun, and as they were Fazila's favourite cigarettes I bought her ten packs. Nil returned to Amasya and I boarded the ship and spent an uneventful evening in my cabin until we reached Istanbul.

Istanbul was under a military curfew. Myshka was about to return to London. Nil still had three months to serve in the army, so I decided to visit my parents in Wales. That turned out to be more difficult than I expected. With the military junta in control, special permission was required to leave the country and it was strictly forbidden to take out foreign currency. Bedii Bey arranged my papers and I stuffed a few precious pounds inside a corset under a pencil slim Pucci dress. The airport looked as though it was under siege. It seemed only a handful of passengers (all foreigners) were travelling, but there were hundreds of armed soldiers and a line checking papers and luggage with a toothcomb. I panicked and pinched my sleeping daughter, who woke up with a yell. The officer in charge looked at me in disgust. 'Let them pass,' he said flicking through my bag and luggage, eager to be rid of a screaming baby. In those days we flew Pan American, a great airline with helpful hostesses who calmed my daughter and soothed my nerves.

Welsh Wisdom

My parents were delighted to see their granddaughter for the first time. The promised telephone calls had never transpired due to Turkey's non-existent telephone system. To make a call, one would first connect to an operator and then wait hours, days – even, to be connected. My parents had received regular 'wish you were here' letters, postcards of Istanbul and photographs of Ceylan but hardly any of those intimate personal titbits they used to receive when I was in London. Loved ones know how to read between the lines.

I was born in Cwmavon, a charming quiet village in South Wales surrounded by woodlands. The youngest of three siblings, we grew up in a healthy, happy home according to rules laid down by our parents. Neighbours were part of the family. My mother took me to chapel every Sunday morning and my father would pick me up after the service to take me for a long walk. My father had suffered from asthma most of his life so was determined his children grew up strong and healthy. I remember plenty of long walks and exercise, no sugar, no cakes, our sugar ration was given to the school so every child would have a birthday cake. We were naive and trusting, my parents were full of hope and expectations that life would be easier now the war had ended. Returning as a mother myself, I realized how much I had missed that intimacy and cosiness, chatting with my mother as she cooked my favourite dishes, listening to the radio and those long walks my father, free from the tension of words and thoughts unspoken. Maybe it was just me, over-sensitive and exaggerating, I thought.

Educated at GlanAvon Grammar School, I was preparing to attend Aberystwyth University when a letter of acceptance from the Central School of Speech and Drama in London arrived. This was the work of my elocution and drama teacher, Miss. Morgan. An ex-student at Central School herself, her dreams of becoming an actress were cut short by a tragic car accident which left her house-bound in a wheelchair.

She began giving private lessons and was such an inspiring teacher she soon had more students than she could handle. We got on really well. I enjoyed the classes and often stayed behind to help. It was she who persuaded my parents to allow me to go to London for the entrance examination at Central School in the Albert Hall, promising that if I wished, after graduating, I could work as her assistant and, upon her retirement, take her students to set up my own school. When she turned on the charm Miss. Morgan was such a delightful, determined lady, no one could refuse her, certainly not my father and I was thrilled.

As luck would have it, the day my mother and I were preparing my suitcase, her godson whom she adored, came to say goodbye. Emlyn Thomas and his wife, Kathleen were singers at the Royal Opera House in London and about to leave for America. I loved Emlyn, he was a kind, friendly person with a smooth honey-toned voice who loved to sing and was content to sing in the chorus at the Opera House while his wife was the epitome of a dramatic opera singer. With black flowing locks, red lips and nails, Kathleen was a solo performer at the Opera House and never let you forget it. She took one look at my clothes, 'This won't do at all, Emlyn drive us into town, we are going shopping'. It turned out to be a fun afternoon with Kathleen choosing 3 suits in different colours, off-white, green and brown (I remember well because I wore them for years!) and giving me and the sales girl a lesson on how to mix and match. Shopping done Emlyn insisted on taking my mother for a celebratory goodbye tea, after all, sang Kathleen loudly, 'We're off to New York and your daughter is off to London'. Emlyn and Kathleen never returned to Wales although my mother received a Christmas card from them until her death. As one of the best dressed girls in my first year at Central School Kathleen's shrewd advice on dressing well, 'Buy one good suit, dress or coat a season then mix and match,' has worked for me throughout my life.

When I was a child my mother and I would attend church every Sunday morning and my father would pick me up and take me for a long walk over the Welsh hills to his elder brother's home. My Uncle William had been a father figure to him and except for his brother, other people's opinions never bothered him at all. On these walks he would point out nature's oddities, a wizened old tree with a room-like hole in the trunk, a river dividing two farms, he knew the names of birds that flew overhead and which mushroom was poisonous. I owe much to my father and those walks, my healthy life-style, quite good sense of direction, love for nature and the art of listening.

A slim, good-looking man, my father rarely smiled but had a sharp wit and spiky humour that caught people off-guard. Besides his two maxims, 'no bad news (meaning school reports) before supper' and 'all I ask is you just do your best and God will do the rest', he made no demands on us. I was told he had been quite a man about town in his youth, which he vehemently denied. Now, racked by asthma but as stubbornly independent and proud as ever, I knew I had disappointed and hurt him deeply but he never once reproached me.

This time we walked slowly arm in arm pass the Round Chapel to rest on a bank overlooking sprawling green fields and the turrets of Margam Castle peeping between a forest of tall trees. Recalling how I had flown the nest instead of returning as promised after Central School to work with Miss. Morgan. 'It was not to be and things don't seem to have worked out as you expected', he paused taking my hand, 'I just want to tell you one thing. Before you walk away from anything, not only a marriage, make sure you have done your best', then with that endearing lop-sided grin I loved so much, he added, 'God will do the rest and no matter what happens, you will have no regrets and can move on with a clear conscience. Let's see how it goes and how you feel before we make a move'. He suggested Ceylan remain with them for a month.

All seemed well on my return to Istanbul and a month later Nil and I waited at Istanbul Yeşilköy Airport for our daughter to be carried off the plane by her carer hostess to take her to Büyükada for a few days. With Nil's military service behind him, talk in the Arbel household was about his future, Afife Hanım had busied herself getting in touch with influential friends on Nil's behalf. The issue became the only conversation or rather argument when Afife Hanım and Bedii Bey came to visit or we joined them for dinner. Nil wanted his mother to finance a project he was considering, so he could set up his own business. To appease her, he even went to Adana to discuss a position with an American engineering firm he had no intention of accepting. He assured me that his mother would give in – 'she always does, be patient, what's the rush? Why are you so up-tight? Don't worry, give her time' and on and on it went.

I discovered a quiet spot between Dolmabahçe Palace and the Mosque. Deserted except for an old man with a tea kiosk, I would park the car and cry into the Bosphorus until the kindly *çaycı* tapped the window with a glass of strong, bitter tea. He never accepted payment. I never doubted Nil's love for me, what hurt, angered me was his indifference to my needs. I respected my in-laws but didn't want them to control our life. That I was incapable of handling Afife Hanım's mood swings, or Bedii Bey in his world-of-his-own or even Nil for that matter who was behaving like a spoilt, rather arrogant insensitive son instead of a husband, didn't seem to bother anyone except me.

On 27th July, Ceylan's 3rd birthday friends arrived with children and presents, Bedii Bey plonked himself on the floor and began singing French songs as the children gathered round clapping and joining in. Everyone was having fun except Ceylan. Afife Hanım was changing her granddaughter's dress because she'd wiped sticky chocolate fingers down the front, Ceylan was crying and Nil was arguing with his mother. I stood there holding a heavy platter of small cucumber sandwiches in my hands that I had spent all the morning preparing for a fun birthday. Listening to them I decided. I had done my best. I wanted out.

That night I told Nil. He was deeply, deeply hurt. Next day Afife Hanım arrived urging me to reconsider, but despite a confusion of mixed feelings, frustration, disappointment, heartbreak, doubt and guilt, I had had enough and knew I couldn't stay. My idea of love was very different, it was simple, generous, happy not complex. I confided in Fazila, spoke for hours to Mehmet, they and friends urged me not to rush into things, accused me of being impulsive and warned me as a foreigner, divorce in Turkey would be difficult, emotional and unpleasant. I did break down in court when the judge gave custody of Ceylan to her father on the grounds that he was Moslem and I was Christian. That evening Nil came to say that he did it deliberately to hurt me and that Ceylan could stay with me. So typical of what Nil would do. He disappeared out of my life quite quickly without leaving much impression as a husband or father to his child. He left for London and never supported his daughter.

Bedii Bey came to take Ceylan to the park. They were so sweet together walking along, a little blonde beauty holding the hand of her white-haired grandfather who called her, Nil. My admiration for Afife Hanım never wavered. That a person, without apology, could be so formidable, capricious, and manipulative yet at the same time so intelligent, charismatic and courageous was way beyond me. To this day she is the most intelligent, complex, fascinating and mystifying woman I have ever met. I always say I divorced my mother-in-law.

In the summer of 1964, I took Ceylan to visit Afife Hanım at Büyükada. She congratulated me on my second marriage to Aydın Erkan whose family she knew well. We had tea on the balcony and she presented Ceylan with a musical box. She was genuinely pleased to see us. Bedii Bey had died, Nil was in London, and most of her friends had left the island. She spoke of loneliness. Taking tea with Afife Hanım in that house full of memories was an afternoon complete in itself – a treasured memory. After tea, she walked us to the carriage. With typical Afife Hanım aplomb, she held my hands, apologised for the past, and said, 'I will never accept another daughter-in-law.' The next moment her face creased into that mischievous smile of hers 'And, is Melike alive?' she asked. Melike Erkan was Aydın's mother. 'No. I never met her, she died in 1958,' I replied smiling. 'I doubt I would have married Aydın otherwise. One mother-in-law in a lifetime is quite enough.' We laughed, loud and together.

That was the last time I saw Afife Hanım. She died in October of that year, one more reason to cherish that afternoon. Nuri Bey was right. Afife was an impossible, irresistible handful but someone I am so thankful to have known and never want to forget.

Amongst the Guardians of the Press

I rented an apartment with a spectacular view of the Bosphorus at Topağacı Nişantaşı near most of my friends. I decided to stay in Istanbul, at least for a while. I felt an affinity with the city, its lively street-life and people, embraced by friends and supported in my comfort zone by the Giz family. Without that support I probably would have returned to England. Instead Nil was the one to leave for London.

Few foreign women walked around unaccompanied, and whenever I took Ceylan for a walk it caused a stir. Blonde, curly-haired with plump, pink cheeks, she had a mind of her own even as a tot. One day when out for a walk she stopped in front of every shop window demanding, 'I want this, I want that.' My patience wore thin and so I walked a few steps ahead, watching her from a distance. Suddenly a Turkish lady assuming I was a nanny, accosted me, saying, 'this is not the way to take care of a small child, young lady. These streets not safe. Hold her hand properly when you take her for a walk or she might fall. I know where she lives and will make it my business to inform her mother,' and off she marched without giving me a chance to defend myself. She did come to the apartment and complain to the kind *kapıcı*, doorman, who promised to tell the child's mum.

I was offered a part-time job at the Daily News, a new English language newspaper. There were five on the staff in a tiny, smoke-filled, garret-like office in a side street at Babıali, the Turkish Fleet Street, where leading newspapers such as Hürriyet, Milliyet and Cumhuriyet had offices. Babıali smelt of paper, ink and dust, its streets thronged with cigarette-smoking photo-journalists, writers, cartoonists and *hamallar* 'porters' bent under heavy loads of paper, plodding from store to store. To enter many of the basement printing houses, you had to lower your head. On street corners, men in matchbox kiosks prepared *köfte* 'meat-balls', or toasted cheese sandwiches to feed journalists scurrying to an event or racing to catch their deadline. Writers, editors, and photographers dropped into the office to share the latest news with my boss.

Emotions ran high. Everyone was passionate, rational or irrational and ready to discuss, defend and argue until midnight. When a newsflash about the ongoing trial of Democrat Party members. A newsflash from Ankara or Reuter concerning the ongoing trials of members of the Democrat Party, clashes on the streets or the military in command sent the indefatigable journalists of Babialı dashing to their typewriters and drawing boards. There was an unspoken camaraderie between workers, journalists, columnists, photographers, editors and owners, and a respect for the freedom of the press cemented by their earthy media humour.

Newspapers were owned by media dynasties. Machinery imported from Europe improved the quality of print and photographs. Articles, depending on the political leanings of the paper, were written without fear or reservation. Freedom of press was of paramount importance. Books, dictionaries, kitchenware and holidays were offered free as incentives to buy newspapers and encourage cultural and social activities. Hürriyet newspaper led the way with the Golden Microphone, a musical competition which encouraged the likes of Barış Manço, Cem Karaca, Ajda Pekkan, her sister, Semiramis, and the delightful Gönül Yazar – stars of Turkish rock and pop music.

The Milliyet Newspaper sponsored international beauty competitions and a Miss Turkey competition which in turn encouraged the founding of modelling schools, advertising agencies, fashion photography and films and drama classes as career outlets for young girls and boys. Cumhuriyet appealed to intellectuals.

One year I was invited to sit on the jury at a Miss Turkey competition by Milliyet Newspaper. I sat next to actor, producer and activist, Yılmaz Güney. Dark, swarthy and handsome in a burgundy velvet jacket, he complained of the heat from the stage lighting but when I suggested he remove his coat, he looked at me with disgust. As poker faced girls paraded past us, I whispered to him, 'I wish they'd smile.' It was definitely the wrong thing to say to my companion. Turning his back to the audience, in earnest whispers he lectured me on the hardship of life in the eastern provinces pointing out I would have nothing to smile about if I had to carry water for miles from a well and give birth without a doctor.

'But this is a beauty competition and the girls are in bathing costumes,' was my pathetic defence. When it came to decision time who should be Miss Turkey, he plonked himself next to me. 'OK I accept you know best and will vote for the girl you choose. Which one?'

Yılmaz Güney was a university student and activist who although untrained in the arts and film-making, wrote scripts, directed and acted in a number of films. He went on to produce many award-winning films including the International acclaimed film, *Yol* (Road) that depicted the life of a world he knew so well in eastern Turkey. He had the capacity for greater works but his dark side got the better of him. Imprisoned for killing a man in a restaurant brawl, he escaped parole and died in exile in Paris.

For months from October, 1960 the Democrat trial made front-page news on every newspaper. Vivid photographs and articles written by respected columnists were discussed in cafes, bars and at home. It was a tense, distressing time for many. Emotions ran high. Every evening at 8 p.m., everyone gathered around the radio to listen to the deep, intimidating voice of Colonel Türkeş: '*Dikkat, Dikkat, Dikkat,*' (Look out, look out, look out), as he introduced and highlighted the day's proceedings of the Yassıada trial.

One evening the prosecutor's lack of respect and unethical behaviour disturbed me. He taunted Menderes and Bayar (who, by the way, sat next to each other but never spoke to each other which I found strange) about their private lives, a dog given as a present and the undergarments of a mistress that I wrote an open letter to the editor. Next morning, I marched into the editor's office and placed the letter on his desk. After all Menderes was the Prime Minister and he and his cabinet was on trial. 'I would like you to publish this letter to the editor, please,' I said defiantly. 'I'll look at it when I have time', came the indifferent reply.

I was about to leave that afternoon when the editor called me into his office. 'I've read your piece and must say that I agree with most of it. You may be right, but, if I publish this, we will both land in jail.' With a tired sigh he added, 'politics is not a subject for a young woman, a foreign woman at that, to write about at the moment. This is not Britain, my dear. Bring me an article on art, cookery, Istanbul, anything, and I promise to publish it.' And looking at me with a grin, he tore up my article page by page, thereby ending my career as a political columnist!

Being part of the media world at Babıali at that time was exciting because day by day, it was the very pulse of the country. The buzz of expectation was infectious; adrenalin was high, people worked long hours for low pay in smoky offices and on the streets. Most of the employees lived in Karaköy or around the Sultanahmet area. As in Ottoman times they were a diverse but fully integrated mix of Turks, Greeks, Armenians, Jews, Kurds, Caucasians and from Eastern Europe. They shared a work place, transport and restaurants in chaotic harmony.

After work, I would walk through the bazaar to Istanbul University to wait for Fazila or take Ceylan to swim at the Karman waterside residence on the Bosphorus, or, go clubbing at Club 12 owned by everyone's friend and fellow English High School school-mate, Tevfik Dölen whose name is synonymous with the music of the 60's and 70's. Tevfik was small, compact and wiry and moved with the grace of Fred Astaire. Cymbals in hand he was last seen at the opening of a new bar in Nişantaşı at the age of 80 gyrating and playing with young musicians who kept a firm but friendly eye on the aged rocker.

In time, the printing presses moved out of Babıali to the suburbs, and newspapers were taken over by large conglomerates and pro-government businessmen. Those dedicated, chain-smoking cynics, journalists and photojournalists, guardians of the press who held that freedom in such high regard lost heart, and with it the voice, vigour and independence of journalism in Turkey more or less, except for a few worthy writers, disappeared.

Ceylan and I spent Sundays with Fazila. She would spread a large blanket on the floor with cushions and toys for Ceylan to play, eat, and often sleep and her school friends from Arnavutköy Girl's School, Maro and Maida would join us for tea with a freshly baked cake, homemade bread or a pot of jam. The group was complete when Dr. Şevket, who had nominated himself Ceylan's godfather the day she was born, arrived with pastries from Park Hotel pastry-shop.

Maro and Maida were Armenians whose private lives belied their sober appearance. Maro was short, plumpish, pragmatic but energetic and bubbly. The reason for this was that Maro was in love and had been for decades. Her life circled around Şabo, her lover, who because of a formidable mother and dependant sister was unable to marry her. This had not dimmed Maro's love or loyalty. Except for Friday, her bridge night, they spent their evenings together until it was time for him to return to the family home.

After Fazila's death, we lost touch until, flicking through an old telephone book one day, I came across Maro's name and on the spur of the moment rang the number, amazingly she answered giggling like a young girl. Her dream had come true, she had married Şabo. She invited me to lunch. It turned out Şabo had proposed when they were in their eighties, on the day his mother died.

They hadn't changed at all, simply aged well. 'If only you had telephoned three months ago. Fatoş was a witness and you would have been the other. All our friends have died,' Maro told me. Şabo smiled, the satisfied smile of man who had achieved his goal. I wished I had called earlier, for they had brought back such happy memories.

Maida Şahbaz was a free soul, a hippy long before it was fashionable. Blond, talented and unconventional, she was the granddaughter of the Ottoman Armenian Mayor of Bakırköy. A love affair with her violin teacher when she was his student caused her life to become entangled with the illustrious Shakir Pasha family, diplomatic, military and intellectual heavyweights during the last days of the Empire and later in Turkish society. This is her story.

Karl Berger was a charismatic Hungarian Jew, a musician-cum-composer who came to Istanbul to escape anti-Jewish aggression in Europe. He soon established himself as violin and piano teacher to the best families in the city. On his first lesson with Füreya Shakir, her aunt, Aliye Shakir, took one look at him and fell in love. He was the lover she had waited for all her life and meeting him was the beginning and end of everything. His dark, brooding good looks and artistic temperament attracted many admirers, but Karl believed an artist should be free to pursue his art, leaving Aliye with no choice but to become a devoted lover, visiting his studio at Narmanlı Han in Beyoğlu twice a week, armed with presents.

Karl Berger had many affairs, but it was Maida who bore him a child, a son she named Charles but called Carol. Proud, discreet and undemanding Maida raised her son renting out a small property left by her grandfather and giving piano lessons. Carol was 4-5 years old when his father died, but remembers visiting him and, on one occasion, being chided for throwing china on the floor in a tantrum.

In 1947, 23 years after they met, Karl did marry Aliye Shakir and they settled high on a hill in Büyükada. But their happiness was short lived. Six months later, while waiting for a boat at the pier, Karl Berger suffered a massive heart attack and died in Aliye's arms. A student of Karl Berger and friend of the Shakir family told me that Aliye was so overwrought with grief she clung to the coffin throughout the night. Aliye insisted that Karl wanted to give the few gold coins he possessed to his son. Her older sister, Princess Fahrelnissa Zeid accompanied her to Maida's house to present the coins.

After the funeral, Aliye went to live with her sister, Princess Fahrelnissa and her husband, Ambassador, Emir Zeid of Iraq at the Iraqi Embassy in London where she was introduced to engraving which became her passion. Home-sick for Istanbul, she returned in 1950 and settled in the studio at Narmanlı Han. In her salon, she worked, exhibited and entertained artists, friends and Istanbul society and was known as Queen of Pera. Aliye Berger decided she wanted to adopt Karl's son. It became an obsession, and so did her pestering. She showered Carol with presents, introducing him to her artistic crowd at her Beyoğlu studio. Maida, fearing that her young, impressionable son would be tempted by her colourful life-style took Carol to America where he completed his education.

Today Carol lives in Copenhagen with his wife and son. On a trip there with my granddaughter, Selina, a few years ago, we met for coffee and he talked about his mother. He told me of her fears of losing him although she had insisted that if he wanted to live with Aliye she would not stop him, despite his constant assurance that she was the only mother he ever wanted. Eventually Aliye Berger faded from their lives and died in 1974.

I never did meet Aliye Berger-Bronai but I did meet her niece, the actress, Shirin Devrim and her American husband, Robert Trainer and we spent the evening talking about her aunt, Aliye whom she had adored.

Maida's last days were spent at the Home of the Little Sisters in Bomonti, cared for by Catholic nuns and visited regularly by Nur Mardin. When she died her son found a note by her bedside, 'I don't want a burial service: no priests, no mourning, just music.' Carol recorded her favourite classical pieces while Fatoş, Haldun and I arranged buckets of flowers, bought from a *çingene* 'gypsy' in the street. Nur was in Europe so was unable to attend the funeral, but she recalled the last time she saw Maida. When she asked Maida if she was taking her medicine, Maida smiled and said, 'just give me a dose of love. That's all I need.'

We sat, a handful of mourners as Maida's favourite music filled the Little Sister's Chapel, a Bach violin concerto, the Cambridge Choir and Ave Mariat, a young Armenian priest read a short but poignant prayer. There was music at her graveside in the Armenian cemetery. A nun sang a French hymn, the priest recited a short prayer, Haldun, a Moslem prayer and I, a Christian blessing and Maida left this world as she had wished, with music and love, in the simplest yet most moving ceremony I have ever attended.

Aydın Osman Erkan

One rather depressing day, a surprise letter from Aydın Erkan suggesting lunch on his return to Istanbul cheered me up. Aydın and Nil had studied together for a few years at the English High School for Boys. Occasionally we would bump into him with his fun-loving younger brother, Akın, whom everyone (including me) adored, or at Club 12. Aydın and Akın were on our Christmas list. Lunch was at a fish restaurant on the Bosphorus and next morning outside the apartment door with the milk and newspaper was a small bunch of wild flowers and an invitation to dinner and a movie.

Aydın Osman Erkan was dark haired, handsome, self-effacing, a quintessential gentleman with a quirky sense of humour. The eldest of four siblings (two boys and a girl) he stayed at his father's apartment in Topağacı when in Istanbul, but principally resided in Aydın where he managed his late mother's estate. Aydın was an Anglophile, he loved everything British, its castles and history, its language and books, British country-style clothes, and obviously British girls. After graduating, he was sent to America to study agriculture, but most of his time was taken up giving talks on Turkey, the Caucasus and Middle East in church halls or Rotary and Masonic Clubs to an enraptured American audience.

He was extremely proud of his Caucasian background, interested in history, politics and the family's antique weaponry which he spent hours caring and cleaning. His father, Hamza Osman Erkan, member of parliament in the Democrat Party, was at that time serving a five-year sentence in Kayseri prison.

Aydın charmed Ceylan with bedtime stories and presents and he charmed me with his unaffected good humour and love. He was kind, concerned, interesting and made me laugh – I enjoy people who can spin a cracking story. We found we had a lot in common and he reminded me of the saying, 'in every man there is a child who wants to play'. My previous relationships seemed to have been complicated with too many people, now there was just me, Aydın and Ceylan. Most Saturdays found us browsing in the bazaar and bookshops around Sultanahmet for old books.

He spoke of his responsibility to his family, his mother's sudden death and father's imprisonment and how the family bank accounts had been frozen by the government. His uncle and mentor, Ekrem Çifçi had come to his rescue. My first husband and Aydın's parents were old friends. In fact, Hamza Bey had lived with the Arbels in Izmir during his courtship to wealthy land-owner, Cemal Çifçi's youngest daughter, Melike, (I am sure Afife Hanım would have been delighted to give her young friend the best possible advice on how to woo a lady).

Fazila invited him to Sunday tea – 'to check you out,' I warned. I needn't have worried. His boyish charm and amiability won Fazila, Maida, Maro and Şevket Bey over after the first cup. His brother, Akın stepped into the role of matchmaker supreme, turned up to baby-sit with a bottle of whisky under his arm, on seeing my surprised expression, he smirked, 'A present, I'll drink milk'. The evening before he was to leave for the farm, Aydın appeared with a present for Ceylan, a bunch of flowers for me and asked me to marry him. During his absence, Akın was at the door to take me dancing and dining and he and I became soul mates.

Fazila's brother-in-law, Hıfzı Oğuz Bekata considered himself as head of the Giz family and decided to take things in hand. One day he invited Fazila and I to lunch. We had hardly sat down before he began making a speech. Quite firmly he said that he did not approve of a young, foreign woman living alone in Istanbul and, although Fazila flew to my defence, he refused to budge. He spoke highly of Aydın's family, especially his father. In fact, so keen was he to marry me off, he offered to finance the wedding. I let him go on for a while before telling them that I had decided to marry Aydın. Fazila was delighted, Hıfzı pleased. Mission accomplished lunch became a celebration after which our host excused himself to attend to more urgent business.

I asked Fazila to be my witness, but she refused: 'I witnessed two marriages, both ended in divorce, and I vowed *never again.*' But she did attend. Determined to do the right thing, Aydın wrote a letter to my parents and his father for permission to marry. My poor mother fainted and my father ordered me home. We telephoned them. I handed the phone to Aydın who, after a long and deferential conversation, managed to calm my long-suffering father with promises of a visit in the near future. They did become the best of friends and my father's antagonism towards Turkey and everything Turkish all but faded.

We flew to Kayseri to receive Aydın's father's blessing.

A Prison Visit

In ancient times, Caesarea was part of the important trade routes, and today Kayseri is known for its successful merchants and businessmen. When I visited, it had a population of 70,000 and was referred to as the city of mausoleums, with countless minarets in its winding narrow streets. I didn't see much of the town on that occasion, but I did catch a glimpse of the huge rock above the town, which had inspired writer, Yaşar Kemal, first Turkish writer to be nominated for the Nobel Prize in Literature, to write, *İnce Memed* (Memed, My Hawk). He wrote a novel in the 1960's called *Tek Kanatlı Bir Kuş* (One Winged Bird), which was recently published 40 years since it was written, about the fear which spreads in society like a contagious disease.

February 1962. The flight to Kayseri was one of the scariest experiences of my life. The plane was full but hardly airworthy, shaking during the ascent and spluttering in the sky. The engine made all the wrong sounds and cabin pressure either didn't exist or didn't work. To reach our seats we climbed over baskets of food, bags of clothing, and books piled high in the gangway. Aydın had brought fresh clothes for his father and I had a large box of Madlen chocolates from the Divan Hotel. Upon landing, I begged that we return by bus or train.

It was February, and a bitter wind swept through the town. Kayseri, ancient Caesarea, was grey and bleak. Our bedroom was over-heated by a black stove and smelt strongly of disinfectant. I could feel the tension in Aydın's body as we approached the prison in the middle of nowhere, a forbidding stone structure surrounded by high fences and watchtowers and observation posts where armed soldiers surveyed the arid land, and the compound where statuesque soldiers stood to attention. There was nothing – not a bush, nor a tree – to soften the menacing landscape. Family members huddled in groups against the cold wind waiting for the gates to open.

Wanting to impress my future father-in-law I had taken great pains to dress in what I thought was appropriate for a prison visit. I was wearing high leather boots, a slim fitting (but thankfully warm) long grey coat over a white polo neck sweater and grey skirt. I looked – and felt – horribly out of place.

The gates opened. We stood shivering in a long line as every bag and basket was searched before being shepherded across the courtyard, up noisy, galvanized metal steps, through corridors, more steps, more corridors, until we reached a series of large rooms where groups of well-dressed men, members of the Democrat Party, waited. Aydın found his father looking very French, with a black beret set at an angle atop his head. He was tall and distinguished looking but worn and tired. He kissed me and hugged his son in a long embrace. Holding my hand, his voice cracking with emotion, he said, 'I am deeply touched and grateful that you came all this way to ask for my blessing, and I apologize for not receiving you in more pleasant circumstances. Thank you for making my son happy.' He went on: 'I accept Aydın's choice with the greatest pleasure. My family and I accept you whole-heartedly as you are, don't ever change for us.' Tears welled up in his eyes and mine, I was deeply moved. That first meeting in that ghastly prison cemented the warm relationship I had with my father-in-law until his death. One by one, he introduced his friends to me using their rightful title. I offered them chocolate and they congratulated us on our engagement.

Except for the barred windows, it might well have been a gentlemen's club: well-dressed, well-educated, well-mannered men, protective of each other, putting on a brave show, smiling and chattering. But their eyes and body language spoke volumes. They held themselves well, but their smiles failed to reach their eyes and could not hide the pain. We visited President Celal Bayar in a private room. Old and bent, yet defiant, he kissed both my hands, blessed our union, and congratulated me for marrying into a fine family. 'When we are free, and free we shall be, come to tea. The British love tea and so do I,' he chuckled.

That evening, huddled in front of a big black *stove* in the hotel dining room, I had never seen Aydın so relaxed and happy. He persuaded the waiter to open a bottle of not-very-good wine to toast our meeting. He thanked me a thousand times for coming, to see his father happy meant so much to him. We dined on Kayseri *pastırma*, a spicy dried bacon.

Hamza Osman Erkan, like many imprisoned for five years, had not committed any offence but was sentenced because he remained loyal to the party and Prime Minister. His words at the trial were as follows: 'I am a parliamentarian, a member of the Democrat Party, and remain loyal to its policies and the party. I am innocent and have not committed any criminal or political crime.'

The next morning, Sunday, we approached the prison to find people shouting and shaking the fence. Women screamed, 'Communists, communists! Let us in! We have a right see our husbands'. It turned out visits had been cancelled without any explanation.

Pointing to a young woman, Aydın said, 'That is Ayla Akarca. Her father died. Some say he was pushed out of the window, others that he committed suicide. Her husband, Turan Akarca, is Member of Parliament from Milas, a friend. Now she is not even allowed to see him, it's a disgrace, a disgrace'. Growling, he moved away from the crowd. I stood watching women crying and shaking the gate demanding an explanation. It was heartbreaking.

An officer inside the compound seemed as though he was walking in my direction caught my attention. On the spur of the moment I gestured to him. He approached. 'I want to see Hamza Osman Erkan,' I said in English, with an authority I certainly didn't feel. He nodded his head towards the gate. I pushed my way through the crowd to the gate, two soldiers opened it just wide enough for me to squeeze through. The officer again nodded his head towards the building. I crossed that huge compound as fast as I could, up those beastly noisy stairs, along corridors and up steps, until I saw an inmate.

'I'm looking for Hamza Osman Erkan,' 'Follow me,' he said and I did, past rooms filled with prisoners conversing in low voices. Just as we were about to leave the last room, I caught sight of my father-in-law's beret and ran towards him.

'Where's Aydın', queried Hamza Bey, looking around.

'He's outside. The visit is cancelled,' I explained.

'I know the visit's cancelled, but I need to talk to him. Go and fetch him.' My father-in-law sounded agitated. 'Please bring him here.'

Cussing my luck and myself I returned down the steps and stairs and across the courtyard, well aware the soldiers in the watchtower were following my every movement. I couldn't believe this was happening to me. The officer was still there. 'Hamza Osman Erkan wants to speak to that man,' I told him pointing to Aydın praying my luck would hold, he shouted at Aydın to come to the gate and the soldiers open it.

'What's going on?' whispered my bemused fiancé.

'I have no idea. Just follow me,' I whispered with a nervous giggle. 'I think the officer thinks your father is the prison warden,' as we climbed the steps to the room where Hamza Bey waited. While father and son conferred, Hristaki Yuvanidis, a delightful Greek member of parliament, still in a state of shock that he had been imprisoned, told me that he was elected only a month or so before the coup, and hadn't even made a speech in parliament.

The following morning the lead article in all the newspapers was that Hamza Osman Erkan had held an engagement party at Kayseri prison for his son and American journalist fiancée. My poor father-in-law was severely reprimanded by the director of the prison. The cause of all that fuss, misery, tears and cancellation: a box of Madlen chocolates. I wondered what the officer who opened the gate thought when he read the newspaper.

My father-in -law had lived a full and adventurous life. He was born, one of eleven children, into a distinguished Circassian family in Mecca, Arabia where his father, Osman Ferid Pasha Commander of the Medina Garrison and Guardian of the Holy Shrine of Medina had been exiled by Sultan Abdulaziz. Following the death of his father in 1912, the family moved to Switzerland where the children completed their education. He along with two of his siblings fought in the battle of Shaiba in Iraq during the 1st World War. After two years as a trainee banker in Paris, Hamza Osman returned to Turkey to become General Director of Iş Bankası, a Turkish Bank and took his first step into politics when he became a Member of Parliament for Afyon in the Cumhuriyet Party. In 1950, Celal Bayer persuaded him to join Adnan Menderes Democrat Party. where he served as Member of Parliament from Kocaelı and Sakarya, an Anatolian province with a large Circassian population. When the 1960 coup occurred Hamza Osman Bey was in Europe attending the World Parliament as the Turkish Olympic Committee General Secretary. On his return to Istanbul, he packed a small suitcase and waited to be arrested.

Marriage and Beşiktaş Konak

Aydın and I were married on March 12th 1962, in my apartment at Topağacı. Şükran, who looked after Ceylan, helped me prepare the sitting room before I went to the hairdresser. On my return I opened the door to screams of 'Surprise, Surprise!' Şükran and Ayşe, her florist friend (with a shop close by) had transformed the room into a garden of daffodils, white roses, greenery and candles. 'We have to take them back tonight', they giggled.

The few invited guests were greeted with champagne provided and served by Akın. Aydın was anxious, the registrar was late when suddenly the door opened and there was Osman, Aydın's other brother, who had flown in from New York on his first visit to Turkey since his father's imprisonment. Aydın and Akın were overjoyed to see their brother and the Giz family gave a sigh of relief that I was getting married. Mehmet and Şevket Bey looked as pleased as punch, Faize and Hıfzı telephoned their congratulations and Mustafa (a photographer friend) took hundreds of shots, then left the camera at the outer apartment door while he went to pick up his car only to find it had disappeared on his return.

Osman had just started his military service with the M.P. military police in Istanbul when the 1960 coup occurred. Walking into the barracks one morning Osman saw his father, hunched in a chair, head in his hands and a small suitcase by his side. He had been arrested. Osman ran to kiss his father's hand when the officer in charged barked, 'What the hell are you doing? That man is a damn prisoner'. He cursed Hamza Bey. Osman punched the officer. He was reprimanded by a disciplinary court and sent to eastern Turkey as a soldier for the rest of his military service. On the day of his discharge from the army, without a goodbye, Osman packed his bag and flew to America.

Aydın had booked the honeymoon suite at the Hilton Hotel, but we never made it. The supposed 'cocktail party' went on and on until someone suggested everyone left. Champagne gives me a headache, I fell asleep, the flowers were whisked away, leaving the brothers in an inebriated fuddle to catch up on their past. Next day, three handsome Erkan brothers and I entered the Hilton bridal suite for a hilarious brunch hosted by our friend, the front office manager.

Aydın took me to the konak at Beşiktaş. Owned by his grand-father Osman Ferit Paşa the large stone villa was in a sorry state of disrepair and home to the elder members of the Shapli family: Uncle Bekir, his daughter Bedia, Aunt Habibe and Aunt Saadet, her son Inal and his wife, Nadia. They lived in separate quarters in rooms filled with antiques, books, swords, old rifles, Caucasian costumes and family photos in silver frames. It was like living in a dilapidated museum. Buckets were strategically placed under cracks in the roof to collect rainwater.

It was in the konak grounds after watching a gymnastic display, '*İdman Müsameresi*' at Tepebaşı Theatre, that the young Shapli brothers, Mehmet Shamil, Hüseyin Bereket and Hamza Osman with 24 young sportsmen decided to open a fencing and boxing club. In those days, permission for meetings of any sort needed the approval of Sultan Abdülhamid. Luckily the rank of their father, Osman Ferit Pasha, Guardian of the Holy Shrine of Medina, Aide-De-Camp to Sultan Abdülaziz, and General of the Imperial Ottoman Army was more than impressive. The request was granted and in 1915, Beşiktaş Bereket Gymnastic Club Boxing and Fencing Sports Club was founded. In 1919, it became Beşiktaş Football Club, one of Turkey's two or three outstanding clubs.

Aunt Habibe, waif-like and slender in an elegant black dress with a Russian brooch pinned at the collar, met us at the door and lead us to a high ceiling vaulted hall, the reception room where Uncle Bekir, his daughter Bedia, İnal, his wife and mother waited. It was a theatrical setting in which Aydın appeared as the favourite nephew. He solved problems, settled unpaid bills and spent most of his time with his cousin, İnal, amongst those dusty heirlooms. İnal's mother, Saadet Hanım was very beautiful, gentle and lady-like with pale complexion, dark hair and dark eyes. I was seated on one of two hard black ebony throne-like chairs, Saadet Hanım offered me Turkish coffee on a small tray. Standing in front of me she directed my eye to a ring in the saucer then winked for me not to reply, '*Buyrun*,' she said '*afiyet olsun*'.

I put the tray on my lap and the ring fell onto my dress. It was a magnificent antique Russian ring set with rubies and emeralds. When I showed Aydın, he grinned. 'She asked me to sell part of her jewellery to pay bills. I refused and paid the bill. This is her thank you gift.'

It became my favourite piece of jewellery which I wore constantly until it was stolen in the robbery from the Aydın house.

A month after our marriage, a month of invitations as Mr. and Mrs. Erkan, we were more than ready to leave, as I said, Turkish hospitality can be overwhelming. We set off in two vehicles: Aydın, Ceylan and I in the Austin Gipsy and Dursun (Aydın's man) with a driver in a van, carrying my belongings. My husband had suggested we live in Izmir where many of his relatives resided and he could commute to the farm. But I like the countryside and thought we should give that a try first.

The journey was difficult and tiring along twisting roads, paved and unpaved, circling the foot of mountains. The problem was not the few cars but tractors, buses and lorries spewing black smoke and chugging at snail's pace up the hills. We stopped for lunch in Bursa, famed for its thermal spas and as a centre for raw silk, a pretty town surrounded by orchards nestling at the foot of the Uludağ mountain where I had previously enjoyed a weekend at the thermal spa and skied on the snowy slopes of Uludağ.

We continued past Izmir towards Selçuk when the sky darkened with heavy clouds and a sudden burst of torrential rain and lightning found us in the middle of nowhere in a raging storm. Traffic came to a standstill. Dursun appeared at the window with news that a bridge had collapsed and traffic was being diverted back to Izmir. As the rain drummed on the roof, I had a premonition: this was a sign that I was not meant to go to Aydın.

Hunched in the seat I noticed lights moving in the darkness and asked what they were. 'Headlights of cars crossing a field,' shouted Dursun. 'The police are about to close the gate. It's too dangerous, there is nothing to do but return to Izmir.'

Voicing my dark thoughts, I said, 'this is a sign, a premonition. Turning back means I am not meant to go to Aydın, that I must return to Istanbul.' Aydın stared at me. 'What? You must be joking.' I shook my head. 'Then you are mad,' he said and jumped out of the jeep. He ran towards a policeman. A few minutes later, screaming at Dursun to remain with the van and without a glance in my direction, he thrust the jeep into fourth gear and swung the vehicle round, straight towards the field, nearly running over an irate policeman struggling to close the gate on the way.

Manoeuvring potholes and keeping close to the grassy bank, vision was so bad he was forced to lean out of the window spraying the inside with rain. Avoiding cars stuck in the mud, the jeep zigzagged, slipped and stopped then ploughed forward for what seemed an eternity, until we hit the main road. Pulling up at the side of the road and shaking the rain off his hair, Aydın turned to me with a wry grin. 'Now you can go back to Istanbul if you wish.' Ceylan had slept through it all.

It was well passed mid-night before we arrived at a house set in a garden in a street, shaded by plane trees above the town of Aydın. The main entrance opened onto a hall with a large sitting room, bedrooms and bathrooms. Stairs led to a lower floor, which contained Aydın's den, his favourite room, a large old-fashioned kitchen (obviously rarely used) which opened onto a walled garden. The den was a long room with a warm glowing fire, a gun cabinet, old settee and comfy chairs and behind the desk, a library. The walls were covered with family photographs, old maps and weaponry. He explained it was his favourite room because without central heating it was warm in winter, cool in summer.

The next morning, half asleep, I entered the kitchen to be accosted by a tall, dark-skinned man who grabbed my hand and nearly gave me a heart-attack. It was Bayram Ay, Aydın's farm manager was descended from one of seven Acarlar families who had made their way from Afghanistan across the steppes of Anatolia selling livestock before settling in a village they called Acarlar Köy – the village of the Acars close-by. Utterly devoted to Aydın, he arrived at sunrise and left at sunset. I called him *Gölge Bey* 'Mr. Shadow'. Acarlars sold cattle, fruit and were merchants rather than farmers. They rarely, if ever, marry outside their own community. Today the village has a population of over 10,000.

Dursun had been employed by Aydın's father and when Hamza Bey was imprisoned, Aydın took care of him but he was not at all happy with the new arrangement, a married couple with a child was hard work compared to an indifferent bachelor. A few weeks later he left and we were fortunate to find Fatma who stayed with us until we moved to Istanbul.

I set to work adding a feminine touch to my husband's bachelor pad and turned the kitchen, which had a lovely old fireplace into a pleasant dining room, added a practical, modern kitchen which opened onto a garden of orange and crab-apple trees so we might dine in the shade in summer. Without disturbing his treasures too much, a new settee, cushions and throws transformed the den into a cosy family room. Time passed quickly – there was much to do, to see, to learn.

Rural Life in the Aegean

The province of Aydın is rich in archaeology, tourism, and agriculture, its fertile soil is irrigated by the Menderes River, the source of which is high in the mountains. As it meanders through valleys and plains it irrigates thousands of acres of agriculture, cotton, tobacco, sunflower, wheat, barley, corn and rye, sesame and peanuts, fruits, olive trees and sweet fine-skinned figs. Its shoreline stretches along the Aegean Sea and its proximity to Greece and the Greek islands makes it home to more antique settlements than any other province in Turkey.

The town of Aydın was quiet and provincial centred around a large square dominated by a mosque, the railway station, Post Office, a very good patisserie and few shops and led to streets lined with neat two storey houses with gardens. But I soon discovered in the back streets there was a hub of noise and workshops where artisans fired ceramic stoves, blacksmiths hammered pots and pans and cooking utensils, sold materials, made shoes and handbags and colourful peasant baggy trousers hung fluttering in the breeze. My favorite was the *yorgancı* 'quilt maker' who sat like a pasha on a raised platform covered with silks and satins of every hue, spectacles perched on the tip of his nose, stitching away at patterns he designed himself – an artist at work. We became friends as he added warmth and colour to our home. His son later reminisced about those years as a boy working with his father. 'In those days, cotton was gold, our textile industry flourished and Turkish cotton was considered one of the best in the world.

The town changed hands many times. Little remains of the city's violent past or its diverse population; the Christian area with churches, *Rum* 'Greek' and Jewish houses were razed during skirmishes between the Greeks, aided by the British and the Zeybeks and Turks until 7th September 1922 when it surrendered to the Turks once and for all. In his book, Meander, Jeremy Seal describes these events as he journeys in a canoe from Dinar down the Menderes River. He draws a vivid picture of Aydın reminding us that it 'had been home, after all, to St. Anthemius, architect of Constantinople's Hagia Sophia Basilica, the very font of Orthodox Christianity.'

And my husband, Aydın was a gentleman farmer, we spent most of our afternoons at the farm in Osmanbükü, a small village off the beaten track. On my first visit to the farm I realized life as a farmer's wife was not going to be at all what I had envisaged it would be. There was no farmhouse, no livestock, no horses, no chickens – but land as far as the eye could see surrounded by distant mountains with a *konak* 'mansion', a walled compound filled with tractors, wagons and farming equipment, home to a migrating family of storks nesting on a telegraph pole who fly from Egypt and are considered sacred. On my first visit, the konak was crowded with villagers waiting to welcome us. Men with cloth caps lined up to kiss my hand while their wives in baggy şalvar trousers and huge squares loosely covering their heads huddled around tables with trays of home-made sweets, baklava and glasses of tea trying to silence giggling children as they waited to welcome the Bey's new foreign wife and offer her tea. It was like a scene at a country fair, noisy and friendly. It was a warm welcome.

Osmanbükü village was made up of high-walled stone houses built around a courtyard where crops, animals, tractors and farming equipment were stored and women cooked and baked bread on black stoves heated with wood. Two, sometimes three, generations of a family shared the same house, adding rooms as the family grew. Every village in Turkey, including Osmanbükü, was made up of a mosque, a *köfteci* 'meat-ball speciality restaurant' and *kahvehane* 'a men-only coffeehouse' which was the nerve and news centre of the community. Nothing happened or was secret from the men drinking tea in the café. There were a few shops selling sweets, chocolates and biscuits and a primary school built by Ekrem Çifçi. No trees shaded the dusty streets from the summer heat and there was no entertainment as such. Social life in a village centres around the family and the community as they celebrate together a birth, a son off to the army, engagements, weddings and a bereavement. Before wedding centres were built, Aydın had allowed villagers to celebrate the wedding feast for the whole village at the konak.

Most afternoons we walked in the fields before taking tea in the konak: men in one corner and we, women, in another. They were chatty and full of humour with a healthy, ruddy complexions, strong rough hands and a ready smile. Cotton is the main crop in the Söke and Aydın *ova* 'plain' which can be rotated with wheat, barley, sunflower or animal fodder every few years to strengthen the soil. During harvest time, I would invite family and friends for a village lunch of köfte, rice, salad and *ayran* 'a cool yoghurt drink', at the konak.

Cemal Bey, patriarch of the Çifçi family and Aydın's maternal grandfather was a prominent Ottoman landlord from Hamzabalı who influenced by his famous young son-in-law, Kazım Karabekir Pasha, during the Republic uprising moved to Aydın and purchased much of the land around Osmanbükü. During the Greek occupation Cemal Bey moved his family to the island of Rhodes and the Çifçi konak an impressive place set in a garden of fruit trees surrounded by high walls in the centre of town was taken over by the Greek Commander.

He built a castle-like folly in the village of Çinçin with gun slits to protect his property from Zeybek brigands who rode from their mountain hideouts to pillage and attack villages. In the master bedroom is an impressive four-poster wrought-iron bed he bought after a stay in hospital in Austria during the 1920's. Osmanbükü was known and is still called by the older generation, *Bey Köy* – Gentleman's village.

Cemal Bey's surviving children and heirs, Ekrem, Nejat and Melahat Çifçi, his daughter-in-law, their children and a few of Aydın's friends made up our social circle and saw to it we were rarely alone. Ekrem Çifçi, the eldest son and head of the family, resided in the konak with his wife, Hümeyra Hanım, and their four children. A typical country squire, Ekrem Bey was hard-working, serious and Greek-speaking and often dropped by to chat with his favourite nephew.

Nejat Bey was good hearted and quick-to-anger with incredible energy. He thought nothing of driving to Kuşadası or Izmir to buy fish, meat and a good bottle of wine for dinner after a hard day in the fields. During his frequent outbursts, his wife, Nevzat *yenge* 'aunt' whom I liked enormously would sit quietly knitting furiously. One balmy evening, Aydın and I were enjoying a quiet drink on the balcony when the doorbell rang. It was Nejat Bey and Nevzat yenge. She plonked herself in a chair, took out her knitting, and began knitting furiously. Aydın and I eyed each other – it was going to be one of those evenings. I served rakı in a crystal glass. 'Nejat Bey,' I said, 'I know you are angry about something, but I bought this set of glasses from an antique shop in Izmir last week. If you feel like throwing something, please go home and break your own glass. Don't you dare break this one.' He looked at me in astonishment then roared with laughter. Nevzat yenge put away her knitting and we spent a jolly evening on the balcony under a starry sky. Soon after, a shiny black Singer sewing machine, stamped by Izmir customs, arrived at the door. It was a wedding present from Nejat Bey and Fatma, chuffed with pride, called in the neighbours to see this amazing machine.

I was invited to monthly 'at home' tea-parties and social gathering given by the wives of the leading families in Aydın. Gossip had it that I was a film star and model until Dursun spread the word I was too skinny to be either. At these soirees I must have gone on about Central School posture and Elizabeth Arden skin care, because later, much later young women, my daughters' age approached me in Istanbul and Aydın to say their mothers used to scold them to sit up straight like Kim Hanım and clean their faces with cotton wool before going to bed. Of course, I am delighted.

The only entertainment in town besides dinners was the open-air cinema. Nejat Bey booked a *loca* 'private box' and bought bags of cabbage seeds to snack on. Eating these seeds is an art I never mastered, but it was hilarious to watch serious grown-ups nibble the shell between their front teeth like rabbits, remove the seed with their tongue, then throw the shell on the floor. The films were black and white and the scenarios much the same, rich boy falls in love with poor girl singing in a casino, alternatively rich girl falls in love with a poor boy working for her father, another popular scenario was of course a wicked landowner abusing his workers. The sets were the same, a village, a villa on the Bosphorus, or the sleazy back streets of Istanbul. Even so, the characters, humour and acting were very true to life and the actresses, Türkan Şoray, Hülya Koçyiğit, Filiz Akın, Fatma Girik beautiful, though heavily made up.

We often dined at Ekrem Bey's konak in Aydın, but it was the *Bayram* holiday celebrations I remember. Religious holidays change according to the lunar calendar. *Ramazan* 'Ramadan', a thirty day fast from sunrise to sunset is a test of self-control. The day began with a drummer banging his way through the streets at dawn to wake the zealous and everyone else for that matter for *sahur* 'morning breakfast', the last meal until sunset when the fast ends with *iftar* 'an elaborate meal shared with relatives and friends'. The fast is broken with a piece of *pide* 'a round flat bread', an olive or soup, followed by special Ramadan dishes.

It is followed by Bayram, a holiday celebration when an animal – sheep, goat, cow – are slaughtered and the meat shared with family, workers and friends. Tables and chairs are set up under the shade of oleanders, olive and fruit trees in the garden of the Çifçi residence. Hümeyra Hanım and her helpers spent days preparing caldrons of rice with pine-nuts and sultanas, meat, cold olive oil dishes, and huge bowls of salads. The ovens were kept hot with trays of 'börek', mountains of pide and gallons of ayran. Trays of sweet syrupy deserts welcomed guests to the iftar feast. Children as pretty as pictures in party dresses, played hide and seek in the garden. Before the guests arrived, members of the family with Ceylan, Aydın and I included, lined up to kiss Ekrem Bey's hand and receive a gold coin. He was one of the last of his generation to practice this tradition and I still treasure the gold coins we were given and remember with great pleasure the iftar feasts in Aydın.

My husband in the first flush of love, fearing I would miss city life and friends in Istanbul, went out of his way to entertain me with trips and surprises.

We drove to Denizli to inspect his orange, fig and olive groves and lunched on fresh trout near a waterfall. We went to markets at Tire and Ödemiş and climbed antique stones at the deserted archaeological sites of Ephesus, Didyma, Sardis and Priene. There were few tourists and fewer guards. Young shepherds lounged on marble beds, one bored eye keeping watch on their flock, the other looking out for stray tourists to sell them artefacts, a marble head or coins from a leather pouch. Before I even got a peep, Aydın shooed them off. 'It's stolen property and should be in a museum' he said pompously.

Aydın never forgave my 'premonition' outburst and one day we drove to Selçuk, up the rough, stony Bülbül Mountain track overlooking Ephesus, past forests of pine and plane trees to a sheltered plateau where stands the House of the Virgin Mary. It is a simple stone building with a stream running nearby where Mary was said to have spent her last days. It was deserted except for a nun who resided in the small church house. When I told her I wasn't Catholic, she smiled, saying the shrine was a place of healing for all religions, and that many Muslims light candles. We sat on a stone bank listening as she related the story of the Virgin Mary then cupped our hands to drink holy water from the spring before wishing her goodbye. On our way down the mountain, with a dollop of sarcasm, Aydın said, 'When you have another premonition, I suggest you come here, light a candle, then tell me.'

A visit by Pope Paul VI in 1967, followed by another by Pope John Paul XI in 1979, has brought millions of pilgrims to the House of the Virgin Mary. Now a visit to the Virgin Mary is included in most Aegean tours and the mountain road from Selçuk is an asphalt highway. The holy water runs from a series of shiny taps. Souvenir shops and cafes surround the car park, but the place remains as serene and energizing.

Then there was a trip to Kuşadası, Bird Island, a sleepy, fishing village with swathes of deserted beaches, wide bays and forests of pine, cypress and fruit trees. In the centre of the square was a dilapidated stone *han,* 'Öküz Mehmed Pasha Caravanserai', later restored by Club Med into a luxury hotel. A café, ice-cream shop, wood bakery wafting delicious smells of hot baked bread, and a few grocery shops selling whisky and American cigarettes under the counter.

We lunched at Kazım Usta, a fish restaurant with a few rickety tables and chairs on the jetty in Kuşadası. There was no menu, just the catch of the day, salad, a few hot and cold olive oil dishes and plenty of *bira* 'beer'and rakı.

Next to the kitchen was a special table for fishermen who were part paid in kind and when not fishing, entertained their Greek fishermen friends. Meat and other products were expensive on Samos, a nearby Greek island, so fishermen crossed over, did some shopping, then joined their Turkish friends to commiserate over the state of affairs between their countries over a 'meze' and 'rakı' supper until, quite inebriated, singing Greek songs, their fishing boat found its way home.

Farming families from Söke and Aydın spent summer months either in Kuşadası or Çeşme near Izmir. On that first visit I had been introduced to two Özbaş cousins and their wives, Halil and Hümayra Özbaş and Ali Rıza and Melike Özbaş so the following year I chose Kuşadası for our summer holiday.

Few people spoke English so I decided it was time to improve my Turkish. My husband was no help, at all, he has never spoken to me in Turkish or corrected my many mistakes. My teachers were Fatma, Bayram and the villagers which is why I became aware of the strong diversity of cultural grammar in the way Anatolian's speak and was fascinated to learn certain rules regarding when, where and with whom it is socially accepted to express emotions. There is a verbal saltiness and cynicism in their words which can be either stingingly sharp or hilariously funny but always blunt and quintessentially Turkish. Cultural grammar is kept alive by word of mouth by the older generation.

Turkish is not part of the Indo-European family of languages, but has its roots in the Turkic Altay region of the Eurasian steppes. With no equivalent for the verb 'to be or to have', person, tense and case are added as an appendage to the word, for example,

'I am in Istanbul' becomes '*İstanbuldayım*'.

This can be confusing and cause quite embarrassing gaffes for beginners. A young English teacher walked into a bakery to buy '*iki tane taze ekmek*' – two fresh loaves of bread but instead asked for 'iki tane taze erkek' – two fresh men! When asked the whereabouts of my husband I would gleefully answer, 'Aydın is in Aydın'.

In 1932, one of Atatürk's reforms was to change the Ottoman Arab Persian alphabet of the court into a Latin alphabet in order to establish the Republic on equal terms with the west and to ensure one language across the country that both the elite and country folk could speak and understand. Aydın's vocabulary contained many words from his father's generation, he always said he learned new words reading journalist and friend, Zeynep Oral's articles in the newspapers. She is one of the few respected reporters still working and writing today.

The introduction of the surname in 1935 gave people an opportunity to choose one with personal and social connotations. The most popular names at the time were patriotic, nationalist, professional, and place of birth. Here are a few surnames: *Çiftçi* – farmer, *Erkan* – blood of a soldier, *Tabanca* – gun, *Erkara* – black soldier, *Mardin* – birthplace, *Hammamcıoğlu* – son of a bathkeeper, *Pirinççioğlu* – son of a ricegrower, *Eczacıbaşı* – head chemist.

The farmers seasons dominated our lives. After a sleepy winter, spring's wake-up call is heralded by chirping birds and wild flowers – time to prepare the soil and plant, free cattle to graze in fields, and replenish the chicken coops, summer and early autumn is spent gathering crops, vegetables and fruits.

Whenever I went to the village, women with a small plate of whatever food they cooked that day would come to visit me at the konak and I served tea and cookies while we talked women's talk. Frugal and practical, they worked side by side with their husbands to add to the family income. They milked cows, made yogurt and cheese, baked bread, worked in the fields and in autumn aubergines, peppers and tomatoes are threaded and hung and sun-dried, fruits are preserved and bottled, all to be sold in the market and ensure a well-stocked kitchen for themselves during the winter months. This was all done, fortified with glasses of tea, chatter and earthly humour, nothing is secret in a village.

We would gather olives by placing a sheet around the trunk of the tree to catch the fruit as it fell when the branches were shaken or beaten with sticks. Each olive was then sliced and thrown into a vat of salt water, which was regularly changed until the fruit was sweet enough to eat. The olive tree is a generous tree. A symbol of peace, its fruit is eaten, its oil used for cooking and salads, and its seed crushed to produce sweet smelling soap.

When it came to picking cotton as the slowest cotton picker in the field, a line or two behind the other pickers, I was usually sacked.

Tuesday was market day in Aydın, the noisiest, busiest and my favorite. For the villager the market place is to earn, not spend, money. Women perch on stools in front of mounds of freshly picked vegetables or fruits encouraging shoppers to touch, smell and choose before purchasing. It is also a time to catch up with friends from other villages, find a husband or wife for an unmarried son or daughter, and chat to town folk. Occasionally Aydın would join me for lunch at Sarıoğlu, a small restaurant in town serving few, but excellent, classic meat or vegetable dishes and a typical Aegean desert, *kabak tatlısı*, 'slithers of golden pumpkin simmered in syrup', and generously sprinkled with crushed walnuts which Aydın thoroughly enjoyed.

Inviting my husband's relatives to dinner was something I rather dreaded. When I was married to Nil, I dared not enter the kitchen now, surrounded by super cooks, I was expected to entertain. Over time, and thanks to Fatma, I did improve; Aydın wasn't difficult to please unlike many a friend's husband. Most Caucasian men possess a healthy, masculine awareness about their looks and Aydın realized my bland English cooking kept him in shape, to the envy of his stout friends. 'Kim keeps me slim', he would say. I never questioned whether it was a compliment or not.

Of course, I had my fair share of blunders. There was the time I asked Bayram for fresh eggs and he arrived with a basket full. Breakfast was scrambled eggs on toast, lunch a delicious fluffy Spanish omelette with salad and supper a light six-egg soufflé. When Aydın removed his shirt that evening, his body was covered with red spots. 'I am allergic to so many eggs', my polite husband wailed. And another time I asked Bayram for two chickens for a barbecue party. He arrived with two large squawking chickens. 'Not live chickens,' I cried and he wrung their necks in front of me. Another very silly mistake was to offer Melahat Yenge English rice pudding in a country which is famed for its milky puddings. Aydın's Aunt Melahat was short and plump, a lively, forceful widow with three children whose husband, Orhan Çifçi, had been mayor of Aydın. She was a *hanım ağa* 'rural landlady' and was driven around in a large black Packard and revered by one and all and always on the go. She liked everything big: she resided in a big 'konak', carried a big bag, hosted large parties with food piled on large silver trays, wore a worthy big diamond on her finger. But the biggest thing about aunt Melahat was her heart. She was friendly, generous and full of life. Why I served her English rice pudding I will never know. 'What's this?' she spluttered. 'unsweetened boiled rice? The English have no taste'.

The next morning Melahat Yenge's driver emerged from the Packard with a tray of Turkish milk puddings from the pastry shop and a note: 'Choose two or three you like and then come for lunch and a lesson on Wednesday.'

But I had some success. When my father-in-law came to stay, I decided to try my hand at his favourite dish, *Çerkez tavuğu* 'Circassian chicken', chicken boiled, shredded and smothered in a walnut paste. Everything was done by hand and it was hard work pressing the oil from the walnuts which added flavour and moisture to the paste. I overheard Hamza Bey ask where I was, to which my spoil-sport husband, replied that I was in the kitchen trying to make Çerkez Tavuğu. 'Hmmm,' came the doubtful reply. 'Let's say it's good and we like it anyway,' was my diplomatic father-in-law's reply.

The expression of amazed delight and sheepish eagerness on my husband and his father's face as they asked for more was sweet revenge enough and well worth the effort. Making Çerkez Tavuğu is a labour of love, I have prepared it four or five times in my life.

Alan Waters, chief engineer/manager at MacAndrew and Forbes Liquorice factory in Söke and his French wife, Pascale, came into my life when, hot and pregnant, I was taking (and passed) a Turkish driving test at the Aydın football field (after driving for years with an outdated International licence). A foreigner, displeased at having failed, approached Aydın to help him translating his problem to the police. As we walked across the field, I felt him eyeing me strangely. 'Where are you from?' he asked.

'South Wales,' I replied. 'So am I,' he muttered, staring at me in disbelief, he stopped. 'Are you Kim, Joan Rees?' I nodded. 'Well I never,' and with a roar of laughter turned to Aydın. 'I attended the same school as your wife. She was prefect of Glyndwr House. She is two years older than me and we had crushes on older girls at school, I had a crush on your wife!' out came another roar.

Alan was tall, slim and good-looking, full of Welsh pride, and amusing stories. His wife was petite, dark, quiet, and very French. They lived in a charming stone house hidden amongst cypress trees on the grounds of the estate. We became friends, spending weekends at a hotel in Kuşadası together snorkelling, exploring caves and coves and returning with shells, strange wood shapes and fish, which the hotel kitchen cooked to perfection. Life was never a dull with Alan around.

One afternoon, driving to Söke with my father-in-law and Ceylan to have lunch with the Waters, a massive *Sivas kangal* 'a huge sheep dog' with a spiked collar bounded out of nowhere in front of us straight into the car. The car lurched as I ran over the monster and stopped. We were relieved to see the dog rise, shake himself, and hobble off across the road to disappear into a field. Hamza Bey, sitting next to me in the front seat, got out to inspect the car. 'Nothing much,' he reported, opening the back door to sit with Ceylan, 'Safer back here,' he muttered. 'Drive on. These shepherds carry guns. If the hound is injured, they will demand to be paid.'

The shepherds were nomads called Yörüks that herd hundreds of sheep, goats or cattle from eastern Turkey to the fresh green pastures of the Aegean. In wintertime they lived in houses, but when they roam the Anatolian plains, they settled in large black tents made of goatskin. They are peaceful and hard working – except for those terrifying dogs. Aydın's Kurdish '*kahya*' once took us to the tent of a relative set on the hillside outside Selçuk. Open on one side, it was spacious and airy with carpets, colourful cushions and blankets piled in a corner, kitchen utensils and three swinging baby-cots. Women smiled in welcome as dozens of children, some with blue-green eyes, ran wild.

Yörük groups dispersed around the late 1970's, settling in villages around the Fethiye area. With dams irrigating the eastern part of the country there was little point in continuing to follow a Yörük life-style. Their pastoral culture, music and traditional way of life is preserved by societies formed by those young children, now adults, who remember with pleasure and nostalgia the times they roamed free and bare-footed.

An Uncomfortable Party

Shortly after his release from prison, my father-in-law came to stay with us in Aydın and Mr. and Mrs. Halil Özbaş invited us with a few mutual friends to lunch. She recalled how she first met the Erkan brothers at the Tennis and Fencing Club in Istanbul, they spoke of friends and relatives, and Halil told risque stories of days-gone-by. After lunch, Hümeyra Hanım and my father-in-law walked arm in arm around the garden. It was a glorious day in beautiful surroundings with good fare and cheerful friends. As we said goodbye Hamza Bey's face, creased with smiles of pleasure, promised to return.

Seeing the pleasure being with old friends had given my father-in-law and Aydın the town being the heartland of the Democrat Party, I suggested we give a party for his Democrat co-fellows. He agreed and next day presented me with a guest list.

The evening before the party, we were all busy checking last minute details (my father-in-law in-charge of guests, Aydın, drinks and music, and Fatma, her two daughters and I, the kitchen) when the doorbell rang. Thinking it was the cake, I wiped my hands on my apron and ran upstairs to open the door – to find Mr. and Mrs. Sırrı Gürsel, dressed for a party. Mr. Gürsel, a leading member of the Democrat Party in Aydın was the elder brother of General Gürsel, President, Prime Minister and Commander-in-chief of Turkey. Mrs. Gürsel, elegant in a black suit with a sparkling diamond brooch on her lapel eyed my floured nose and apron in astonishment. My heart sank 'Hello', I whispered. Then, shouting downstairs, 'We have guests.'

'*Hoş geldiniz, sefa geldiniz, welcome*' boomed my father-in-law, climbing the stairs and ushering them into the sitting room. Of course, I was blamed, although I did wonder why only one couple arrived on the wrong evening.

The men fell into amiable conversation while Mrs. Gürsel and I smiled at each other in silence until she suggested that we went to see what was going on in the kitchen. Chatting with Fatma cheered her up and putting on an apron, Mrs. Gürsel set us to work. By the time her husband was ready to leave she had produced four local specialties and forgiven me.

The following evening, the actual night of the party, was choked with emotional hugs, and tears between those released from imprisonment and their loyal supporters. Rakı, whisky, and beer flowed, Fatma's 'mezes' disappeared fast and Mrs. Gürsel pointed out her dishes. The party was in full swing as we danced to the Beatles and Frank Sinatra records in smoke-filled rooms when I was called to the door to welcome latecomers from Izmir. A lady member of parliament whose name I've forgotten had arrived with her houseguests, Mr. and Mrs. Ethem Menderes. He handed me a bottle of champagne, apologizing for being late, 'You're very welcome. It's frightfully noisy,' I laughed, leading them downstairs to.........silence. Everyone froze.

What on earth has happened, I wondered, looking around for help. Hamza Bey was deep in conversation with Necip Postacı and Aydın was nowhere to be seen. Mrs. Menderes, small and slim, wearing black, pulled at a string of magnificent pearls as though they were prayer beads. Mr. Menderes stared into the fire. Thankfully Aydın appeared with drinks and inquired after their son named Adnan named after the late Prime Minister, Adnan Menderes who was a school friend. I turned on the music and asked Ethem Bey to dance, nodding to Aydın to follow. It was horribly embarrassing; Ethem Bey was stiff, his body tense. Mrs. Menderes clung pathetically to Aydın's arm. A few couples joined us others moved to the dining room. Aydın had prepared a speech but decided not to read it. Desserts, cake, coffee and Napoleon brandy failed to ease the atmosphere or sweeten grim expressions enough to save the party. Everyone left. Closing the door on the last guest, I threw myself on the sofa. 'What on earth was that about?' I asked in exasperation.

Hamza Bey explained. Ethem Bey's father worked in some capacity for the late Adnan Menderes's family from Çakırbeyli Köy. Adnan and Ethem, both born in 1899, held similar interests, and a desire to serve their country. So intertwined were their lives that Ethem, at some point, changed his surname to Menderes. He became mayor of Aydın then a Member of Parliament in the Democrat Party. With his friend and mentor, the Prime Minister, Ethem rose swiftly through the ranks, first as Minister of Interior, then Minister of Defence. Just before the May coup, Ethem Bey was exposed: a number of letters from the military headquarters expressing concern at the mounting unrest in the country were found in a drawer in his desk. At first the letters were polite, cautionary words from worried army generals, but as time passed, upon receiving no reply, the tone became urgent and less friendly. The last letter demanded that the government take immediate action to stabilize the country – or else. For reasons known only to himself, Ethem Menderes did not give these letters to President Celal Bayar or Prime Minister Adnan Menderes his life-long friend and mentor. When the letters became public it was rightly considered an act of betrayal against the Prime Minister and the party.

Another strange incident involving Ethem Menderes was that he was sharing a room with Dr. Gedik on the night he died. Rumours of suicide or that he was forcefully pushed out of the window were rampant. Whichever is true, Ethem Bey must have known what happened.

Sentenced to ten years in prison, Ethem Bey was released after three and a half years (along with my father-in-law, who had been sentenced to five years). He was ostracized by the Democrats, especially loyal party members such as Necip Postacı who stunned by his sudden appearance had gestured to everyone to leave. My father-in-law prevented this dramatic exodus by telling him that he would consider it an insult to his family if anyone walked out of a party given in his honour by his daughter-in-law.

The evening was the talk of the town for months, years.

A Trip, Birth and Lesley Blanch

It was 1963, the end of May and we decided to take a trip along the coastal road to Antalya, to (Attaleia), before we would return to Istanbul for the birth of my second child. Hamza Bey was delighted. Travelling in those days was an adventure more than a holiday. I packed a pillowcase and two bed sheets for each of us, powdered milk, Nescafe, biscuits, mugs, glasses and toilet paper. Ceylan and I sat in the back of the roomy green Pontiac Aydın had purchased from Turkish film star, Ayhan Işık, after being cautioned by my doctor that bouncing in a jeep was hardly appropriate for a heavily pregnant woman.

We drove along narrow country roads at the foot of the Taurus Mountains, winding up wooded hills, past olive groves, fig gardens, oranges and apple orchards, fields of wheat, barley and melons, and down into bays, inlets and small coastal villages. My father-in-law pointed to a sign that said *ev yemekleri* 'home-cooking'. We stopped, and a plump woman leaned out of the kitchen window and beckoned us into a garden with a few tables set up under apple trees, a vegetable plot and flowers in cans. Her husband welcomed us and reeled off the menu.

Hamza Bey had a habit of tipping waiters when he entered a restaurant. 'That way I am sure of good service. Why tip when I leave if I am not satisfied?' was his argument. This time he didn't tip, but said to the woman, 'as the best cook in this village you will choose our lunch.'

The same red-faced woman served goat's cheese, garden tomatoes drenched in thyme and olive oil, crisp fried aubergines, home-made yoghurt, freshly baked 'börek', followed by cracked wheat pilav and köfte. A few locals wandered in to listen to Hamza Bey expound the merits of farming, Atatürk and democracy, as though he was on an election trail. By the end of the meal, the garden was crowded and the good woman was positively bursting with pleasure as Hamza Bey thanked her and shook hands with his audience.

We drove on to the Sacred Pool at Pamukkale, formally Hieropolis, a Roman spa of white calcium cascades frozen in stone. We settled into the only hotel there with a swimming pool on the edge of the plateau. Next morning, we swam in the warm, mineral water overlooking the fertile plains below. It was wonderland, shimmering white, verdant green, and utterly peaceful. We decided to stay an extra night to explore the ruins while Hamza Bey kept Ceylan occupied in the shade of pine trees and wisteria in a perfumed tea garden.

We were in no hurry and leisurely made our way through the untamed scenery of Fethiye's dense forests, bays and inlets, to Telmassos and then the glorious bay of Gökova. To please his father and very pregnant wife, Aydın stopped at any pretty place that caught our eye – not his usual way of travelling at all. We swam in the crystal turquoise sea with the snow-capped Babadağ, part of the Taurus range, in the distance. We ate the freshest fish in tiny fishing hamlets and scrambled over antique sites at Kalkan, Kaş and Patara, birthplace of Apollo, to swim amongst sunken ruins. It was these places that Freya Stark had in mind when she wrote, 'There are not so many places left where magic reigns without interruption.'

We arrived at Antalya, a town of 40,000 people, late one afternoon and strolled down the cobbled street in Kaleiçi to find lodgings at the only Ottoman guesthouse in town. There is an amusing story about the rich ladies of Antalya; it was a tradition that boys inherit the more fertile land, so that they could support their family when they marry. Girls most likely would be supported by their husbands when they marry, and therefore inherit the less productive bits of land sandy beaches, swamps or dry stony ground. When tourism hit the magnificent Antalya coastline and a string of Miami-like hotels and golf courses mushroomed on its beaches and swampy stony land, you can imagine the wry stories about the rich ladies of Antalya. Today Antalya means location, location, location. Its Mediterranean climate, crystal-clear blue sea, luxury hotels and easy access make it Turkey's most popular tourist resort, connected by fast-lane roads, an international airport, yacht harbour and port. It is a sprawling city of high-rise hotels surrounded by golf courses and magnificent resorts, home to a mixed population of over two million local and foreign all-year-round residents.

Ten days after our return, we piled into the Pontiac to drive to Istanbul to wait for the birth of my second child. Dr. Mehmet Giz, having made all the arrangements was waiting to take us to Güzelbahçe Clinic where Dr. Kazım Arısan welcomed us warmly. 'Delight to see you again my friend, and you, Mrs. Arbel looking so well, we have your details, so a few check-ups will suffice,' he said. Mehmet jumped in. 'Kazım – when I told you we want everything the same, I forgot to mention there is one slight change. The husband. Meet Mr. and Mrs. Erkan.' They roared with laughter at my husband's confusion.

On July 9th 1963, at breakfast I felt contractions. The hospital was nearby, Hamza Bey and Aydın were so agitated and over-wrought I felt obliged to calm them. Aydın held my hand in the operating room until the next contraction then he'd rush out and come back until Dr. Kazım bellowed, 'Either stay or leave, your causing a draft'. Aydın disappeared. He looked more exhausted after the birth than I did. Around lunchtime, Rana Nefiset Erkan was born. Faize was the first to take the baby in her arms and after a close inspection she announced, 'Rana is a beauty, like her sister.' How right she was. I chose the name Rana, which means 'unique or queenly, and Aydın chose Nefiset his paternal grandmother's Caucasian name. This time I was well prepared with dozens of *nazar boncuğu*, 'evil eyes' for her cot and blanket. Our room opened onto the garden, and for my whole stay in hospital, four or five days of being spoiled and cared for, it became a meeting place for Kazım Bey, Hamza Bey, Fazila, Mehmet, Şevket Bey and their doctor friends.

After a few weeks we drove to Aydın, the weather was oppressively hot, perfect for cotton picking but not for me. In mid-September, we decided to spend a weekend at Tusan Hotel in Kuşadası, Alan and his wife joined us. We literally moved the nursery into the hotel but as it was nearing the end of the season, the staff were understanding. It was deliciously cool, fresh with a light breeze blowing across the bay, there was ample shade for Rana to sleep and for Ceylan to build sand castles while I indulged in one of my greatest pleasures that is to swim early in the morning before breakfast. We dined on the balcony overlooking the shimmering moonlit sea on fish caught by Alan and Aydın with enough for us and the staff. It was bliss. Young girls working at the hotel vied to play with Ceylan and care for Rana, and the manager offered us an amazing weekend rate until the hotel closed which we could hardly refuse.

In the summer of 1964, we drove to Istanbul to attend the funeral of Saadet Shapli, İnal's mother and Aydın's favourite aunt. Her sister, Zübeyde, flew in from Indonesia. A few days later Zübeyde telephoned to say that Lesley Blanch, journalist, biographer and travel writer, had visited her and wished to meet the family. Her last book, *The Sabres of Paradise*, was the biography of Shamyl, Imam of Dagestan, great grandfather of the Shapli and Erkan families.

Aunt Zübeyde was a formidable lady. In an old newspaper, the Indonesian Observer, she gave an interview when her husband was the first Ambassador of Egypt in Indonesia and it was headed 'The blood of heroes runs in my veins'. A journalist by profession, aunt Zübeyde spoke and wrote in French, English and Turkish and had married Egyptian Ambassador, El Amroussi, an intellectual with a deadpan sense of humour. Aunt Zübeyde did not ask; she commanded – in the nicest possible way – so Hamza Bey and I were at the konak at 3pm sharp on the day of the visit with flowers, chocolates and a cake to help with preparations while Aydın picked up Madame Blanch from the Park Hotel at 4pm sharp.

Lesley Blanch was known as a woman who never ceased to be the star of her own life. In *Looking Back*, Lesley Blanch describes her first meeting with Aunt Zübeyde to writer, Shusha Guppy:

'I wrote *The Sabres of Paradise* in Los Angeles in the late fifties. My research often took me to Turkey and the Caucasus, but when I finished it there seemed to be something missing, a gap, and I decided I must go back to Istanbul, where Shamil had lived briefly in exile after his defeat. I had a feeling I had to go and find Shamil's family... I had to go to Beşiktaş along the Bosphorus. The area was different then – old dilapidated houses and beggars, a most desolate place. Today it has been tidied up and rebuilt. I asked the beggars, Shamil, Shamil Imam? One of them finally pointed to a dead-end alley. I went down and found a broken-down door and pushed it open. A woman looking very Caucasian with slanted eyes and dark hair came out, tight-lipped. She spoke French and I asked her if it was possible that Shamil had ever lived there? She gave me a look like a steel dagger and said, 'Why do you want to know?'. I said I was writing a book about him. She looked me up and down and said, 'He died in Mecca'. 'I know,' I said. Then she said something, which I contradicted, and she responded by saying: 'I see you know your subject – you can come in'.

She was Shamil's great granddaughter leaving that very night for Jakarta where her husband was the Egyptian Ambassador. She had only come over for her sister's burial, so you see another couple of hours and I would have missed her, hence my premonition. She said, 'I'll stay,' and did. We became great friends. She gave me all sorts of papers and letters and other original material. I became a friend of the whole family."

Family silver, locked in a trunk for years, was taken out and polished. The ebony throne-like chairs were placed near a table covered with a pristine French tablecloth and laid for tea with differing Limoges cups, a silver sugar bowl and milk jug on a massive silver tray placed next to a magnificent silver Russian samovar stamped with the Imperial seal, a gift from Tsar Nicholas I to Imam Shamil during his exile in Russia. Aunt Zübeyde looked splendid in a knee-length Circassian jacket over a long black skirt arranged the flowers while Aunt Habibe, chic in a black dress with a Russian brooch on her lapel, fussed.

Lesley Blanch looked stunning in a burnt gold kaftan, her short blond curly hair framed a pale, round face and startling blue eyes. A well-seasoned traveller and artist, her body language and words added drama to her speech. 'All my life I have waited for this moment – to be in the home of Shamil's family. It is a great honour,' she said, addressing each member by their Circassian name. She and Hamza Bey sat on the thrones while Aunt Zübeyde, Habibe, İnal, Aydın and I gathered round. The whole scene delighted Lesley (and me) as, caressing the samovar, she recalled her travels in Circassia and Russia.

My father-in-law told her of their life in Switzerland with his mother, Nefiset Hanım, Shamil's granddaughter. Aydın served wine in crystal glasses. We were about to leave when Aunt Zübeyde announced how delighted I would be to take Lesley to the bazaar the following morning. Actually, I wasn't that delighted, as she'd hardly spoken a word to me all afternoon.

Nevertheless, I arrived at the Park Hotel the next day to find Lesley, in shirt and slacks, having breakfast with the manager after an early morning walk along the Bosphorus. I drove as she quizzed me about the family and life in Istanbul, then she began telling me of her years as features editor at *Vogue* magazine, briefly touching on two previous husbands – both British, the last an army officer. 'I was not cut out to be an officer's wife, darling,' she said. She found her soulmate, a man she would love forever, in the French diplomat and novelist, Romain Gary, whom she married and later divorced after he took up with actress Jean Seberg.

As we strolled through the bazaar, her love for all things oriental was obvious. She stopped to fondle silks and velvets, crushed cushions to her face, tried on kaftans, and perched on carpets, haggling over prices as she drank tea. Delighted with her purchases (two cushion covers, a small prayer rug, a water jug and metres of striped Turkish cotton), she blew kisses to the shopkeepers. We strolled down the hill to the Egyptian Bazaar, bought herbs and tisanes then on to Pandeli at the entrance of the bazaar, a well-known restaurant decorated with Ottoman blue tiled walls and for its Ottoman food specialities.

Relaxed by a cool glass of white wine, she spoke of life with Romain Gary. 'It was the most productive time of my life; we were very much in love. He was an exceptional man, an astute diplomat, a brilliant writer and intellectual. We travelled, wrote books, hosted presidents and prime ministers.' There was a dramatic pause. Then, in a rather loud voice she went on. 'One morning in bed, reading my French newspaper, I came across an interview by Jean Seberg denying that she was the cause of the break-up of our marriage. She even had the audacity to say that Romain and I had not shared the same bed for months before he met her. At that moment, Romain was asleep beside me – in our bed. I rolled up the newspaper and banged him on the head to wake him.' People at the next table giggled until Lesley's withering glare silenced them. Then as though she was speaking to herself, in a quiet voice, she said something I have never forgotten, 'love does not expose faults, it covers them.'

The evening prior to her departure, my father-in-law invited us to a fish restaurant on the Bosphorus. Lesley, magnificent in blue with silver jewellery and a stunning silver Circassian belt (a gift from Aunt Habibe), presented him with a signed copy of her book. Hamza Bey was in great spirits. He showed us two photographs with

British officers – one as enemies during World War One, and the other, arm in arm, friends in World War Two. Conversation and wine flowed to the gentle lapping of waves beneath the wooden floor of the balcony. It was a heavenly, balmy evening. Lesley flirted and blushed at Hamza Bey's compliments and funny stories.

At one point, startled by the sound of gurgling and splashing in the water, she cried out, 'Aydın! Aydın! It's a dog, he's drowning. Save it, be quick.'

Horrified at the thought of leaping into the dark water, Aydın leaned over the side with a candle: 'it's a man, not a dog.' 'Oh, then don't bother, darling', came the flippant reply as she turned to ask Hamza Bey yet another question about his family.

She kept in touch, sent articles, wrote notes (always inquiring after Hamza Bey), invited us to her home at Garavan in France, and made plans to return. She sent a copy of *The Sabres of Paradise* to Aydın, signed, 'for Shapli Aydın O. Erkan, from a proud new member of the family, Shouanette[11], the author Lesley.' Her escape in life was the romantic world of her imagination, inspired by the mysterious traveller and Russian theatre director, Theodore Komisarjevsky, a friend of her parents who made a deep impression on her and became her first lover when she was 17 and he 39. She lived out her dreams in her travels to the wilds of Caucasia and the Middle East, and survived passionate love affairs – all of which demanded a fair amount of stamina and a core of steel, which I found admirable. She remained on good terms with Romain Gary through the tragic suicides of his son and wife. Deeply hurt by tragedies and the divorce, she would say, 'learning how to deal with pain is the most important thing in life'.

Hamza Bey had obviously made an impression on Lesley. Now they had both mellowed with age and were alone, I felt Lesley had a vulnerable need for love and companionship and a little matchmaking might be just what was needed. One day I approached my father-in-law and suggested we invite Lesley to Aydın and Kuşadası. But Hamza Bey, with a knowing look, shied away. 'All I want now is a quiet, uncomplicated life with my books and family,' he said. Aydın warned me not to interfere.

In 2016, I received an email from Georgia de Chamberet, Lesley Blanch's god-daughter and the inheritor of her estate, papers and library, inquiring about the relationship between Hamza Bey and Lesley. I emailed back what I knew of their meetings. She then sent me the copy of a letter written by Aunt Zübeyde dated 25th October 1962, a week after his release from prison, which included a few words from Hamza Bey. It was an intimate letter of Hamza Bey's love and affection, implying he was thinking of marriage and that he had addressed Lesley as his fiancée to friends. Aunt Zübeyde was a compulsive romantic and obsessed with her brother. A romance between him and Lesley Blanch, writer of *The Sabres of Paradise*, the biography of

1 Shouanette was the beloved wife of Imam Shamil.

their great grandfather, Imam Shamyl, religious leader and warrior who fought the Russians armies from 1834 to 1859, would have been a dream come true for her. As for Hamza Bey, what a boost to his morale, after years in prison, to learn that Lesley Blanch found him attractive. Knowing his sister's love for romance and matchmaking, I am sure he played along from a safe distance but shied away from a more serious relationship. Had they had met before he went to prison, the outcome might have been different.

Lesley lived to be 103 and will be remembered as much for her love of life, and flamboyant sense of style as for her romantic novels. Born to shine, Lesley Blanch left the world a greyer place.

Kuşçubaşı Eşref Bey and His Daughter

Once a month we drove to Izmir, formally Smyrna, second largest port and third most populous city in Turkey for a weekend. My first port of call was the American Bazaar to stock up on a few luxuries such as instant coffee and baby products. In the evenings we joined Aydın's cousins for dinner. Most of the hotels, restaurants and nightclubs had live bands and we danced the night away. People in Izmir are open-minded, gregarious and extremely hospitable. The women have a reputation for being quite flirtatious, gained in the 19th century when the city was the foremost Levantine trading centre for Europe enjoying privileges forbidden to other cities. English, French, Dutch and Italian Consulates were used as trading centres, flying their own flags with their own quays and ships to transport the abundance of tobacco, cotton, figs, grapes and raisins from the Aegean to the West. (Philip Mansel's fascinating book, *The Levant*, tells the story of Smyrna's multicultural past and its influence on the local population, especially Turkish women. Moslem women although still behind the veil moved in a freer, cosmopolitan society. Watching European women stroll arm in arm with their husbands aroused an awareness of European modernity and their own femininity)

Today Izmir's population is predominately Moslem. Most of the wealthy Levantine and Greek families moved to Europe leaving a few families, the Whittalls, Girauds and La Fontaines who still reside in mansions set in English gardens at Buca and Bornova.

My first trip to Izmir was a near perfect day spent with Kuşçubaşı Eşref Sencer. Eşref Bey, a sprightly eighty years old charmer, his wife, Pervin Hanım, Aydın's relative, and their two daughters, Cuyap and Diktam. Eşref Bey was a close friend of the Shamil family and had telephoned and written letters of encouragement and hope to Aydın during his father's trial and imprisonment.

Kuşçubaşı Eşref had fought side by side with Enver Bey in the Balkan wars, Afghanistan and Egypt against the British. He described himself as 'an Ottoman, a Turkish speaking Ottoman citizen not a Dağıstanlı with dreams of establishing national Circasia nor an Arab nor Greek, but a man who believes and trusts Enver Paşa.' Returning to Arabia with Enver Paşa's Third Army in the east, Eşref Bey commanded the *Bedevi Birlikeri* in Libya. He understood the harsh beauty of the desert and like the Beduins lived in caves, spoke their language and escaped arrest so often he was known as Şeyh-it-tuyyur, *uçan şeyh,* 'the flying sheikh'. A fearless guerrilla who fought against Lawrence of Arabia.

He established the Teşkilat-ı-Mahsusa, *MIT*, 'the Turkish Intelligence Service', initiating an elite and powerful network of spies, mostly Circassians, which included my father-in-law and his sister, Zübeyde. He spoke of Atatürk with respect, '*Herkes savaş kazanabilir. Ama devrim yapamaz. Atatürk her ikisini başarmıştır,*' 'Anyone can win a war. But not everyone can revolutionize. Atatürk accomplished both,' adding '*Ben teorisyen değil eylem adamıyım*'. 'I am an action man, not a theoretician'.

Diktam was 3 years old when she last saw her father, and 17 when he returned. She recalls his first words: looking with admiration at his young daughter he said, 'I can't be a father to you. You're grown up. But I can, and would like to be, your good friend.' Diktam's husband, Sedat Aktay recalls his father-in-law with deep affection and admiration. 'He was an amazing human being, to have compressed so much into one life time is mind boggling.' He was modern open-minded intelligent, humble in thought and behaviour with a keen sense of humour and fun. He told a charming story about his exploits with Hamza Bey and El Amroussi (Aunt Zübeyde's Egyptian Ambassador husband), which I love because it was so typical of El Amroussi.

On one occasion, the three friends, tired after their visits to the mosques and antique bookshops in Sultanahmet sat on a park bench to rest before walking through the Spice Bazaar for lunch at Pandeli. El Amroussi removed his new, bespoke Italian shoes, placed them under the bench and closed his eyes. When he opened his eyes, his shoes had disappeared. Hamza Bey was furious, but El Amroussi remained calm. 'Whoever took them needs them more than I do,' he said and in his stocking feet, walked calmly across the square to the nearest shop to buy another pair of shoes.

'I shall never forget the sight of my dear friend, Ambassador, El Amroussi immaculately dressed, swinging his cane nonchalantly as he walked across Sultanahmet Square in his stockings.' Eşref Bey chuckled.

I was fond of El Amroussi Bey. He addressed me as 'Aydın's better half' and on one occasion he presented me with an English Koran.

Fearless and fortunate that he lived so long, Kuşçubaşı Eşref Sencer spent his last years with his wife and family and aged with humility, humour and wisdom. He died in 1964 the year following our first meeting.

Diktam surprised everyone by accepting (with no experience) the management of BP Mocamp (camping site) at Kuşadası. A classic Caucasian, slim, dark haired and well-mannered, her determination, hard work and sense of humour kept the camp in pristine condition. She treated campers the way she would treat house-guests. She always said she learned everything there was to know about camping from foreign campers. Her husband would rush from his office at NATO headquarters in Izmir to mow the lawn, water the grass and trees before settling down in a comfortable chair to smoke his pipe. Ceylan, aged 13 or 14 helped out until Diktam tired of shooing away a stream of young admirers from the small office, had no choice but to ask her to leave.

In the evenings, Rana, her cousins, Halil and İrem and friends refused to go to bed until Aydın returned from the farm to tell them a bedtime story. They would sit on the grass, mouths open, eyes glued on the storyteller, listening to tales of scary, haunted campsites, wild animals in the forest, or brave Caucasian knights fighting for freedom against wicked Russians.

Diktam managed the camp for thirteen years until the tragic war in Yugoslavia closed the roads for mobile homes. The land was sold by BP and Diktam and her family retired to their charming summerhouse on the hill of Kuşadası.

I often visit Diktam and Sedat in their lovely moated farmhouse, (actually on an island due to a freak turn of the Menderes River) and set in beautiful grounds and gardens of fruit and flowering trees in Söke. Diktam has hardly changed except for her greying hair and Sedat now in his 90's, still potters around the garden, collects fruits for jam-making and is as good company as ever chatting away about political, cotton prices, family goings-on, the past and certainly the future.

The Last Sultan's Granddaughter

The social scene in Kuşadası was delightfully hosted by two members, cousins, from the same family, Halil Özbaş and Ali Riza Özbaş were the grandsons of Haci Halil Pasha, a highly respected wealthy landowner who originated from Eğin on the Fırat River in the province of Erzincan, but who made his home and fortune in Söke. Hacı Halil Pasha accompanied his father to Söke when his father became *müftü*, the religious authority of a province appointed by the Sultan. There he married and had five children from Fatma Hanım, a wealthy lady and source of his wealth from Özbaşı Village. After Fatma Hanım's death, Hacı Halil Pasha married Zeyda Hanım from Kuşadası and fathered three children.

When the surname law was introduced in 1934, it is interesting to note that Fatma Hanım's children took the name of their mother's village Özbaş while Zeyda's children chose Fırat after the Fırat River and birthplace of their father.

Halil Özbaş married Suade Hümeyra Hanım Sultan, who, on her mother's side, was the granddaughter of Sultan Mehmet VI, last Ottoman Sultan and on her father's side, granddaughter of the last Grand Vizier, Tevfik Pasha (Ahmet Tevfik Okday), owner of the land on which the Park Hotel in Istanbul was built.

Hümeyra Hanım referred to her husband as Halil Bey. Theirs was a complex relationship with twists and turns but it was respect and a deep emotional bond for each other which stood the test of time and helped them weather many marital storms and give birth to two children, Halim and Hanzade. A generous, gregarious couple they settled in Söke and spent summers at the modest home he built on the Akyar peninsular which he had given as a gift to his wife. Whenever they were in residence, a blinking red lamp summons friends and we all run down the hill.

Halil was good-looking, a natural raconteur with a stream of stories. He worked hard, drank hard and played hard – as did most men from the Söke and Aydın area, except my husband. Halil managed the farm and fisheries at Bafa Lake nearby, presenting us with the finest *balık yumurtası*, 'fish eggs from sturgeon' sealed in wax at Christmas time. As rare as caviar, when held to the light it should be translucent. It is an acquired taste, rather salty, but delicious sliced paper thin and eaten on buttered toast. Underneath a gruff pretence, Halil was kind, generous and unboreable. After a hard day's work, drink in hand, he adored to entertain guests with stories. Surrounded by a captive audience he'd begin with 'When I was in America…'

My favourite story was when he landed in New York after sailing on the first ocean liner to cross the Atlantic after the Second World War. His mother had sown thousands of dollars for tuition and living expenses into the lining of a heavy, black overcoat. Fearing it would be stolen he refused to take it off, even under the hot Mediterranean sun. Once the ship anchored in New York harbour, he unstitched the precious dollars, dropped the coat into one of those help the soldiers clothes boxes on every street corner, left his suitcase at the train station, and headed for the only address he had in New York – a dance hall where a friend promised that he would meet the prettiest girls in America.

Halil, being Halil, bought a roll of tickets, sought out the prettiest girl and danced the afternoon away. Being a Turkish gentleman, he insisted on escorting his date home safely, so come the end of the night, he hailed a taxi. It was far, an hour and a half drive's – far by the time the taxi pulled up outside her home.

As it happened this taxi-driver was a streetwise, good-natured Italian. Listening to this young boy chatting away at being in New York, he felt empathy for this young stranger in town, the same age as his son, and invited him home to supper. Halil felt at home in this noisy Italian household. Beaming between mouthfuls of pasta, he said 'Italians and Turks have a lot in common – football, good food, beautiful women, you must come to Turkey,' while the comely mother and her son warned him against the pitfalls of New York's bright lights, dance halls and sleazy night life. They insisted he spend the night on the sofa. Next morning the taxi driver drove him to the train station then to Princeton University, waiting to ensure that Halil enrolled, before wishing him goodbye.

'If it hadn't been for that Italian taxi driver, all my dollars would have gone on dance tickets,' he roared (And it's true – they probably would have.)

Hümeyra Hanım's childhood was shaped by the collapse of the Ottoman Empire and birth of a new Republic. Her father's marriage to Mehmet V1's eldest daughter was not a happy union and after a few years, İsmail Hakkı, an officer in the Ottoman army left the palace to join the freedom fighters, *Milli Mücadele*, under Atatürk. He received two *İstiklal Madalyası* – medals for bravery.

On 3rd March 1924, members of the Ottoman House, including six-year old Hümeyra, boarded a train for the journey into a life in exile. For a little girl, what an adventure that was. Skipping up and down the corridors, she wondered why her mother looked sad and nanny was crying. They resided in Italy, then the south of France, before settling in Egypt.

When her father was Consul General to Moscow in the new Republic, he appealed to Atatürk to allow his daughter to return to Turkey. Atatürk sympathized, but reminded his friend that his hands were tied, and new laws had to be passed which could take time. Atatürk suggested she accompany him on his diplomatic passport from Moscow to Turkey, which she did.

Young Hümeyra was thrilled to live with her Aunt Zehra, in a city she called home but hardly remembered. She became a member of the Tennis and Fencing Club and was soon winning trophies presented by another ardent tennis player, Foreign Minister Şükrü Saraçoğlu. It was there she met the Erkan brothers, Şamil, Hamza and Bekir. When Atatürk stayed at the Park Hotel, he made a point of socializing and dancing with guests in the ballroom. On one occasion, Atatürk asked young Hümeyra to dance.

It was with great dismay the *Milli İstihbarat* 'secret police' learned of her presence and she was arrested. She recalls bitterly being exiled a second time and the arranged marriage to a young student, Fahri who was leaving for America. The marriage was short-lived. Hümeyra, not one for self-pity, set about looking for work which she found – teaching at Princeton University, where she met civil engineer Halil Özbaş, who brought her back to Turkey.

When Halil's father, Hüseyin Avni Özbaş, authoritarian patriarch of the family received news of his son's intended marriage, he called his close friend, Şükrü Saraçoğlu, to inquire about this young lady. Şükrü Bey was delighted to champion the relationship. With the enthusiasm of an old admirer, he spoke in glowing terms of the bride-to-be especially her prowess at tennis.

One stiflingly hot afternoon, Hümeyra Hanım telephoned ordering me to turn on the TV at once and watch the bad guy a blond actor in an old Hollywood film. No sooner had the film ended, giggling like a teenager, she telephoned and told me the bad guy was none other than her first husband, Fahri.

During one of his many terms in office, Prime Minister, Bülent Ecevit announced his intention to nationalise the fisheries at Bafa Lake. Naturally upset, Halil made an appointment to see him. They were classmates at Robert College and in a way related in that Ecevit's aunt had married Hümeyra Hanım's father. Full of good intentions, on time Halil arrived at the ministry in Ankara to be told that he should wait. He did. An hour and half later, according to Halil before a secretary appeared to say the Prime Minister would see him. Halil replied he had changed his mind and walked out. The fisheries were nationalised, failed miserably as a cooperative, but fortunately were later saved as a nature reserve.

Halil built the first Kısmet Hotel in Izmir. When a law was passed (probably enforced by the Ecevit government), making coastal land public property, Halil build a second Kısmet Hotel on the peninsular. One evening at dinner chuckling wickedly, he whispered in my ear, 'I'm going to build a hotel here, then these free-loaders will have to pay for their drinks.'

Ali Rıza Özbaş married beautiful, blond Melike from İstanbul. He had studied in Miami and was so impressed by the ocean-front resort hotels there, he decided to build one in Kuşadası at the opposite end of the village, on the shore of *Kadınlar Denizi,* 'Women's Beach'. On September, 1965, Kuşadası was a buzz of activity as the Imbat Hotel and Kısmet Hotel opened their doors the same day and we were driven from one hotel to the other by horse-carriage. The hotels were quite different in concept. The Imbat had a Miami resort feel with 40 large, comfortable rooms, modern facilities, out-door swimming pool and long sandy beach, while Kısmet Hotel was a 24-room family-run boutique hotel in a lush garden of pines, olive trees, oleander and bougainvillea with steps going down to a rocky beach and sea.

Never one for sentimentality, Hümeyra Özbaş, petite with short blond hair and Ottoman features decided to take on the management of the hotel. Her family connections attracted royalty, international and local celebrities whose photographs lined the walls of the lobby. Queen Elizabeth and Prince Philip, the Queen of the Netherlands, and the King of Sweden chatting to their hostess to mention but a few. When friends of ours, the Earl and Countess of Arran set down their luggage in the lobby of the hotel, Tom Arran, who sits in the House of Lords, seeing the photographs, grinned, 'Ah, Ah, a rogue's gallery similar to the one we have in the House of Lords' and when Hümeyra Hanım asked if he and his charming wife, Nell, would be photographed for the gallery, they accepted with pleasure.

Hümeyra Hanım's natural charm and integrity added much to the success of the Kısmet Hotel. One satisfied guest was overheard to say, 'the warmth and hospitality makes you feel you're at home – until you get the bill', another, 'who on earth is that woman shouting at the staff?' Guests returned year after year, charmed not only by the ambiance and service, but the hostess, Hümeyra Hanım's graciousness. Uniquely rooted in her past, her journey from Ottoman Palace, career woman in New York, to running the Kısmet Hotel is proof of her adaptability, energy and courage. 'I am a hands-on mother figure house-keeper,' she'd say proudly. She called every staff member by their first name, shared their problems, paid health-bills and saw that many positions passed from father to son.

And their devotion to her spoke for itself. One summer Hümeyra Hanım flew to Switzerland for minor surgery. I came across the head gardener relaxing under a tree smoking. 'If Hümeyra Hanım caught you smoking here you'd have your ears boxed and a jolly good scolding,' I said.

He sighed. 'Ah! Ah if only she was here to scold me, I'd be a happy man. Now I am not happy, I worry and pray for her quick return.'

One day Hümeyra Hanım rushed down the steps to the beach bar to warn us of a group of young Italian girls coming to the beach to swim topless. 'No ogling or funny remarks,' she said, knowing full well the raunchy humour of most husbands. Topless bathing was frowned upon except at the Club Med. By the time the Italian beauties bounced down the steps, eager husbands were already positioned, swimming or sunbathing on the rocks under the midday sun. My dear husband sat reading his newspaper until I found he had cut two holes to spy.

Hümeyra Hanım's first trip to London was hilarious, so typical *à la* Hümeyra. She had lived and knew every European capital except London and I teased her mercilessly. 'London is the most exciting capital in the world and you have never been there, shame, shame.' One day when I was in London, she rang to say that she was coming for her granddaughter's graduation and that she wanted to see the Changing of the Guards at Buckingham Palace and the crown jewels at the Tower of London. Off we went to Buckingham Palace. Elegant, perfectly coiffeured in a Burberry mackintosh, silk scarf and leather gloves, we joined the crowd outside the palace gates. She shooed those who blocked her view and (surprise, surprise) they moved away politely as she clung to the railings watching the changing of the Guards.

As we filed pass the magnificent regalia, crowns and jewels in the Tower of London, her loud comments attracted people around her until she had quite a following: 'that diamond is not as big as the one in my grandfather's fez at Topkapı Palace,' 'just look at the sparkle in that ruby, magnificent,' and 'I have a photo of my cousin, Hanzade Sultan wearing a similar tiara at a ball in Egypt.'

'Who is that lady?' whispered those around us.

The tour ended at a small shop, sparkling with copies. 'I'll buy all my presents here,' she announced and was soon filling a basket carried by a tall, elegant man in morning suit who explained the story behind each piece of fake jewellery while she replied with its Ottoman version. The bill, I remember very well, came to just under 700 pounds. The shop hadn't sold that amount since opening! Her platinum credit card didn't register. She tried and tried insisting, 'It's not possible. My card is limitless, limitless.' The assistant was practically in tears, I offered her my card, but after much fuss, 'You buy lunch' she handed over all her cash to the cashier who sighed with relief.

I took her to the roof restaurant at Liberty's, a well-known store, which had opened its doors one year before the discovery of America. In those days it had dark wooden panelled walls, wide stairs and was known for its classic merchandise. As we walked through the needlework department, Hümeyra Hanım insisted on trying her card. She bought a few packets of pins and needles, the card registered, and needless to say, she kept on buying.

The following day, Lord and Lady Arran invited Hümeyra Hanım, her daughter, Hanzade, and granddaughter, Neslişah, to the House of Lords for lunch. One could see how deeply impressed Hümeyra Hanım was by its historic heritage and architecture as we walked along the corridors of power listening to Tom's explanation as he stopped in front of many of the paintings especially that of his father. Lord and Lady Arran were delighted with their guest, 'She understands and appreciates what this house is all about', and in the panelled walled dining room over-looking the Thames, Hümeyra Hanım looked very much at home. She fell in love with London, its traditions and historical past. For months after she'd whisper: 'Halil is still paying my credit card. He is angry I spent so much money and says I am never to go to London again. But don't you worry, I will come. When are you next going?'

Rosie Baldwin and Rose Cottage

I always think of Rosie Baldwin tossing her head of silvery blond hair and hearing her laughter. Tall, slim and attractive with perfect posture, an English beauty, Rosie belonged to that generation in which the socially conventional mingled with left-leaning artists, writers, actors, spies and politicians. All you needed was to be beautiful, intelligent, artistic and witty.

One day, Hümeyra Hanım telephoned Aydın to say she was bringing a Mr. and Mrs. Ken Baldwin to lunch, adding, 'She is an admirer of your great, great grandfather, Imam Shamyl and everything Caucasian and wants to meet you.'

Hümeyra Hanım had been a witness at the Baldwin's recent marriage and invited them to honeymoon at the Kısmet Hotel. Rosie had met Ken Baldwin when she accompanied Prince Bernard of Holland, President of the Wildlife Society and his party on a trip to establish the existence of leopards in the mountains of south Turkey. Ken acted as their guide. Ken was a young, good-looking American exiled to Kuşadası by a military court because of his involvement in American goods illegally sold on the Turkish black market. Rosie took it upon herself to clear Ken's name, which she did. Then she married him.

A passionate gardener, Rosie loved nature, wildlife and all things beautiful. Her first marriage had been to Peter Calvert, father of their three daughters. Her second was to Commander Taffy Rodd, wartime head of naval intelligence in Alexandria and uncle of my friend Mary Rodd. After the war they settled in Italy Rosie created a terraced garden in their country house at Ansedonia, opened a restaurant in Porto Ercole, and landed a role as fortune-teller in Fellini's unforgettable film, *La Dolce Vita.*

Rosie was delighted to meet a descendant of Shamyl, one of her heroes, while Ken was more interested in organising a hunting party. Aydın, impressed by her knowledge of the Caucasus and Russia, brought out family photographs and papers,

Shamyl's seal and handwritten, six-sided Koran in its silver embellished box, which hung from the pillion of Shamyl's horse when he was going to war. That afternoon sealed their friendship as they pored over trophies of the past.

Hümeyra Hanım had found a barn in an olive grove on a hill opposite Kısmet Hotel, which Rosie and Ken rented and renovated into the nicest higgledy-piggledy home, Rose Cottage, full of as she said, 'All you need, darling, to make a home are books, beautiful carpets and kilims and Rosie had them in galore. Ken built a small flat on the upper floor to accommodate friends who arrived in droves and stayed for months. Under the shadow of a huge oak and tall pine trees, Rosie created a natural wild garden of sweet-smelling honeysuckle, climbing roses and lavender. Herbs, mint, thyme, and basil grew between peach, apple and olive trees. They bought a boat to ferry passengers from Kuşadası to Samos and were soon part of the local community. Ken was an easy-going, friendly guy who spoke Turkish, looked after the boat and cottage, drank with fishermen and kept on the right side of the harbour-master. Meanwhile his wife arranged excursions, entertaining her huge circle of friends who came to visit and accommodated a stream of backpackers, children of friends, who arrived unannounced on her doorstep. She was a born romantic and matchmaker. I know of more than one couple who tied the knot after spending time at the cottage.

But at the same time Rosie was quite capable of twisting the arm of an official on matters dear to her heart, such as conservation, keeping Kuşadası clean, and relations with Samos. She worked tirelessly to preserve the natural beauty of Turkey's shores, forests and wild mountains, and was a great believer in the medicinal properties of royal jelly. In spring, armed with a long list of orders we would drive beyond the forest to Davutlar where bee-man, Hüseyin and his family prepared and sold honey, pollen and royal jelly, which Rosie bought and sent to friends. It was to him that I rushed in 1979, when Ceylan lost so much weight after a thyroid operation.

She encouraged Aydın to write, gave him books, sent articles on the Caucasus, and often dropped by unexpectedly with friends after a trip to Lake Bafa or the mountain markets of Tire and Ödemiş. She would telephone him at all hours of the day asking him to write a letter in Turkish or translate an article. Happy to oblige, he was impressed by her generous spirit and passion. One day I mentioned Aydın had a fever during a telephone conversation with her. An hour later the doorbell rang and there was Rosie and Ken with ashes from Indian guru, Sri Baba, which she placed on his forehead while he slept.

And it was Aydın Rosie turned to when her marriage broke down after twelve years. Ken returned to America, and a few months later Rosie left for Australia, leaving Aydın to sort out her affairs, letters and the cottage. I was thrilled when we took it over. At the farewell party we gave for Rosie I asked the name of the owner. 'Oh, an old man on a donkey, darling. I told him you were my niece and will live here during my absence,' came the flippant reply. That summer I greeted every old man on a donkey that passed the house until one day an old man marched up the olive grove yelling,' Rosie, Rosie, Rosie.' I introduced myself as her niece. Aydın sealed the arrangement by increasing the yearly rent to his satisfaction.

Australia didn't work out. Rosie telephoned to say that she was returning to Turkey to stay with Rahmi Koç. I told her the cottage was hers, but she refused. I gave her the keys, but she never used them. Rosie possessed that rare quality of moving on without the baggage of the past.

Turkey was Rosie's greatest love. She worked hard to establish a nature reserve on Bafa Lake. She inspired the Turkish Wildlife Society and, despite a heart operation, continued as unofficial guide, bringing journalists and writers to Turkey, travelling to off-the-beaten-track sites, and climbing mountains. She died in 1992 at the age of 75 after a remarkably varied and full life. She left behind a legacy of friends, gardens and good works. Her ashes are scattered on Bafa Lake. Ömer Koç wrote in a profile of Rosie Baldwin for *Cornucopia*, the magazine for connoisseurs of Turkey, that 'she immediately became a member of our family. She filled the garden with flowers and plants and the house with books.... She did more than anyone else I know to promote Turkey and help the Turks appreciate and save the beauty of their coastline and countryside. For me her death is an irreplaceable loss, as it is, I am sure for all her friends.'

A week or so after we had settled into Rose Cottage, a telegram arrived at the Kısmet Hotel for Rosie from Julie Dodson, wife to the newly appointed British Ambassador, Sir Derek Dodson: 'Dearest Rosie, been seriously ill. In need of sympathy and a few days of sun before facing Ankara. Arriving on the 10th.'

I replied in haste: 'Rosie has moved to Australia. We have taken over the cottage, you are very welcome to stay.'

'Arriving Saturday afternoon around five at the Kısmet Hotel,' was the reply.

Born into a diplomatic Bostonian family, Julie Dodson had a strong presence and quick, dry sense of humour. After she had settled in, I invited her for a drink, she stayed for supper, plying us with questions about Istanbul society. That night there was a sudden rainstorm. A banging on the door woke us up. 'Roof's leaking, need buckets' shouted Julie above the noise. Aydın put buckets and bowls under the dripping ceiling. Luckily the roof over her bed was dry. Next morning, armed with new tiles to replace broken ones, Aydın crawled onto the roof. Julie climbed to the top of the ladder after him shouting instructions as he worked. By the afternoon the roof was as good as new and the two workers stood pleased as punch, admiring their work. I suggested dinner at the Kısmet Hotel to celebrate. Hümeyra Hanım appeared, Julie was duly introduced as wife of the British Ambassador, by the end of the evening, as I thought, Hümeyra Hanım and Julie had become friends and Sir Derek and Lady Dodson were added to the August guest list at the Kısmet Hotel.

One cold April evening the police telephoned to warn of terrorists hiding in the hills. They suggested we stay at a hotel rather than Rose Cottage, which was pretty isolated. Instead we decided to sleep in the upper flat near the car. Aydın loaded a sawn-off shotgun used to hunt boar. I was curled in an armchair, flicking through a magazine in front of the glass front door, when a mighty blast of hot air and shards of glass hit me. 'I've blown my finger off, get towels,' Aydın yelled, blood pouring onto the floor.

I wrapped his bloody hand in towels, tying a belt as tightly as I could around his wrist and we ran to the car. My hands shook so badly I couldn't open the car door. There was blood everywhere. I drove like mad to the first aid centre at Kuşadası. Aydın was taken inside, I was told to wait. A little later İbrahim, Ali Rıza and Ergun rushed in. I broke down when I saw İbrahim. We were taken to Söke Hospital where Aydın's finger was cleaned, sown and bandaged. Ali Rıza insisted we stay at the İmbat Hotel. The following day I was driven to a specialist in İzmir where x-rays showed that I too had been hit – sprayed by sixteen pellets in the arms, legs, feet and face, but, thank God, not one had touched a nerve. The rest had smashed the glass door behind me.

Aydın was devastated at the thought that he might have killed his wife. He could not forgive himself for pointing the gun in my direction. News travels fast, the telephone never stopped ringing. Jenni Franco, my doctor friend, assured me that pellets would 'voyage' to the surface of the skin. Another friend gave me the number of her cosmetic surgeon. Yet others came up with bizarre, not very nice gossip, which upset Aydın dreadfully. I asked the operator not to connect calls.

The following day two policemen arrived at the hotel to take a statement. Melike Özbaş bounced in, she was really sweet and teased Aydın relentlessly. 'Kim, this is your chance. Either he gives you 10,000 dollars, or else,' she kept saying, keeping up this light-hearted banter to put my husband out of his misery. The policemen walked into the room with black book and pencil at the ready, but I told them in fluent Turkish: no thank you, I do not wish to file a complaint against my husband. It was an accident. Believe it or not they looked disappointed, Aydın breathed a sigh of relief, leaving Melike pretending to be disgusted, 'We could have gone to Rome for a holiday, silly woman'. For a long time Aydın's moods swung between anger at his own carelessness and depression at having lost a finger – Circassian vanity!

Pellets do work their way to the surface of the skin and can be removed. Two pellets caught my sweater; two were removed from my foot and one from my leg, leaving eleven still 'voyaging.' After suffering needle-like pains in my foot for weeks I visited a Harley Street specialist recommended by Julie Dodson. Peering at the x-rays the doctor asked me what had happened. 'My husband is Turkish,' I joked. After a thorough examination I was told there was 'nothing to worry about' and that 'men who fought in the war walk around with bullets too dangerous to remove all the time. The pain will pass, let me call your husband in.' Dismissively he explained that the body protects itself from foreign objects by forming mucus around them. He then sat down with Aydın to discuss guns and his time in Ankara during the Second World War. Addresses were exchanged. Two years later Aydın received a telephone call. The surgeon and his wife were on a cruise ship anchored at Kuşadası. Aydın took them to Ephesus and then Kazım Usta for a fish lunch where they continued their Second World War stories.

Some pellets are still there all but forgotten. They don't buzz when I pass security machines at airports and the one that skimmed my eye has 'voyaged' to my jawline. Years later, after a fall, I had an x-ray on my foot. The young doctor asked for a second one, but was still dissatisfied. 'There is something there,' he insisted looking puzzled. 'Have you had an operation?' Rana and I thought and thought, then in unison laughed: 'the pellets.'

Cotton

Farmers are a patient lot, they pray when they plant a seed, pray when they tend the crop, and pray for a bumper harvest and good prices. When it doesn't happen, they pray that next year will be better. Walking with Aydın in fields of cotton, wheat, barley or sunflower, he would smile and say, 'look at this magnificent crop. This year we'll be millionaires', I'm still waiting.

Planted in April, cotton bursts into soft, white, fluffy cotton balls in late September/early October ready to be picked by cotton-pickers from eastern Turkey. Previously cotton pickers came from near-by villages around Aydın and Denizli, but as their standard of living improved, they stopped picking cotton and Kurdish cotton pickers from the east moved in.

Lorries, with families perched atop mattresses, rumbled through the village to set up camp near the fields. Aydın was quick to point out that cotton picking in the Aegean was a pleasant place to earn money. People were friendly, water was plentiful and the climate fresh with cool breezes blowing over the fields and trees for shade from the midday sun. The river bank was a fun place for children to play. The headman, *kahya* of an extended family with approximately twenty to forty members was in charge. His word was law and it was his duty, at the end of the season, to bargain for an advance payment for the following year to support his family through the difficult winters. Aydın and the kahya had worked together for years. Deals were sealed with a shake of the hand over a glass of tea at the konak.

Early in the cool of the morning, women and young girls strapped baskets to their backs and began to work the rows picking the six-flowered balls of cotton in one clean sweep while listening to the sound of loud Arabesque music and followed by a water carrier. Baskets full, the cotton was weighed and registered by Bayram and the kahya, then put into bales. Boys jump in to stamp down the cotton until the bale was full, it was then sown and piled onto the *remork* 'wagon' to be taken to the konak.

Cotton pickers are paid by the kilo – the more they pick the more they earn. They are fast, clean workers – no easy feat, and I speak from experience as the slowest cotton picker in the Aegean. At midday they would eat and rest under the shade of the trees then continue until sundown. Children ran bare-footed around. Each year a woman offered a baby: 'You take him, you can call him Aydın. I have plenty.' She'd say.

Cotton pickers were a boisterous, chatty lot and brought a fairground atmosphere to the otherwise sleepy village. There was lots of horseplay, babies, children galore, young boys (who didn't know how to swim) jumped and splashed in the river. Wrinkled old crones would prepare meals in large black pots over a few burning sticks, blowing hard to keep the fire alight. Bayram was a popular figure and cheered when he arrived with a weekly tray of 'baklava' or 'börek'. As dusk fell, fleets of tractors piled high with bales bumped along the dusty road to the barns. The men would jump on the last tractor to spend the evening at the village café drinking tea, talking politics, watching football and catching up with the local news. With three pickings of cotton a year, pickers moved from field to field.

I liked the friendly cotton pickers so every afternoon Aydın and I drove to the fields. He sat with the men while I went for a long walk and chatted to the women. Walking through a field, one day I heard a meowing sound. 'Strange,' I thought, 'cats never wander this far from the village.' I pushed the cotton plants aside and there, on the ground, was a baby wrapped in a blanket next to a bowl of milk, swarming with flies, a dirty spoon on top. 'Whose baby is this?' I shouted, a girl, no more than a child herself, appeared from nowhere, picked up the baby and ran off, just as the foreman appeared shouting in Kurdish.

The next day I drove to the fields armed with a bundle of Rana's baby clothes, a thermal flask of hot water, a bottle, baby milk and a plastic washing tub. I filled the tub with cotton, covered it with a clean sheet, then called the painfully shy child-mother over to showed her how to add formula to warm water, feed the baby from a bottle, and cover everything with a clean sheet.

Eager to see how the child-mother was getting on, I drove to the fields to find no tub, no cotton, and the baby on the ground. I was disappointed and called the mother who stared at the ground without saying a word before picking up the baby and running off. Aydın chided me when I told him what had happened: 'You have no idea of the hardship these women suffer. Life in the east is difficult. They carry water for miles from wells. There are few schools, little education, and medical attention. They give birth to lots of children knowing some will die. Dr. Spock will not work here.' (Dr. Spock was the bible of childcare for my generation).

'You can't change people's habits overnight. All you've done is embarrass that poor girl in front of her family and got her in trouble with the kahya'. That was last thing I intended. I didn't get much sleep that night, but I woke up with a plan.

In the morning I drove to the fields with an old plastic tub which I covered sparingly with cotton, mixed powdered baby milk with cold water in a plastic bowl with a plastic spoon, and covered them with old netting. I put the baby in the basket and carried her to the old woman who prepared food then called the kahya. Without looking at the woman, I told him I would pay her a few liras if she fed the baby in the basket so that her mother could earn money picking cotton. The kahya nodded, we shook hands, and he told the old lady the deal who smiled a toothless smile. That afternoon on my walk, I waved to the child-mother and smiling shyly she waved back and the women around her nodded their approval.

The fertile plains in the Aegean changed forever when the land was levelled as flat as a pancake to accommodate massive cotton-picking machines instead of cotton pickers. The shady tree-lined canal, Söğütlü, a favourite picnic spot, was felled and replaced with a concrete irrigation system. A new seed yielding one crop a year was imported from America. It meant goodbye to the cotton pickers. Those unfamiliar with country life and ways decry the practice of farm labour. They believe in one scenario: wicked landlord, poor peasant. But that was not the case in the Aegean. Cotton pickers from eastern Turkey were sad to leave, they were earning money and were well treated. Later during the exodus from the east in the 70's - 80's, many cotton pickers set up villages in the province of Aydın.

A good crop means a farmer can buy a tractor, cow, hunting rifle or invest in gold bracelets, which not only pleases his wife but provides ready cash in an emergency. I rather fancied those slim plain gold bracelets and had purchased two myself. One day a woman in the village noticed them. 'Hmm,' she said, rolling up the sleeve of her cardigan to display an armful of gold bracelets. 'My husband bought these for me,' she smirked. Whatever would she have thought of me, had she known I had paid for them myself?

The Flood

In 1966, hopes were high for a bumper harvest, the fields were snowy white with fluffy balls waiting to be plucked and cotton pickers on their way. One late afternoon the sky appeared strangely overcast with storm clouds moving in the direction of the fields. It was an ominous sign, Aydın looked worried, and villagers became apprehensive, animals restless, as cracks of thunder rumbled in the distance. It was sticky and hot as we walked in silence in the fields.

That night the heavens exploded, lightning flashed, and windows rattled. A branch from the plane tree crashed down onto the garden table like a gunshot, we jumped out of bed, the telephone rang. It was Bayram. A flash flood had hit the bank of the Menderes River at its widest curve near Çinçin and the water was heading towards the fields.

Pulling on wellingtons and raincoats we drove through sheets of torrential rain to the fields, but got no farther than the bridge. We stood aghast: instead of a sea of white cotton, it was a sea of water, a lake. Villagers in tiny rowing boats flashing torches searched for lost animals, cows, sheep, even horses. I saw one lamb rescued from the branch of a tree. We drove back to the village stopping outside the crowded café for Aydın to shout, 'Follow me Çinçin, Çinçin' and sped off. We found Aydın's uncle Nejat Çifçi wrapped in oilskin staring at the surging water. 'If that river changes course, acres of farmland, villages and families are at risk,' he stated ominously. We stood in the pouring rain mesmerized by the fast, flowing water. It was the most frightful scenario a farmer could imagine.

There was not a moment to lose. Desperate telephone calls to the Department of Agriculture in Ankara of the fate of seven villages under threat proved to be of no avail. No help was forthcoming. They failed to respond to the urgency of the situation. The following morning village *muhtar* 'head-men', landowners and farmers decided to take matters into their own hands. A unanimous decision was taken to strengthen the banks of the river immediately in order to save the villages and land,

and a committee to organise the operation was set up. Nejat Çifçi's castle folly in Çinçin became headquarters. Landowners were required to pay a certain sum per *dönüm* 'one and a half acres', provide tractors, equipment and workers. 'Muhtars' were put in charge of co-ordinating villages and villagers to work in shifts. Fatma and her daughters set up a working kitchen providing nonstop tea, coffee, soup, 'börek' and biscuits. Under the teeming rain crocodile-line of men, naked except for underpants, carried sandbags on their head down to the water's edge and handed them to a second team, standing in the swirling water, to place one on top of the other along the breaks in the bank. A convoy of tractors supplied spades, sacks, sand, sandbags, stones, equipment, drinking water, food, towels and dry clothes. One group followed another until darkness fell, only to begin at the first break of light.

Crisis brings out the best community spirit in Turks. Their fortitude, determination and spirit to overcome the most arduous task is impressive. I had never seen such a force of togetherness as volunteers kept turning up to work in the cold, wet and muddy river until a sandbag wall appeared out of the water. Cafes became crisis centres. Old men and children sewed sacks and plaited thongs of rushes, which, when wet was stronger than the thickest of ropes. The women kept the stoves burning producing mountains of warm food.

Aydın would leave at dawn and return in the evening often with his uncle for a hot soup and rakı. One of Fatma's daughters looked after the children in the mornings so I could buy the list of things which Aydın gave me every evening; I'd drive to Çinçin help Fatma until lunchtime and return so her daughter could leave to help her mother. The sandbag barrage held. The rain began to subside. A fence was built on both sides to strengthen the sandbank ditches that would ensure the water flowed into the Menderes River. Seven villages and thousands of acres of land were saved by hundreds of villagers, farmers and their wives.

The Department of Agriculture began work on strengthening the bank of the river in May, when the flow of water was at its lowest.

Elation over nature's quirky storm soon gave way to gloomy faces, reality and debt. Spirits were low in the café as they moaned about loss of the harvest, sheep and cattle and agricultural equipment and debt to the bank. Rural communities complain, grumble then shake their heads and accept. That acceptance, *kısmet* 'religious belief' – call it what you will – comes from an inner patience and resilience that is lacking in the West. '*İnşallah*, God willing, next year will be better,' they sigh, and move on.

In the whole province of Aydın, only two people, Nejat Çifçi and my husband, repaid their debt to the bank on time. A few weeks later, the Ministry of Agriculture announced that the debts of farmers in the Söke and Aydın province were to be written off. The bank did not return Nejat Bey and Aydın's money, but sent them a letter of thanks. I framed Aydın's and hung it over his desk.

'How can you? You didn't sell any cotton!' I cried in despair. When Aydın announced his intention to send his father and brothers their due share of money they should have earned but had not that year.

'They depend on me. That is their only income. You'll manage,' was the despondent reply.

How? I wondered miserably. To keep my sanity and not harm my husband, I did what English people abroad in need of money always did, teach. I began teaching English and drama at the small private school Ceylan attended.

One morning, checking the mail at the post office box, I found a letter from Jane White, a friend from Central School who lived in Cyprus and had visited me in Istanbul and Büyükada. Now she had decided to return to London and wanted to stopover on her way home. I read her letter over and over then in a flash, it occurred to me, Aydın and I could do the same. Why hadn't I thought of it before? We could go to England. Jane had answered my prayers.

I rushed home pulled Aydın into a chair, blurting out a plan as it formed in my mind. We could rent the land for a year and go to London. I had a little money there so the children could go to school. We would work, live in London, or in Wales with my parents, instead of spending a depressing year feeling sorry for ourselves. At the end of the season there would be capital enough to farm. Why hadn't I thought of it before? Now Aydın was an extremely cautious man but it didn't really take much to persuade him. After telephoning and discussing it with his father, he agreed. We spent Christmas and New Year in Istanbul with my father-in-law (who was more than encouraging,) before flying to London in January. After three cold, wet weeks in Wales, we left for London. I thanked the Lord – and Jane.

I had lived in Aydın for four years. They were happy, full years spent in a friendly, farming community with people who accepted me warmly as a 'yabancı gelin', shared my Christmas parties and Easter egg hunts as I shared their religious feasts and Bayrams. I am a practicing Christian, Aydın is a Muslim. Like every married couple we argued about everything under the sun except religion. We respected both religions and brought up our children to think likewise. Religion was never a subject of discord in the family or the village, on the contrary, villagers went out of their way to include me as much as possible. In those days there was no transport from the main highway to Osmanbükü, villagers would wait outside the coffee house for a lift. We often picked up the Imam who would join us for tea before climbing the stairs to the balcony of the mosque for the call of prayers. Aydın and I held the same belief that all religions have much in common, ethically and morally, and that the heart and philosophy of religion is love, peace and unity, 'for love is wise'. In a world which is becoming so closely interconnected it is vital to find common ground.

London

We rented a flat in Ladbroke Grove. Notting Hill Gate. Ceylan was enrolled at the local primary school and Rana became number six at a kindergarten in a mews house nearby, the home of a lovely young mother of two children. She was a teacher and had wisely decided she might as well look after another four making it six to earn a little pocket money. The schools were within easy walking distance from the flat, which meant we were able to take them to and from school. Aydın had a letter of introduction which assured him an acceptance at the Turkish Tourism Office on Conduit Street, and after reading an article about Elizabeth Arden in a Sunday paper, I applied for the course and a job. After three weeks at different department stores, I worked in their Bond Street office. My parents were delighted, we visited them and my mother came to London.

Belinda Bather was Aydın's supervisor at the Turkish Tourism Office and had lived in Ankara for years. We were sure that there was a love story there, but dared not ask. Belinda spoke fluent Turkish. In fact, she looked Turkish, with her black hair, red lips and dark red painted nails. At work, Aydın was conscientious, first to arrive in the morning and last to leave at night. His one real pleasure was lunching at different nearby restaurants until one day he invited Belinda to an Italian bistro. After lunch she brought out a calculator and proved that he was spending more money on lunches than he earned in a month. Aydın was miserable at the thought of sandwich lunches. That Italian restaurant is still there, and on our visits to London, we ate there for old time's sake.

The Turkish Ambassador, Zeki Kuneralp had met the Erkan family during his student days in Switzerland, and Yusuf Mardin, Director of Turkish Tourism, in some way, was related to Aydın's mother, (Melike Hanım). Our names were added to the Embassy guest list which meant we could attend official functions. A regular and charismatic guest at these receptions was Nubar Gulbenkian, a wealthy Armenian businessman and socialite born in Istanbul. A larger-than-life, eccentric with a pointed beard and monocle, a fresh white orchid in his buttonhole, he resided at the Ritz Hotel and ensured his entrance to every party would be the highlight of the evening.

Time flew and weeks turned into months. Life was hectic but pleasant, many times I had to sprint that last mile from the tube station to collect Rana from kindergarten. At weekends weather permitting we took the children to feed ducks at Hyde Park or to London Zoo and in the evening entertained or visited friends. A treat for me was a night at a theatre, for Aydın it was time to browse in the old bookshops in Notting Hill Gate. News from the farm was encouraging, all was well.

One evening Aydın arrived home late after a meeting at the Turkish residence with the Ambassador and Yusuf Bey. They had asked him to stay on in London and consider a career in the Foreign Service. Tourism in Turkey was growing fast and they needed men with his background and knowledge. I was about to jump on him with excitement, but stopped mid-air.

'I know you'd love to stay here, and more than anything in the world I want to make you happy,' he said to me not looking at all happy or enthusiastic. 'If you want to stay, I'll accept the offer. It's up to you. You don't have to answer now.' Giving me a peck on the cheek, he disappeared into the bedroom. When he had applied for the job, he told Yusuf Mardin that it was for a year. Never having worked in an office, having a boss or taken orders from anyone, Aydın was horrified of making mistakes. He was over-conscientious and took his responsibilities far too seriously.

Politics would have been Aydın's first career choice had his father not insisted he oversee his mother's estate instead. Hamza Bey did not want Aydın to enter politics: 'for generations our family has served their country: in the Caucasus, the Ottoman Empire and the Turkish Republic,' he had said to Aydın. 'In return we suffered nothing but injustice. My great grandfather, Imam Shamil, grandfather, Ghazi Mohammed Pasha, father, Osman Ferit Pasha, and now me, were all unjustly dishonoured, forced into exile or imprisoned. That is more than enough for one family. Tend to your mother's estate. Enjoy your life.'

And at heart Aydın was a country squire. Farming allowed him the time and freedom to write, read, hunt, help villagers, support Caucasian and local causes, and follow politics from a distance. As president of an anti-communist group he had continued to write and give talks, even after receiving threatening letters.

I decided to talk to Belinda. She knew everything that went on in the office. We met for lunch. 'Yusuf Bey has received thank-you letters and telephone calls from influential clients saying how pleased they are with Aydın,' she told me. 'He's polite, intelligent, has perfect English, the right background and is good-looking. Of course, they want him to stay. He's just what they and Turkish diplomacy needs. But I'm not sure it is what he wants. He told me you were to decide'.

I was sure Aydın loved me enough to accept any decision I made, but I also knew I would suffer the brunt of his frustration and stress. Would he be happy? He was one of those rare people who valued their personal freedom more than success or financial gain. He loved London, being with our friends, but not under these circumstances. After a few soul-searching nights, I came to the conclusion it would be difficult for Aydın, a man set in his ways whose character was impeccable but, in many ways, old fashioned, to change his life-style for his wife. More difficult for him than for me with my more flexible and spontaneous personality to live in Turkey. If only he were an English gentleman farmer! One evening I packed the children off to bed and greeted him at the door with a glass of wine to toast his success at work and my decision to return to Turkey. He was ecstatic, smothering me with kisses, dancing me around the room, promising the world. I did have two conditions, however: we were to move to Istanbul and take annual trips to England. Since I accepted to return to Turkey I have only myself to blame so I can hardly complain!

Belinda gave a splendid farewell party for us, attended by the Ambassador and Mrs. Kuneralp, and Yusuf and Mrs. Mardin. 'The offer still stands, think it over. I will be in Istanbul over the holidays. Maybe we can get together with your father and ask his opinion?' said the Ambassador. Mr. Mardin did not hide his disapproval, tutting and muttering that Aydın should remain in London. But I knew my husband, amiable, solicitous and polite as he was, in the long run, it was his independence and languorous life-style and space in his own country with his father that made him happy.

Belinda had longed to visit Istanbul, so we invited her. To conquer a fear of flying she ordered a stiff whisky at the airport before boarding. As usual, the plane was late. Belinda continued to drink, arriving at Istanbul Yeşilköy Airport dishevelled, drunk, and without the faintest idea of where she was. But after a good night's rest she recovered enough to enjoy her stay especially a visit to an old colleague in Ankara.

After we returned to Turkey our trips to London became even more meaningful. Aydın prowled antique bookshops and I would go to a theatre or a concert. But the time he and I enjoyed most was being with friends and the pleasure of going to Wales to be utterly spoiled for a few days.

Istanbul

A week or so after we arrived back in Istanbul my father-in-law told us Sıdıka Bilimer had invited us to tea at Narmanlı Apartment in Nişantaşı, a prestigious building within walking distance of his apartment. She and Melike Narmanlı, her niece, met us at the door of an empty apartment on the first floor. It had a long, dark corridor with rooms opening on either side, which led into a large, high-ceilinged room at the end. Sıdıka Hanım handed Aydın the keys of the apartment with a contract for a year, a present from his father. It was so unexpected and such a surprise. I walked from room to room, wondering how on earth we were going to furnish such a large place until Sıdıka Hanım assured us, 'Bring what you have, I will provide the rest as long as you promise to take good care of them.' Sıdıka Hanım was known for her vast collection of antiques and we were fortunate to receive beautiful pieces until we moved twelve years later.

Hamza Bey and the Narmanlı family went back to the early 1930's when, as a young manager, Hamza Erkan was sent to open a bank in Erzurum, a small town in Eastern Turkey. For a young man who had spent his youth in Switzerland and Paris moving to eastern Anatolia with no friends, no heating, no running water, was devastating. 'I will die here,' he wrote to a friend.

One snowy evening, an elderly man, muffled in furs, marched in just as the bank was about to close. Shrugging off the snow he placed two leather pouches on the desk. 'What is this?' inquired the manager.

'Gold coins. Put them in the safe,' came the gruff reply.

'I'm sorry, Sir. But you will have to come back tomorrow. The bank is about to close,' replied Hamza.

'Then be quick,' came the reply.

Hamza pulled himself up to his full height. 'I am sorry, Sir. For me to provide you with the necessary receipt I have to count these coins. It's late and the bank is about to close. Please come tomorrow.'

'It's not too late for me, young man. I don't need a receipt. Just put them in the safe.' His tone defied objection as 'Hacı' Mustafa Narmanlı removing his coat, settled in a chair. 'You had better start counting,' he commanded. Defeated, miserable, the young manager began to count the coins while Mustafa Bey told Hamza the story of his life and so began a life-long respect and friendship between the young banker and the old man.

Mustafa was born in the village of Narman near Erzurum, when the city had a vibrant Armenian community and served as provincial residence for the Archbishop of the Armenian Apostolic Church. Mustafa's mother, an uneducated but far-sighted woman, sent her eldest son to work for an Armenian who made Ottoman *fez* 'a headwear for men' 'He will teach you a trade,' she urged. In spite of being ridiculed, bullied even, by the other lads in the village, Mustafa persevered in his work until the day came when, disturbed by growing political tension and unrest, his Armenian boss decided to move to Istanbul. He left the atelier in the hands of two Armenians and Mustafa.

They worked hard, travelling far and wide to Istanbul and St. Petersburg to sell the Ottoman fez red, felt headwear. A few years later, they decided to set up a textile business in Samsun and the three partners prospered.

When his first child, a son called Sıtkı, showed an early interest in music at the age of six, his delighted father decided to buy him a musical instrument on his next trip to Istanbul. Marching into a music shop, Mustafa Bey demanded each instrument be played so he might choose one for his son. He finally heard an instrument with a sound he liked. It was a violin. Later Sıtkı became a student of violist and teacher, Karl Berger.

As the situation in eastern Turkey continued to deteriorate, Mustafa Bey decided it was time to move his family to Istanbul. He set off alone, taking forty days to cover the distance and after days of wandering around the city he invested in land, purchasing corner lots in strategic locations. He went on to build *hans* 'caravansaries', *konaks* 'mansions', apartments and business blocks. He employed the best Armenian architects and used the highest quality construction materials, marble and stone, and imported wood from the forests of Bulgaria. He installed elevators from Italy and central heating, adding classical decorative touches and bronze statues. Hacı Mustafa's business thrived. At that time the family settled in a large konak on the Asian side at Üsküdar, his sons attended the French Galatasaray Lycée and later the American Robert College while his daughter, Sıdıka was taught at home by a governess. In 1932, Hacı Mustafa built Narmanlı Apartment an imposing building which dominates a busy corner of Teşvikiye and today is home to many members of the family.

Following the death of her parents and her husband, Sıdıka Bilimer, unassuming in manner, but a presence that demanded attention, took charge of the Bilimer and Narmanlı family affairs and worked tirelessly to preserve their property and maintain their Anatolian traditions. She was renowned for her vast knowledge of antiques. She carried a well-worn black address book in her handbag containing names and telephone numbers of the finest craftsmen, artisans and the most reliable stores in town. Generous with her knowledge, she put me in touch with the best polishers, repairmen and decorators and in keeping with their father and his artisan friends, she instilled a love of art, antiques and architecture in the younger members of the family.

With the help of Hamza Bey and Melike's delicious dishes delivered each day for the first week, we settled happily in Narmanlı Apartment. Most afternoons my father-in-law would walk from his apartment to ours, stay for supper or to baby-sit and Sıdıka Hanım, more often than not would dropped by to chat with her old friend. Melike's daughters, Yasemin, Nilüfer and Aslı and my daughters, Ceylan and Rana grew up together at Narmanlı apartment and are as close today as ever. Since returning to Turkey had been my choice, I was determined to make it a success and the high-ceiling, spacious sitting room was just what I needed to begin. I organized a twice weekly gymnastic group and in an interesting round room off the sitting-room, set up a beauty parlour. Hazel Sporel, my friend Feyhan's mother was one of my best clients, saying it remained her of her days in England and she often stayed for tea recalling stories of her youth and family in Smyrna and Moda and of her amazing great, grandmother, Magdalene Whittall who had 256 direct descendants when she died.

The children attended Nilüfer Hatun Primary School which was within walking distance. Aydın commuted to the farm and when he was in Istanbul busied himself writing articles for Caucasian magazines. In 1968 he was asked to write a column on agriculture but often used the column to express what was then a controversial question, global warming, for a new daily newspaper, Günaydın, part of the Hürriyet group. I was invited to join a group of Turkish and foreign professionals at L.C.C, a Language and Culture Centre which taught languages and drama and was about to set up a model course with fashion shows. I met Flora Aksel, Irena Kutbay, Grace Bezmen, Julie Katırcıoğlu and Hilary Nowell and with our husbands, we formed close, lasting friendships. When school closed for summer, we piled into the car to drive to Rose Cottage.

On 29th February 1968, Hamza Bey decided to host a family dinner party for his sister, Zübeyde who was returning to Egypt. He was in great spirits as he greeted his brother and sister, Bekir and Habibe, niece Bedia and daughter, Güneş and her husband. We, Aydın, Akın and I kept the kitchen, drinks and music going. During dinner I thought aunt Zübeyde and my father-in-law were up to something because I caught her adding whisky to his Coca Cola in the kitchen and found them whispering mischievously together just before she left. It was a delightful evening and Hamza Bey had thoroughly enjoyed himself, and he chatted with Aydın while I helped tidy up before, last to bide our happy host goodnight, we left.

At around four o'clock in the morning the telephone rang. It was Akın, he had returned home to find his father lying on the bathroom floor. Hamza Bey had died of a heart attack.

A few weeks later, on March 5th 1968, my own father died. I left for Wales to attend his funeral. In a short space of time I lost two men who had played such an important role in my life, my father who had taught me most of the good things in life and my father-in-law who always took my side against Aydın which pleased me no end. I loved, respected and valued our companionship. I miss them but celebrate their lives and the legacy they left behind.

Aydın suggested my mother came to live with us after my father's death but she refused, 'I will miss my home and friends, you can visit me', although she did come to stay with us. She died in November 6th 1976. No matter how old you are, when you lose both parents you feel like an orphan. In 1979 when Rana became a boarder at Queen's Gate in South Kensington, we bought a flat in Redcliffe Gardens. Handing me the keys, Aydın, with a rueful smile, said 'You deserve a key in your own country after all these years with me in Turkey'. We still own the flat.

Beşiktaş and the Bosphorus

The 'konak' at Beşiktaş was a prime property and its sale would have provided more than enough money to re-house each member of the family comfortably, but the inheritance process was complicated by the descendants of their grandfather. In 1971, it was finally sold to a crafty Black Sea contractor who, as part payment, offered apartments to each member of the family further up Serencebey hill, Beşiktaş. In 1979 we moved to Şamil Apartment and it was there that I fell in love with, as Gyllius called it, 'the strait that surpasses all straits because with one key it opens and closes two worlds, two seas.' I woke to golden dawns, retired with silver moonlight shimmering on eerie dark silhouettes of submarines and boats, and watched the rain and winter winds whip the waters of the beautiful Bosphorus.

The Bosphorus is central to Istanbul's busy life ferrying passengers to work, motorboats skim around huge tankers on their way to foreign ports, and flocks of *yelkovan* 'shearwaters' or *yelkovan* 'wind chasers' follow the fishing boats then fly off in formation. On the wooded Asian shore, cars line up for the car ferry at Kadıköy or Üsküdar to cross to the European shore, where busy cafes at Rumeli Hisarı and Bebek do a roaring breakfast trade. I practiced yoga and meditated in view of the ever changing, ever moving, waters of the Bosphorus.

Şamil Apartment was a family apartment, the family simply moved up the hill with its antiques, weaponry, books and paintings. İnal, his wife and son, Şamil, Aunt Habibe, and Aunt Zübeyde, when in town, lived in Şamil Apartment, while Uncle Bekir and his daughter, Bedia at the adjoining, Bereket Apartment. Aydın continued caring for his aunts especially Aunt Habibe who popped in at all hours, more to chat with Mürvet Hanım, our help. I arranged a catch on the door so she didn't have to ring the bell. Aunt Habibe was an elegant Caucasian lady, proud but poor. She would still offer guests cakes and expensive chocolates on a Russian silver embossed dish and present them with small presents and tell magical stories of her past. She never married and always spoke and thought in French.

İnal Şaplı, Aydın's cousin was an eccentric with a mystic group of followers, Turks and foreigners frequently came to visit and it was through him I met two yoga teachers. One, a tall, intellectual aesthete German who, after living for ten years in an Indian ashram, was on his way home to Germany, the other a young, slight, dark-skinned Indian on his way to Tibet after three years training and teaching in London. I took yoga lessons from both in the sitting room. The Indian used to teach wearing just a white cloth wrapped around him like a baby's nappy. One day, standing on our heads at the end of a session, in walked Aunt Habibe. She screamed, Mürvet Hanım came running. I collapsed in hysterics while the yogist remained on his head until calm prevailed, then slowly folded down. Aydın suggested I take lessons elsewhere.

In May with the arrival of Spring we enjoyed a blaze of pink and purple trees along the hills of the Asian shore from our sitting room window as the Judas Trees, Love Trees, the *erguvan*, blossoms on both sides of the Bosphorus. Indigenous to Istanbul, the Judas Tree is known as the flower of Byzantine and was a symbol of the Ottoman Empire. Its trunk is used to make walking sticks and its flowers used to flavour and add colour to Ottoman cuisine. The *erguvan* has a short season, and people rush to parks or enjoy romantic boat trips along the Bosphorus when it is in flower. One year, Cemile Garan invited us for a picnic lunch and *erguvan* tour on her boat. It was like an old-fashioned technicolor film, a feast of colour and beauty.

Another popular event, stretching through April and May, is the International Istanbul *Lale Festivali*, the Tulip Festival, which takes place in Emirgan Park and in parks around the city. It is a reminder of the *Lale Devri*, the Tulip Era during the reign of Sultan Ahmet III in the 18th century. The tulip originally grew wild on the Asian steppes and was later introduced in Europe.

Sadly, crowds and traffic now make it impossible to enjoy this event.

The Crimean Memorial Church, Christ Church

On many Sunday mornings I walk along the cobbled side streets in Şişhane on my way to Christ Church, the Crimean Church which stands in a garden on the slope of a hill leading to Karaköy. Şişhane is one of those colourful hidden pockets in the city which mushroom up when restored, usually on a shoestring, by young entrepreneurs. Once home to a flourishing non-Muslim community, these tall, imposing but derelict bay-windowed, 19th century houses have become home to artisans, craftsmen, designers and young entrepreneurs who run trendy galleries-cum-cafes, hip hotels, antique shops, cool coffee bars, tiny corner cafes, restaurants, jazz clubs and shops with designer clothes at affordable prices. The shops are much more attractive than any in the shopping malls which dot the city at every turn. The neighbourhood has become a vibrant mix of young, liberal-minded artisans, poor conservative locals, lost migrants, curious tourists and affluent foreigners. And as the muezzin calls Muslims to pray, church bells ring inviting its followers to Christ Church.

In 1855, a promissory note of 100 pounds by Lord Stratford de Redcliffe, then British Ambassador to Constantinople, and Dr. Tomlinson, Bishop of Gibraltar, began an appeal to build a church as a memorial to those who died in the Crimean War on land presented to the British Government by Sultan Abdülmecid. The church, a cathedral-like Gothic building was designed by Victorian architect, C.E Street.

For more than thirty years, the Reverend Canon Ian Sherwood OBE has been vicar and chaplain of the Crimean Memorial Church, St. Helena's Chapel in the grounds of the British Consulate, and All Saint's in Moda on the Asian shore. Educated at Trinity College Dublin, he was auditor of the Theological Society, the oldest debating society in Ireland, and his sermons attract a healthy Sunday congregation. With a middle-to-high Anglicanism and panache for seventeenth and 18th century hymns our vicar is a source of comfort to all who ring the parsonage bell in Istanbul, a city he loves and calls 'the Great City.' During his years in charge, more than 2,000 homeless persons and refugees have received a welcome bed at the chaplaincy hostel of St. George. Many have repaid this kindness by helping to rebuild the church while their children received basic education from a team of volunteers.

Life at the parsonage embraces its Christian community in a city of mosques and minarets, in a neighbourhood at times friendly, at times, hostile. Ian Sherwood is a modern man-for-all-seasons who makes a robust, dapper figure going about his daily duties, tending the needs of refugees, visiting prisons and the sick, organising fund-raising events, feeding ducks, hens, a tortoise and cats in a cloistered garden, as well as partaking in the social life of the city. His keen Irish wit and love for Havana cigars and the written word make him a natural diarist. His account of life, the pleasures of the table, the endless stream of visitors and friends, some of whom 'make you feel there is nowhere in the whole world a soul would rather be,' are filled with amusing, endearing anecdotes, peppered with more than a few critical home truths.

Canon Sherwood is a constant presence in times of crisis – and believe me there are many in the Great City. Following the 1999 earthquake, the chaplaincy erected forty community huts. Following the tragic bombing of the British Consulate, Canon Sherwood comforted the grieving and organised the clean-up operation, for which he was awarded the OBE by Queen Elizabeth in 2003. Particularly close to my heart is the fact that, since 1989, he is solely responsible for saving and restoring four Grade-A buildings in Istanbul: The Crimean Memorial Church (1991); the Parsonage (1991); All Saint's Moda (1992); and following the Consulate bombing, St. Helena's Chapel was saved, re-built and re-consecrated (2006). This has been a massive undertaking, involving petitions to both houses of Parliament in Westminster, newspaper articles and letters by influential friends to MPs.

Strange as it may be, the powers-to-be in the Church of England, instead of commending his long, rewarding service, trim his stipend and frustrate the church council with visitations. As a member of the church council we wonder why? when in the words of Oliver Goldsmith, Canon Sherwood is one of those rare clergymen able 'to preach a better sermon with his life than with his lips.'

Philanthropy

A chance encounter with Vehbi Bey holds a special memory for our family. Aydın and I flew to Istanbul to meet my father-in-law on his release from prison hospital on 18th October 1962. It was an emotional homecoming. Tired and fragile, Hamza Bey embraced his sisters, Habibe and Zübeyde, his brother Bekir, and sons, Aydın and Akın. After a while, he retired to his room. Aydın had arranged his books and personal belongings the way he liked them, and he and Akın sat by his bedside until he fell asleep. Next morning, after a comfortable night, he appeared relaxed in a white shirt and pants, eager to greet his daughter, Güneş, and take telephone calls from well-wishers.

Hamza Bey took great pleasure in eating well, he was a large man with a large appetite, he told us in prison he only dreamt of food. But he was diabetic and his sister, Habibe was a stickler for 'doing the right thing'. Determined to follow doctor's orders, Habibe served tasteless, salt-less dishes that Hamza Bey, not wishing to hurt her feelings, ate obediently. On the third day after his release, Aydın suggested an outing and asked his father what he would like to do. 'Visit your mother's grave,' came a quick response. Then, checking to see his sister was out of the room, he added, 'and lunch at the Divan,' his favourite restaurant.

Aydın, Hamza Bey and I entered the Divan Hotel, owned by the Koç group, at the same time as Vehbi Koç. Delighted to see his old friend released from prison, Vehbi Bey insisted we join him for lunch. Summer neighbours at Büyükdere on the Bosphorus, they had much in common and were soon chatting away. Orhan Kutbay, *maître d'hôtel extraordinaire* served dish after dish and my father-in-law ate his way through seventh-heaven cuisine. Vehbi Bey chided him for sending Aydın to manage the farm – 'waste of the boy's potential, send him to me.' Taking a long, hard look at me, his cat-like crinkly brown eyes smiling, he mumbled something – obviously at my expense – for they both roared with laughter. That sharp business brain is spiced with a sharp wit, thought I.

It was a happy lunch, perfectly presented by Le Maitre Orhan Bey, who joined in the conversation. Aydın was delighted to see his father, on his first outing, beam with gourmet and friendly satisfaction as he thanked our gracious host. Vehbi Bey insisted Aydın call him and, holding my hand, invited me to come to visit him after I had learnt Turkish.

From that time on, whenever we met, no matter how crowded the room, Vehbi Bey would stop to ask me, 'haven't you learned Turkish yet? You haven't come to visit.'

Three years after Atatürk established his headquarters at Ankara – 'a small town of no importance' – it replaced Istanbul to become the capital of Turkey, on 13th October 1923. The great and famous – Kazım Karabekir, Ali Fuat, İsmet İnönü, Halide Adıvar, her husband, Dr. Adıvar – would come and go. Designed as a planned city, Ankara underwent phenomenal growth throughout the 20's 30's and 40's to accommodate a rise in population from 3,500 in 1924 to 286,781 by 1950 and more than 4 million today. At the same time *gecekondular* 'shanty towns' mushroomed on the surrounding hills. This resulted in a surge of energy in construction, production and manufacturing never seen before and attracted young entrepreneurs prepared to work hard. Philanthropy and entrepreneurship flourishes during a period of growth, change and opportunities and what better a time than the new Republic?

Ankara in the1900's was the right place and the right time for Vehbi Koç, a quiet, unpretentious young boy to be born. Son of a grocer, at the age of 16, he chose to work at his father's grocery store. It became evident even at that young age that his quick and clever mind was endowed with a remarkable acumen for business when he saw the golden opportunity that was on his very doorstep. In 1926, he founded Koçzade Ahmet Vehbi Company which with time became one of the major building suppliers in the capital's building boom. In 1948, in partnership with General Electric, Vehbi Koç established a bulb factory and moved to Istanbul. In 1963, the companies and commercial partners were registered under one name, Koç Holding A.Ş. which became the nucleus of the future Koç Empire and which to this day holds its place amongst the world's largest enterprises. In his autobiography titled 'My Life' and numerous national and International publications, Vehbi Koç's achievements as entrepreneur and philanthropist are well recorded.

Despite his great wealth, Vehbi Bey was known for his personal frugality and simple lifestyle. Everyone has an amusing anecdote about Vehbi Bey's thriftiness. People identified with his humility, admired him as an astute businessman with a relentless work ethic, and respected his efforts to spread and promote education throughout Turkey. He was singularly apt at surrounding himself with the best brains in Turkey and was known to treat 'yes-men' with contempt. A strong sense of tradition and social responsibility induced him to pledge eight per cent of the Koç Holding fortune to philanthropic causes. In 1969, he established the Vehbi Koç Foundation for the purpose of 'institutionalizing the vision of social responsibility to further education and social services to support and maintain a healthy Turkish society.' The Vehbi Koç Foundation focuses its philanthropic activities on three areas: education, healthcare and culture.

Vehbi Bey remained at the helm of the Koç Empire until his death in 1996. His son Rahmi became chairman and with his siblings, Semahat, Suna, and the late Sevgi Gönül, they continued their father's work ethic and philanthropic interests.

Philanthropy in Turkey is an age-old custom, the continuation of what was then called a *vefa borcu* 'a debt of gratitude', giving back to society. A *vakıf* is a charitable foundation in which a portion of a person's wealth cannot be sold. Instead, the revenue from the property is distributed according to the *vakıf* document – either to family members or the poor. A 'vakıf' is inherited, two shares for males, one share to females, and passes from one generation to another. It is a means of preserving the family wealth for future generations and helping the poor. Most Imperial mosques have hospitals, schools, and public baths supported by foundations that were commissioned by Ottoman royalty or military pashas. The 'vakıf' of Yeni Camii at Galata Bridge was commissioned by two queen mothers, Valide Sultan Safiye and her daughter-in-law Türkan Sultan who finished the mosque when her son Mehmet IV was enthroned as Sultan and she became Queen Mother. It includes the income from *Mısır Çarşısı*, 'the Egyptian Spice Bazaar'.

The Koç family's love for collecting began when their mother, Sadberk Hanım took her children on trips on a steamboat trip from Büyükdere to the bazaar at Kapalıçarşı. What started as a pleasant past-time and hobby developed into a passionate interest in all things Ottoman and Anatolian: 19th century textiles, embroidered silks and velvets, clothes, and bed linen. Sadberk Hanım accumulated a rich collection and a desire to exhibit it in a museum. Unfortunately, she died before the first private museum in Turkey, the Sadberk Hanım Museum, opened its doors. Her daughter, Sevgi, proved a worthy curator during her lifetime after which Ömer Koç, Sevgi's nephew and Sadberk Hanım's grandson, became curator. The late Mrs. Koç's boat trips and her influence on her children and grandchildren was philanthropy at its best. She inspired them with a passion to preserve and collect beautiful things and they, in turn, opened museums.

Ömer Koç has created an impressive library which has received international acclaim. In a review by Philip Mansel on the 'Impressions of Istanbul, Voyage to Constantinople 1493-1820 for the magazine, *Cornucopia*, he writes, 'some libraries are declarations of love. Ömer Koç's library of books on Istanbul and the Ottoman Empire shows the owner's love for the Empire and its capital'.

When Rahmi Koç retired, his eldest son, Mustafa Koç became chairman of Koç Holding. An all-round sportsman, Mustafa was a popular figure around town. He rode, played golf, sailed and was a devoted Fenerbahçe football fan. He patronized many charities, and one evening told me how he had overcome strong opposition from the board at Madame Tussauds Waxworks Museum in London to replace a model that bore no likeness to Atatürk with one sculptured by a Turkish artist. During the Gezi Park Protest (a protest which initially began in May, 2013) when a few activists protested against a project to fell trees in Taksim Square, Mustafa and his brothers opened the doors of the Divan Hotel as a safe haven to receive wounded victims. His sudden death of a heart-attack on 21st January, 2016 at the age of 55 was a frightful shock and touched the hearts of people from all walks of life. The huge outpouring of love, condolences and respect from ordinary people demonstrated the very special place Mustafa held amongst the public in Turkey and abroad. Today Ömer Koç is at the helm of the Koç Holding and the Koç Foundation.

The Koç family are leaders of much of the social diary in Istanbul. An invitation to one of their many charity functions is legendary and much coveted by those who have attended over the decades. Suna Aksu and I have enjoyed many evenings as guests and have appreciated their generosity and attention to minutiae which has never changed.

There were many entrepreneurs, business-men and families breaking boundaries and setting up philanthropic foundations. The Sabancı family were generous hosts, especially on one occasion, May 21st 1999, when I organized a dinner for certain prestigious members of the World Monuments Fund led by my friend, the late John Julius Norwich at Atlı Köşk, Emirgan, home of Türkan and Sakıp Sabancı, chairman of the Sabancı Holding, a leading industrial and philanthropic conglomerate. Sakıp Bey was a popular figure, a charismatic extrovert with a great sense of humour who charmed foreign guests with stories of his family and Turkey.

In his book, *Turkey, Changing and Developing*, he writes, 'in 1921, my father, Hacı Ömer Sabancı, an Anatolian villager, arrived in Adana from the Kayseri village of Akçakaya, after walking and travelling by donkey for 10 to 13 days. He found work in Adana as a cotton worker. He later engaged in cotton trading. After that he bought a ginning machine – a workshop which could extract the oil from the cotton seed – 30 years later he became the owner of BOSSA Flour Mill and laid the foundations of the BOSSA textile factory. He founded a private bank, Akbank'. Then Sakıp Bey goes on to write, 'With the business sector in the hands of Turks following the exodus of minority groups, I predicted a rosy future of thousands of Hacı Ömers and Vehbi Beys'. How right he was.

In 1974, he with his brothers co-founded the Sabancı Foundation which manages more than 100 charitable organisations in Turkey.

Today the residence with its impressive calligraphy collection is home to the Sakıp Sabancı Museum in Emirgan. After the death of Sakıp Bey, his niece, Güler Sabancı succeeded as chairwoman of the Sabancı Holding. Our paths rarely cross, but when they do, she is as friendly and accessible as ever. Recently named one of the most powerful women in the world by *Fortune* magazine, Güler, who is pragmatic and earthy with a great sense of humour, is a powerful voice in the fight for the rights and empowerment of women in Turkey and one of her goals is to raise the number of women in the workforce, especially in senior managerial positions.

Notes from the 70's

Theatre lovers like myself will never forget December, 1970, the day that the *Atatürk Kültür Merkezi*, 'The Atatürk Cultural Centre', went up in flames.

In 19th century Istanbul, fires regularly scorched districts of wooden houses, and the fire brigade's warning bell never ceased ringing as it raced through the city. Edmondo de Amicis wrote, 'the word fire means for the inhabitants of Istanbul every misfortune, and the cry, *yangın var,* fire, fire, is charged with a dread meaning, terrible, fateful, carrying with it dismay – a cry at which the entire city is moved to its very depths, and pours forth as at announcement of a scourge from God.'

That was how it felt on 12th December 1970.

The Atatürk Kültür Merkezi was a spectacular arts centre, one of the largest and most modern theatre buildings in the world. The construction, begun in 1946 took 23 years to complete at a cost of 106 million Turkish Liras. With a capacity of 20,000 people, a jubilant crowd including Aydın and I waited at Taksim Square for its doors to open in April 1968.

A year later a silent crowd stared in horror at the burning building. The following morning, Aydın and I joined those in Taksim Square, the stench of smoke and charred wood filled the air. We had watched *Fiddler on the Roof* there a few weeks ago. It was too awful, the destruction of such a fine building completed and opened but a year before.

Our neighbour, journalist, Hikmet Bil reported a conversation he had with Şükrü Kaya, Minister of Internal Affairs, at the time: one day Atatürk, journeying to Istanbul from Yalova, paused at the outskirts of Haydarpaşa to gaze at the city. After a while the President turned to Muhittin Üstündağ, Mayor of Istanbul, and said 'when you look at Istanbul you can visualize Byzantium with its aqueducts and the Hagia Sophia. The Ottomans stamped their seal on the city with elegant minarets, magnificent domes and beautiful palaces. But although I have looked carefully, I see nothing of the Republic in Istanbul.' That conversation inspired the in-coming mayor, Dr. Lütfi Kırdar, to lay the foundation for the magnificent opera house and cultural palace worthy of the Republic in Taksim Square.

An evocative description of the fire was published in an issue of *SES* magazine at the time:

> *'It was the last days of Ramadan, a Thursday. The third act of Arthur Miller's Crucible was underway when one of the designers leapt on the stage shouting "there is a fire." Actor Nihat Aybars looked up to see the sofita, the area above the stage, in flames. He screamed, "lower the steel curtain, lower the steel curtain" in order to divide the stage from the auditorium to contain the fire, but the steel curtain could not be lowered, it did not function. The clock showed exactly 10.48 p.m. A small flame from the sofita was able to burn the huge Palace.'*
>
> *'At the rehearsals of the Crucible I had wept with joy. How could I have not? We had waited 23 years. Every time I came to Istanbul I thought, 'Will it ever be possible for me to act on this stage?' I am crying now but this time from my deep distress. Just imagine – even the fire extinguishers were not working. There wasn't a single fireman to extinguish the fire. I started to cry in the midst of flames. Who was supposed to be responsible? Fire departments from close by arrived within short intervals but the water pressure was so low that not a single windowpane was shattered and the water returned from the windows.'*

With less splendour, the *Atatürk Kültür Merkezi* re-opened in 1978, home to the Istanbul Philharmonic Orchestra. A dear friend, the late Mükerrem Berk, brother-in-law to Prime Minister Turgut Özal and father of Ahmet Çifçi's wife Tülay played the violin and his second wife, Sevim played the harp in the orchestra. Concerts were held on Saturday and Sunday mornings. We would meet up with friends at the concert on Saturday and lunch together afterwards. I had noticed that the male members of the orchestra wore day shoes on stage which bothered me. I was told, 'More important things to discuss and spend money,' but I persevered and with the help of my music lover friends we collected enough to present to Mükerrem Bey so he might buy shoes for the orchestra. The following Saturday we sat in the audience smiling as the orchestra walked onto the stage in black patent shoes.

The Atatürk Kültür Merkezi in Taksim Square was closed and remained boarded-up waiting to be restored. For those aware of its historical past and those who love the theatre, it is an eye-sore, a sad sight and a sensitive public issue. In 2019 work for a new opera house began.

An Ambassador's Invitation

Our introduction to Saudi Arabian Ambassador was as undiplomatic as you can imagine, but it cemented a close friendship. One afternoon Betül Mardin, a friend, rang sounding most agitated. The new Saudi Arabian Ambassador to Turkey was expecting her to take him to dinner that evening in Istanbul, but she was stuck in Beirut. She begged us to help. As we had no plans for the evening, I agreed. Betül told me she would arrange for the Ambassador telephone us upon his arrival at the Hilton Hotel. I popped out for a few minutes without telling Aydın and as luck would have it, the telephone rang while I was out. Our family is known for playing practical jokes, so when a strange voice announced, 'I am Anas Yassin, Ambassador to Saudi Arabia,' Aydın thought it a joke and replied with 'As-selaam'u alaykum, I am Aydın, Prince of the Caucasus.'

'Oh, selam,' came the surprised voice at the other end. 'Mrs. Mardin asked me to telephone Mrs. Erkan.' Still unable to recognize the voice, Aydın went along with the hoax, 'Ah, ah, she did, did she? Well, Mrs. Erkan will be back in a few minutes if you wish to call back.' 'Thank you, I will,' came the bemused reply.

Aydın was furious when I told him the caller really was the Saudi Arabian Ambassador. A short while later the telephone rang. I apologized and explained to the Ambassador, who, thank heavens seemed to have a sense of humour and accepted our invitation for dinner. We had booked a table at the Süreyya restaurant in Bebek. Brushing off Aydın's apologies he did admit sheepishly that he had telephoned Ankara to ask them to check up on a 'Prince Aydın of the Caucasus.'

Anas Youssef Yassin was darkly handsome, educated in America, immaculately dressed and recently divorced. He wore a watch with two faces, one telling the time in New York, the other in Saudi Arabia. His daughter lived with her mother in Beirut and he missed her dreadfully. He spoke with pride about his late father, a lawyer of distinction, educated in Switzerland, the first non-royal to be include in King Saud's inner circle. Anas was astonished to learn that Aydın's family had close connections with Saudi Arabia and that they were people whose names were familiar to him: Shamyl, Imam of Daghestan and his son Ghazi Mohammed Pasha were buried in Medina, his grandfather, Osman Ferit Pasha had spent 22 years as Commander and Governor of Medina; and his father, Hamza Erkan was born in Medina. This sealed a friendship and they talked for hours.

We had watched the Atatürk Bridge being built from the window of our apartment in Beşiktaş. Massive concrete blocks, gigantic coils of thick, black wire, tall, spindly cranes taller than an apartment moved at a snail's pace along the waterway on wide tugs surrounded by boats. The bridge which span the Bosphorus Strait from Ortaköy on the European side to Beylerbeyi on the Asian side was the fourth longest bridge in the world and had taken more than 20 years to come to fruition at a cost of 23 million 213.000 dollars. Completed in 1973 a day after the 50th anniversary of the Republic we were delighted to be invited by the Ambassador to join his table at the roof of the Hilton Hotel in the evening.

We watched the inauguration ceremony from the comfort of our sitting room as masses of people congregated on both sides of the Bosphorus to see the opening ceremony hosted by American comedian, Danny Kaye. President Fahri Korutürk, Prime Minister Naim Talu, members of Parliament, ambassadors, foreign guests and journalists led the walk across the Bosphorus, pursued by a horde of excited citizens, who swarmed the bridge with such force and weight it began to sway. Poor Danny Kaye was pushed aside, losing a shoe and his aide. He was not amused and we feared the bridge would collapse. For the first four years the bridge was free and pedestrians were allowed to walk across, but an increasing number of suicides put a stop to it and it became a toll bridge.

It was a glamorous, star-studded evening with Eartha Kitt the star attraction. Her rendition of '*Üsküdar'a Giderken*' (on the way to Üsküdar) received wild ovations. Darvaş, a popular local violinist and everyone's friend, moved from table to table playing requests. Anas asked me if he would play the theme song from *Love Story*, which he had listened to while recovering from an operation in hospital. I jotted the name of the song added my name and gave it to a waiter. Darvaş, usually so accommodating, seemed to avoid our area. Excusing myself I walked to the bar where he was speaking to the manager. Giving him a peck on the cheek I asked, 'Darvaş, didn't you get my note? My friend wants you to play *Love Story*.' Putting my arm through his, I lead him to the table where he played for the Arab Ambassadors. Darvaş was Jewish.

After dinner everyone moved to the casino, which caused Aydın to hesitate as Turks were not allowed to gamble. Anas brushed aside his misgivings. 'Tonight, is a special evening, and anyway you are my guest.' Handing us a bag of chips, he ushered us inside. I whiled away the time at the machines. For the first time in my life I was winning when an agitated husband whispered in my ear, 'we have to leave now, come on.'

'Why? For the first time I'm winning,' I beamed.

'The manager recognised me and asked me to leave quietly without causing a scene,' breathed my desperately embarrassed husband.

'I'm British, I can stay,' I teased. He was not amused. Pretending a sudden headache, we made a quick getaway.

A second suspension bridge, the Fatih Sultan Mehmet, was built 5 km north of the first bridge spanning the Bosphorus from Hisarüstü on the European side to Kavacık on the Asian side. At the opening ceremony on 3rd July 1988, Prime Minister Turgut Özal was the first person to drive his official car across the bridge.

The third and most expensive bridge, built at a cost of $3 billion, is the longest and comprises two rail lines and eight motor lanes. Styled after the Brooklyn Bridge in New York, it was built at the most northern tip of the Bosphorus between, Poyrazköy and Garipçe. President Erdoğan oversaw the inauguration on 26th August 2016 and named the bridge *Yavuz Sultan Selim* (known as Selim the Grim). Serious concern over damage to the environment and the felling of thousands of trees has disturbed many people.

The name of the first bridge recently changed to *15 Temmuz Şehitler Köprüsü* (15th July Martyrs' Bridge).

I call the bridges First, Second and Third.

Mingling with the Stars

In 1973 the Istanbul Culture and Arts Foundation, *İstanbul Kültür Sanat Vakfi* or IKSV, was founded by pharmaceutical philanthropist, Dr. Nejat Ferit Eczacıbaşı.

When Dr. Şevket Bey telephoned me to ask 'Are you busy?' I thought it was to stand in for a teacher at Darüşşafaka and was about to say no, when he went on, 'a friend urgently needs an English person to help out for a few weeks during a music festival and I told him I know just the person. Are you free this afternoon?'

That was how I met Nejat Eczacıbaşı. Born in İzmir and educated in Germany, Nejat Bey had a passion for classical music and after years of deliberation decided to make his dream a reality by establishing an art and culture festival in Istanbul. It was a gamble, an audaciously ambitious venture in a city without proper auditoriums or concert halls and limited hotel accommodation. 'I believe it is the right time. Istanbul and its citizens are ready for an art festival'.

The following day Nejat Bey introduced me to his team: artistic director Leyla Turgut; director of administration and ex-president of the Basketball Federation, Turgut Atakol and to my delight, director of public relations, Betül Mardin, a close friend.

Leyla was a slim, highly-strung conventional rather than conservative lady who spoke about seven languages fluently. She was a chain smoker with old-fashioned manners and lived with her equally ascetic brother, an Istanbul gentleman. One day she showed me a faded black and white photograph of her late father, the Ottoman Governor of the province of Iran, climbing into an open carriage helped by an Iranian soldier standing stiffly to attention by his side. 'That,' she said, pointing to the soldier, 'is Reza Shah Pahlavi, father of the present Shah of Iran, Mohammed Reza Shah Pahlavi.'

Leyla was a stickler for the small print, while Turgut Atakol, an easy-going ex-sportsman was skilled at rallying young people, solving problems, and keeping everything rolling. I called him Mr. Quick Fix. He and Betül Mardin got on like a house on fire. Betül decided to take me under her wing, my job was to take care of the foreign artists and guests and over a working lunch, we went over my schedule of names, dates, arrival and departure times, hotels and cars for the duration of the festival. As we rose to leave, peering over her glasses she said,' You will have problems but you will have to work them out yourself, don't bring them to me, I shan't even have time to sleep, D-day is nearly upon us'.

Betül Mardin's personal style signifier is a classic trouser suit with her dark hair drawn back in a bun at the nape of her neck and brown inquisitive eyes peering above glasses perched on her nose. She is the 'grand dame of public relations,' one of three siblings born into a renowned Ottoman family of diplomats. The early death of her sister from TB marred much of a rather lonely childhood. Her younger brother, Arif Mardin, became a well-known pop music producer in America. She married twice; her second husband is actor/director Haldun Dormen. She has two children.

Betül was working at the BBC in London when, on a flight from Ankara to Istanbul she sat next to an old friend, Nejat Eczacıbaşı, who (true to form) began explaining his festival project. Impressed but doubtful, she argued that it was beyond the scope of the city. By the time they had landed, he had convinced her of its success. A few days later she received a letter from Nejat Bey with an offer to become public relations manager of the festival at an attractive salary. It was *kısmet*. Betül, at that time, was at her wit's end trying to raise that exact amount to pay her son, Ömer's school fees at the Austrian school. Without a second thought she accepted and flew to London, resigned from the BBC, packed her bags and headed home. With limited time and on a tight budget she set to work printing 50,000 brochures and leaflets, which she and her assistant, Cevza, handed to incoming passengers at Istanbul Yeşilköy Airport. She persuaded passport control officers to place a brochure in every passport they stamped: 'this is not a *karpuz* (watermelon) festival! It is a music and arts festival and you should be proud to help,' she scolded.

The first festival, in 1973, was organised on the fiftieth anniversary of the founding of the Republic of Turkey, ran for a month in midsummer and had an impressive list of national and international artists performing, including the Austrian-British soprano Elisabeth Schwarzkopf and Turkish artists Suna Kan and İdil Biret. It was a month of music, opera, ballet and song, the likes of which had never been seen before in Istanbul. As to be expected, there were more than a few horrific hiccups but these were quickly resolved by Betül, Turgut and of course, master of ceremonies, Nejat Bey. Tickets sold like hot cakes to Turks and foreigners of all ages, flocking to support the festival.

I accompanied guest of honour, Scottish historian, Lord Patrick Balfour Kinross looking distinguished in a dress suit to the opening night reception at Topkapı Palace. His biography of '*Atatürk, The Rebirth of a Nation*' written in 1964, is considered the definitive work on the life of the founder of the Turkish Republic. The entrance to Topkapı Palace looked magnificent. I asked the driver to drive past the 'No Entry' sign so Lord Kinross would not have far to walk, but we were stopped by a policeman. I told him the gentleman was the guest of honour but he was not impressed, telling us that his instructions were to not let any vehicle, plane even a bird fly past that point. I flashed my pass it didn't sway him, as a last resort I reprimanded him in Turkish for not being hospitable to a man of his age, 'he is a guest, who has difficulty walking and you are going to make him walk quite a long way, shame on you.'

Shaking his head ruefully the policeman allowed us to pass. As we got out of the car, Lord Kinross took my arm and began to limp. 'Better act the part, dear. He might be watching,' he chuckled wickedly.

Being a close friend of Mina Urgan, Lord Kinross knew his way around Istanbul. Handing me a list he said, 'I don't have much time, dear but let's see how much we can get done tomorrow'. We did purchase most of his list and then he invited me to the fish restaurant, his choice, under Galata Bridge and it turned out to be one of the longest and most enjoyable luncheons I have ever had.

Dame Ninette de Valois, grey-haired and petite, dressed in country tweeds, seemed rather jittery as we waited for her luggage to be cleared at Istanbul Yeşilköy Airport. It turned out she had a radio for a friend in Ankara stashed in her bag. Knowing full well the strict laws forbidding certain products (radios being one) from being brought into the country, she was anxious. Luggage was randomly searched. Should her radio be discovered, not only would it be confiscated, we'd have to hang around for hours filling in forms and answering silly questions. I ran to the porter, took the case, and waited in line for the customs official. Showing my pass, I nodded in the direction of Dame Ninette de Valois, telling the official of her great service to Turkish ballet and the country, while she nodded with a regal smile. The suitcase was ticked with white chalk and off we went.

Dame Ninette De Valois spent her formative years at the Ballet Russes, where she trained under the great impresario dancer and choreographer Serge Diaghilev. She established the first ballet school in Ankara in 1947, persuading the likes of Margot Fonteyn, David Blair and Michael Soames to make guest appearances. In 1965 she produced and choreographed the first full-length ballet for the Turkish State Ballet, titled *Çeşmebaşı* 'At the Fountain', incorporating elements of Turkish folk dance and music composed by a famous Turkish composer Ferit Tüzün. Referred to as 'Madame', she had a fearsome reputation as a manager with zero tolerance when it came to dance, but in private was, so said a loyal friend, 'witty, delightful, intelligent and one of the most informed of companions.'

Having helped her shop, I suggested brunch before she went to the theatre for a rehearsal. Settled in Rejans, a Russian restaurant in Beyoğlu she told me of a trip to

Moscow to bring Galina Ulanova to Covent Garden. I remembered the incident in 1956 as a student in London. It was at the time of the cold war when Russians were not allowed to come to Britain and the political climate between the West and Russia was cold. It was the lead article in newspapers for weeks – 'It's on' – 'Its off'. Everyone held their breath in anticipation of the Russian Ballet of Moscow dancing at Covent Garden. There was a frenzy to get tickets, queues at the stage door stretched around Covent Garden a week before the performance. It was the most dramatic cultural episode, not only for ballet lovers, but also for everyone else due to the political dimension of it all. I was incredibly impressed that it was she, Ninette de Valois, then Director of the Royal Ballet and David Webster, (Director of the Royal Opera House) had pulled off such a magnificent feat. Everyone in England knew the name, Galina Ulanova, the first Russian ballerina they had ever seen.

I accompanied Dame Ninette De Valois to the train station and as she climbed on the train to Ankara to see her friend, she smiled, 'Be sure to see that I am invited next year to the festival, dear.' And off she went.

Paul Taylor was a champion swimmer before becoming a choreographer/dancer in his late-twenties and studying under Martha Graham. In 1954 he formed his own company, the Paul Taylor Dance Group. His signature style was muscular and stamina-powered, but amazingly fluid and natural. At 6 foot, Paul was tall for a dancer, as was his favourite partner, Bellie de Jong, a beautiful dancer with a long, slim silhouette. They were an unusually self-deprecating group, cool and easy-going in the stressful world of ballet. He was eager to go to London to work with Rudolf Nureyev who had personally requested to dance in one of Paul's work, *Aureole* at Sadlers Wells.

Yehudi Menuhin arrived a day late. I whisked him straight from the airport to Darüşşafaka, a school concert hall, where the orchestra was rehearsing. I sat in the hall remembering my days at Central School when we would creep into the forbidden upper floor of the darkened Albert Hall auditorium to listen to him and other artists rehearse. It was an eye-opener into artistic temperaments. Dressed in weird outfits, conductors would shout, throw tantrums and batons, star musicians and singers would swear, curse, march off the stage in a rage or tears. But on the night the show must go on, and all was perfect.

On the night of his performance, Menuhin told me, 'During the interval, please see that I am not disturbed, I meditate.' In 1952 he had befriended yogi B.K.S. Iyengar in India, and was instrumental in bringing him to Europe to teach in Paris, London and Switzerland. I attended one of Iyengar's lectures and had taken a few yoga lessons from his assistant at a studio in Knightsbridge, London.

Custodian to the great, I plonked myself outside Menuhin's dressing room door, daring anyone to enter. Shortly, an apparition in flying red chiffon approached. 'I'm sorry, but you cannot enter. Mr. Menuhin has requested not to be disturbed,' I said with authority.

The chiffon settled on a svelte, tense body. 'Not be disturbed?' said the chiffon beauty staring at me in disbelief. 'Not be disturbed? I am Mrs. Menuhin. I do not *disturb* my husband.' Pushing me aside, she slammed the door behind her. She was none other than the British ballerina and actress, Diana Gould, known for her fiery and temperamental disposition. Cringing with embarrassment, I prayed the earth would open to swallow me up.

After the concert, I pushed my way through the crowd of admirers to congratulate Yehudi Menuhin and apologise to his wife, which she graciously accepted. He smiled, squeezed my hand, and thanked me for taking care of him. The following day, after they left, his driver brought me a parcel. It was an old, signed copy of Iyengar's book on yoga with a thank you note.

The Bolshoi Ballet, orchestras from Austria, Germany and Britain, and soloists from all over the world flocked to Istanbul to perform with the best Turkish artists. My favourite was Turkish violinist, Suna Kan, a tall, impressive lady with magnificent stage presence, who played with such energy and emotion. I also loved the young and intense Fazıl Say at the piano, who played his own compositions and a superb rendering of *Rhapsody in Blue.*

Rushing from one venue to another for a musical month, brushing shoulders with artists, listening and watching performances by first class modern ballet companies and musicians was a huge pleasure – as were the tantrums and first night nerves. In those halls where the acoustics, microphones and flooring were far from perfect, once on stage, performers gave their best. In turn, they were handsomely rewarded by loud applause and standing ovations from appreciative audiences, who filled the seats night after night.

Nejat Bey nurtured the festival into an event of stature. He and his wife, Beyhan, (who turned out to be none other than the lady I met on the boat whose fur I had carried; after she chided me for not getting in touch, we became friends) hosted every performance, greeting the audience as they walked to their seats in the front row.

On the 15th Anniversary of the festival, in his opening speech, Nejat Bey said that 'the progress of the Istanbul Festival is a testimony to the Turkish people's aspirations for what is good and beautiful.' I would like to add that it is also a testimony of one man, his, vision and determination to establish an art and culture festival in the city he loved.

I worked for the festival for four years, met fascinating people, watched magnificent performances and thoroughly enjoyed myself and am proud that it has become an established part on Istanbul's social calendar, attracting young musicians, loyal fans, supporters, and music lovers young and old. Its success pioneered other festivals. In

1984, the first Film Festival, 1986, a Jazz Festival and the first International Exhibition in 1987, the Biennial of Contemporary Art; 1989 saw a successful Theatre Festival and in 2012, the Design Biennial.

Whenever possible I attend performances at Hagia Eirene, St. Irena, my favourite venue. On a warm, summer evening, what could be more satisfying than a glass of wine on the lawn of the outer court of Topkapı Palace before settling under the high dome of Hagia Eirene, nesting home to musically inclined birds who perch in silent reverence as music fills the air in one of the most beautiful Byzantine churches in the city? In June 2016, caught in a torrential downpour I waded my way to Hagia Eirene to attend the last evening of the festival with American soprano, Angel Blue and the Borusan Orchestra. Neither thunder and lightning, nor the fact that wine is no longer served before a concert, could dampen the beauty of the leafy green outer court of Topkapı Palace, the simplicity of Hagia Eirene, or Angel Blue's rich, throaty tones. An extra pleasure was seeing Mükerrem Berk's son and daughter, Murat and Leyla, playing in the orchestra.

Today the Istanbul Foundation of Culture and Arts is chaired by Nejat Bey's son, Bülent. His wife, Oya, founded the first modern museum in the city, the Istanbul Modern, which was, until recently, housed in an old warehouse on the Bosphorus. Betül Mardin remained director of public relations at the festival for 25 years. After attending a concert sponsored by Marks and Spencer at Windsor Castle in England, she convinced Aydın Gün of the financial benefits of sponsorship for the festival and that was how it started in the Istanbul Festival.

Aphrodisias, a Love Story

Aydın and I were introduced to Professor Kenan Erim by Hümeyra Hanım at the Kısmet Hotel, Kuşadası when she gave a luncheon in his honour. Conversation turned to the meaning of the word *kısmet,* its oriental belief of destiny, fate and acceptance. The professor believed his destiny was to come to Aphrodisias and Hümeyra Hanım believed meeting her husband in America was her destiny. I suggested kısmet might have played a role in bringing us together in this small Anatolian fishing village – Kenan and Hümeyra Hanım from America and me from Britain.

A week or so later Professor Erim, Director of Excavations, invited us to Aphrodisias. We drove to Denizli, past fig gardens, orchards of oranges, mandarins and apples listening to Hümeyra Hanım as she filled us in on the gaps about Kenan's life, his family and idiosyncrasies. The son of a diplomat, he was born in Istanbul, educated in Geneva and lived in New York where he was professor at the Department of Classics at New York University. She had brought a basket of goodies, warning me, 'whenever you're invited to Aphrodisias, make sure you take a full hamper' (I always have). We turned off the highway onto a winding track past fields and villages, sheltered by the Babadağ snow-capped mountain, until columns, half hidden amongst tall poplar trees, a vast stadium, and city walls came into view then we turned into a road lined with pomegranate trees to Geyre. Kenan was waiting for us dressed in his signature outfit, a well-worn, navy-blue sweater and patched blue jeans. 'There is just time for a walk before lunch,' he said, handing us sticks with a sharp nail attached to the end and a large plastic bag to collect rubbish as he talked us around the site.

Our host had a scholarly face, high forehead and serious brown eyes and of medium height with a rather stiff upright posture. He was multilingual and had a powerful baritone voice with an aristocratic British accent (honed by a British tutor in Switzerland). A quintessential Ottoman man, Kenan's wide range of interests included classic and popular art, music, theatre and films. He had an impressive collection of old film posters, which decorated the stairways and corridors of the excavation house.

He told us of his first discovery, 'I looked down a drainage ditch the villagers had started to dig five years before and suddenly found myself staring straight into the face of a marble head, It was a beautiful woman's head with a broken nose and curious headdress like a tiara, but with sculptured shapes of towers and city walls crowning it. She was Aphrodite. That day, Latif, the watchman came out carrying a piece of marble with traces of Greek letters. He fitted it into the side of the statue. The inscription: Polis – the City. It was a sign. Aphrodisias, it was kısmet'.

Kenan Erim believed that 'kısmet' guided him on his first reconnaissance trip to this Greco-Roman city in south – western Turkey as it had the Emperor Augustus who was known to have said 'I have selected this One City from all of Asia to be my own'. Kenan Erim had selected Aphrodisias to be his own and from then on dedicated his professional career and life to Aphrodite, goddess of love, life and fertility. As John Julius Norwich wrote in his introduction to Kenan's second book, *Aphrodisais, City of Venus, Aphrodite*, 'Kenan Erim loves Aphrodisias as a man loves a woman and his commitment is total.'

Over a frugal lunch I met Joyce Reynolds from Newnham College and Nathalie de Chaisemartin, University of Bordeaux, American sculptor, Peter Rockwell, a few students and Turkish officials. There was a marble head with a bunch of sweet-smelling wild flowers in a glass tumbler as a centre-piece on the plastic tablecloth. After lunch Kenan, Aydın and I followed Peter up the slopes of Salbakos to the ancient quarry where huge blocks of translucent white marble with fine blue veins were roughly hewn into shape before being taken down by ox-cart to the city below to be sculpted. Many of the techniques and tools used by the Romans are similar to those Peter uses today. Drinks on Kenan's balcony to the strains of classic music ended a magical day and cemented our friendship with Kenan.

Kenan drew us into his world and insisted I become a member of *The Geyre Vakfi*, Foundation. Aydın and he found they had a lot in common, both shied away from strangers but were gregarious, entertaining and funny in private. He would telephone on Mondays, their day of rest, to see whether we were at the farm or in Kuşadası. He preferred the farm – having suffered from TB in his youth, he disliked the sun, never swam in the sea, and even on the hottest days wore the navy-blue sweater. He invited us to Aphrodisias for weekends. Living accommodation was basic to say the least, but the cold, out-door showers, rock hard pillows and frugal meals were forgotten as we gathered to listen to classic music and drinks on his balcony. Kenan held court at the table, slipping from one language to another, on topics ranging from David Hockney to marine archaeology off the coast of Italy.

Up at dawn, Kenan worked until dusk with workmen, archaeologists and students under the hot Aegean sun. Even when his unconventional, bull-headed nature got the better of him and he behaved like a kahya, he inspired his workers who over the years become accomplished artisans. In winter, as well as teaching at New York University, he set up Friends of Aphrodisias Societies in Paris, Izmir, Istanbul, London and New York. Making a gruelling tour of the capital cities in Europe, he would give lectures, beg, bully and cajole for funds. He wore a silver bracelet inscribed *Aphrodisias.*

In 1982, Mrs. Dorothe Gould-Pratt, a wealthy American historic-motif textile designer lived in Kuşadası for a few years. She was one of the first to block designs dresses on calico and cotton in black and white and export them to the States. With Mrs. James Moffett and members of the Izmir Friends of Aphrodisias, she financed the publication of a fund-raising cook-book which included a recipe from the Director himself. Anyone who has had the pleasure of drinks on Kenan's balcony will enjoy his recipe:

> *'This is the first attempt on the part of this writer to commit cooking practices to writing quantities, and ingredients are more generally descriptive than methodically presented in their listed amounts and sequences. The reader's indulgence is consequently, de rigueur! for an Aphrodisias Cocktail.*
>
> *'Pomegranate trees are strikingly abundant in and around Aphrodisias. In early summer their vermillion-red flowers add a bright note to the white marble remains of the site whilst their dark-red fruits literally bursting with pink seeds contrast handsomely with yellowing-green foliage in October. There are at least two varieties of pomegranates at Aphrodisias, one producing a sweet, the other a sour juice when squeezed. The juices of both are used in preparing the following cocktail, often served in early autumn, after a hard day's work at the site or in the storerooms.*
>
> *'For one glass or serving: 2 1/2 jiggers of Vodka, 2 jiggers of sweet pomegranate juice, 2 jiggers of sour pomegranate juice. Ingredients are well mixed in a blender. If a sweeter drink is preferred, a tablespoon or two of confectioner's sugar can be added. Serve over crushed ice or with ice cubes. Lemon juice could be substituted for sour pomegranate juice if this is not available.' Kenan. T. Erim, Aphrodisias.*

When I was in London in the spring of 1984, Robin Murray-Philipson invited me to the Serenissima Travels office in Sloane Square to meet eighty years-old film producer, Bill Burnside (whose claim to fame was unpublished photographs he took of Marilyn Monroe) and Robin Lowe from RLP, a British film company. They were discussing the possibility of making a TV documentary for Television South West about Aphrodisias. Which was to be financed mostly by Asil Nadir, a Turkish Cypriot millionaire and chairman of Polly Peck.

Film director, Christopher Miles had gathered an impressive crew John Julius Norwich had agreed to be narrator with Kenan Erim and American sculptor, Peter Rockwell, as well as archaeologists, students and workers. Robin asked if I would be project co-ordinator.

In August I received a letter from Robin Murray-Philipson about travel arrangements and the schedule emphasizing, 'knowing the red tape in Turkish customs, we envisage every kind of problem in getting them and their equipment through customs. I have always found Turkish customs far more difficult, in fact, the most difficult, of any I have ever come across in my life.' It went on, 'making a film is always extremely expensive and the one thing you simply have to do is keep a very tight schedule. Moreover, Lord Norwich can only remain in Turkey for about four days (because of his many commitments) and so if there is any delay in getting through Izmir Airport on 2nd September it is going to throw the whole project into jeopardy. The schedule for shooting the film has been set at between 3rd and 16th September.'

Aydın and I spent a day at Izmir Airport and the harbour custom offices going over permissions, papers and signatures etc with the authorities. They assured us that there would be no problem.

A few days before the film crew were to arrive, Kenan telephoned insisting we come to Aphrodisias the following day at 7 a.m. sharp, but refused to say why. I feared the worst and Aydın, not at all happy at such an early wake-up call and didn't stop grumbling the whole way to Karacasu. When we arrived, Kenan was talking to workmen under a tree outside the compound door. He rushed us into the Sebasteion. There, between two masonry blocks, lay a perfect marble statue of a woman; we stared in silence fearing to wake her, awed by her beauty, which had not seen the light of day for centuries. Kenan caressed her face. Aydın suggested not disturbing her until the film crew so Kenan gently prepared her for her film role. It was a moment, a scene I will never forget in my life.

Two days later I was at Izmir Port to meet film director, Christopher Miles and his wife Suzy, producer, Bill Burnside and Chelsea photographer, John Bignall. Within an hour the Land Rover, camera-car and equipment were on their way to Aphrodisias. On the evening of 2nd September, I waited at Izmir Airport to greet John Julius Norwich, Alistair Cameron and the camera crew. The flight was late. I was sitting with the airport manager in his office talking about the film when he was handed a telegram. He read it, looked puzzled, then handed it to me. It was from the Ministry in Ankara specifying that any equipment for the documentary film was not to be released unless custom taxes – amounting to thousands of liras – were paid in full. I was nonplussed. 'Someone in Ankara doesn't like Kenan Erim,' I growled, and telephoned Ankara. Of course, at that hour there was no reply. The plane landed. John Julius Norwich and the crew were grateful for hot tea and savouries as, so they thought, we waited for their luggage – though in reality we were stranded until we could contact someone in the Ministry. It was well past midnight and we had a four-hour drive ahead of us.

I telephoned Aydın, he told me the only person who could help me would be the airport manager. I walked into his office. The telegram was still on the desk in front of him, 'That gentleman over there,' pointing to John Julius, looking quite exhausted, 'is Viscount, Lord Norwich, an aristocrat, Byzantine scholar, writer and friend of Turkey. He and the crew are here for five days to film a documentary on Aphrodisias. Instead of being welcomed with usual Turkish hospitality, they are confronted with a custom bill for thousands of liras for equipment that will be out of the country in five days. It doesn't make sense. I tell you, this is the doings of a mean, little man in Ankara, jealous of Kenan Bey. It didn't happen at the harbour customs office and that Land Rover was carrying far more expensive equipment. I'm sorry, but I cannot explain to my friends at this hour of the morning that someone in Ankara has caused this ridiculous mess. As manager of the airport, it is your duty to tell them'. Picking up the telegram, I held it out to him. 'Please'. Shaking his head and raising his eyebrows to heaven, he took the telegram, opened the door and shouted to the porters to carry the equipment to the bus. Placing the telegram in the drawer, he said, 'What could I do? The telegram arrived after you had left the airport.' And with a conspiratorial wink signed the release papers. I hugged him with all my might. It was past 4.30 a.m. by the time we arrived at Aphrodisias.

Everyone was shocked when we were told how Bill Burnside had financed the film. At a final meeting with Asil Nadir who was to provide three quarters of the funding, his wife, Ayşegül had inquired who would play the goddess of love since the film was about the city of Aphrodite? Whereupon, Bill turned to her and said, 'I think I am looking at her….' and Ayşegül Nadir was on her way to play Aphrodite. Kenan was furious.

An afternoon siesta was broken by a car honking at the gate. Then a voice, 'Helloooo.'

Kenan, from his bower, boomed out, 'Who is it?'

'Aphrodite,' sang a happy reply.

We held our breath, straining to hear Kenan's reply. 'There is only one Aphrodite and she is made of stone!'

It was Ayşegül Nadir, a statuesque, beauty with large sensual eyes and long black hair, known for the flamboyant parties she hosted at her Çengelköy Yalısı on the Asian shore of the Bosphorus.

Kenan was beside himself with fury. He refused to speak to Bill and threatened to cancel the film. The team put their heads together to find a workable solution, while Suzy and I took Kenan on long walks around the site. Ayşegül's entrance gave Christopher an idea. Ayşe had arrived with a photographer and two assistants perhaps she could play a model posing as Aphrodite for a photographer to start the film off.

Kenan had no choice but to accept. The crew followed Ayşegül, who looked magnificent, as she stepped over one ancient marble stone to another in a divine, flowing white Grecian robe.

Furious as he was, Kenan behaved with courtesy and diplomatic correctness towards Ayşegül – even when he caught her chauffeur carrying half a wardrobe door with a mirror attached to it up the stairs. As the sun set behind the hills and shadowy columns, and tall trees mingled into one, beauty and tranquillity embraced the site, and tempers cooled. Bathed and refreshed, we gathered on Kenan's veranda, drinks in hand. Charmed by the music and atmosphere, Kenan, with Ayşegül on his right and John Julius on his left held court at a table graced with the latest find: a singularly elegant foot. I had made sure there were more than ample trays of Turkish specialities, 'böreks', meat, olive oil dishes and baklava for dessert to ensure pleasant evenings. Impervious to the under-currents, Ayşegül was friendly and generous, inviting the crew to a fish restaurant by the edge of a stream and offering them the use of her car until, with a fanfare of 'let's keep in touch,' she was driven away.

Credit for the film is due entirely to Christopher Miles, not only as director but for handling the behind-scenes dramas. In the Director's Comments, Christopher wrote, there was still no script from the producer. However, John Julius knew his history and Kenan knew all there was to know anyway, we ad-libbed the rest of the film which gave it a freshness and spontaneity.

A private premier of the film was held at a Soho theatre in London, after which Lord and Lady *Camrose*, generous patrons, hosted a reception at their elegant home in Eaton Square. Laurence Kelly fell into Aydın's arms when he heard he was a descendant of Imam Shamyl, Suzy Miles became *peintre en résidence* at Aphrodisias, and Linda Kelly, John Julius, his wife, Mollie, Timothy and Patricia Daunt became life-long friends.

Bill Burnside's mishandling of the project resulted in a holy row between Asil Nadir and Robin Lowe and the film was never released on Television South West.

Extraordinary treasures unearthed over his thirty years as Director of Excavations at Aphrodisias have more than repaid Kenan Erim's passion and dedication as did the satisfaction from the appreciation, accolades and awards he received for his achievements and the icing on the cake happened during his thirtieth season at Aphrodisias, thanks to his devoted friend, Madame Madeleine Lejwa.

In 1987, the First Lady, Semra Özal, accompanied by a group of charity ladies called *Papatyalar* 'daisies' travelled to New York to promote an exhibition of Sultan Suleiman, The Magnificent at the Metropolitan Museum. My daughter, Rana accompanied them.

Madeline lived in an East-side brownstone, choc-a-bloc full of precious artefacts and paintings. Her home was a much-sought-after address for cultural soirees and meetings by those in the art world. To promote Kenan and persuade Semra Hanım to visit Aphrodisias with her husband Madeline organised a party in Semra Hanım's honour inviting the New York Friends of Aphrodisias and other impressive names in the New York art world.

Describing the evening to me later, Madeline complained: 'my dear, they did not stop smoking. The air was thick! I was kept busy emptying ashtrays – which weren't ashtrays but Ming bowls – opening and closing windows as my precious paintings disappeared in a mist of smoke. It was exhausting, but Mrs. Özal has promised to take her husband to Aphrodisias. If that happens it will be well worth my efforts for darling Kenan.'

Three years later Mrs. Özal kept her promise. On October 12th 1990, the President of Turkey, Turgut Özal and his wife flew in by helicopter to honour Professor Kenan Erim at the unveiling of the Tetrapylon on Kenan's 30th anniversary at the site. I was unable to attend but Aydın told me it was a warm, balmy autumn day as Kenan and Madeline led President Özal, his wife, members of the presidential party including Ahmet and Tülay Çifçi, local dignitaries, workers and villagers to an open green space where, in all its glory, stood the Tetrapylon – a magnificent marble – columned gateway. It had taken twenty years to find the original pieces and six years for Austrian architects, Gerhard Paul and Thomas Keifer, to reconstruct. The President was so impressed with the site he promised to return. That visit turned out to be an act of fate, as kısmet, within a few weeks, would play its final card in the life of Kenan Erim.

The Divan Hotel was Kenan's home in Istanbul. For years Kenan and I had two fixed lunch-dates at the Divan Pub: one the day after he arrived from New York, the other the day before he left Turkey for New York. He would talk and I would listen, mostly it was about monies promised but not received.

On this occasion he telephoned to say that he intended to spend two days with the British Ambassador, Sir Timothy Daunt and his wife, Patricia at the Embassy in Ankara then come to Istanbul. Late that evening the telephone rang. It was Timothy Daunt, his voice trembled as he told me Kenan had had a heart attack, fallen in his bedroom and died. Who should he call? I gave him the telephone number of Cenan Çamoğlu, his sister, in London. I telephoned Aydın and sat in bed wiping my tears on the sheet, thinking our lunches would never again take place.

Kenan Erim died in Ankara on 3rd November 1990. Turgut Özal, President of Turkey, signed an official document which would allow him to be buried on site at

Aphrodisias. There were two ceremonies: one in front of the Ministry of Culture in Ankara, and another at Aphrodisias. Soldiers in white helmets, khaki uniforms and white spats from the local barracks guarded the coffin in front of the museum. Zeybek folklore dancers mingled with the subdued crowd of Kenan's team, foreign and Turkish colleagues, workers, villagers, and friends who greeted each other in silent embrace. We walked behind the coffin to his grave at the side of the Tetrapylon, where he now rests in peace. The sky was red, the sun a ball of fire, as Aphrodisias honoured Kenan Erim.

His sudden, early death was a devastating shock. But his legacy has inspired colleagues and friends. Most of the excavation team had worked with Kenan since their university days. Professor Bert Smith, Lincoln Professor of Art and Archaeology at Oxford University was appointed Director. He met Kenan as a student at Princeton University in America and first came to Aphrodisias in 1985, Dr. Gerhard Paul arrived in 1983, and Dr. Thomas Keifer in 1989. Sevgi Gönül proved a pillar of strength in those confused, sad days as Bert Smith and his team prepared for the immediate future. Research papers were properly documented, books and papers published, the museum has been renovated and the Sevgi Gönül Hall houses the reliefs and sculptures excavated from the Sebasteion and restored by the late Trevor Proudfoot.

With Ömer Koç chairman of Geyre Vakfı and with Professor Smith and his team in charge of the excavation, Aphrodisias is in safe hands and well on its way to becoming one of the most magnificent, exciting open-air museums in the world.

In 2017, Aphrodisias was included as an UNESCO site and the Director, Professor B. Smith said, 'Inscription as UNESCO World Heritage Site is great news for Aphrodisias as it recognises high level work over more than 50 years as well as the intrinsic importance of the site and its monuments'.

In London circles whenever Aphrodisias is mentioned, Lady Patricia Daunt, writer and wife of former ambassador, Sir Timothy Daunt comes to mind. Patricia first came to Turkey in September 1960 to take up her post at the British Embassy in Ankara. There, she met and in 1962 married 3rd secretary, Timothy Daunt and spent the first 2 years of their married life exploring the country. When Sir Timothy returned as Ambassador in 1986, an introduction to Kenan Erim resulted in a long and fruitful relationship and Patricia's defining interest, Aphrodisias, as they became ardent patrons and members of Kenan Erim's intimate circle. In 1993 Patricia established a London Friends of Aphrodisias Trust which she has chaired with huge success ever since. A collection of Patricia's travels and writings for Cornucopia has been collected in a beautiful book, *'The Palace Lady's Summerhouse and other inside stories from a vanishing Turkey'* published by Caique Publishing Ltd.

Ara Güler

Ara Güler died on the 17th October 2018, after this chapter had already been written. I decided to leave it as it is.
He will be deeply missed.

What was it that inspired Kenan Erim to set off on that first signature expedition to Aphrodisias? That brings me to the story of photographer, Ara Güler.

When Dacat Güler presented his mischievous son, Ara, with a camera on his tenth birthday, little did he realise that he had just put his son's future into his hands. Nor is it a wonder, born on Tosbağa Street, Beyoğlu, that his photographs reflect the lives and world of ordinary people. All Ara had to do was open the front door of his house and there was Istanbul, at its best and sleaziest, on his doorstep: elegant ladies wearing hats walking arm in arm with gentlemen along fashionable Grand Rue de Pera, sip tea in tearooms, and dance at embassy balls, while the alleyways and back-streets teemed with suspicious characters roaming the nightclubs, restaurants and crumbling, over-crowded apartment houses where locals worked and whores, smoking cigarettes, waited for customers.

Born in 1928 into a progressive Armenian family, Ara Güler's father, a pharmacist, was part of the artistic and theatrical crowd who gathered in Beyoğlu's *meyhanes* and coffee houses. Young actors, including Muvahhit Bey and his wife Bedia, spent hours in the backroom of his shop experimenting with creams, powders, pencils and colours for theatrical make-up.

In 1958, Ara, then director of photography for *Hayat* magazine, a Turkish weekly, was assigned to photograph the opening of the Kemer Dam in the province of Aydın. The Governor of Aydın provided him with a car and driver to cover the difficult inland journey to Kemer. A large crowd gathered for the opening, farmers and villagers stood listening to long-winded politicians praising the achievements of the government, and bureaucrats in black pin-striped suits applauded. Ara photographed it all, then sat back to wait for one last shot of the setting sun simmering on the dam's water. It was dark by the time he was ready to leave. The irate driver suggested a shorter route back along the slopes of the Karıncalı Mountains. After hours bumping along rough roads, it was clear that they were totally lost. Ara, tired and hungry, insisted that they spend the night at the next village.

They stopped in front of a village cafe in a square. The doorstep was made of white marble and the inside was dimly lit by an oil-lamp hanging from a wooden beam held up by a marble column. The air was thick with cigarette smoke. Men played cards, dominoes and 'tavla' and drank tea on round wooden boards resting on carved marble bases. Ara was amazed. The 'muhtar' offered him tea and cigarettes, sending a young boy scuttling off to prepare a meal and room.

'What's the name of this village?' Ara inquired.

'Geyre Köyü,' came the reply.

Too excited to sleep, Ara waited for the first light of dawn sitting on a bench under the shade of a magnificent plane tree outside the cafe. He shot marble fragments embedded in stone walls of houses, marble block stairs leading to wooden balconies, colonnades supporting stable roofs, and carved sarcophagi serving as grape-vats, water troughs for animal fodder, and laundry tubs. Come daybreak, men led the ecstatic young man past tall plane trees, pomegranate bushes and vineyards, where capitals, statue bases and upside-down friezes lay in long grasses. Ara shot roll after roll of women carrying firewood tied to their backs, children playing on ancient marble blocks, the sheep, goats and cattle grazing amongst ionic columns until, hit by a photographer's nightmare, he ran out of film.

Once back in Istanbul Ara learned that Geyre village stood on the site of a Greco-Roman city. Brief excavations had been undertaken in 1904 by Paul Gandin, a French engineer and Director of the Izmir Railway, and later by an Italian, Guilio Jacopi, in 1937, but they were cut short by the outbreak of the Second World War. The photographs roused little interest in Istanbul, but did attract the attention of *Horizon* magazine, a prestigious American publication. The editor recognized the archaeological interest of the photographs and cabled Ara for more, as well as an article. Photographs from his second expedition showed Turkish villagers living in the ancient city.

Armed with photographs, Ara went to the Archaeological Museum to research the site for an article, but found little information. However, the Director did suggest he get in touch with Kenan Erim, a young classical art and archaeology scholar at Princeton University in America. Ara cabled Kenan's details to the editor.

In the course of his studies, Kenan had been fascinated by a theory that he'd read suggesting evidence of a school of sculpture in Aphrodisias during the first centuries of the Christian era. Imagine his surprise when he received a call from the editor of *Horizon* magazine asking him to write an article on Aphrodisias.

Kenan Erim made plans to visit Geyre in the summer of 1959. Before setting off on his first reconnaissance trip, he called on Ara Güler at his studio in Beyoğlu. They poured over the photographs, talking well into the night. Two years later Kenan Erim organized his first exploratory campaign under the sponsorship of New York University. The rest is history.

Although quite different personalities, Ara and Kenan developed a close professional bond. Whenever Kenan needed a photograph, he called Ara, and Ara, aware that he was one of the privileged few given *carte blanche* onsite, spent hours wandering amongst the ruins at Aphrodisias with his camera in hand.

Ara Güler with his grey white beard and piercing eyes is a larger-than-life person with a big heart and strong opinions on most subjects and no qualms about voicing them. He has photographed the world. He worked as Middle East photographer for Time and Life, Paris Match and Der Stern until Henri Cartier-Bresson invited him to join the Magnum Agency in Paris. 'I live by my eyes,' he once told me, he often travelled with his late wife, Suna 'my best friend,' across the hinterlands of Anatolia in search of 'that perfect shot.' As a photojournalist he documents both the lives of ordinary people and places, as well as the rich and famous. Each photograph is a one-off composition seen through a sharp eye with a steady hand and a depth of passion. Portraits of the rich and famous or humble and poor, make no difference to the time and concentration taken to capture that moment of truth – Winston Churchill, Pablo Picasso, Bertrand Russell, Marc Chagall, Salvador Dali, Indira Gandhi, a fisherman, quay workers, street children or villagers in the field.

I associate him most with photographs of the city in which he is rooted. His black and white photographs of Istanbul in the 1950's and 60's captured the street and people in familiar places. Poignantly gentle in retrospect, low-key, comfortable, a little seedy, the photos show the streets exactly as I remember and record a sense of the passing of time. No matter how often I look at them, I find something new, something fresh. Ara makes the ordinary, extra-ordinary. His portraits now hang in museums throughout the world and his work has received awards galore, including Master of Leica, Légion d'Honneur and the Grand Prize of Culture and Arts Leica Award.

As he ambles along the streets of Istanbul, hat set at a rakish angle and cigarette dangling from his mouth, neighbours greet him with a respectful smile. The family home is now an office and art gallery next to a café where Ara can be found most days, surrounded by young students discussing new techniques, digital cameras, planning an exhibition or the publication of a book. Whenever I went to Beyoğlu I'd drop by the café or gallery for a chat and cup of coffee and Ara would show me what he was working on or talk me around the gallery. Listening to him made me aware of the quirkiness and fragility of nature and human beings that lies hidden within the photographs. He'll stop in front of one to tell a story – hilarious, shocking or sad – about the sitter and the sitting.

Now when I go to Beyoğlu I miss my extra-ordinary friend.

No Politics Before Breakfast

Two subjects which raises the blood pressure of Turks are discussions about their favourite football team and politics. It is a subject you cannot get away from in Turkey. I have often cheerfully announced when we have guests, 'No politics at the table please' but it rarely worked.

Aydın's passion for politics came to the fore when in 1974 Turkey invaded Northern Cyprus in what Prime Minister Bülent Ecevit called, *Kıbrıs Barış Harekatı*, 'The Cyprus Peace Operation' in July and a second attack launched on 14th August of that year. This came about because Greek Cypriot islanders decided to unite with the mainland's ruling military Junta which resulted in fierce conflict and fighting on both sides in the village communities. Aydın covered the dining table in our Kuşadası house with a large map of Cyprus and glued tiny Turkish flags onto pins, tied to a ball of red wool, to follow the movements of the Turkish army – a system he had seen used by the British government in the Second World War in the War Rooms, London. Friends and cousins came for breakfast and stayed for supper. A victorious combat was met with loud cheers and flags were moved forward. Defeats were met with sober silence.

When British Foreign Minister, later Prime Minister, James Callahan criticized the Turkish invasion, I became public enemy No.1 so I decided to take a stand. Drawing a line on the floor I announced, 'This is British territory. Whoever wants lunch had better think carefully!' My giggling daughters nestled up to their father waving Turkish flags. Taffy, our Yorkshire Terrier, ambled across the line towards his bowl. 'That's it, kitchen's closed,' I decreed. Picking up Taffy I drove to the Club Med to spend an idyllic, war-free afternoon.

Rosie Baldwin was cheered as she drove around town with a Turkish flag tied to the antenna of her red Fiat, flying high in the breeze, and Nelson Rockefeller on a short stopover at the Kısmet Hotel with his wife, Happy, noted a broken pier jutting out of the water. 'Greeks, I suppose?' he inquired. 'Oh no,' Hümeyra Hanım was quick to point out. 'The Turkish navy destroyed the pier in fear of Greek submarines.'

Melina Mercouri, feisty Greek star, singer and political activist was forced into exile by the Junta in the late 1970's. With her husband, Jules Dassin, a French American film director, she stayed for weeks on many occasions at Kısmet Hotel. 'This is the closest I get to my beloved country,' she cried, breaking into a Greek dance, her wild blonde locks blowing in the wind, cursing the day the Greek Junta came to power. Following the overthrow of the Junta, Melina Mercouri returned to Greece to become Minister of Arts and, if I remember correctly, accused the Turkish Ministry of Antiquities of archaeological misdemeanours.

In November 1983, one third of the island was declared the Turkish Republic of Northern Cyprus. Turkey is the only country to recognise this state. Even though both countries are members of NATO, disputes have nevertheless brought Greece and Turkey to the brink of war on two occasions. On May 1st 2004, Cyprus was accepted into the European Union, and in 2008, its currency changed to the Euro.

Nikos Konstandaras, a Greek journalist writes, 'despite new dangers, decades of separation seem to have worn away at the desire to fix the problem. It has lost its will to find a solution.' Not only have they lost the will – these drawn-out problems have become more complex with time and have taken on a different impetus.

But away from politics and religious dominance most Greeks, especially island Greeks and Turks get on quite well and have much in common.

At a lecture I attended at Istanbul Kadir Has University, a researcher said, 'Every political power wants to leave a legacy on the urban landscape so their work reflects the ideological power at work at the time. What is happening in Istanbul and Turkey is no different'. That might be so, I thought, but it is certainly more obvious here than elsewhere.

During the 1960's and 70's, massive migration took place from Anatolia. Trainloads of Turkish workers travelled to Germany and at the same time, thousands of Anatolians descended on the hillside periphery of Istanbul, Ankara and Izmir to live in hurriedly built, illegal *Gecekondu* shanty towns built at high speed and low cost by crafty contractors with no infrastructure, water, electricity or roads by spectacular views of the Bosphorus in Istanbul, the city in Ankara and the Aegean Sea in Izmir. *Gecekondu* means 'put up at night.' If the roof was in place by midnight, apparently it could not be demolished. Turkish artists captured these 'journeys of hope' in evocative paintings of workers in search of a better life departing from Anatolian city train stations to Germany and 'caravans of hope' arriving to the outskirts of major cities.

Villagers became city dwellers over-night, influencing the social aspects of the city as they settled in districts where relatives could help find employment, schools, and medical services and attending the same mosque as part of the community. Many opened restaurants promoting local specialities named after their birth place: Bursa Kebabı, Adana Kebabı, Kayseri Pastırması, Maraş Dondurması. Merchants came from Kayseri, construction workers from the East, cooks from Bolu and Menemen, taxi drivers from the Black Sea, and gardeners from southern Anatolia.

Hardly any 'Gecekondus' exist today, most have been bulldozed to make way for high-priced modern apartment blocks with spectacular views.

Between the late 60's and 70's the lack of stable governance, security and the rule of law dominated conversation as the population fell into disarray between fractions on the Left, Right, Islamists and Nationalists. Thirteen coalition governments vied for power, not one party or leader was popular or strong enough to gain sufficient votes to form a one-party government. There was Bülent Ecevit, a graduate from Robert College who wrote poetry and had studied journalism and politics in America leading the Republican Peoples Party, engineer Süleyman Demirel leader of the *Adalet* 'Justice' Party, a pro-western, centre-right party, the pro-Islamic Welfare Party was founded by Necmettin Erbakan, and Colonel Alpaslan Türkeş led the ultra-right National Party.

It was at this time that Robert College and its magnificent campus founded in 1863 by a body of Americans was taken over by the government to become Boğaziçi University.

Students took to the streets while coalition parties continued arguing and pursuing a policy of self-sufficiency which practically took the country to the brink of political and economic collapse. With hardly any foreign investment and a lack of foreign currency, businesses were left with one option, black market profiteers. One evening, dining at Süreyya's with Atif Aksel, his wife, Flora, Sedat Kutbay and his wife, Irena, Sedat was complaining at having to deal with corrupt black marketeers to keep his business afloat when the waiter came along to ask him to lower his voice because a minister was sitting at the next table, Sedat was so upset we left before finishing our meal. Daily clashes on the street between police and students became violent. Troops moved into universities to keep the peace. In March, 1971, the military forced Prime Minister Demirel to resign and imposed martial law in many cities, including Ankara. The military remained the power behind the scene for thirty months without disbanding parliament or dissolving political parties.

To keep my head-strong, teenage daughter, Ceylan off unsafe streets I would invite her school friends for tea after school. We ate and talked, 'Mummy you don't understand, you are British', was as far as I got but at least they were safe. Our local *bakkal* 'grocer' complained to Aydın that I was feeding the whole school.

Finally, out of despair, I arranged for her to take her A-levels at St. Clare's College, Porthcawl, a Catholic School quite near my mother and brother. And later I was able to send Rana to Queen's Gate School in London as a boarder for her A-levels.

A business friend helping me transfer funds, telephoned, 'Have you heard, the lira has just devaluated 70%', he said. I broke the news to Aydın as we walked in a field of sunflowers. He smiled reassuringly. 'Don't worry,' he said. 'This field will pay their school fees.' He lifted one drooping sunflower head after another, to find that birds had eaten the seeds. Help! On top of that frustrated by a third robbery in the house in Aydın, he had sold the house and was about to convert a barn in the konak into a village house in Osmanbükü. There was nothing to do but hope for the best.

Inflation reached 120%, oil prices increased, and the economy was on the verge of collapse. İsmail Hakkı Aydınoğlu, head of the Turkish Central Bank, wrote, 'every country in the world reacted realistically to the oil price increases but Turkey continued to act as if nothing had happened.' By the end of 1977, the country had accumulated the largest debt of any banking system in the world. In his book, *From the Bosphorus to Bradninch,* Sidney Nowill wrote, 'Ecevit was rightly confident in the ability of his countrymen to withstand privations and shortages which in any Western country would be unthinkable except in time of war. The Turkish population have shown fatalism, resignation and a fair measure of good temper and even humour in their current straits.'

Shortages and a lack of basic goods affected all our lives in different ways. The lack of foreign currency, diesel fuel, kerosene, liquid gas for cooking, petrol, coffee, butter and margarine meant empty shops so the black market thrived. Water and electric cuts lasted between three and eight hours a day. A friend travelled to Cyprus once a month to use the telephone and buy coffee, later she bought a house and settled there. A designer friend is convinced that her frustration and anger inspired her best ever collection and one friend, fearing for the safety of her three sons, bodyguarded them around town, driving them to school, football and sports practice, while another became so exasperated with the electricity cuts, she learned how to make candles in her kitchen. Her hobby developed into a fruitful career, and she turned professional, handing over a thriving candle business to her son when she retired. Mothers feared for their children's safety, fathers worried about inflation and business, and everyone had money problems. Carrying foreign currency and, heaven knows why, Marlboro cigarettes, could land you with a night in jail. Atif Aksel deliberately banged a packet of Marlboro cigarettes on the bar at the Divan Bar, much to the amusement of the street-wise barman, who could spot a civil policeman a mile away and with one stroke of his hand, the packet of Marlboro disappeared.

With the children at boarding school, Aydın and I spent weekends with friends or at the farm. The boot of the car contained an overnight holdall, torch, supply box of biscuits, nuts, dried fruits and water in case we missed curfew hour. The more unpleasant life became, the more effort Turks made to sustain their good humour. People organized their lives around the curfew. Suppers ended half an hour before the curfew and parties began half an hour after the curfew with an overnight stay.

One evening, an hour or so before curfew hour, I was driving home alone along Barbaros Boulevard in Beşiktaş when a car full of young hooligans passed me. The windows were open and the radio was blaring. I saw the one sitting next to the driver had his hand hanging outside the window holding a gun. Seeing me he shouted to his companions, 'woman alone.' The car skidded to a stop but it had passed the turning into a dark road where trucks and large lorries parked at night that led to Yıldız Palace and our apartment. They began to reverse. I swerved into the road, pulled in between two huge lorries turned off the headlights, stopped breathing, and started praying. For the first time in my life I felt fear. The car passed radio blaring, shouting and I heard two shots. The shouts die down, I don't know how long I waited there before I rolled down the window and plucking up the courage to drive those few yards home. Aydın believed I had a guardian angel who protected me from my impulsiveness, that evening she was certainly beside me. I didn't tell Aydın of the incident.

Most of us complained, blamed someone else, but as usual in Turkey, the circumstances brought out the best in most people and the worse in a few, they never lost that street humour or love for a companionable rakı table. Frayed tempers turned to sarcastic humour as we queued in cars for a tank of petrol or to fill a bottle of water. One morning at my father-in-law's apartment, there was no drinking water. Everyone was asleep, so I took two large water jugs to a nearby street fountain in Nişantaşı. Even at that early hour there was quite a long line and I took my place at the back. A few minutes later a lady from the front of the queue walked up to me and said in English, 'Please come and fill your bottles.'

'No, thank you,' I replied. 'I'll wait my turn.'

'We,' gesturing to those in front, 'don't want a guest in our country to queue for water,' she replied.

'I'm not a guest,' I replied in Turkish. 'I live here and have the same problems as you.'

Taking my arm, she led me to front. 'Even so, we don't want you to queue. It's embarrassing. Whenever you come here, you will not queue.' '*Evet, evet, yes, yes*,' chorused the line as she filled my bottles. Whenever I went, which was not often, smiles would lead me to the front of the queue.

By September, 1980, a chilling 5,000 people had been killed and more than 40,000 wounded. There was talk of civil war. The army in Turkey, unlike those in other countries, flex their military might only when governments are unable to control outbreaks of violence and divisions within the country, and they did so then.

On September 12th 1980, General Kenan Evren gave the order for a pre-dawn coup. According to *Time* magazine on September 29th 1980, Kenan Evren stated, 'despite warnings by the military, personal feuds, and interparty quarrels, silence and indifference continued. When all warnings remained unheeded the Turkish armed forces, as a last resort, carried out the duty entrusted to them.' This military intervention brought order and peace without a single shot being fired.

After so much uncertainty, rampant inflation and bloody terrorism, many, including Aydın and I, felt a sense of relief. 'People feel safer, but it's not the end of the danger', said one university professor.

Kenan Evren and the five-man military junta considered the 1961 constitution far too liberal and set about drawing up a more authoritarian constitution which of course displeased a great many liberal and socialist groups. In 1980 new parties began to emerge to replace the ones which had been banned. The Motherland Party, led by Turgut Özal, won the elections. He had served in the World Bank and was former economic adviser to Süleyman Demirel. Within three years his liberal economic program, with the help of the International Monetary Fund and World Trade Organisation, resulted in economic growth of 7.8%. It was a financial miracle.

Turgut Özal's liberal economic policy paved the way for a modern consumer society as well as improving the country's status on the international stage. A brilliant negotiator, he was able to navigate peaceful relations between Turkey, the West and neighbouring Asian countries. He applied for membership to the European Community in April 1987 with the slogan, 'Trade not Aid'. Turkey's application remains on the shelf to this day. Turkey survived. The business community and workforce rallied, exports surged, business boomed, taxes for workers were cut, foreign goods filled the shops, and construction work on infrastructure, roads and rail began. Within an amazingly short period the country was on the road to recovery.

Sidney Nowill in his book, *'From the Bosphorus to Bradninch'*, quotes British Ambassador, Sir Timothy Daunt's assessment of Turgut Özal, 'The man displays unusual tenacity and projects an air of sincerity which disarms the people he is talking to… his position in Turkey today seems unassailable, he is the one pivotal figure and perhaps, a flawed genius certainly, the most influential personality since the Atatürk revolution'.

When Turgut Özal and his wife travelled within the vicinity of Kuşadası they lunched with Ahmet and Tülay Çifçi, Mrs. Özal's niece at their summer-house. On one occasion Turgut Bey chided Aydın for his lack of political involvement: 'You have no right to criticize the state of the country unless you participate. Come to Ankara, I wait you in Ankara.'

Kenan Evren and his military junta remain a contentious issue to this day. Thousands lost their jobs, were put on trial, jailed and tortured during the time the military were in power, it was said more than 43,140 arrests were made. Artists, writers, socialists and liberals demanded justice against those who had participated in the suppression of civil rights and later Evren and General Şahinkaya, his second-in-command, were stripped of their rank and sentenced to imprisonment – considering their age and health, though, the sentence was more or less symbolic. Until his death, Kenan Evren never faltered in his conviction. A Turkish journalist in an open letter to a British newspaper wrote whether you like it or not, the cold hard truth of the matter is that Evren and Şahinkaya saved the nation from civil war and untold bloodshed. Drastic times call for drastic measures.

The 90's also proved to be a decade of survival for most people in more ways than one.

We welcomed the first woman prime minister, Tansu Çiller but disillusionment soon set in and she resigned after two years or so to disappear from the political scene. Necmettin Erbakan, known as *hoca* 'teacher' planted the seeds of pro-Islamic politics by strengthening ties with the Muslim world rather than the West. In the 1994 local elections, two candidates from his party, the Islamist Welfare Party, became mayors of the most important cities in Turkey. Recep Tayyip Erdoğan became mayor of Istanbul, and Melih Gökçek became mayor of Ankara. Covering the head with a head scarf had become a political problem.

In times of trouble, creativity often fills Turkish cracks and in the 1990's, the number of festivals, theatres, books published and cultural events supported by enthusiastic crowds, grew. Turkish contemporary and modern art began to attract interest from the global art market. Exhibition halls and galleries opened in towns and resorts. Turkish artists and films went on to win international awards and the names of Turkish fashion designers appeared in international fashion magazines and their designs sought-after by exclusive stores in Europe and America.

Immense construction has resulted in a thriving modern city. But the Turks' 'love for concrete' has destroyed much of Istanbul uniqueness and its magnificent sky-line has not been improved by high-rise buildings and skyscrapers. In many parts of the world, the state role is to safeguard the interests of the public when negotiating with private developers. In Turkey the state is the biggest developer.

Digging anywhere in Istanbul, or in Turkey for that matter, one is more than likely to hit an ancient ruin. It was no surprise then, when layer after layer of artefacts and history, testament to the city's long past and identity were discovered during the construction of the Marmaray project, an undersea rail tunnel. Construction work began in 2005 with an expected completion date of April 2009. However, when the world's richest collection of medieval shipwrecks dating back 8,500 years was found, progress was delayed by four years. It proved to be one of the most important marine archaeological finds of the century. Remnants of 37 ships, Byzantine black wooden boats with cargo intact, animal remains, pottery and artefacts were discovered. In the early stages of the marine excavation we were shown around the Harbour of Theodosius, part of the walls of Constantine the Great. It was amazing. They had found details of the commerce of the port and evidence of a settlement and details of the lives, religion and economics of a minority group who farmed arable land dating back to 6,000 BC. The first phase of the Marmaray was finally completed in October 2013.

There is no rush hour traffic in Istanbul since every hour is rush hour. One of the main problems is many inner-city roads end at inadequate junctions, roundabouts, or narrow streets, causing congestion and bottlenecks.

I rarely use taxis, but whenever I do, I enjoy chatting to taxi drivers who usually come from eastern Anatolia. Conversation generally begins with: 'Are you German? How come you speak Turkish?' They see me, like themselves, as a stranger from another place.

One evening I was invited to a cocktail party at 6 p.m. in Galata. Expecting traffic to be heavy, I drove to Beşiktaş and parked the car to take a taxi the rest of the way. A taxi stopped and out got a man, woman and child, crying. I hopped in and gave the address. We hadn't moved 100 yards when we stopped at some red lights. The driver turned to me. 'I have a terrible head-ache,' he said. 'I want to go home. I picked up that couple from the American Hospital. The child never stopped crying and the parents did nothing to console her. I want to go home. I'm sorry.'

I got out to hail another cab. The driver was young. I gave the address and he drove across the roundabout – and then saw lanes of traffic at a stand-still. He stopped. 'It will take us hours to get to Galata, why are you going there?'

'I'm trying to go to a party,' I replied, rather irritable.

'The party will be over by the time we get there. Please, let me drive you home. All roads to Galata are congested. You can have a comfortable drink at home. Please,' he begged. I got out and telephoned my hostess to apologise.

'Silly you. Why don't you use the *metro*?' was her reply.

The Last of the Ottomans

Most people who have been exiled carry the scars of a life in exile, and the Ottoman family were no exception. Following the chaotic outcome of the First World War, empires became republics and exiled royals from Russia, Germany, Austria-Hungary and the Ottoman Empire moved from one country to another across the Americas, Europe and the Middle East. The Ottoman royal family fared rather better than most because of their close ties with royal families of the Middle East. Some led charmed lives, others suffered hardships but all intuitively grew up with a feeling something was missing, an unfulfilled entitlement, birth-right claims and a nostalgia for what might have been.

The guest list at Kısmet Hotel, Kuşadası during the month of August reads like a page from Burke's Peerage as Hümeyra Hanım prepared to entertain her cousins for a month in the sun. First to arrive were the beautiful, widowed sisters, Neslişah Sultan, Hanzade Sultan and Necla Sultan, grand-children of Sultan Vahdettin. Bonded by a turbulent childhood, they were protective of each other and delighted to be together.

Neslişah Sultan was born in 1921 in Istanbul and spent her youth in exile until she was married to Prince Muhammed Abdülmünim, son of the Khedive of Egypt. With her husband, the Prince she returned to Istanbul in 1964 after an absence of 40 years. Like her cousin, Neslişah Sultan had suffered the humiliation of being twice exiled, once from Turkey and then from Egypt following the overthrow of the monarchy there. Neslişah Sultan was a handsome woman, tall, statuesque with silver-white hair rolled at the nape of her neck. She had the energy, physique, and posture of a professional sportswoman. Always last off the snow slopes, she also rode with the skill of an equestrian rider and excelled, like her sisters, at water sports.

She smoked cigarettes until the end. 'Allow me to enjoy the few pleasures left to me,' she'd snap when chided. Zeynep Osmanoğlu, wife of Osman Efendi once brought a carton of her favourite cigarettes as a present from New York. Her daughter quite rightly requested she came to lunch but didn't give the cigarettes. The telephone rang. It was a royal command: 'Come to lunch, with the cigarettes.'

At the age of 16, Hanzade Sultan, against her elder sister's wishes to escape her parents rather frugal lifestyle married an older but kindly Egyptian Prince, Muhammed Ali İbrahim and her sister, Necla Sultan married his brother, Prince Amr İbrahim. Hanzade Sultan resided in Paris and Necla Sultan in Switzerland. Hanzade Sultan was exceptionally beautiful, her black hair framed a heart-shaped face, finely shaped mouth and rather sad, pensive blue eyes. Her voice was soft and manner demure and every personal story she told had a tinge of regret as though she had not been able to live life as she would have desired. When Aydın mocked my belief in my gut feeling, my premonitions, one day she flew to my defence 'Don't mock your wife. Sensing trouble is a premonition of sorts,' then went on to tell how she had felt full of misgivings, fear even when her daughter Princess Fazila who became engaged to the young King Faysal of Iraq in 1975 was preparing to visit her fiancée. The following year in 1958, a few months before the wedding, the king was assassinated.

Days passed quietly on the beach at the Kısmet hotel, swimming, reading and sunbathing with a few trips to Samos, local markets, Tire and Ödemiş or the bee-man for royal jelly at Davutlar. Every market day, a lady from the village would bring a tray of *gözleme,* 'a delicious, large round thin pancake filled with cheese, herbs, spinach or potato' to the hotel for lunch. My companions were all excellent swimmers and I could never keep pace with them. One day watching them prepare for lunch I thought how constrained they carried their nobility and how modest they behaved. Rising to leave I said laughingly, 'Do you realise I am the only untitled person in a bathing costume on this rock'. Neslişah Sultan was standing next to me and to the delight of her sisters and with a, 'Silly girl' pushed me back into the sea. Evenings were spent with relatives and friends at a fish restaurant, in their homes or at the open-air Kısmet dining room overlooking the sea hosted by Hümeyra Hanım and Halil who would turn the evening into a jolly party. We gave candle lit barbecue parties in the garden of Rose Cottage. They were, out of necessity, quite informal gatherings so everyone was happy to give a helping hand before lounging on cushions in a garden lit by candles under a starry sky. In those days, music was played on the gramophone and although Aydın had a large collection of romantic and military records some guests brought their own records to listen to.

In 1992, Osman Ertuğrul Osmanoğlu, forty-third head of the Imperial House of Osman was granted permission to return to Turkey. His first remark was, 'Democracy works well in Turkey.' With his second wife, Zeynep (Tarzı), a descendant of the Afghan royal family, he chose to celebrate this momentous occasion with his relatives at the Kısmet Hotel. Hümeyra Hanım was delighted. On the day of his arrival, she sent word to the beach bar to inform us that Osman Efendi intended to join us for lunch. I slipped into a long beach dress. Aydın disappeared – he had a maddening habit of disappearing to a quiet corner in the garden with a book. I was just going off to search for him when he came flying down the steps, dressed in slacks and shirt. 'I didn't want to meet Osman Efendi in bathing trunks,' he spluttered to Hümeyra Hanım's delight.

Osman Ertuğrul Osmanoğlu was an Ottoman gentleman who spoke four or five languages fluently and loved opera. An engineer by profession, he had worked and met his first wife in South America before retiring to New York. His modest life-style was reason enough, perhaps, for his complete lack of entitlement or the slightest touch of nostalgia for past glories. Chatting at a dinner given by Neslişah Sultan, he once said to me, 'I can't decide whether you are an English lady or a Turkish *hanımefendi* – but I find the combination attractive.' I've loved him ever since.

Their aunt, the austere Princess of Berar, Dürrüşehvar Sultan, daughter of Sultan Abdülmecit, had married the son of the Nizam of Hyderabad and on occasion joined her nieces at the Kısmet. Her life had revolved around grand palaces and Europe's cafe society, but her last years were spent at an elegant apartment at Queen's Gate in London, a few blocks from Rana's boarding school. The walls of her flat were covered with paintings, including one impressive life-size portrait of Sultan Abdülaziz in uniform. Tall, elegant with strong Ottoman features, her photographs taken by Cecil Beaton, graced international society and fashion magazines.

One evening, desperately late to an invitation at Sotheby's, I ran up the red carpeted stairs of the auction house. Just as I reached the top an authoritative voice boomed out, practically sending me tumbling down the stairs: 'Ah, in London! Why haven't you telephoned?' There, a sibyl of chic, cane in hand, was the Princess about to leave. I mumbled my apology, I had every intention of calling, but had just arrived. She handed me one of those small, stick-on addresses with a promise to call, before she walked down the stairs.

Whenever Aydın and I were in London, the Princess invited us for a tea of bite-size cucumber sandwiches and cake. She complained of loneliness, wanted to visit Istanbul and the Kısmet Hotel, 'but I cannot manage the steps to the beach. I must tell Hümeyra to install a lift.' She would show my grandson, Alican, photographs of her childhood. 'I don't want him to be bored,' she smiled.

Aydın entertained Dürrüşehvar Sultan with stories of his family's adventures in the 1930's, when his father, a trainee banker at *Le Bank Ottoman* and shared an apartment with his brother, Bekir and sister, Habibe. Habibe was an intimate friend of Samine Sultan, daughter of Prince Abdul Halim and became part of the royal party accompanying them to exclusive restaurants and private clubs to listen to fabulous artists such as Josephine Baker at the Café De Paris.

One day Samine Sultan confided to Habibe that her father felt unwell and that their finances were in dire straits. The next day Habibe asked permission to speak to the Prince. She presented him with a bag stuffed with French notes. Prince Abdul looked affronted, chiding her angrily, 'I cannot accept money from you.'

'Efendim, it is not my money. It's yours. Its half the gratuity you left at restaurants and clubs. You are too generous. Each time I took a few hundred francs to put in this purse.'

The Prince was deeply touched, taking her two hands, he kissed them warmly. 'My dear child, Habibe. What a loyal friend you are to my daughter and her father, thank you.' Aunt Habibe was known for her frugality.

One day Prince Abdul asked Bekir to take a jewel-encrusted dagger to a certain antique dealer to sell. The dealer examined the exquisite dagger, carefully peering at the handsome young man who had brought it to him over his horn-rimmed glasses. 'A rare, beautiful piece indeed,' he said. 'I have a client that I am sure will be most interested in it. Please wait while I telephone him.' Within a few minutes two French policemen burst into the shop to arrest poor Bekir.

Dürrüşehvar Sultan would often speak of her father, his love for art and painting, and how much she adored him. She never spoke of her marriage. It had obviously not been a happy life. The last time I called her, she was eager for news of Neslişah Sultan and Hümeyra Hanım. She asked when I would visit her and I promised to telephone the following week. I did, but was told she had died.

Cucumber Sandwiches

One summer during an August month of *Ramazan,* Princess Fawzia (Fevziye) Fuad of Egypt, daughter of King Fuad, sister to King Faruk, first wife of the late Shah of Iran, Mohammad Reza Pahlavi, (a lady of titles) came to the Kısmet Hotel with her Caucasian husband, Colonel İsmail Şirin, and their nineteen-year old son, Hussain on their way to Egypt. At dinner, in their honour, Aydın sat at one end of the table on the left of the Princess, whose face was hidden behind large, dark sunglasses. She hardly spoke and I could see Aydın trying hard to keep the conversation flowing while at our end of the table, her husband, İsmail Bey kept us in hysterics with tales of escapades in Paris with the late Shah. Looking across at his wife, İsmail Bey told us, 'I fell in love with Fawzia the first time I set eyes on her.' He beamed. 'She was standing at the top of the grand stairs of the palace next to the Shah of Iran, her husband, a long white fur draped over her shoulders. She was Queen of Iran. I was a besotted young officer serving in the Egyptian army.'

His son whispered into my ear: 'And he is still as besotted as ever.'

Aydın was upset that he had not been able to entertain the Princess and was still talking about her at breakfast, 'it's most off-putting conversing with a beautiful woman when she is wearing dark glasses. I rambled on and she hardly said a word, just yes or no. She was probably bored.' and mumbling to himself, he left for the farm.

An hour or so later Hümeyra Hanım telephoned to say the Princess, her husband, and son intended to come to tea with us. They were to arrive at five and stay until the car came to take them for *iftar*, 'the evening meal'. I told her Aydın had left for the farm, 'then tell him to come back', I phoned Aydın and got to work making small cucumber sandwiches and a cake, strawberries and ice-cream – a decent enough summer tea.

They arrived. As they climbed down the uneven steps, Princess Fawzia removed her glasses and not wanting to fall held out her hand to Aydın. She was incredibly beautiful with violet eyes, white alabaster complexion, fine features and lush, black hair. Looking around she smiled. 'Hümeyra told me so much about Rosie and this cottage,' and turned to Aydın. 'Last night you said....' and so began a lively conversation. Hussein and the girls explored the olive grove then sat on Rana's balcony until tea was served.

Hussein chided his mother for not teaching him Turkish – after all it was his mother tongue. 'We were not allowed to speak Turkish at court, darling. Your grandfather insisted we speak Arabic or French. If you want to learn Turkish why don't you spend a summer here?' she said, throwing a biscuit to the dog.

Colonel Ismail was fasting, he looked at the sandwiches then smiling mischievously said 'Can I take two cucumber sandwiches to break my fast? They remind me of my days at the Egyptian Embassy in London when I used to take pretty English girls to tea at the Ritz.'

The driver arrived. No one moved. I panicked, fearing they might stay for dinner. The driver appeared again to remind them of the time. Regretfully they got up to go, Princess Fawzia handed Aydın her card and invited us to visit in Switzerland before flashing a disarming smile, the Princess disappeared behind the dark glasses.

In the eyes of the world, Princess Fawzia was the epitome of glamour and beauty with an oriental mystique. The Egyptian writer and poet, Adel Sabot described her as a 'shy, supremely naive, over-protected girl, mobbed by adoring servants, aunts and ladies–in-waiting, rarely allowed out or to socialize.'

Her first marriage at the age of eighteen to the Shah of Iran was a dynastic arrangement, loveless and unhappy. After six intolerable years of sickness, bouts of malaria and other ailments, she left Iran never to return. As the plane was about to take off, her daughter was forcibly kidnapped by the Shah. Five months after her divorce from the Shah, she married Colonel İsmail Şirin, diplomat and officer serving under King Farouk. Marriage to Colonel İsmail gave her a freedom and privacy she had never known in the claustrophobic world of royal intrigues. For a shy, beautiful princess, sunglasses were protection from inquisitive eyes. At the age of 92, in July 2013, Princess Fawzia Fuad Şirin died as she lived, quietly at her home in Alexandria. She was buried the following day in Cairo.

Hümeyra Hanım died on 20th May 2000. A few days earlier we had spent Saturday at the beach before my late flight to Istanbul. As we said good-bye, she gave me an unusually long hug. 'I loved Aydın like a son,' she said, 'and I am happy he married you. Now I love you.' I was touched. On my way to the airport I stopped at the florist in Kuşadası and ordered a bunch of flowers to be delivered to her the following day, Mother's Day. A few days later, when Alican telephoned with news of her death, I was shocked.

I flew to Izmir to attend the funeral and found Halil sitting in the little house with a relative. After a while he said, 'you know, I think Hümeyra loved me in the end. On

Mother's Day we argued. I left the table in anger and went to the farm. That evening she telephoned, apologizing for making me angry. She said she hadn't meant to. That was the first time Hümeyra ever apologized to me.'

'Halil, Hümeyra Hanım always loved you,' I replied, 'and you, deep down in your silly old heart, loved her. That's what kept you together all these years.' He gave a wry smile and began reminiscing about the time they met. Halil spent most of his time at the bungalow in Kısmet Hotel, Kuşadası until he died.

Within a relatively short period of time, Hanzade Sultan, Necla Sultan, Osman Efendi and, finally at the age of 91, Neslişah Sultan, the oldest surviving member of the Ottoman dynasty, died. It was the end of an epoch.

The Kısmet Hotel is now managed by Hanzade and Halim Özbaş.

In the early 1990's, the old man on a donkey died. His three sons decided to sell. Aydın offered to buy Rose Cottage and the garden, but they were intent on selling the property with the olive grove for a huge sum. They found a buyer, a man from Denizli. The only thing I remember about his visit was that he was wearing white nylon socks.

Some places have good vibes. Rose Cottage set on a hill alone at the end of a dirt road nestling under the shadow of a spreading oak tree with its cobbled path, deep well and tangled over-grown garden, olive and fruit trees was one. It had a special charm, you either loved it or hated it. Thank heavens everyone who visited, loved it. For fifteen years we had entertained our friends, Rose's friends and friends of friends, Turks and foreigners, artists and artisans, Princesses, Lords and Ladies, diplomats and statesmen, the rich and the down-and out, conservatives, socialists even a delightful Italian communist couple came to visit. Captivated by its quaint charm and Fatma Hanım's welcoming smile, they too became a part of Rose Cottage and hoped to return.

We gave a splendid goodbye party and were not too sad to move on before the bulldozers and construction workers descended on the village.

And what of Kuşadası? That sleepy little village where we spent our first summer holidays has all but disappeared. It is now a vibrant sea-side resort with a population of more than 110,000, a major port of call for huge cruise ships, a touristic centre with modern hotels galore, apartment buildings, hospitals, two-lane boulevards, shops and supermarkets, cafes and restaurants for holiday seekers, home to Turkish and foreign residents year-round, a busy economically vibrant town.

One evening, sitting in Kazım Usta Restaurant, I watched crowds of holiday-makers browsing, bargaining in well-lit shops which were doing a jolly good trade, and I thought to myself: the old fishing village might have gone, but these tourists know Kuşadası as it is now – a lively summer resort in the Aegean with a wide promenade, cool blue sea, delicious food, within easy reach of the most splendid antique sites and an international airport. A few thousand palm trees, empathy for whatever natural beauty remains and sensitive city planning could still work wonders.

Travel Tales

Aydın was a 'in books I have travelled not only to other worlds but into my own', person and except for his yearly visit to London, which he looked forward to, he preferred to entertain people at home, while I loved travel. From my very first days in Turkey, friends had sent friends seeking assistance to book a hotel, a good restaurant, interview a politician, and research for a book they were writing. I had organised trips for Serenissima Travel, the World Monument Fund and other private tour companies. But it was a surprise call from Rana's mother-in-law, İnci Pirinççioğlu, founder of V.I.P, asking if I would stand in for her as guide on a tour to Scandanavia that was the start of a decade or more traveling with a small Turkish group to destinations of my choice during the 1980's and 1990's. It was an opportunity to see the places I had dreamt about. I was overjoyed. The fact that my family seemed more than happy to be rid of me did give me pause to think, but I put it down to mid-life crisis. Sometimes it's better not to question why, but go with the flow! Aydın was a huge help with itinerary details, map reading and timing distances to allow not only for 'must see' sights, but to absorb the local atmosphere, wander around, meet people, eat locally and perhaps lunch with a famous local personality. That was the way I liked to travel.

Before 9/11, travelling was much more enjoyable. There was less security, better service, acceptable regulations and benevolent customs officials who would turn a blind eye to the extra kilos of shopaholic ladies. Turks are good travellers – no penny pinching for them, travel was a time to shop, eat well and be entertained and see the sights. They are generous and open to suggestions. Except for minor frustrations and the odd hair-raising incident, each journey enriched my life in a way I could never have imagined.

My first organized tour was to China with twelve Turkish ladies and it was an eye opener to quite a different civilization. Our pretty Beijing guide was proud of her mother who had walked the long walk and bowed to Mao Tse-Tung's dictates by giving birth to eleven children. Her own expectations were very different. 'I approve of the one child policy and less government control,' she said reciting the modern communist doctrine. 'My son's childhood is better than mine was. He has a clean home, is well fed, attends a good school and knows he is loved.' Our guide in Xi'an was adamant that 'tiger parenting' for children to attain a better life was necessary in Chinese society. 'My friends and I will be millionaires before our thirtieth birthday,' he announced with conviction.

Walking on the snake-like fortifications of the Great Wall, stretching over hills and valleys along the northern border of the country was mind-boggling. Considering the immensity of the task, that the first emperor of China, Qin Shi Huang was a thirteen-year-old child when, under his command, work began on the terracotta army in Xi'an, an extra-ordinary tomb of life-size sculptures of soldiers and horses, each face with a different expression. The tomb itself is sublime but what I found rather unsettling was the men on the streets pulling carts and riding bicycles wore the same weary, pained facial expressions as the men in the terracotta army. Life was never easy in China.

There were only four other passengers besides our small group on the plane to Lima in Peru and we were about to land when I was called to the pilot's cabin by an air hostess. In a hushed tone, the pilot told me not to be alarmed, but I was to ensure the group make a quick exit from the airport building because the Shining Path guerrillas, a Maoist group, were going to attack the airport any moment. The airfield was surrounded with Peruvian soldiers. I peered out of the window. Sure enough, short, menacing soldiers with guns stood along the periphery of the airport. Having read of the brutality of Shining Path guerrillas, it was frightening.

Lights in the airport were dim. The group, oblivious of any danger were pleased to climb into the waiting bus, revving for a quick get-away. I gave a sigh of relief. The next morning the receptionist at the hotel informed me that the airport was closed, flights cancelled and that there had been fighting. He shrugged his shoulders: 'It happens all the time, *no problema, no problema*' - the Peruvian answer to every problem.

Brazil is magnificent: nature's wonderland of giant trees entwined with every type of creeping plant and green carpets of lush vegetation cover the ground. The Amazon Rainforest is home to one third of every species of plant, bird and fish in the world. In crocodile line our guide led us along a forest path by the broad and brown Amazon River. The forest pressed in on all sides, ants, scorpions, butterflies of every hue, jumped, fluttered and scrambled around us. It was hot, humid. No jungle Jane, I felt extremely uncomfortable.

Our guide, a wildlife conservationist over lunch one day spoke of his country as rich with natural wealth, minerals in the mountains and mines, medicinal properties from the trees in the forests and rivers swarm with fish. Then he added, 'Yet we suffer. We did not have an Atatürk to save us,' he sighed, to everyone's delight. Atatürk is hugely admired throughout South America as a leader and saviour, with statues erected in his honour in many town squares.

Checking into Hotel das Cataratas, an impressive Portuguese colonial residence set in the Iguazu National Park, a stones' throw from the magnificent waterfalls when the Asian manager checked my British passport, he asked me to wait. After he attended to the group's rooms, chuffed with pride, he told me that just the day before Princess Anne and her party had departed after three days at the hotel and that her stay had been a huge success, the Princess left happy with everything. He led me to a grand suite with a vast drawing-room decorated with massive carved furniture, three enormous bedrooms with bathrooms and a breath-taking panorama of the forest and falls. 'From now on, this will be known as our Royal Suite. As you are our first British guest after your Princess, you may stay here,' he bowed low before closing the door behind him.

It was splendidly spacious. I felt lonely so invited the group for cocktails every evening at the Royal Suite.

There is a Welsh settlement in Argentina's Chubut province along the coast of southern Patagonia, Puerto Marin. Established at the turn of the century during the depression in Wales and Scotland, a statue of Captain Lewis Jones, who set sail with 200 immigrants to establish the colony, dominates the square in Puerto Madre, sheep farming country. For more than 150 years, this Welsh colony has protected its language and customs. We drove past flat, arid lowlands to Gaiman, a small town of two-story houses in gardens bursting with flowers. Signs in Welsh swung over the gates of Welsh tea-houses, *Plas y Coed*, where pretty girls in Welsh costumes served traditional tea in rooms decorated with flags and posters of Wales.

'Now for a touch of Welsh hospitality,' said I, proudly, as we entered one. Although I am proud of an O-level in Welsh, I failed to impress the Welsh speaking Argentinians – but they were gracious enough to give us a discount on what would otherwise have been an expensive tea. The group thought it hilarious consoling me with, 'never mind the Welsh, Kim. We Turks still love you.'

On a trip to Petra Jordan, I met the daughter of Marguerite van Geldermalsen, a New Zealand backpacker who fell in love and married a Bedouin. She had given birth to three children and lived in a cave with her husband's family. Watching the handsome Bedouins gallop bareback on magnificent stallions across sand-hills, robes and headdresses flying in the wind, it wasn't difficult to understand why Marguerite had succumbed! When our guide pointed her out to me sitting with friends in a café cave, I was warned her daughter shied away from inquisitive strangers, I sat at the next table and began chatting not her but to her friends. I told them my daughters celebrated both Christian and Muslim holidays, she piped up to say so did she and joined in the conversation saying her mother was from New Zealand. Salwa was fair-haired with light coloured eyes and dressed in an Arab robe. She told me they had visited Istanbul, spent summers at Kaş in the south of Turkey, and looked forward to returning. 'We moved to New Zealand to live with my grandparents, but became home sick for the Bedouin life-style, even my mother, so we returned after a year,' she explained. The family settled in a nearby hillside village where her mother writes and cares for the sick. The family is well known in Jordon.

Welcoming in the new year with a Singapore Sling at the longest bar in the world at Raffles Hotel before a hilarious rickshaw race through the streets at 3.00 am, swimming with rainbow fish in crystal waters in the Maldives on the day that America declared war on Iraq, and watching the sun shimmer – but not set – at the tip of Norway, are but a few of my unforgettable memories with a group of great travellers, Turks who became friends.

Freya Stark wrote, 'A journey in Turkey without history is like a portrait of an old face without wrinkles.'

What makes Turkey unique and complex to understand for me is the contrast and diversity within its own geographical borders. For centuries Anatolia's colourful past, culture and religion has been charted by diverse, roaming tribes, galloping across its plains, plundering, warring and leaving behind layers of civilizations. At times, it seems scary, but at its best, it is awe-inspiring. I have journey to most parts of Anatolia, met fascinating people and enjoyed its local specialities.

Quite a few of our trips in Anatolia were shared with the late Lord and Lady Monson. Intrepid travellers, we met Ivan and Emma when we dined at the same table on a Turkish mail ship from Izmir to Istanbul. Aydın was suffering from hay fever. Lady Monson produced a magic pill. When the ship docked, cards were exchanged and so began a long and intimate friendship in England and Turkey which lasts to this day.

On one trip, tired, hungry and longing for a bath and supper, we drove to our hotel near Lake Dalyan to be told the official opening of the hotel was not for another week. The embarrassed manager insisted we stay – we had no choice but to do so. We sat rather miserably beside an empty swimming pool, making plans for the following day, when other guests arrived and a pianist began to play. Music, a delicious meal and French wine soon revived our good humour especially when I realized the friendly, well-dressed guests were members of staff.

Next morning, a Turkish country breakfast gave us the energy we needed to plunge into the sea and waiting as we emerged out of the sea was a row of waiters with large towels. It was hysterical. The manager insisted we remain for our stay, two nights. 'Please stay,' he begged offering use of the hotel's boat as a bribe. When I queried the guests, he laughed. 'It's no fun eating alone. By the way, they're looking forward to joining you tonight.'

We sped across the Dalyan Delta, past labyrinths of tall, thick tightly rooted reeds to salty İztuzu Beach, flanked on one side by the fresh water of the Dalyan Delta and on the other by the salty Mediterranean Sea. Almost 5 kilometres long, it is the perfect breeding ground for loggerhead sea turtles to lay their eggs. We crossed on to Caunus to see the great tombs carved out of the cliff and climbed the hill to the theatre and on to Sultaniye, where Emma and I covered our bodies with natural mud spouting from a pool, sunbathed until it caked, then washed it off in a nearby stream. Our skin felt smooth and moist.

Later I learned the reason for the cock-up with the hotel was the girl in charge of our hotel bookings had been fired that morning – we bore the brunt of the girl's revenge against the travel agency!

Whenever Aydın and I drove pass Muğla, we'd spend a night at Dalyan. The reeds are less thick and the natural mud pools now enclosed in smelly public baths, but İztuzu Beach has been saved. In the early 1980's, this fragile breeding ground, threatened by mass tourism, was saved thanks to June Haimoff, a British environmentalist and long-time Dalyan resident. Between 1984 and 1988, June and a group of like-minded environmentalists, including Nergis Yazgan, chairwoman of the Turkish Wildlife Society appealed to Turgut Özal and Prince Philip (then President of the Wildlife Society) for support. They got permission to establish a Sea Turtle Conservation Foundation for the protection of the breeding habitat of loggerhead turtles, those lovable *caretta caretta.* June's work was honoured by Queen Elizabeth in 2011 and in 1997 she wrote a charming book, *Kaptan June and the Turtles*, about her life at Dalyan.

On one trip with the Monsons to Cappadocia at Göreme and Ürgüp with its lunar volcanic weird landscape, fairy chimneys and rock houses, we explored the churches and subterranean tunnels leading to underground cities. Then climbed 400 steps to Ihlara, a valley green with shrubs, poplars and pistachio trees where early Christian monks and hermits took refuge in the 4th century. Finally, wilting from heat and exhaustion we went in search of a decent place to lunch. Aydın drove into a square dominated by an impressive building which I was told was an old Greek Church that had been converted into an Ottoman Post Office, then a depot and now a hotel by Yıldız University, Istanbul.

The snooty young man at the desk was adamant – no, we could not have lunch. The appetizing smells wafting from the kitchen was supper for Greek guests staying at the hotel on a pilgrimage to Greek churches. Just then a corpulent man wearing a cook's hat ambled past. 'Hello,' said I, sniffing the air appreciatively. 'Delicious smells, what's cooking?' True to form, the cook reeled off the dishes in the oven. When I told him of my dilemma and my hungry aristocratic British guests sitting in the car outside, he gave the young man a withering glare and insisted I call them in.

The nave of the church had two long coloured windows of the Virgin Mary and saints set in wood panelled walls. Beams of warming sunshine filtered through the windows. Bach played softly. Four places were set for us at one end of a long trestle table. We sat speechless as we were served a generous slice of freshly baked cheese börek, tender lamb on a puree of aubergines with pilaf, salad and a milky pudding desert, all washed down with cold beer.

The chef joined us for coffee with stories of bearded, mad-hatted, religious fanatics who want to live in caves, hot air balloon experiments and projects for cave hotels; as we thanked him and said good bye, he gave me a box of sweet baklava he had just made for our journey. I will never forget the jolly chef of Cappadocia.

Windsor Castle

Lord and Lady Monson arrived in Istanbul in 1994 at the start of one of our yearly trips to Anatolia. Emma with obvious delight, presented Aydın with a catalogue of photographs from the private Royal Photographic Collection at Windsor Castle and explained the story behind it. The Monsons had donated a collection of photographs of Lady Augusta Monson (1870-1910) to the Windsor Castle Archives. As they chatted over tea with the curator of photography, Miss Frances Dimond, she showed them a copy of that same catalogue for her next exhibition. It was called *Presenting an Image*, 'a selection of photographs from the Queen Mother's personal collection to be shown to the public for the first time'. You can imagine their surprise to see the first photograph was of Shamyl, Imam of Daghestan (1796-1871) in St. Petersburg 1859, and the second, his son, Khazi Mohammed, Aydın's great, great grandfather and great grandfather.

To Aydın's delight, a few weeks later we received an invitation for a private tour of the exhibition and Windsor Castle. Off we went. Frances Dimond was thrilled to meet Aydın, insisting he pose in front of the photographs. Having spent months researching each image she had learnt that they were taken by Andrei Denier, after Shamyl's captivity, during his exile in Russia. The photographs, the provenance of Queen Victoria, were inscribed to the Queen in Arabic and French and sent by Shamyl himself. The Caucasian battle for Independence against the might of the Russian Army was seen as a romantic fight for freedom. In Britain Ladies at court knitted woollen socks, gloves and scarves to be sent to the brave mountain guerrillas. It was a splendid occasion of magnificent rooms and back stairs, 'short cut,' puffed Frances. For Aydın it was an epic experience to see his ancestors honoured at Windsor Castle. The following evening Ivan and Emma gave a splendid party at their home in London to honour the occasion.

Murder

1st November, 1998 began like any other day, except that after weeks of rainy weather, the sun peeped through a clear sky. It was 7am I jumped out of bed to telephone the gardeners who were waiting for a fine day to sow grass in the garden of the house at Demirciköy near the Black Sea. I promised to join them at lunchtime.

At 10.30 a.m. the telephone rang. I knew it was Aydın. Whenever we were apart, wherever I might be, he would telephone on a Sunday morning for a long chat. He sounded pleased to have finished the final chapter of a biography he was writing in English about his paternal grandfather, Osman Ferit Pasha.

His brother, Osman had asked him to go to Izmir together but Aydın preferred to work on the book. He suggested I come but as he was coming to Istanbul the following Tuesday it was hardly worth it. We spoke about the children and Demirciköy. When I inquired about the cotton, his voice took on the usual farmer's moan: early rains had affected the crop, prices were down and, on top of that, Şevket Çetin's cotton had been returned by the co-operative because of dampness, sounding relieved he said he had fired him. About time too. Aydın and his father, Hacı Çetin, had been partners for years without any problem except for Hacı Çetin frequent complaints about his son's work and behaviour and his persistent request that Aydın should speak to him about it. In the midst of a bad season, Aydın decided enough was enough and fired him.

With a 'see you on Tuesday,' we hung up.

An hour or so later, the telephone rang again. It was my son-in-law calling for Ceylan, asking if I had spoken to Aydın. What an odd question, I thought but replied I had. The telephone rang again. Raw howls filled the room.

'Kim *Abla*, 'sister' Kim *Abla*, Kim *Abla*.' It was Bayram, Aydın foreman.

'Bayram, what's the matter? What happened?'

'Kim *Abla,* Kim *Abla*, Kim *Abla.*'

'Where is Aydın Bey? Give the telephone to Aydın Bey.'

'*Öldü! Öldü! Öldü!* Dead! Dead! Dead!'

The telephone fell onto my lap. I could hear Bayram's howls *Kim Abla, Kim Abla, Kim Abla.* Carefully I placed the telephone onto its receiver, the howling stopped. I couldn't breathe. I tried exhaling puffs from my mouth to ease the tightness in my chest. It was hot. The telephone rang. It was Rana. I said, 'Your father is dead'.

'I know. Who told you? We're coming,' she said. The telephone rang and rang and rang. I let it ring.

Ahmet Çifçi, Aydın's cousin had telephoned Rana. Devastated as she was by news that her beloved father had been murdered, she insisted on breaking the news to me herself, hence that strange call from her husband. When they arrived, Rana and I fell into each other's, arms crying and hugging. Arrangements to fly to Izmir had been made. My elder daughter, Ceylan was supervising a university examination so could not be reached. She would take a later flight.

The doorbell rang and there was Ceylan, as surprised to see her sister and husband as we to see her. She told us she couldn't concentrate, felt restless and asked a teacher to stand in for her supervising the exam. Rana told her sister what had happened without a word, she walked to the window and stared out at the Bosphorus. My seventeen years old grandson, Alican at boarding school in Switzerland told me later that he couldn't sleep that night but had tossed and turned until morning not knowing why.

We flew to Izmir. I stared at the clouds floating past the window. We drove to farm at Osmanbükü, together but alone, no one spoke, no tears fell. The konak was full of family members and villagers. Bayram, that proud upright man, sobbed into my hands until one of his sons took him away. A fire burned in the house. Three bullet holes had cracked the wall behind Aydın's chair. He died instantly. Şevket Çetin had shot him and given himself up to the gendarme, military police.

Ceylan's ex-husband Erol and his father, Ali Rıza were first on the scene. It was they who spoke to the police, had the house cleaned then drove to the airport to meet us, but we had missed each other.

I stood detached, insulated by my thoughts, hand out-stretched accepting condolences from a line of grim-faced, silent men before I went inside to sit with red-eyed women who sobbed loudly into the tea they served, sobbed as they threw wood on the fire. I stared at the bullet holes in the wall. I couldn't believe it. This wasn't happening, it wasn't possible. Aydın murdered in his Osmanbükü house, in a village where nothing ever happened, a place he called his sanctuary, safe haven, where he was loved and respected? I couldn't cry, couldn't speak, couldn't feel but then no-one spoke to me, they just kissed my hand and walked away.

The coffin arrived men gathered in groups as prayers were said. In convoy, we drove out of the village, the streets were full of people. As we passed the house Şevket

Çetin's family lived, I shouted, 'Stop the car! I must know how this happened.' Şevket's stepmother was a small, slight woman. She came flying, screaming down the steps, arms outstretched and held me in such a stranglehold I couldn't breathe. She was hysterical and so strong she wouldn't let me go and they couldn't pull me away, one man held her while another huddled me into the car. For days I felt those arms and that iron grip around my chest and heard her screams.

We sat in the cold, empty hangar at Izmir Airport staring at the coffin: a wooden box with no name, no markings. I wondered aloud what would happen if we went to Istanbul but the coffin went to Ankara? Or, what if another coffin came, and we took the wrong one with us? Whipping a VIP tag off her bag, Ceylan banged it onto the coffin. 'Now it will come with us,' she growled.

News travelled fast. The house was full. Ceylan, Rana and her friend, Aslı served me endless cups of tea and plates of food, which I, in turn, offered to whoever sat next to me. I remember an American woman inquired whether I would go back to England now. I hadn't thought of that. The telephone didn't stop ringing. A call came for Ceylan, 'He says he is your father', to which Ceylan replied,' My father is dead'. It was Nil, her biological father, telephoning from London. My daughters sighed with relief when I finally went upstairs. The next day they told me the food and tea they offered me had been spiked with enough sleeping tablets to put an elephant to sleep. Poor guests. Headlines on the front page of Turkish newspapers read, 'English wife forgives man who murdered husband.'

Şevket Çetin had waited for Bayram to leave before coming to the house to ask Aydın to take him back. They argued but Aydın had had enough. Not for the first time had Şevket Çetin's work been below par, kilo per acre average low. That the cotton had not been accepted by the cooperative was just too much in a bad year. Out of sheer frustration, Aydın had said things he shouldn't have.

Şevket had taken out a gun and shot him three times.

Ceylan Pirinçcioğlu attended to the funeral arrangements, for which I am deeply grateful. My only request was we kept in line, in some sort of order. Silent faces filled the crowded courtyard of the mosque as we lined up to accept condolences. Many lowered their eyes as they passed. The Imam read eight-year old Emrecan's letter, written that morning to his beloved grandfather and which Rana placed on the coffin.

Alican flew in from Lyceum Alpinum his boarding school in Switzerland. Fighting back tears, clutching my hand, he whispered, '*Dede,* grandfather would be proud. He died like a soldier.' Muhsin Fazıl, Aydın's favourite Iraqi cousin, marched into the courtyard beside himself with rage and grief, kissed me and marched off.

Nesligah Sultan held me in her arms. 'I grieve with you, Aydın was a lovely man. There is nothing to say,' and walked out of the mosque.

We followed the hearse to the cemetery. People trampled over graves, walked on flowers.

Muslim funerals take place a day or two after death and follows specific rites; this includes repeated prayers for the deceased on the 7th, 40th and 52nd days. Those days of mourning are shared with family, friends, and neighbours, who arrive with offerings of food. Deaths are announced in newspapers in cities and in villages the Imam, acting as town crier, announces the death and time of funeral from the minaret of a mosque. I am a practicing Christian, even so, those rites and the love of my family was a huge comfort.

The 7th prayer day found us at the farm in Osmanbükü. Cemal Çifçi, Aydın's cousin had organized the prayers and refreshments. There was a table for the Imam, chairs for men in the courtyard while the women sat indoors. Before the Imam began his service, I asked if I might address the crowd. I ordered anyone carrying a gun to leave. More than a dozen or so left. Many men in Anatolia possess shot guns and hunting rifles, but a sudden surge in the sales of revolvers and pistols was encouraging people to carry weapons under their jacket, giving them a false sense of confidence.

Hümeyra Hanım greeted me at the door, distressed at not having attended the funeral in Istanbul. The front office manager at the Kısmet Hotel knowing how distraught she would be, had removed the page about the murder from the newspaper, telling her it was an advertisement for the hotel. When the same thing happened the following day, she was not amused and demanded they buy two newspapers. Luckily, her husband, Halil arrived to break the news. 'They treat me like a child,' she complained petulantly. 'Of course, I would have come to Istanbul for the funeral.'

The 40th days prayer was held at Ceylan's house where Aydın had spent many a happy hour playing with Alican.

The 52nd prayer was held in the village mosque in Osmanbükü. We did not attend.

For weeks I felt a hole in the pit of my stomach like a Henry Moore statue. One morning, I woke with tummy intact but an excruciating pain across my shoulder blades, as though they were attached to a steel band. I had had the same, inexplicable pain when my father died, and was the reason I took up yoga. No amount of exercise or massage eased that pain for months.

Life doesn't stop when someone dies. I was numb to the things going on around me. Everyday chores continued but without any participation on my part. Brought up to get on with it, here I was – incapable. I have always been a light sleeper, while Aydın only had to put his head on a pillow. Now I fell asleep the moment my head touched the pillow. I had inherited Aydın's sleeping habit. Daytime was the nightmare.

Mundane tasks exhausted me. When I felt about to explode, I drove to Demirciköy, climbed the cliff, and sat on the edge, watching the mighty Black Sea waves roll, crash and break into white, twirling spray on the rocks below. It was bitterly cold and windy, the sky and sea grey, angry, and lonely, like me. Black cargo ships waited in line to enter the Bosphorus then sail on to an Aegean, Mediterranean or European port. Demirciköy reminded me of South Wales. Birds squawked on cliffs, it was cold and wild, but familiar and somehow comforting, and when the sun came out it warmed my back. It was my place to cry.

Coming to terms with death needs time, a closure but there is no closure in murder. Murder puts mourning on hold until a sentence is pronounced in the trial. Rana recalls that year as a year of vengeful thoughts.

The family flew to Aydın on March 1st 1999, my birthday, to attend the last court hearing when the judge was due to pronounce sentence. Waiting in the crowded hall outside the courtroom, I looked at the men from the village. I knew many by name but they shied away from my gaze. Years of a shared way of life had been shot away from the barrel of a gun. I sat with Ceylan and Bayram at the back of the courthouse. Bayram, suddenly a broken old man suffering from cancer held my hand. The judge sat. Lawyers spoke their piece, twisting the truth into that age-old scenario: rich landowner, poor villager. Rana, ashen-faced, fought back tears as she rose to speak in defence of her father. I wanted to speak, but choked. I couldn't breathe. I slipped out of the courthouse and crossed the street. There was nowhere to sit. I leaned against a car in the car park, silent tears fell. Anger and betrayal surged through my body. I was so alone, grieving in a town that I came to 36 years ago, but still did not belong. I was the outsider, the *yabancı.* An old man offered me a glass of tea. I returned to the courthouse as the judge was reading the verdict. Şevket Çetin was sentenced to sixteen years imprisonment. As we walked out of the courtroom someone behind us said Şevket would be out in a year or so. Bayram swung around and grabbed the man's jacket: 'Tell him I will be waiting for him with Aydın Bey's gun,' he shouted. Bayram died a year later.

I needed to be alone. On the pretext of checking an itinerary for an upcoming tour of historical sites for members of the American World Monument Foundation, I set off on a journey from Aydın to Antalya with a dour mini-bus driver, Mehmet not at all pleased at having to drive across Anatolia in cold, wintry March. There were no springs in the suspension and at each crossroad Mehmet took the wrong turning. Once we landed half way up a snow-topped mountain. Battered, bruised, cold, and hungry after bumping along rough roads for hours, I made superficial inspections of sites and hotels before falling into bed.

We arrived at Olympus in the late afternoon. The climb to the top would take thirty minutes. Mehmet grumbled it was too late and about to get dark. I told him to wait, and set off at a brisk pace. I climbed the winding stony path in a forest of bay, oleanders and pine trees. Far below, vineyards and green fields disappeared in the rising mist. The chief deity of Olympus was Hephaestus, god of fire and blacksmiths. As if on a pilgrimage, I quickened my steps, desperate to see the eternal flame called Chimera after the mythical monster with the head of a lion, the body of a goat and the tail of a serpent, who roamed the woods spouting fire. The nearer I got, the more eager I became to see something eternal.

I reached the top to find the eternal flame was covered with a big, black kettle and a young boy, portable radio glued to his ear was listening to a football match. Falling to the ground in exhaustion, I laughed and laughed until laughter turned to sobs. The boy kept bringing me tea and paper napkins to cry into, as he kept up a running commentary on the match. Darkness fell. 'I'll put these away. We'll go down together,' he said. I watched him lock the glasses and kettle into a large, heavy tin trunk, freeing at last the eternal flame. I prayed to Hephaestus. It was dark and bitterly cold. He put his coat over my shoulders. 'Let's go,' he said, and taking my hand, he led me down the hill.

As though sobbing women were regular eternal flame visitors, he hadn't asked why I was crying, but instead comforted me in the only way he knew – with glasses of tea and a running commentary of the football. He was a young Samaritan, holding my hand tightly as we ventured down in the dark. I slipped, he picked me up, 'Opps' and laughed, his natural kindness and humanity for one so young comforted, warmed me. As he handed me over to Mehmet, I thanked him with a tip that brought a huge smile to his freckled face. We said goodbye, I didn't even know his name but the eternal flame had worked its magic. I felt calm.

My last port of call was Antalya. After a light supper, I collapsed in comfort at the Divan Hotel. The next day I lunched with the curator of the Antalya Museum and Orhan Akyavaş before flying back to Istanbul.

Super-sensitive, vulnerable, fragile, you name it I felt it, I preferred being alone although Ceylan, Rana, Nur and Fatoş stayed close-by. When terrible things happen, it is surprising who turns up to help and who doesn't. 'Do what you have to now, because later you'll feel very tired,' was my friend, Ayşe Sılan's wise advice when she telephoned.

And how right she was, grief is emotionally, mentally and physically exhausting. I knew I had to reconstruct my life, but I didn't have a clue where to begin – nor did I have the energy. It was an *annus horriblis* – a year my daughters and I never speak of.

I would sense people whispering as I entered a room: 'Her husband was murdered.' Being an object of pity is unpleasant, it's offensive. I did not want my husband's murder to be part of my identity – nor did I want Aydın to be remembered because of a violent death. It is painful enough to lose someone you love without gossip. Murder happens to other people, in newspapers or films, not to Aydın in a quiet village. Murder has a stigma. Murder has no closure.

But you survive and little by little things get back on track as daily necessities draw you into the present. My first evening out was dinner and a film with Fatoş and Haldun Erkman. The opening scene in the movie was a man being shot. Haldun was mortified and scolded poor Fatoş throughout the film. 'How was I to know,' she whispered miserably. In the darkness, I grinned at its black humour.

Fleeting moments of guilt at being alive came and passed but I was overcome with the deepest sense of loss as I arranged Aydın's library in Rana's house, a rare collection of titles specializing on the Caucasus, Russia and Eastern Europe which he valued so much. Some were inherited, others bought after a long search in antiquarian bookshops in London and Istanbul. It took me three days. Books have their own special intimacy and smell, they become part of your life and it's sad when they are gone. But life moves on, time blurs that lingering sadness into acceptance, you change and become a different person. After all death is part of life and bad things happen to good people.

But after the bedroom door is closed and you are alone you miss the intimacy and cosiness of sharing your day with someone you know so well and have been married to for more than 37 years. You miss the pillow talk I suppose.

Aydın left a lasting impression on everyone he met. In his introduction to Aydın's posthumously published book, *Tarih Boyunca Kafkasya*, Laurence Kelly wrote, 'in 1998, Turkey was deprived of one of its most talented, original and unusual personalities by the violent death of Aydın Osman Erkan'.

Rana's Poem written in February 1999:

He had books
Dusty, bound in leather and gold
He had stories
Chevaliers, princes, princesses
He had heroes
Fearless, proud, lonely,
He had dreams
Hazy, distant, unreachable
He had ideas
Honest, decisive, wise
He had collections
Meticulously kept, protected, valuable
He had songs
Old, melodious, joyful,
He had ancestry
Aristocratic, proud, brave,

He had style
Modest, responsible, gentlemanly,
He had friends
Few, trustworthy, private
He had loved ones
His wife, daughters, grandchildren
He had values
Honesty, respect, loyalty
He had pleasures
His farmhouse, fields, peasants
And he had guns
Locked, unloaded, licensed
He had fears
Bigotry, poverty, ignorance
An ignorant peasant shot him in cold blood
Without reason, without pity
He had a life
The life he lived.
The life he gave.
And the life he will live forever.

Dedeye son mektup

Aydın Osman Erkan'ın eşi Joan Kim Erkan, torunu Alican Özbaş'la taziyetleri kabul etti.

CİNAYETE kurban giden VİP Turizm'in sahiplerinden **Rana Pirinçcioğlu**'nun babası ve Çeçen Halk Kahramanı **Şeyh Şamil**'in ikinci kuşaktan torunu olan **Aydın Osman Erkan,** dün Teşvikiye Camii'nde kılınan öğle namazından sonra Zincirlikuyu Aile Kabristanı'nda toprağa verildi.

Aydın'ın İncirliova İlçesi Osmabükü Köyü'nde 25 yıldır tarlasını kiraya verdiği, ancak bu yıl anlaşamadığı **Şevket Çetin** tarafından öldürülen 66 yaşındaki **Erkan**'ın cenazesinde, turizm, siyaset ve iş dünyası bir araya geldi. Camiye getirilmeyen 8 yaşındaki **Emrecan**'ın dedesinin ölümü üzerine yazdığı şiirin tabutun üzerine konulması duygulu anlar yaşanmasına neden oldu. "Aydın **Dede seni çok seviyorum. Hatta inanılmaz seviyorum. Sana en son hediyemi verdim. 1 Kasım Pazar 1998 yılında öldün. Biraz daha yaşasaydın. Bir-iki yıl, bir-iki ay, en azından bir-iki gün daha yaşasaydın. Artık çok geç. Ya cennete gideceksin ya da başka bir hayatla dünyaya döneceksin**" diye yazan **Emrecan**'ın şiiri namazı kıldıran hoca tarafından da okundu.

■ Cahit AKYOL
Mustafa KÜÇÜK / İSTANBUL

Rana's Tears

Reprieve, September, 1999

Mrs. Rahşan Ecevit, wife of Prime Minister Bülent Ecevit was on a prison visit when she was overcome at the sight of a baby in the arms of an inmate. She decided, there and then, there should be an amnesty for non-political prisoners: an *af*, 'a general reprieve', no matter what crime had been committed. It seemed that law and justice were over-ruled by the whim of a woman without any political authority or clout, other than that she was the Prime Minister's wife. There was widespread outcry from judges, lawyers, journalists, teachers, and doctors who sent emails, signatures and letters galore to the government condemning the proposal, but to no avail.

Night after night, Ceylan and I watched Rana on television at meetings with other family members who had suffered at the hands of criminals crying, raging, appealing against the injustice and illegality of such a decree. I could stand it no longer and begged Rana to stop. She didn't.

This is an extract from an article written at the time by Zülfü Livaneli, composer, singer, writer, columnist and film director in the Sabah newspaper;

> *'I always see Rana with a big smile. Be it on TV, the street or at a party, her beautiful warm smile would welcome us. So, I was shocked to see her tears, crying on TV, for the first time. She cried because her heart ached. They were tears of anger, resentment against the release from prison of the man who murdered her father... Next to her sat others who suffered the same injustice, their tears burned deep in the hearts of thousands of families whose loved ones had faced similar ordeals at the hands of criminals. They cried 'is this a penalty for believing in justice? Only we have the right to forgive...' Would Rahşan Ecevit be as forgiving had it happened to her husband, Bülent Ecevit? This amnesty called 'penalty reduction' will not serve social justice, but further increase injustices in the country. The state*

does not forgive crimes committed against the state, but forgives murderers who kill the fathers, mothers and children of its citizens. While writing this I learned that those convicted of torture were covered by this amnesty. There is nothing left to say… We declare we are on the side of Rana and relatives of victims; we respect their pain and strongly condemn politicians who forgive torturers. Public conscience will never forgive you.'

One day the telephone rang. An uncouth, dark voice demanded to speak to Rana. The man was an inmate in a prison in Anatolia who began threatening her to stop her campaign against the reprieve – or else. With extra-ordinary composure, Rana explained, as though she was speaking to a child, the reason she was against the decree. She spoke of a need for justice, her love for her father. 'If you had a daughter wouldn't she do the same?' she asked.

The caller listened without interruption. Then, with a little more restraint applauded her loyalty and love for her father, cursing the man who had caused her so much suffering and wishing her well – but adding that he and his mates still wanted to be set free. After a pause, the menacing tone returned as he told her that there was a way to satisfy them both. All she had to do was say the word, give the name and the prison, and it would be dealt with… Rana thanked him, but declined the offer.

For a while Rana went around with a bodyguard, who took it upon himself to guard her every movement. After bumping into him, arms folded, in front of the loo door at the Conrad Hotel, she decided she was safe enough.

The reprieve passed. Şevket Çetin was freed after one and a half years in prison. Another *annus horriblis* for us and others in the same position as perpetrators walked free and prison gates swung open. Thousands of inmates were released onto the streets many to return within months. The mother and child were not released.

I had insisted on going to the farm alone. Ceylan and Rana weren't keen, but wise enough to comply rather than fuss. Bayram had chosen his elder son, Zeki, to take over as farm manager. A few months later Bayram died, not from the cancer that racked his body, but from a broken heart. The konak gate at Osmanbükü was rusty. The house was in dire need of a coat of paint; the walls were flaked with dampness and gutted by three bullet holes. I was presented with scraps of paper – expenses. I asked for a meeting with Aydın's *ortaklar*, partners. There was a lot to do which helped me overcome my own grief and vulnerability.

Six sombre farmers sat uncomfortably around the table in the garden of the konak drinking tea with the widow, foreign at that, of their murdered Bey. I had prepared a little speech, that I had no intention of selling the farm but would keep farming and wanted them to work for me as they had for Aydın. I had two conditions. I would not work with anyone who carried a gun nor would I pay any bills without proper

ZÜLFÜ LİVANELİ

Dünya Değişirken

e-mail: livaneli@sabah.com.tr

Rana'nın gözyaşları - Rana's tears

Rana Pirinççioğlu'nu hep gülerken görmüştüm. Ekranda olsun, günlük hayatta olsun, iyiniyetli, aydınlık bir gülümseme yüzünden hiç eksik olmazdı.

İlk kez kendini tutamayıp gözyaşlarına boğulduğunu görünce sarsıldım doğrusu.

Ağlıyordu çünkü içi yanıyordu.

Babasını öldüren adamın sokaklara salınmasına isyan eden gözyaşlarıydı bunlar.

Yanında **Boray Uras** vardı: **Ölmeyi ve öldürmeyi düşündüğünü anlatıyordu.** Kızını yitirmiş olan babanın bu sözü son derece önemliydi: Ölmek ve öldürmek noktalarına sürükleniyordu Türk insanı.

Mustafa Ünsal ve **Mümin Karaca** da Boray bey gibi, kızlarını trafikte kurban vermişlerdi. Onlar da ölmeyi ve öldürmeyi düşünmüşlerdi herhalde.

Nazan Odabaşı'nın ağabeyi kurşunlanarak öldürülmüştü.

Ayten Arslan bıçak darbeleriyle can veren kızının acısıyla toplantıya katılıyordu.

Bu yaralı insanlardan yükselen çığlık **Or-An** semtine ulaşamıyordu ama yakınlarını kurban veren binlerce aileyi kezzap gibi yakıyordu.

"**Adalete güvenmenin cezasını çekiyoruz!**" diyorlardı.

"**Yıllardır her gün ölüyoruz!**" diyorlardı.

"**Sadece biz affedebiliriz!**" diyorlardı. "**Bülent Ecevit'e bir şey olsa Rahşan Ecevit yine affeder miydi?**" diye soruyorlardı.

★★★

Artık iyice ortaya çıktı ki ceza indirimi dedikleri bu af, sosyal barışa değil, tam tersine bu ülkedeki adaletsizliğin artmasına yardım edecek.

Devlet, kendisine karşı işlenmiş suçları affetmiyor ama yurttaşların çocuklarını, eşlerini ana babalarını öldüren katilleri bağışlıyor.

Böylece dünyanın en saçma, en haksız, en adaletsiz affına imza atıyor bu hükümet.

★★★

Oğlu **Erdim**'i canilere kurban veren **Metin Sertoğlu**, binlerce kurban adına bu affa isyan ediyor. Diyor ki: "**Aldığım yüzlerce mağdur aile mektuplarından esinlenip isyan bayrağını çekmekle kendimi görevlendirdim. Bu yazdıklarım, haksızca öldürülen insanların ruhlarına armağan olsun isterim.**"

★★★

Bu yazıyı yazarken, işkence suçlularının da af kapsamına alındığını öğrendim.

Pes!

Rahşan hanımın bir sözünün, koskoca ülkeyi böylesine bir adaletsizliğe sürükleyebilmesine hayret ediyorum.

DSP'deki arkadaşlarımız, bu işi nasıl içlerine sindirebiliyorlar?

İçleri yanan mağdur ailelerinin acısını bin kat artıracak böyle bir haksızlığa nasıl göz yumuyorlar, neden seslerini yükseltmiyorlar, neden itiraz etmiyorlar anlayamıyorum.

Diktatörlük mü burası!

O arkadaşlarımız arasında sol geçmişleriyle, insan hakları mücadeleleriyle övünen kişiler var.

Niye susuyorlar?

Biz kalemimizle **Rana**'nın ve mağdur yakınlarının yanında olduğumuzu ilan ediyoruz.

Onların acısına saygı duyuyor ve işkencecileri affetmeye uğraşan siyasetçileri şiddetle kınıyoruz.

Halk vicdanı sizi affetmeyecek!

receipts. No more little bits of paper. They listened in silence, nodded in agreement and with a '*Başınız sağ olsun* – our condolences', we shook hands and they left.

The house was cold and damp, even though a fire burned. I sifted through bundles of old papers, bills, read letters and looked at old photographs. I didn't cry, nor was I overwhelmed with sadness. Since that telephone from Bayram I had felt detached from everybody and everything – until the electricity was cut.

Everyone had an Aydın Bey story: the electrician and iron-smith who came to repair the gate told me how Bey had bought them a football and allowed them to play in the konak and how during difficult years Bey would give the third pickings of cotton to his partners. A white-haired man dropped by to tell me that Aydın Bey wouldn't harm a fly, said a prayer and left: an old lady came crying into the food she brought me as she spoke of days gone by when most of the villagers including her family were married at the konak.

I listened to these good people digging my nails into the palm of my hand until it hurt to stop me screaming out, 'then why was your Bey murdered?' I had the iron konak gate painted green with Aydın Osman Erkan written in black.

I flew to London where Turkish Ambassador Özdem Sanberk and his wife Sumru Sanberk graciously hosted a memorial service for Aydın's friends at the Turkish Embassy in Portland Place. Özdem Bey is highly thought of as one of the most distinguished Turkish Ambassadors to be posted to London.

Reading an article about Swedish biopath and reflexologist, Gudrun Jonsson in the Sunday Telegraph, I telephoned for an appointment only to be told that there was a long waiting list. I was leaving London in a few days. The secretary asked where I lived and, as it was quite close, suggested she call if there was a cancellation. A few days later around 10 p.m., she called asking if I could be at the surgery at 8 a.m. the following morning.

There was no time to fill in the four-page form of personal data before I found myself in the presence of Gudrun Jonsson, a healthy, blond Swede. She immediately set to work on my feet. It was agony and so painful I cried. Miss Jonsson raised her eyebrows. This was followed with a pencil-like electric instrument placed between my toes and fingers. She didn't say a word throughout the treatment. After she had finished, she gave a deep sigh, sat back piercing me with those eyes, then taking my hands in hers, gently asked, 'Tell me what happened. Your body is on red alert, your immune system near collapse. If you hadn't come to me today, you would be in hospital within a few weeks.'

I told her. She listened without interruption, then she explained how the mind and body handles stress. Continuous stress puts pressure on the nervous system and weakens the immune system. The more stressed you are, the more care you should take of your body. I was on the edge of a collapse.

I returned to Istanbul with a suitcase of organic products, a personalized diet and telephone number to report progress. Determined not to collapse I became a dedicated Gudrun Jonsson patient, following her advice and booking my yearly appointment well in advance until she retired to India a few years ago.

Şevket Çetin had returned to the village. I did not change my routine but continued to go to Osmanbükü only leaving the konak to walk around the fields with Zeki close by my side. Neither did I greet any of the villagers.

An interest in organic food and Christmas hampers brought Ceylan to the farm. Without a thought, in her usual easy-going manner, she gathered the village women to the konak to teach her how to dry vegetables in the sun, pickle cucumbers, preserve jams and paint boxes. The iron gate of the konak was flung open, and in doing so, Ceylan healed my relationships with the villagers. I was touched and more than a little ashamed of myself when my neighbour, Ilknur, who had looked after Aydın tearfully related how my cold attitude towards the women had upset them so much they were about to ask Cemal Çifçi to act as intermediary.

21th Century

There was little for the government in Ankara to celebrate in the 21st century, overwhelmed as ministers were with uncertainties. It was a sad state of affairs indeed to begin a new decade and was not helped at all by public clashes and disputes between President Ahmet Necdet and Prime Minister Bülent Ecevit. The lira had lost half its value, there was a sharp decline in foreign investments, bad credit interest rates rocketed, the stock exchange plunged and banks closed or were taken over. And citizens, weary of economic instability and warring political parties demonstrated their frustration at the up and coming election when Turkish politics dramatically changed.

On the 3rd of November 2002, 'the Justice and Development Party', *Adalet ve Kalkınma Partisi, AKP*, a newly formed party won the general election with 34.3 % of the ballot and 363 seats, more than enough to form a government. The first single party to do so since 1987. Years of political uncertainty ended with hope that a one-party government would bring the stability needed to encourage growth and economic reform within the business sector. AKP, a party which claimed to be secular Muslim democrats, not unlike Christian democrats in Europe and America, came to power with Abdullah Gül as prime minister. In 2003, Recep Tayyip Erdoğan became prime minister.

At first AKP was conscientious, Istanbul became cleaner and greener but they were not slow in introducing changes. In accordance with demands made by the European Union Committee to be considered as a candidate, a number of laws were passed. Many were passed but few put into practice. I certainly couldn't follow what was going on, but when a friend was having problems to spend his rightful time with his son because of a wife behaving badly in an ugly divorce, I advised him to apply to the European court under the 'father's right' law. His lawyer didn't even know it existed.

It soon became clear that many of these reforms and laws involved the start of a cultural movement and change of direction in Turkish politics. Amazingly, the most visible change occurred in woman's fashions. By 2013, to the relief of the headscarf groups, the ban on wearing headscarves was lifted and being covered become the norm. Students, covered or not, walked arm in arm in schools and universities, worked as government employees and in the private sector.

This demand for headscarves and ankle length, more subdued dress-wear not only changed the female countenance on the street, but has become a thriving business. Throughout history, fashion has been a communicative power which defines personality and status, how one acts and presents oneself. Fashion makes a public statement which can be social, political or religious and therefore might be controversial.

In 2014, after serving three terms as prime minister, Recep Tayyip Erdoğan was elected President.

As in many countries in Europe and America there were large scale demonstrations in Turkey against the war in Iraq.

Family Life

Family life can be messy. Its saving grace is its spirit, that love and support which is able to overcome the ups and downs we all experience at some time. As a person who had never strayed far from my comfort zone, a family, I desperately needed that support and empathy to face the future.

Most people were unaware that Ceylan and Rana had different fathers. Aydın sufficed them both. We never thought about being good parents perhaps we weren't. I did have one maxim which worked and that was, 'Let's have a cup of tea and think about it'. We did what came naturally, loving and scolding as seemed fit. Ceylan and Rana belong to a generation that don't blame parents for their own faults and failures.

With politics in the 70's disrupting education and life, Ceylan was sent to Wales to take her A-levels at St. Clare's Catholic School in Porthcawl (at her graduation, the Head Mistress said, 'Ceylan fitted into our school well, she is a lovely, intelligent girl, what a pity she is not Catholic!'). In her first year at university, she eloped to Miami with her childhood sweetheart, Erol Özbaş, Ali Rıza and Melike Özbaş's son. What a drama that was! They both graduated in hotel management and economics from Florida International University, after which they returned to Turkey to work in the family-owned, Imbat Hotel in Kuşadası. When they were three years old, Ceylan and Erol fought over a tricycle. After their marriage, too young, too wild, they loved and fought until the marriage ended in divorce soon after the birth of their son, Alican.

Ceylan with her son moved to Istanbul and she began work as Public Relations and Advertising Manager at the Sheraton Hotel until she decided on an academic career. She taught Tourism and Hotel Management at Marmara University, Yeditepe University, and also lectured at Istanbul University.

While teaching at Istanbul University, a memo was sent around decreasing the course timetable from 14 hours to 9. Ceylan was concerned, and being Ceylan fought the decision tooth and nail. She raved to anyone who listened that the course was incomplete and students would graduate without the necessary tools for a successful career in the hospitality industry. One evening I stopped over at her flat at Gümuşsuyu to find a dozen or so students sitting on the floor. Beaming triumphantly, she explained: 'I decided to give those extra classes to anyone who wants them at home.' And so, until the end of term, I saw that hungry students eager to learn had tea and sandwiches to sustain them. Today those students hold managerial positions in Turkey's leading hotel sector. After resigning from the university, Ceylan organised seminars for private companies.

Ceylan was born blond, blue-eyed and beautiful and today, without making the slightest effort, remains so. Intelligent, fun, brave and stubborn, her emotional energy and outbursts cloak a free-spirit. Ceylan has no personal agenda – you get what you see with Ceylan – which can be exhausting and exasperating. Like my mother, she is a hoarder; her home is full of books, bric-a-brac, old photographs and clothes she never wears. Whatever catches her attention at that moment, be it teaching, lecturing, travelling, gardening, organic food, jam making, or Christmas hampers becomes the centre of her life (and from necessity, ours too) until something else comes along, that is. Ceylan is a loyal friend with a lioness protective instinct towards the family. She judges a person by their eyes: 'he doesn't have smiley eyes,' she'll whisper and often she is right.

Rana went to an English boarding school in New Milton. She was 11 and has never forgiven me! At the end of her first year she refused to return to school. Having paid a term in advance, I insisted. Folding her arms, an unusually determined look on that sweet, round face, she told me: 'Then I won't go to school. Children who are unhappy at home go to boarding school. I am very happy at home, thank you. I can read and write. That's enough for me.' I lost my deposit. She attended the English School for Girls in Istanbul, which, by the way, is an excellent school, but a scary shoot-out in İstiklal Avenue, Beyoğlu shattering the windows of her classroom as students took cover under their desks proved me point that politics was disrupting education. Older and wiser she graduated from Queen's Gate School, London. One day she telephoned her father nearly in tears. In class, the history teacher had read a chapter from a history book about 'the barbarian Turk…' Frightfully embarrassed she wanted to know why. Aydın promised to research the incident and wrote a four-page paper relating events from the Turkish standpoint. Rana presented it to the history teacher, who was so impressed she read Aydın's paper to the class and apologised to Rana.

Her working life began at VIP Tourism, a family owned company when she married Ceylan Pirinçcioğlu. Around this time, Cem Hakko, a close friend had set up a music radio station called Power FM and he persuaded Rana to DJ a breakfast show called 'Coffee Time'. The show was hugely successful and made her a household name. She possesses that rare natural broadcaster's voice – beautifully modulated, rounded and warm – and expresses herself with clarity and originality. Those years on the radio and later television served her well throughout her career as DJ, TV presenter and Master of Ceremonies.

How many mothers can say, 'My daughter danced with Nureyev?'. When Rudolf Nureyev performed at the Atatürk Cultural Centre, a private party was given in his honour and there she did dance with Nureyev; she was so inspired she ended doing the splits. The next morning, she telephoned in agony and was rushed off to the American Hospital for an appendix operation. Nureyev sent a sympathetic note with a huge bunch of red roses.

Rana is dark haired with hazel eyes that crinkle when she smiles, beautiful, loving and generous to a fault, respectful to elders and like her father honest to the core. A multi-tasker, she has a strong sense of responsibility and believes everyone has the same high principles and standards as herself, which of course often backfires. She is quick-witted, funny and versatile and tends to see the funny side of life. Rana will go out of her way to please family and friends but keeps her own feelings well in check. Even when she was a teenager, she had a natural eye and contained refinement which over the years has developed but no changed much and which expresses her style and personality, simple, monotoned elegance (her daughter, Selina has inherited her style).

Aydın and I were besotted grandparents and it has been a privilege and joy to be part of their lives. Our first grandson, Ceylan's son, blond, blue-eyed Alican Özbaş, was born on January 11th, 1983 in Izmir. One golden autumn afternoon walking across a field of wild flowers and butterflies behind Rose Cottage with Maço, her German shepherd dog looking young and vulnerable in a simple cotton smock, Ceylan stopped at the top of the hill, stretched her arms out wide and shook her long blond hair. Lifting her face to the sky she shouted, 'Dear God! I feel so full of love for the world, I am going to burst,' and whirled into a dance.

Glowing and cuddly plump after the craziest baby shower ever, Rana and I set off to London to prepare the flat for the birth of her first child. I sewed a splendid Moses basket in blue satin for my second grandson. Rana said I was difficult, menopause-ish and having an affair with Peter Jones. All utter nonsense – Peter Jones is the name of a shop in Sloane Square! I put it down to her over-active hormones. Her son, Emrecan Pirinççioğlu, dark-haired with big expressive eyes was born on the 4th of July, 1990 at the Lindo wing of St. Mary's Hospital in London. Grandparents and siblings flew in from Istanbul to celebrate. I prepared mountains of cucumber and salmon sandwiches to serve with a celebratory glass of wine.

Surprise, surprise, ten years later, Rana gave birth to a beautiful baby girl, Selina Pirinççioğlu, born on 1st September, 2000, at the same hospital as her brother. Out came the Moses basket covered, this time, with pink satin ribbons and bows. Selina's birth brought hope, love and joy into our lives.

Two great-grandsons followed when Alican and his Swiss wife, Chantal, his school sweet-heart at Lyceum Alpinum in Swizerland gave birth, first on 2015 and then on 2019 to two gorgeous blond, blue-eyed boys, Erol Emil and Oskar Ali Özbaş. Alican and Chantal had settled in Kuşadası and while Alican busied himself with the family business, Chantal with her partner, Monica Özkaya set up Bird Island Farm, an animal sanctuary in the hills of Kuşadası. There, these two young animal lovers with Turkish husbands, work very hard indeed training dogs and caring for animals who have been badly mistreated by us, human beings.

On August 17th 1999, I caught the last flight from Bodrum to Istanbul, arriving home at Beşiktaş well past midnight. I showered and collapsed into bed only to be woken by what I thought was someone shaking the bed. There were shouts, someone was banging the door, ringing the doorbell, shouting 'get out, get out, earthquake, earthquake.'

It was 3 a.m. I pulled on a tracksuit, reached for my handbag, and made for the stairs. It was pitch black I felt my way down guided by my hand on the wall until a torch shone in my face. The park and street in front of the house was full of people, some still in their pyjamas, strangely quiet as they busied themselves carrying chairs, blankets and cushions to women comforting babies and small children clinging to their skirts. Car doors flew open for the sick and old. As daylight broke, we were told to move to Yıldız Mosque, a few metres up the hill, where food, water and tents were being set up. I knew that buildings on the hill of Beşiktaş had a rock foundation and instead, returned to the apartment. A quick inspection revealed not even a crack in the walls. With Ceylan and Alican in Bodrum, Rana insisted I stay with her in Vaniköy on the Asian side of the Bosphorus.

The earthquake could not have hit at a worst time, when everyone was asleep. The epicentre hit the densely populated industrial urban province of Kocaeli and Gölcük, eastern Marmara, at 7.4 on the Richter scale. The after-shock lasted 35 seconds. The official death rate was 17,480 but believed to be much greater. 43,000 were wounded and more than 600,000 left homeless in and around Kocaeli, Sakarya, Yalova and Istanbul. Fearing that the next earthquake would hit Istanbul, people slept outdoors in makeshift tents, in sleeping bags on park benches, and in cars for weeks. There was a rush on crisis earthquake bags, dried foods, blankets, first aid kits and cash.

The government was slow to react, but volunteers turned up in droves. Ceylan, with her university team collected and sent truckloads of food, clothes, books, toys and medical supplies to distributing centres, hospitals and schools. Rana, her husband and friends joined forces with *CYDD*, 'the Association for the Support of Contemporary Living', founded by the late Prof. Dr. Türkan Saylan. Early in the morning they flew to Izmit to return late in the evening then sit in front of telephones cajoling, begging, demanding donations to build pre-fabricated houses.

One day, after taking hours to save and settle a wounded man in hospital, Rana discovered watches, jewellery and cash stuffed in his pockets. 'He was looting,' she cried. 'I should have left him there.'

I kept my eye on Emrecan, who thought sleeping in a tent in the garden, great fun. One evening sitting on the balcony, a fresh breeze blowing across the Bosphorus, ships silently passing by, Rana reminded us how fortunate we were when there was so much destruction and suffering. On November 12th 1999, another major earthquake erupted at Düzce, 7.2 on the Richter scale, resulting in 900 deaths.

The Marmara disaster aroused earthquake awareness in Turkey. There had been warnings beforehand, but these were ignored. Shoddy construction, poor workmanship, unsuitable locations and a complete lack of building regulations and safety laws were the main cause of much of the destruction and high death rate. Building regulations were put into force and today buildings require official earthquake proof certificates to be insured. People have short memories, though, and unethical contractors, given half a chance, are still far more concerned with a profit margin than safety. More has to be done to ensure earthquake awareness is kept alive. After all, Turkey is earthquake country.

Alican was a student at Lyceum Alpinum in Switzerland and found a way to contribute to the emergency by collecting money in a way which impressed all of us including his IB Co-ordinator, Peter Pasquill, who wrote this letter to his mother:

Dear Mrs. Arbel,

This is a short message to let you know how proud we are of Alican's work for the earthquake victims in Turkey. Yesterday he worked non-stop until late in the evening selling kebabs at a market stall in St Moritz along with other Turkish students. It was a freezing cold afternoon and evening, but Alican was untiring in his efforts and was a shining example to them all. He deserves the highest praise… The students collected over SFr 2000 – all of which will be donated to the earthquake relief fund.

Bombs

On November 15th 2003, suicide bombers in two trucks carrying bombs blew up the Bet Israel and Neve Shalom synagogues at Galata, Beyoğlu, blasting the buildings, killing 27 and injuring 300. The busy, narrow street was left a rubble of concrete, shards of glass, and blown-off doors. It was an evil, premeditated act, designed to kill as many innocent people at prayer as possible. There was rumour that this attack was linked to Al-Qaeda.

Five days later, on November 20th, a crisp Thursday autumn morning, my daughter Ceylan and I met for coffee in Nişantaşı before I was to collect my grand-daughter Selina, then 3 years old, from Papatya, an English pre-school. It was an ordinary, quiet morning. We sat watching shoppers strolling past and the 'simit-man' set up his glass-covered tray of fresh 'simits' in time for the lunch-break at his usual place next to the flower-seller. Suddenly a horrendous explosion made us jump, black smoke billowed in the distance 'British Consulate bombed,' came a shout. Chaos and confusion broke out. People screaming into their mobile phones ran, cars drove on pavements. We rose to go to the Consulate when a louder, nearer explosion and more black smoke billowed in our direction. 'The HSBC Bank in Levent,' screamed a voice. That was close enough to Selina's school for us to panic. Ceylan jumped in front of a taxi as it pulled out. She wrenched the door open, pushed me inside, and ordered the driver to take us to the school. The drive was horrendous. The roads were blocked so eventually we got out and ran down side streets. Arriving at the school, the yard swarmed with parents. Children held hands in small groups huddling around their class teachers who, striving for calm, would hand out children to their parents as they arrived. Rana had already taken Selina. To get there so fast, Rana must have flown, swum the Bosphorus, or already been in town. Relieved, Ceylan and I collapsed on the wall watching frantic mothers and angry fathers swoop away offspring, leaving those brave teachers to comfort the remaining few.

Innocent people died and buildings were destroyed. Amongst those killed was popular actor and singer Kerem Yılmazer, waiting at a traffic light to cross the road. I dropped Ceylan home then walked to the British Consulate until I was stopped by police. A suicide bomber had driven a lorry of bombs into the gate, killing 30 and wounding 400 British and Turkish people. I could taste dust, smell burning, hear police whistles, firemen shouting orders, and ambulances screeching. So much confusion and pain I felt sick – how easy it is to destroy, blow up a building, drop a bomb, pull a trigger, kill, take a life. It was dark. I went home.

Two days previously I had attended evening prayers at the Crimean Church for leaders of all Christian faiths in Istanbul, presided over by the then-Archbishop of Canterbury, Rowan Williams. Afterwards there was a reception at the home of the Consul General and his wife, Roger and Victoria Short, on the hill of Beşiktaş just below our apartment. The elderly, corpulent Christian leaders, resplendent in strange garb with long beards and large appetites included the Greek Patriarch, Armenian Archbishop, Catholic and Church of England priests, Jewish, Sephardic and Syriac made short work of the grand dinner prepared by their hostess. Rowan Williams and I got on famously, exchanging stories of our Welsh childhood. As I was leaving, I thanked Roger for a splendid evening. 'Yes indeed,' he enthused. 'You know, I think it is one of the best parties I've ever given.'

It was to be the last party he ever gave. Just two days later, Roger and Victoria drove from their Beşiktaş home to the Consulate. Before turning into the grounds, Victoria got out of the car to buy milk. Roger Short was killed by the bomb, Victoria was saved.

In 1968, Roger Short, then a young diplomat, had driven his shiny Triumph Spitfire through Europe to Ankara to take up his first post, unaware, as his daughter wrote later, 'how deeply Turkey would plant roots in his life.' Victoria and Roger were engaged in Istanbul and married in England and later, with his wife and three children, Roger Short returned to Istanbul as Consul General. A seasoned diplomat, he used his estimable business skills to promote trade and investments between Britain and Turkey. He presided over an extensive expatriate community and was a popular figure within the diplomatic circle where he and his wife had many foreign and Turkish friends. So strong were their ties and particular love for Turkey and its Ottoman heritage that the Shorts were considering making their home in Istanbul after Roger's retirement.

After Roger's death, Victoria did remain in Istanbul while her children attended boarding schools in England. She resides in a lovely apartment over-looking the Bosphorus near the Crimean Church. An active member of the church council and British community, she is a much sought-after landscape gardener who tends to the British Consulate garden as well as many other private gardens in Istanbul.

With her three children and friends, they set up the Roger Short Memorial Fund at University College Oxford, which offers grants and travel awards to promote inter-culture exchange in keeping with Roger's ideals and motto, *eruditio permeat limites* 'education transcends boundaries.' Travellers, usually students, are given grants to research, form friendships, absorb cultures and return home with a greater understanding of Turkey and the surrounding region.

Happy Days

'When someone you love dies, you will find something else to love.'
Aydın Osman Erkan

I had moved in with Rana and her two children after her divorce in 2003. At one Christmas party, I noticed two strangers in business suits sitting alone in the library, I was busy in the kitchen so I sent my bubbly friend, Ayla Gedek to entertain them. After a while just as I was struggling to take the hot, heavy turkey out of the oven, she rushed into the kitchen. 'Kim, Rana bu adamı kaçırmasın, he is handsome, has perfect Anatolian manners, Rana kaçırmasın'. Now *kaçırmak* means to run away, escape, I was more concerned that the turkey was about to escape, fall on the floor, than a man escaping from my daughter before dinner. 'Hum, hum', was my reply, 'find out if he is married, has children, what does he do, but don't bother me, tell Rana'. Ayla was right, this was the man who was to start a new chapter in our lives, a chapter of happy days.

Erol Tabanca was born in the city of *Eskişehir*, (the ancient Phrygian city of Dorylaeum) in central Anatolia which lies along the Porsuk River. Its history dates back to ancient times when thundering hordes Hittites, Lydians, Persians, Romans, Byzantines and Ottomans rode through leaving behind traces of their culture and a diverse population. One of four siblings born to Zeliha and the late Mehmet Tabanca, Erol was the tallest boy in class so he carried the Turkish flag on November 10th to commemorate the death of Atatürk in school parades and carried his mother's shopping basket to market. He studied architecture at *Ankara Devlet Mimarlık ve Mühendislik Akademisi* and played professional basketball for M.T.A, *Maden Tetkik Arama Enstitüsü* Ankara during his university days. After completing his military service and working in Istanbul for a while, an offer by a Turkish company to work in Türkmenistan sealed his fate. 'It was kısmet'.

Rana had met Erol at a charity function which she hosted as Master of Ceremony. Usually when her work was done, she would leave and come home but that evening Esat and Mehpare Edin insisted she join their table and there she was introduced to Erol Tabanca. Kısmet at work!

As a family we love surprises and Rana came up with a brilliant one for Erol's 50th birthday on March 15th, 2007. Recalling the pleasure his days at university playing basketball had given him, she decided on a 'super bowl' basketball match with his old teammates. For this she needed the assistance of Erol's partner and best buddy, Cem Siyahi and her close friend, Esra Özsüer, owner of Maya Sports Centre. With Erol away in Türkmenistan and Esra and Cem sworn to secrecy, they spent weeks planning, inviting guests, organising a hotel for team members and their wives in Istanbul and the venue for the match and party at Maya Sports Centre.

That morning at breakfast as presents and hugs were presented to Erol, Emrecan and Selina could hardly contain their excitement, they knew about the surprise and had been sworn to secrecy.

Picture the scene that evening: it was hilarious, when Rana and Erol entered the basketball court after more than two decades, there stood his team mates prancing around in shorts and numbered T-shirts, some slim and fit, some portly, some white-haired, some bald cheered by dancing cheer-leaders of ALL ages (including yours truly). Erol shed a surprised tear before changing into his shirt and shorts for a robust game. Excitement over, we gathered for the birthday supper arranged by Esra. Her son was ill with a high fever. As we walked to supper, I told her to go home but she insisted on staying which I thought very strange when her son was so ill.

What we didn't know was that Erol Tabanca is far more skilled at the art of surprise than we are. Erol supposedly working in Türkmenistan had actually been busy orchestrating a different scenario with his partners in crime: double agents, Cem and Esra. The next scene was beyond belief, the plan and its execution worthy of an Oscar. Suddenly the Mayor of Şişli, a friend of Erol's but not on the guest list appeared and gave an amusing after-dinner speech insinuating Erol should propose to Rana. Erol obliged and Rana, giggling like a teenager said 'yes.' In walked a registrar followed by two men carrying a white-clothed table with a short veil and flowers on it and four chairs and Rana was married.

I was standing between Dodo, an antique dealer and his friend at the back of the crowd. Dodo said, 'darling, they ARE getting married.'

'Don't be silly, it's a rehearsal,' I replied.

'*Burası İstanbul, her şey olabilir*', 'This is Istanbul anything is possible,' laughed his friend.

Rana shouted, 'Mummy' and Rana was married there and then in jeans and a white T-shirt, amidst roars of laughter and cries of joy. Everyone was crying from happiness, except me – I was in shock. Emrecan rushed up to give me a hug, shouting above the noise, 'this is the happiest day of my life.'

Rana radiant and starry-eyed, in shock, disappeared in a crowd of kisses, hugs and congratulations. It was the most amazing, bizarre, ridiculous, romantic wedding ever, and talk of the town for months.

Selina had gone home after the game so missed her mum's wedding. Next day we had a repeat performance at home just for her. Dressed in Fatoş's black university gown I led Rana, wearing the white veil, followed by bridesmaid, Selina, in her prettiest party dress and carrying a bouquet of flowers down the stairs to the dining table where Erol, the smiling groom, waited for me, the registrar, to perform a wedding service. 3 years old Selina jumped and danced around the room.

On Rana's birthday, 9th July, Mr. and Mrs. Erol Tabanca, beautiful and handsome in evening dress hosted a reception at Sunset Restaurant over-looking the Bosphorus to celebrate their marriage. 'Buy one, get 5 free,' joked Rana: Emrecan and Selina, two dogs, and, believe it or not, a mother-in-law, joined Erol's daughter, İdil, and her dog to made up the new family.

One of the first presents Erol gave to his wife was a book he had published of her poems. Erol and Rana make things work so that this colourful ménage can live happily ever after in the lovely house Erol built.

Erol had realised that Türkmenistan was a country with a future for a man prepared to work hard, and he wanted to be part of it. In 1995 he returned to Turkey and founded Polimeks, a construction company, with Cem Siyahi, his best friend from primary school in Eskişehir. Abdullah Gözener, a fellow student at Ankara joined later.

Turkish entrepreneurs are risk-takers, prepared to work hard and travel thousands of miles. Erol had the initiative and resourcefulness to take the less-travelled way, his own way, which made all the difference.

It was Henry Ford who wrote, 'one individual can make an extraordinary difference, but coming together is a beginning, keeping together is progress, and working together is a success.' This is a fair description of the growth of Polimeks, from its modest beginnings to its place today as one of the leading construction architectural and engineering companies in the world. It wasn't an easy ride. Entrepreneurism and leadership is not for the faint-hearted. There were huge setbacks and high risks, desperate days and lonely nights of sweat and doubt, but Erol and his team persisted.

The secret of Polimeks success is hands-on role-model management. First to arrive and last to leave the office or site with directors prepared to go that extra mile. Erol's years playing basketball taught him the importance of being part of a team, and it is this team spirit and commitment that has created a communal energy, family atmosphere and an amazing degree of loyalty within the company. His work ethics apply to himself and partners as much as to his employees. Constantly travelling, Erol's schedule is relentless. No matter how stressful his work might be, whenever

I ask, how he is, his answer is always the same: *'her şey daha iyi olacak'* – everything will be better.

Tall, sporty and handsome, Erol's self-discipline, energy and capacity for work is phenomenal. He radiates an unaffected friendliness, has a competitive spirit and ready earthy humour, and is an amusing dinner companion – especially when his favourite desert is served. He will build a house around a tree and, while talking on the telephone, doodle away creating new designs and ideas. Success comes to those with passion and a sense of his or her own place in the world – a person who lives his dream and that, I believe, is what makes Erol Tabanca tick. In the early 50's he became interested in art especially Turkish artists and so began his art collection.

As a couple, Erol and Rana share similar interests. His passion for art merges perfectly with her more eclectic tastes in furniture, colour and fabrics. For Rana price is irrelevant. A junk shop purchase, if she falls in love with it and it fits, receives the same status as a prized antique in their comfortable, elegant homes. No object is out of place. Notwithstanding their busy schedules Erol and Rana are family-orientated. Dates are reserved well in advance for Tabanca get-togethers at Bayram holidays.

Erol's daughter, İdil, moved to New York after graduating film school where, in the competitive, cut-throat world of publishing, she published an edgy avant-garde magazine called *Bullett* as owner-editor-in-chief. But the urge to return to script writing remained. Exiling herself from the hustle and bustle of New York, she moved to a quiet, green paradise in Costa Rica to write. Selina went to visit and fell in love with her house with a tree growing inside. İdil has now returned to live in Istanbul.

Eskişehir, a town meandering around the Porsuk River means Old City which it certainly was, but today with a population nearing 900,000 it is a modern, vibrant university city, home to 60,000 thousand students who fill its cultural centre, streets and parks with youthful buzz in restaurants and coffee houses which remain open until well after mid-night. The oldest residential area in Eskişehir is Odunpazarı, a timber market of old with classic wooden houses acclaimed as an UNESCO Cultural Site. The town and its two universities, Anadolu University and Osmangazi University are synonymous with the names of two remarkable men, Professor Orhan Oğuz and Professor Yılmaz Büyükerşen, who played such an important role in the growth and modernization of this charming Anatolian town.

Gezi Park

A high price for a green space.

On one side of Taksim Square there is a small urban park shaded with old trees, one or two benches, and a small teahouse. No Hyde Park, it lies in a heavily congested area of shops, apartments, hotels and traffic. Even so, it is a leafy patch of nature and fresh air on hot summer days for office workers and shop assistants to lunch on simit sandwiches, for mothers to walk dogs while watching their children play, for students to study or chatter on the grass and for old folk to sit on benches watching the world pass by. Alican and I often walked his dog there. One day the little rascal ran off. After searching for hours, we stuck reward photos on the trunk of every tree. That evening a lady called and we ran to the park to claim the naughty dog. That is Gezi Park.

In 2013, as part of the controversial Taksim Square Pedestrianization Project it was announced that trees in Gezi Park were to be felled in May, (not the time to fell trees). On May 27th a group of 50 young, environmentalists set up camp to organize a peaceful protest to protect the trees. Three days later, while they slept, police ripped down the tents in an aggressive dawn raid, spraying the sleeping protestors with tear gas. The incident triggered a huge public reaction, never before seen in Turkey. Was there no one, no official anywhere, to discuss this problem with these young people before sending in the police?

Within hours, people of all ages and from all walks of life, with different political leanings, in an unprecedented display of support for the demonstrators swarmed the park to join the protest. 'It is our obligation to support these young people protecting our trees,' announced a middle-aged, middle class lady in a loud voice in the bank I was in.

I went to the park. Crowds had gathered to protest against such unacceptable, heavy-handed police raids. What began as a social, civic outcry in Istanbul turned into a political protest in most cities around the country, with more than 2.5 million people involved, 8 killed and hundreds injured. Like most meetings in Turkey it had begun as a good-natured get-together in the park. Everyone brought gifts, blankets, helmets, torches, and pillows for the protesters. So much food arrived there were cries of 'no more food please, we need fridges.' The next day, vans rolled up with refrigerators, gas masks and medical supplies. Doctors, students, and office workers spent the evening in the park. Housewives cooked in the morning so they might bring their children and food after school. Hawkers, jumping on the bandwagon selling simit, balloons, and lemon cologne to soothe the burning effect of tear gas. Turkish street humour rose to new heights, with hilarious but cuttingly sharp remarks as social media kept the rest of the country in touch. TV and film stars came to entertain, they spoke and sang words of encouragement and families at home spent the evening banging saucepans and frying pans on their balcony. Comedians sang, '*Tencerem var, tavam var, Çapulcuyum havam var*,' – 'I have a saucepan, I have a frying pan, because I am in the mood to be a looter' responding sarcastically and humorously to a remark by a politician.

Each clash with the police enraged more protestors, not only in Istanbul but in Ankara, Izmir and Eskişehir. Anger and frustration filled the air as people were injured and exhausted by tear-gas attacks, tanks and barriers. One rainy, wet evening we stood listening to David Martello, an Italian pianist and activist singing emotive songs of love and peace, next day police removed his piano.

Watched by the world on international TV and social media as it unfolded, the Gezi Park protest became a symbol of sociological and political discontent for millions of people. Urbanisation, construction, congested traffic, political frustration, religious reaction, whispers of a secret agenda, a lack of transparency in the government, uncertainty and anxiety were taking its toll on another-wise docile, middle class population. People were concerned. As a foreign travel writer put it, the Turk's love for concrete was having an effect on the majority of the population. I recalled Gudrun Jonsson's words on stress, and believe that what had triggered the Gezi protest, as well as the desire to protect a few trees, was stress, enough is enough – the straw that broke the camel's back.

I remembered how I had crossed over the busy, two-lane Barbaros Boulevard in Beşiktaş via the over-head bridge late one evening. Next morning, I had to cross the bridge again, but couldn't find it. I walked up and down, feeling an utter fool, until, out of sheer frustration, I approached a policeman and asked what had happened to the bridge. 'It was removed last night,' came the nonchalant reply.

The dynamics of the protest turned ugly as armed attacks increased. Between 1st and 15th June, eight people were killed. The Divan Hotel opened its doors to the wounded, and police followed in with tear gas. A cousin and her husband spent nights in the park to be close to their doctor daughter working in the midst of the fray. Tanks rolled through the streets. Protesters, unable to withstand the force of such heavily armed police intervention, dispersed on 16th June. It was over.

Hatem Ete and Coşkun Taştan wrote in the introduction to *The Gezi Protests* that it was one of the most striking social-political developments in Turkey in recent history, triggered by serious social fault lines, which will continue to occupy Turkey's social-political agenda in the future'. The first civic social movement which unfortunately had to end as a political one.

Ceylan's neighbour, the late Professor Nazan İpşiroğlu, art historian, and writer whom we loved dearly said that this was the first civic protest she had seen in Turkey. In an article in the Radical Newspaper she wrote how amused and proud she was to be part of the protest and, at 90, to be called a *çapulcu* 'looter'. Nazan Hanım was convinced that the Gezi Park movement had aroused an awareness in young people of policy changes which might affect identity and secularism in the country in the future.

Brief Encounters

Partly out of necessity, my time is spent following the seasons which allows me to keep in touch with old friends in the Aegean. In March I usually set off for Aydın and the farm in time for planting. There is no privacy in a village, they knew exactly when I arrived, and an hour or so later, someone would turn up with a plate for dinner.

Spring is a pleasant time to drive around the country-side and I made the most of it with visits to Aphrodisias, lunch and a walk around their garden with Sedat and Diktam Atay in Söke, and in order to spend a night at the Marinette Hotel, a charming wooden villa hidden with ivy and vine, I would drive to Karacasöğüt Köyü, a small bay embraced by dark green pines growing out of the sea.

Gökova Sailing Academy and the hotel belong to Hasan Karamanoğlu, known as Uncle Hasan and his British wife Christina. Hasan is a sprightly man with a white beard, a healthy tanned complexion and twinkling eyes, and the look and heart of a seafarer. Multi-tasking Christina is the camp's *anne* 'mother', housekeeper and shopper. The club, which Selina thoroughly enjoyed for five summers, is a safe, healthy haven for children to learn to sail run by the Karamanoğlu children, Derin and Deniz.

In 2013, after the students had displayed their sailing skills, they jumped back into the sea, overturned the boats and, scrambling on top, began waving Turkish flags. Many, including Selina, fell into the water only to scramble back to wave more vigorously. Two red lifeboats with a wide portrait of Atatürk stretched between them slowly circled the boats of the cheering flag waving graduates across the bay. There wasn't a parent with a dry eye. This sporting tribute by these young students was deeply touching. We all agreed this is how the world should be, nature in all her glory, enjoyed by healthy children and appreciated by grateful parents. It was a magical afternoon.

Hasan Karamanoğlu wrote in the Academy's magazine, 'when we look back on the 10 years as Global Sailing, I think that in our own way we have fulfilled most of the objectives laid out by our great leader, Atatürk. I think that his ten-year sermon lights the way for any Turk who loves his country. Our primary aim is to teach the children of this country a love for the sea and our surrounding nature, to help them become responsible individuals who protect these resources and as a result of this become positive useful individuals... Educated children can easily have a positive effect on their surroundings, friends and even educate their parents to change their views.'

Following my yearly April and May, stay in London to spend precious time with friends, see a theatre, exhibition and concert and visit my family in Wales, summer is upon us. My home base is the farm in Osmanbükü, so I can keep an eye on the cotton, and be within driving distance to Alaçatı and Bodrum to stay with Rana and Erol, Alican and Chantal and Ceylan. And by late September I am back on the farm for the harvest before I finally fly to Istanbul.

Alaçatı is seventy kilometres from Izmir on the Çeşme Peninsula. Cooled by constant winds, washed by the sparkling Aegean Sea, and scented with picture perfect fields of purple lavender, herbs and artichokes, its cobbled narrow streets are lined with 19th century stone houses, mostly in their original state, with painted doors and shutters hidden in gardens of olive, mastic, fig and almond trees. Besides its undoubted village charm, Alaçatı's appeal and pulling power is its offshore winds which make it a paradise for out-door sports-windsurfing, kite surfing, paragliding, and sailing world-wide. For non-surfers like myself, sipping a cool drink at the beach café, watching the antics of surfers riding the board is great fun.

One year, in the overgrown garden of an old, dilapidated stone house, Rana hung a chandelier on a branch of a spreading oak tree, placed settees and armchairs underneath it, spread throws and cushions on the grass, and lit candles on a table groaning with local delicacies and wine. It was a magical evening and inspired Erol to build a very special boutique hotel called *Alavya* 'A word Rana coined meaning I love you' which opened its doors in June, 2013.

Alavya Hotel has twenty-five rooms, a spa and swimming pool in five original stone houses set in hidden gardens. The interior designer, Hakan Ezer worked so closely with Rana that in many ways the hotel reflects her signature style, tastefully decorated with a blend of art pieces, touches of rural charm, pebbles and stones and homely comforts, books near at hand and the fragrance of lavender. There is a feel-good romantic air about the place. Expect to meet a few famous foreigners and many people from Istanbul enjoying the delicious local and fusion cuisine, breakfast feasts and the friendliest, smiling young staff to pamper you.

Alaçatı's Saturday market must be the most satisfying to market in the Aegean in that it offers the natural wealth of the countryside's food products, rural crafts and culture. Its abundance, variety and low cost never cease to amaze me. Pass the kitchen, house-ware and beauty products section until you find blowing in the breeze, your summer wardrobe of flimsy cotton dresses, blouses, jackets, trousers, and scarfs. Believe me, as the best dressed lady at summer parties all from Alaçatı market!

Aydın and I have happy memories of evenings at the excavation house in Selçuk with the Austrian archaeologists working in Ephesus and of our first visit to the mountain village of Şirince in 1962, a bumpy adventure in the jeep up the stony, dirt track from Selçuk. We reached the top of the hill to find, hidden amongst swathes of purple and green forests, Judas and pine trees, wild oleanders and violets, a church and crumbling, terraced timber houses, and, in the distance, the blue Aegean Sea. It was an artist's paradise, utterly peaceful and remote. The few remaining Greek families were friendly, eager to tell their story for the price of a bottle of thick, dark olive oil, a bar of rough olive oil soap, or a basket of fresh vegetables.

Şirince Köyü was established by local Greeks in the 15th century – possibly after the collapse of Ephesus and the flooding of the Menderes River. In those days it was called *Çirkinceköy*, 'ugly village', a ploy by the Greeks to ward off nosey Turks from neighbouring villages. In 1924, when the Exchange Agreement between the Greek and Turkish governments was signed, most Greeks returned to the mainland or the islands. Visiting in 1926, the governor of Izmir was astonished to find such a charming village nestling amongst in a forest and renamed it *Şirince Köyü* 'Pretty village'.

Şirince Köyü was rediscovered in the 70's and luckily conserved by a group of environmentalists, including the Narin sisters, Oya and Miniş, friends of Rana. Oya is partly responsible for transforming the village into a unique mountain retreat, now a protected area. She fell in love with Şirince Köyü on her first visit. Captivated by its energy, beauty and stillness – similar to that of the House of the Virgin Mary on the opposite hill – she decided it was her kind of place and set about renovating a few old houses into a delightful motel, Güllü Konaklar.

An Appreciation

This tragedy affected everyone I know. I include it in my memoirs as a thank you and appreciation to the family and those friends who faced this appalling tragedy with inspiring dignity and steadfastness and who, today, still meet to celebrate a life well lived.

Kemer Country is a community of elegant townhouses, apartments and timber villas, a small shopping centre, sports and social centre, golf club and riding school. This community concept, country-living in style, a first in Turkey, was masterminded by the late Esat Edin and his team and built in Belgrade Forest, north-west of Istanbul on the European shore of the Black Sea. The forest covers vast stretches of rolling countryside lakes, ponds Byzantine structures and an Ottoman aqueduct built by Mimar Sinan – the last aqueduct to supply water to the city. So-called after its founders, a band of Serbian settlers in the 16th century and later home to Muslim refugees fleeing the Balkan wars.

Esat Edin and his wife Mehpare married in 1993, they were a golden couple, socially popular and culturally active, especially when it came to children for the Edin's were parents to four siblings, Murat, Cem, Serra and Aliye. A bright, well-known young businessman about town, Esat was quick-witted of average height with crinkling laughing eyes while Mehpare was a dark-haired, down-to-earth practical beauty.

The Edins and Tabancas were close friends. In fact, it was Esat and Mehpare who introduced Erol to Rana. Mehpare's amusing but pragmatic approach to life and in handling her children and indefatigable husband came from her German mother, Rosie Taki. Every Christmas I would buy a dozen tickets for a pantomime put on by the British Community charity theatre group, Bubbles, for Selina, the Edin children and a few friends. Once Aliye was so small we lost her in the crowd during the interval.

In 2005, Mehpare was diagnosed with cancer. Weeks turned to months of anxiety as the illness advanced requiring more intense treatment and hospitalization. We all prayed for Mehpare. In those dark days, Mehpare's remarkable courage and determination to see her children lead a normal life inspired those around her. She never lost her sense of humour for the ridiculous, once turning up at the American hospital for a session dressed as super woman.

Mehpare and I often met at Papatya, the British school which the children attended. One day, watching her brood play in a muddy garden, I said, 'If I were you, I'd hose your lot down in the garden then throw them into the swimming pool.' 'Oh, I often do that - but bath time is fun. Except on Fridays, then it's a nightmare with 80 nails, hands and toes, to cut,' she grimaced.

At Christmas time, 2007, I met Rosie at a shopping mall. We chatted then I queried tentatively after Mehpare. 'Well, she has to be well, she has four children to look after,' came the positive response from her stalwart mum.

Mehpare Edin died in the spring of 2008 at the age of 40. She was deeply, deeply mourned. Family, friends and neighbours at Kemer Country proved a constant support and comfort to the family. Murat, the eldest, was sent to Bishop's Stortford College in England as a boarder. Esat, faced with pressing financial problems, locked himself up in his office trusting the care of his children to Rosie, a devout catholic who rolled up her sleeves and, as devoted grandmothers do, got on with looking after her grandchildren.

Six months after Mehpare's death, in October of that year, Esat took the children to England to visit Murat and on their return to Turkey to Hızır Camp near Edremit for a short camping trip in one of the tree houses. They set up a tent at the side of the river and on the last evening decided to sleep there. In the small hours of the morning, a flash flood swept the sleeping family and the tent into the swirling, torrential waters.

Rana burst into my room. 'Esat and the children have drowned – we don't know what's happened,' she cried and left. I telephoned Natalie Sadıkoğlu, the manager of Kemer Country Sports Club, whose husband was a relative of the Edins. I asked if it was true about Esat and the children. 'Yes,' came a weepy whisper, 'we are at Bodrum Airport waiting to fly to Istanbul.'

It was too shocking, too heart-breaking. Rana rocked Selina in her arms as she explained the terrible tragedy as gently as possible to a small child. She spoke of Murat, safe at boarding school, and how he was saved to carry on the family name, so there would always be an Edin in their lives to remind her of her little friends.

Selina marched into my room, her sweet face white, eyes red with tears. She climbed onto the bed and holding my hands in her lap repeated, word for word, what her mother had said with such innocence and belief I had to fight back my tears. We never went to a pantomime again. Throughout those days of unbelievable shock and sadness Mehpare's friends embraced Murat and Rosie with stalwart love, generosity and kindness. The city mourned the death of that young, beautiful family: Mehpare, then Esat – 48 years old, Cem – 12, Serra – 10 and little Aliye, just 7.

Rosie rented an apartment at Bishop's Stortford, near Murat's school. The headmaster, teachers and staff provided the daily normality and structure that Murat so badly needed, and regular visits by aunts, uncles and friends from Istanbul inspired continuity and emotional support for the young boy. Murat insisted things remain the same, which included his birthday celebrations at Şirince at the home of Oya and Miniş Narin.

That year Rosie and I met in London and went to an exhibition at the Queen's Gallery. We lunched at Partridges in Sloane Square then returned to the flat for tea. Rosie spoke of the next phase in her life now that Murat was off to America. Ruefully she confessed that she had enjoyed her stay at Bishop's Stortford and would miss living in England and how Mehpare had planned that both sons would attend an English boarding school. After some hesitation, I asked her how she had felt and reacted when she first heard the news. She was in Germany at the time. After a long pause with a slight smile she replied, 'Faith – my faith in God gave me strength. I thought of my mother how she would have coped. She lived through the Second World War looking after me and my siblings in dire conditions. Yes, I decided to do what my mother did for us'. Faith means waking up day after day with a good attitude, and Rosie is a shining example.

Embrace the Unexpected

When an English friend remarked, 'we live in interesting times' I don't think she imagined how interesting or uncertain it was going to be, or that it would be such a tumultuous year of political changes. In June, the British were stunned by Brexit, the vote to leave the EU after 43 years, causing a Prime Minister to resign, the pound to plummet, and Scotland to demand a second independence vote and on November 9th, American electors voted Donald Trump as President, causing more global shock waves.

For Turkey, 2016 was a sad year indeed and will be remembered for the string of terrorist attacks that continued over the year, killing and wounding hundreds of people and ending with the saddest of all, an attack on New Year's Eve at an exclusive nightclub, Reina, where innocent young people were dancing, having fun and welcoming in a New Year. It left 39 mostly foreigners dead and 69 seriously hurt. There were bombs at Atatürk Airport, military personnel attacked in the heart of Ankara, a double bombing targeted police after a crowded football match at Beşiktaş Vodafone Stadium, and, unbelievably, the Russian Ambassador was murdered in front of an audience in Ankara. This violence severely affected the population, economy and tourism.

On the 15th July 2016, Ceylan and I were in Osmanbükü when news of the attempted *coup d'état* by a faction in the army reached us. It was around 9 p.m., tanks blocked the First Bosphorus Bridge and Istanbul Atatürk Airport. Within a few hours, it was a failed coup; the soldiers and tanks were captured and taken away. The government declared a state of emergency, which lasted until 2018. The coup was blamed on Fethullah Gülen, a self-exiled cleric with a living in Pennsylvania America. Those in his organisation, and those military personnel, businessmen, bureaucrats and academics said to be in Fethullah Gülen's employ were purged, imprisoned or lost their jobs. Not long after the name of the Bosphorus Bridge was changed to *15 Temmuz Şehitler Köprüsü*, 'The 15th July Martyrs' Bridge'.

April 1st 2017 marks an extremely important day in Turkish politics. It was the day the country went to the polls to vote in a constitutional referendum to change 18 proposed amendments brought forward by the AKP and the MHP parties which would change the governance of the country from a parliamentary system to a presidential system and grant President Recep Tayyip Erdoğan sweeping new powers. The presidential system won by approximately 51.41 percent yes votes compared to 48.59 no votes.

I must admit feeling apprehensive about the results. I believe in a separation of legislative, executive and judicial powers and control over checks and balance. I remembered what a friend had once said, 'We might have preferred things differently however we are where we are and need to act accordingly'.

October 1st was the anniversary of my husband's death and it was the first time in years I happened to be in Osmanbükü with Ceylan, Alican, Chantal and Erol Emil. Erol Emil's startled blue eyes still looks at the world as if to ask, 'am I on the right planet?' Like his father, Erol Emil is a pleasant, happy child, no trouble at all and Chantal is bringing up her son to love animals, nature and life on the farm. Ceylan is a fun grandma who takes him on morning walks to see cows, goats, chickens, ducks and chat to the villagers. Erol Emil is the village mascot.

It is a custom to hold a *mevlit,* 'Islamic memorial service' and this was carried out in the proper tradition by Zeki and the Imam. Since I and other members of the family were present, I thought I should do something different and asked my neighbours, İlknur and Selma Hanım, who suggested *lokma*, 'a sweet, round doughnut', after the prayers. Ceylan and Alican arranged the 'mevlit' with the Imam, and the 'lokma' with the 'muhtar'.

It was a warm sunny day. At 11 a.m., a van from Aydın drove up to the square outside the mosque. The women in the village set up tables with paper plates as the young men threw small rings of sweet pastry into hot fat until they turned golden brown. The first batch was offered to the Imam and those coming out of the mosque. They were delicious – not too sweet, fresh and crispy. We chatted to the villagers, Imam, 'muhtar', and headmaster of the village primary school who came to take a tray full for his students as cars, mini-buses, motorbikes, tractors, horse and cart stopped to receive their lokma before going on their way. It was a friendly occasion which pleased everyone.

That afternoon I walked around the village. The streets are paved and clean, and most houses have a car parked outside but actually the village had not changed over the years although now it has become a *mahalle*, 'a district' of İncirliova. Not that it made much difference. The cafés are still crowded by the same men, older and white-haired drinking tea and complaining about cotton prices. What had changed dramatically was the attitude and the way women think and see themselves. Technology, social media, computers, mobile phones, TV had changed their mind-set, they were more self-confidence, open-minded and may I say it, more demanding. They had embraced change with more enthusiasm and were eager for discussion and for their children to go to university, many drive cars and discard the *şalvar* 'traditional loose pants' for skirts and coats when they go to town alone. During engagements, weddings or other social functions which are now held at hotels in town or the wedding hall in the village, they appear beautifully made-up and modern.

A highlight in 2017 was my birthday, a big one with a zero, on 1st March. Rana and Erol orchestrated the evening perfectly. When Rana asked what I wanted for my birthday, I said I wanted a relaxed evening, finger food and jazz music my friends could enjoy and that was exactly what I got. In the lovely wood and stone art gallery owned by Erol, eighty friends and relatives danced and enjoyed great jazz and solos spots by my white-haired relatives, both architects, who after they retired had returned to their first love – music. İlder Tokcan is lead singer and guitarist in a band called The Bebek Blues, and Haldun Erkman, with his deep, baritone voice, sings soul love songs with his group of retired fellow musicians. It was a glorious evening and ended quite dramatically, but thank heavens not seriously, when our nearly-ninety-years-old doctor friend, Warren Winkler after too much champagne and dancing, collapsed and was taken to hospital in an ambulance. Thankfully he soon recovered. When Erol laughingly ensured me at my next party, there to be two ambulances at the door. I decided since one cannot improve on a perfect birthday, this should be my last.

Nihat Odabaşı

I certainly did embrace the unexpected when one day Turkey's most celebrated fashion photographer, Nihat Odabaşı telephoned his friend, Rana and told her he was working on a project for the winter collection for the fashion house, Gizia and instead of using professional models he wanted the theme to be women of the city and the first person he thought of was me! Rana doubted I would do it but told him to get in touch with me. He did and I of course, agreed.

On July 4th 2019, I spent a thoroughly enjoyable day in a large studio full of young people and rail upon rail of beautiful clothes. It was a hub of busy people running to and fro with dresses, lights and scenery and cups of coffee. In one corner in front of a walled mirror, hairdressers, make-up artists and dressers prepared models for their photo-shot. In the centre huge lights and cameras lit a background stage setting for the shot. Watching Nihat and his crew at work was a master class in fashion photography. Without pause he kept the action rolling and the adrenaline high, checking every tiny detail until, silence, and he began to shoot and direct the model. It reminded me of my carefree modelling days in London except that in those days, fashion photography was a Leica camera and not much else.

Pandered by kind professionals, surrounded by young, beautiful people and wearing gorgeous clothes it was certainly a day to be treasured.

And it is thanks and by courtesy of Nihat Odabaşı that I include his beautiful photographs in this book.

Odunpazarı Modern Museum

By the end of summer 2019, the Tabanca family were on the move. Emrecan was off to Valencia in Spain to complete the final years of his university studies as an architect and Selina was looking forward to settling in London to begin the first year of her university studies in social anthropology. Both cities were marked with a red circle to visit in my dairy once the cotton harvest was over.

But first was the anticipation and excitement of a long-awaited event, the opening of the Odunpazarı Modern Museum in Eskişehir on the 7th September.

My son-in-law, Erol Tabanca has had a portfolio of dream projects for many years and a museum in his hometown was the reality of his first dream, and his way of giving back to the community.

Designed by Japanese architect, Kengo Kuma and his associate, Yuki Ikeguchi, the OMM is a stunning structure of interlocking timber blocks (which turn golden in sun-light) in harmony with its surroundings, the Odunpazarı, an old timber market with residential wooden framed konaks on a Historical Urban Site. Included in the complex is a delightful OMM INN of 12 suites housed in 3 adjoining konaks around an outdoor courtyard of cafes and restaurants.

Erol Tabanca's private collection of more than 1,000 modern and contemporary art pieces, mostly by Turkish artists, is on display to the public for the first time. The collection will rotate and takes its place alongside other temporary exhibitions and art pieces which include, amongst others, an exciting bamboo installation by Tanabe Chikunnsai IV.

The opening of the OMM was indeed a grand affair, attended by 1,200 guests who made their way from one gallery and hall to another guided by smiling young hostesses, mostly art students, dressed in red futuristic costumes. And who better to have organised this magical evening but the Chairwoman of OMM Foundation, Idil Tabanca, Erol's daughter. It was a splendid, a spectacular evening and to add to my delight, I met English writer, Roger Norman and his wife, Sibel who reside in Eskişehir.

Eskişehir is a university city in the centre of Anatolia, buzzing with a rich and diverse community of young students and a steady flow of visitors. It is rare to see art and the natural world combine in harmony but by its very design and spirit, the OMM with its community – inspired, ecological and progressive sustainable vision is certain to contribute to the city's growing cultural significance in the international art world.

A Time for Reflection

The cotton was harvested and sold and the farmers back in the coffee house voicing their complaints. And rightly so with cotton prices down and expenses high, they were left with little to show after months of hard, honest work.

I enjoy breakfast in the garden, its peaceful and smells of fresh grass and nature. One morning over an introspective cup of tea watching birds fly in to drink water and search for seeds in the grass, my thoughts took me to the past. I remembered the cosiness of chatting with my mother, walks with my father to Margam Castle, of Aydın and I in front of a warm fire on a cold evening on the farm and my daughters and friends gathering in the garden at Rose Cottage. It seems so long ago, another time another life a different world and I wondered about the future.

Interesting times had become times of seismic change with global warming in the fore of an ever complex, divided perhaps dangerous world over which we have little or no control. I recalled how my mother would sigh and say that the world was not all good or all bad, but patchy adding, 'so let's get on with it as best we can'. Technology, the internet, digital advertising, fake news in such a globally connected world demands a different approach and mindset to 50 years ago.

Then my thoughts turned to Turkey where I have spent most of my life. Turkey's achievements are there for all to see. Istanbul the city port my ship sailed into in 1959 has all but disappeared in a concrete revolution even so the city has, amazingly, not lost its uniqueness and secrets nor its Burası Istanbul - This is Istanbul appeal and charm making the places that remain all the more precious. Turkey's population has more than doubled to 80 million plus and Istanbul has increased ten-fold, they say 16 million but I am sure it is much more (not forgetting 5 plus million Syrians). Fashion has radically changed on the streets. Technology and social media work well, although I doubt people are aware how much technology has changed the rules of life. Most homes throughout the country including those in the lower income bracket own a TV, washing machine, mod cons, have a car parked outside the door and children glued to their mobile telephones.

But something has gone wrong.

Many people young and old in cities, rural areas and villages feel anxious and filled with doubt as to where and which way their country is headed. A series of policy changes and laws affecting the identity, moral and social aspect of their culture and life-style has aroused conflicting emotions and unease, and polarised communities. Some rally behind a political party, others may not. Politics cannot change human nature nor the unique traditional characteristics and customs that sets a nation apart from other countries. For decades Turkey had a reputation for being a secure, prosperous, secular country with resilient, hard-working, open-minded, hospitable citizens and it is these qualities that set the Turkish people apart from its neighbours in the Middle East.

Peace at Home and Peace in the World was their mantra.

Unfortunately, within the last few years a shift in geo-politics has influenced the global and political landscape and drawn Turkey into the tangled politics of the Middle East, the most dangerous and complex place in the world. I remember the conversations I had with Nigel Ryan, a charismatic correspondent, Director of TV programmes and Reuters writer I met during his travels in Turkey in 1888 and 1989 to co-write, 'The Scholar and the Gypsy' with James Howard- Johnson and what he wrote, 'What I was to discover.... was that the Turkish mind-set was not a European one nor yet a wholly Asian one. It was Turkish, a fascinating blend of great talents and defects, of sensibility and warmth. But the energy and enterprise of the humblest of individuals, the pride and generosity of the countryman, the extraordinary surge of market forces and the success of the state in modernising the infrastructure of the whole country win the traveller's admiration'.

I agreed with him then and still hold the same opinion. Regardless of what is happening politically, may the spirit of komşuluk 'neighbourhoodship unite communities throughout the land in keeping with their true identity, culture and traditions as a tolerant secular country with a friendly, hospitable society'.

Then came the Pandemic - March, 2020 saw the beginning of a pandemic which has sweep through every country in the world. The Covid-19, an unknown virus is causing the loss of millions of lives, an economic catastrophe with life-changing civic and social modifications. Governments ordered quarantine, curfews, lockdown and social distancing. Hospitals, doctors and nurses worked around the clock desperate to save lives while we were brain-washed to wash our hands, wear masks and stay at home. Normality was put on hold as shops, businesses and travel was forbidden. Mixed messages from professors, scientists and politicians in the media and on TV and a serious lack of leadership and effective action at the very beginning to contain the virus caused confusion and uncertainty, fear even amongst the public. Information, laws and restrictions keep changing. It has been a year of two steps forward, three steps back for everyone especially governments as they grapple with the need to procure a vaccine and prioritize public health without adding further risks to the economy.

I was at the farm in Osmanbükü when the lockdown was announced. That evening a car whisked me off to Bird Island Farm, the private animal sanctuary on the hills of Kuşadası founded by my grandson's Swiss wife, Chantal. Ceylan arrived from Izmir and we remained there for two and a half hectic but full of fun, months. Early in the morning Erol Emil, aged 5 and Oskar Ali, 2 years old my great-grandsons came running into my bedroom to wake me up, and so began a day of chasing and feeding children and animals within the farm compound. In the evening we would gather for supper on the balcony overlooking rolling hills of olive trees and the calm, blue Aegean Sea and red stunning sunsets while nature, animals and children, unaffected by the pandemic, slept.

Rana arrived and she and I drove to Bodrum where I remain to this day. It is easier to lead a near normal life in the country-side than in a crowded city, even so we are careful and vigilant. As we learn more about Covid 19, there is hope of a vaccine the near future. Out of necessity we have learnt to adapt and evolve within this new norm of social distancing, working from home and students studying with computers instead of teachers. One positive act to cheer during these trying days of pandemic fatigue has been the creative use of technology. It has brought music, dance and art, zoom weddings and comforting face time chats for families to keep in touch.

It is twelve months on and Selina has left for her final term before graduating at Goldsmith University, London, the family commutes to and from Istanbul for business and I have received my two vaccines and am happily settled in Bodrum - the Halicarnassus of Caria in ancient times, famed for housing one of the Seven Wonders of the World, the Mausoleum of Mausolus and for Bodrum Castle of St. Peter built by Crusader Knights in the 15th century. The town has a population of 430,000 but the pandemic has increased this number three-fold to over one million three hundred. Bodrum Peninsular is like the fingers on your hand, spread out with winding forest roads leading to charming bays and modern marinas. The Tabanca residence is situated in a quiet bay on the sea-shore surrounded by forest, besides the family and dogs, a few friends come to stay. I was told winters in Bodrum were mildly warm with sunny days but this winter we had some quite fierce stormy weather with thunder and lightning, heavy rains and even the fear of flooding. The Aegean Sea looked more like the Atlantic Ocean as its loud, grey, rolling waves crashed on the shore and the fonds of palm trees in the garden bent and whipped wildly in the wind. Boats were taken to a safe harbour and cars driven further inland. It reminded me of the Welsh coast and I loved it. But was it a warning from Mother Nature? Emrecan and I prepared cosy suppers in front of the fire and were delighted when Idil joined us.

Having been brought up to 'do your best' (although I am well aware that if there is such a thing as a life school report mine would read 'could do better',) Even so, I am cautiously optimistic about the future especially when I am in the company of young people. They are unafraid, they care about the world and most of them are eager to do something about eco, gender and social problems, the environment, conservation and sustainability.

Embrace Your Age - I thoroughly enjoyed my birthday on March 1 which I spent with Erol and Rana. It was a day with flowers, delicious food, excellent wine, presents, music, lots of laughter and birthday greetings from family and friends. Since the world started to close down due to the pandemic and the future still seems uncertain, I have learned to EMBRACE MY AGE, live in the Now, and keep myself busy and occupied enough so I have a reason to get out of bed in the morning. Every birthday motivates me to be the best I can at that age. Being healthy and fit makes you feel good so it has become a priority. My mornings are taken up with a brisk walk along the seashore, or an hour in the gym or dancing in my room or best of all a heavenly early morning swim in summer. Besides the dark place I found myself in when Aydın was murdered, I am not one to dwell on the pain of the past. Regrets I have a few, everyone has, but my sense of humour, inherited from my father, keeps me from sinking into despair at the extraordinary goings-on in the world. Being naturally curious about most things, my life in Turkey might have been out of the ordinary, but it has been interesting, mostly enjoyable and I appreciate the good people who have shared it with me. Its tragedies made me stronger.

Aydın used to say I had a guardian angel that protected me from my mad impulses but I believe it is the love, faith and an inner security my parents gave me as a child growing up in Wales. Our world has changed so much during the last year, many of the things we took for granted have or are disappearing leaving us with no choice but to re-balance what we need to hold onto and what we must let go. I know what I want to hold on to - Hugs, small acts of kindness that will make someone smile; I want to share the joy of being alive and healthy and I want to learn from my grandchildren all about sustainability and the new technology which will surely be on the market in the near future.

Death does not bother me, no plugs, quick and painless please. Until that time comes, family, grandchildren and friends are all the boaster energy injections I need to sustain a healthy, deeply grateful attitude to life.

In his poem, The Mower, Philip Larkin said it all in two lines, 'We should be careful of each other, we should be kind while there is still time'. And bash on as best we can.

I wrote 'Lady Kim' to preserve what I thought then was the vanishing places, traditions and times that I lived in Turkey. Now it seems very obvious that my generation, past and present, has not only failed but added to the global problems of population and damage to the earth and the seas because of a lack of ethics and decent leadership. Climate change is here and now. My hope for a brighter, fairer future lies in the digital age generation. These young people are active and support public protests to raise awareness to these global challenges. They are socially conscious and environmentally responsible so who better to have the *last word* in this book than my beautiful, activist, granddaughter, Selina.

In my 20 years of life, Kim, or Mummy to me, has injected me with her love for life and appreciation for every moment, which I am eternally grateful. I grew up learning from her how the best and the worst moments can come together to make up this short but incredible experience we call life. My Mom and Mummy have been the biggest influence in my life, so I felt distraught when I kept finding out the horrible things that we did to *all* our mothers- *mother nature.* Initially, my hopes were sky-high, thinking we could save the world simply by refusing plastic straws or choosing to consume less meat. The more I learnt the more pace there was to lose hope as I realised how important systematic change is needed to change this fast-paced world we live in. I long for the time my Mummy lived in, when things were slower, simpler, and we hadn't destroyed over half the world's forests. I want to grow up with all our current digital age opportunities and live with the nature that she saw and surrounded her. I don't know if that is too much to ask. Mummy's generation might have failed as the guardians of our planet, yet they have allowed us to make our craziest imaginations work and come to life. I take this as a gift, a sign of hope.

It grieves me deeply to see our forests ablaze, our seas heating up by the year and animals being killed. However, there is life after death. This is certainly no time for denial or depression which to me seems the easy way out. This is a time for collective healing, finding a solution and taking action to resolve these pressing global problems. I trust my generation to create the energy for this hope and to move forward. It was not our fault, but *now* it is our responsibility. Thank you for following my grandma's journey and I hope you will join us and become a part in the fight for a brighter, healthier future for your children and grandchildren too.

Further Reading

Atatürk: Rebirth of a Nation by Lord Kinross, K. Rustem & Brother, 1964.

Looking Back by Shusha Guppy, British American Publishing, 1991.

The Scholar and the Gypsy by James Howard-Johnston & Nigel Ryan, Sinclair-Stevenson, 1992.

Turkey, the Quest for Identity by Feroz Ahmed, Oneworld Publications, 2003.

Istanbul, A Traveller's Reader edited by Laurence Kelly, Robinson, 2005.

Turn My Head to the Caucasus by Aydın Osman Erkan, Çitlembik, 2009.

Places in Turkey by Frances Russell, Frances Lincoln. Ltd, 2010.

Levant: Splendour and Catastrophe on the Mediterranean by Philip Mansel, John Murray, 2011.

South from Ephesus by Brian Sewell, Tauris Parke Paperbacks, 2012.

Meander by Jeremy Seal, Vintage, 2013.

The Fall of the Ottomans, The Great War in the Middle East by Eugene Rogan, Basic Books, 2015.

From the Bosphorus to Bradninch by Sidney E. P. Nowill, Bradninch Books, 2015.

Prisoner of Geography by Tim Marshall, Elliott and Thompson, 2015.

The Circassian: A life of Esref Bey, Late Ottoman Insurgent and Special Agent by Benjamin C. Fortna, 2016.

Turkey, A Short History by Norman Stone, Thomas & Hudson, 2017.

My father...

My father, Alfred Fredrick Rees and my mother, Ivy Edna Rees

London, 1958

Nil Arbel / London, 1959

Mrs. Afife Arbel

Ambassador Bedii Arbel, seated, with friends in Büyükada

Professor Fazıla Şevket Giz

With Ceylan / İstanbul, 1962

Mr. and Mrs. Erkan / 1962

Aydın Osman Erkan, 1960

Aydın's family, 1963

Aydın Erkan in front of his jeep / İstanbul,1962

Fun in the barn / Osmanbükü, 1964

Cotton pickers

British Ambassador, Sir Timothy Daunt with Aydın

The Erkan Family; me, Aydın, Rana and Ceylan, 1963

Aydın

My father-in-law, Hamza Erkan with Ceylan and Rana

Rana with her father

Professor Kenan Erim and Lady Daunt in Aphrodisias, 1984

Professor Kenan Erim, Mr. and Mrs. Laurence Kelly in their London garden

Lord and Lady Monson

Professor Bert Smith, Sevgı Gönül, Trevor Proudfoot and Aydın in Aphrodisias Museum

L.C.C. YILIN İLK MEZUNLARINI VERDİ

Genç ve güzel kızlar, tertip edilen kokteylde diplomalarını Grace BEZMEN'den aldılar

L. C. C. Manken ve Zerafet Kursları, yılın ilk mezunlarını vererek bu vesile ile de güzel bir expozisyon tertip ettiler.

Mankenlik ve Zerafet dersleri gören genç kızların bu kurslardan ne kadar faydalanacağını belirtmek gayesiyle tertip edilen bu expozisyonda bütün hocaları ve velileri, misafirleri önünde birbirinden güzel makyaj yaparak kırıla dökü̈le yürüyen kızlarımızın kaliteleri açıkça görünüyordu.

L. C. C.'nin yakışıklı ve entellektüel sahibi Mesut Üstünel sade ve kısa bir konuşma yaptı.

Mankenlik ve Zerafet bölümü müdüresi genç güzel Grace Bezmen ise sertifikaları dağıttı.

Diğer hocalar ise birbirinden güzel ve zarif görünüşleri ile misafirlerin hayranlığını kazandılar.

Yardımcı öğretmenleri Sema Akıncı ise o gün hayli faaliyet gösterirken çok zarif ve ölçülü hareketleri ile cazip bir genç kızdı. 20 ye yakın talebe arasından ancak 3 tanesini «Manken olabilir» diye ayıran müessese ne kadar titiz davranıyor böyle?...

Genç nesle hayli faydalı bilgiler ve görgü kazandıran L. C. C. ayni zamanda bazı imkânlar da yaratmış oluyor.

Tiyatro bölümünde kıymetli sanatçı Ayla Algan ve eşi Beklan Algan bütün günlerini, bilgilerini ve eforlarını esirgemiyorlar genç talebelerinden...

Ayşe Gül Sihirli Ülkede

Kent Oyuncuları ilk defa müzikli bir çocuk piyesi sahneye koydular.

"Ayşegül Sihirli Ülkede" isimli bu temsilin müziğini çocuk Doktoru Sami Uçar yazdı. Müzik bilgisi ve fevkalâde keman çalışı ile dostları arasında temayüz eden genç Dr. Sami Uçar, böylece olumlu bir faaliyete girişmiş oldu. Her yaşta çocukların zevkle seyredebileceği oyun muvaffakiyetle devam ediyor. Sami Uçar'ın yine Çocuk Doktoru esmer güzeli eşi Güler Uçar ne kadar mutlu olsa hakkıdır ..

İRENA KUTBAY .: Suat Aysa'nın mankeni. L. C. C. nin yürüyüş hocası. Varşova manken okulu mezunu. Sedat Kutbay'la evli, bir oğlu var.

FLORA AKSEL: Okulun başarılı bale ve estetik jimnastik hocası, Londra Royal Akademi mezunu, Atıf Aksel ile evli. İki de şirin kızı var.

GRACE BEZMEN : Manken ve Zerafet bölümü müdürü, New-York'ta idarecilik tahsili yapmış. Fevkalâde güzel ve cazip bir kadın. Pamir Bezmen'le evli.

KİM ERKAN: Makyaj hocası. Narmanlı Apartmanında makyaj salonu var. Aydın Erkan'la evli. 2 kızı var. Londra'da Elizabeth Arden kurslarına devam etmiş.

Irena Kutbay, Flora Aksel, Grace Bezmen at LCC, Language and Cultural Centre

Member of the jury for Miss Turkey Beauty Contest in Istanbul 1970

Windsor Castle

Members of the Ottoman Royal Family, 1986

Dining in a fish restaurant in Kuşadası, 1986

Mrs. Nur Bekata and her sister, Professor Fatoş Erkman

Selina at the Queen's Gallery / London

Ceylan, Alican and Chantal

The Erkan Family with baby Emrecan, 1991

My daughters and grandchildren, 2003

The Tabanca Family

A suprise wedding, Erol and Rana

Erol, İdil and Emrecan, 2018

Rana and Selina at her graduation from Bryanston School, 2018

Rana and Rodi

A man and his best friend, Rodi

Ceylan with her grandsons

Chantal, Alican and Erol Emil in London

Rana and Ceylan

Erol and Rana at their farm on her birthday / Bodrum, 2019

OMM, Odunpazarı Modern Museum

Erol and Rana hosting the Opening of OMM / Eskisehir, 2019

London, 1958

Photo by Nihat Odabaşı, İstanbul, 2019

Shapli Family

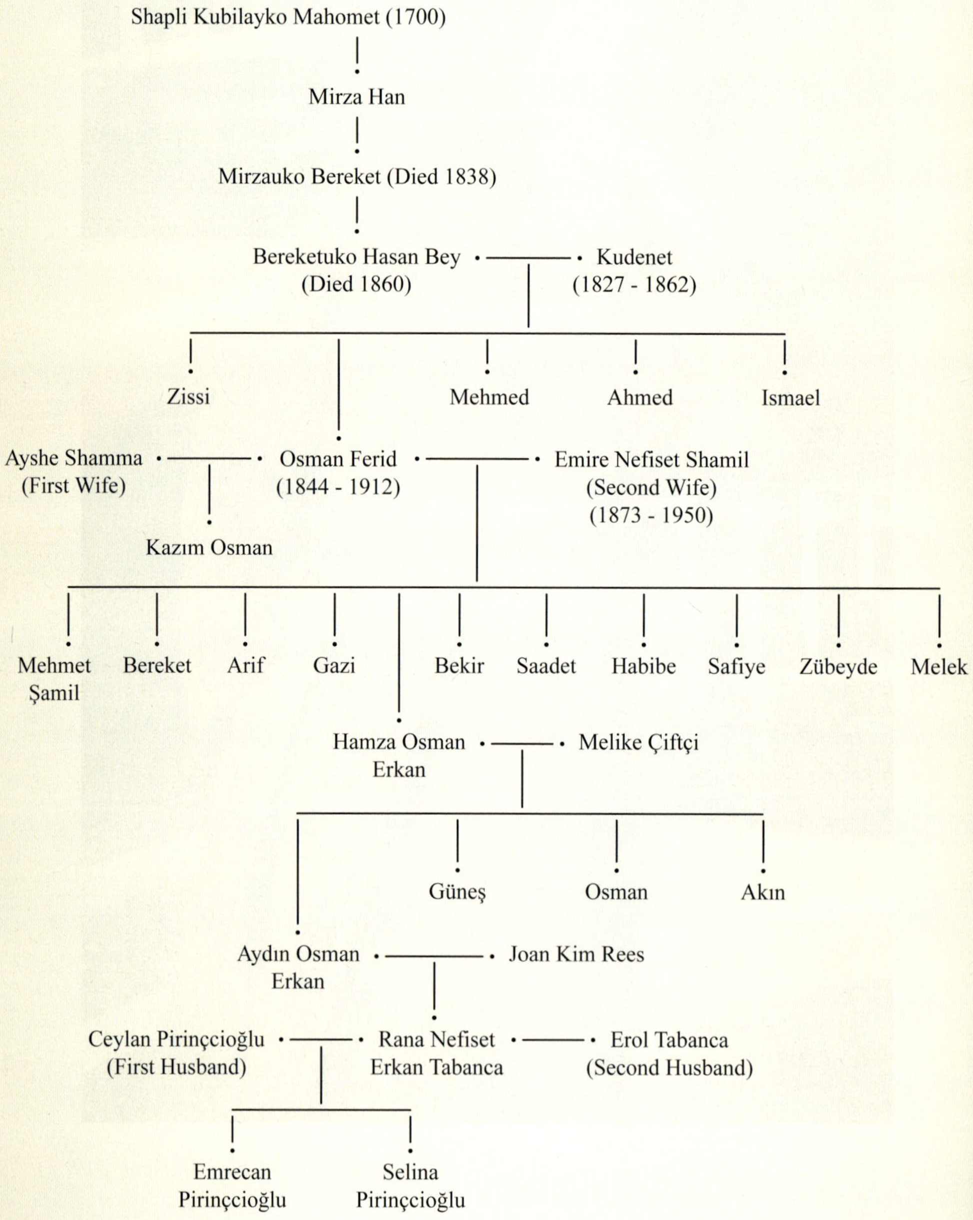